SECURING AVA

What Reviewers Say About Anne Shade's Work

Love and Lotus Blossoms

"Shade imbues this optimistic story of lifelong self-discovery with a refreshing amount of emotional complexity, delivering a queer romance that leans into affection as much as drama, and values friendship and familial love as deeply as romantic connection. …Shade's well-drawn Black cast and sophistication in presenting a variety of relationship styles—including open relationships and connections that shift between romance and friendship—creates a rich, affirming, and love-filled setting…(Starred review)"—*Publishers Weekly*

Masquerade

"Shade has some moments of genius in this novel where her use of language, descriptions and characters were magnificent."—*Lesbian Review*

"The atmosphere is brilliant. The way Anne Shade describes the places, the clothes, the vocabulary and turns of phrases she uses carried me easily to Harlem in the 1920s. Some scenes were so vivid in my mind that it was almost like watching a movie. …*Masquerade* is an unexpectedly wild ride, in turns thrilling and chilling. There's nothing more exciting than a woman's quest for freedom and self-discovery."—*Jude in the Stars*

"Heartbreakingly beautiful. This story made me happy and at the same time broke my heart! It was filled with passion and drama that made for an exciting story, packed with emotions that take the reader on quite the ride. It was everything I had expected and so much more. The story was dramatic, and I just couldn't put it down. I had no idea how the story was going to go, and at times I was worried it would all end in a dramatic gangster ending, but that just added to the thrill."—*LezBiReviewed*

Femme Tales

"If you're a sucker for fairy tales, this trio of racy lesbian retellings is for you. Bringing a modern sensibility to classics like *Beauty and the Beast*, *Sleeping Beauty*, and *Cinderella*, Shade puts a sapphic spin on them that manages to feel realistic."—Rachel Kramer Bussel, *BuzzFeed: 20 Super Sexy Novels Full of Taboo, Kink, Toys, and More*

"Shade twines together three sensual novellas, each based on a classic fairy tale and centering black lesbian love. ...The fairy tale connections put a fun, creative spin on these quick outings. Readers looking for sweet and spicy lesbian romance will be pleased."—*Publishers Weekly*

"All three novellas are quick and easy reads with lovely characters, beautiful settings and some very steamy romances. They are the perfect stories if you want to sit and escape from the real world for a while, and enjoy a bit of fairy tale magic with your romance. I thoroughly enjoyed all three stories."—*Rainbow Reflections*

"I sped through this queer book because the stories were so juicy and sweet, with contemporary storylines that place these characters in Chicago. Each story is packed with tension and smouldering desire with adorably sweet endings. If you're looking for some lesbian romance with B/F dynamic, then these stories are a cute contemporary take on the bedtime stories you loved as a kid, featuring stories exclusively about women of colour."—*Minka Guides*

"Who doesn't love the swagger of a butch or the strength and sass of a femme? All of these characters have depth and are not cardboard cut outs at all. The sense of family is strong through each story and it is probably one of the things I enjoyed most. *Femme Tales* is for every little girl who has grown up wishing for a happy ever after with the Princess not the Prince."—*Lesbian Review*

"All of these characters have depth and are not cardboard cut outs at all. The sense of family is strong through each story and it is probably one of the things I enjoyed most."—*Les Rêveur*

Visit us at www.boldstrokesbooks.com

By the Author

Femme Tales

Masquerade

Love and Lotus Blossoms

My Secret Valentine

Her Heart's Desire

Securing Ava

SECURING AVA

by

Anne Shade

2022

Credits
Editor: Cindy Cresap
Production Design: Susan Ramundo
Cover Design By Jeanine Henning

Chapter One

Ava groaned as her phone vibrated loudly on her nightstand. "Who the hell is calling at this ungodly hour?" she grumbled as she answered.

"It's nine thirty in the morning and we had a meeting scheduled for a half hour ago," her father responded on the other end.

"Shit!" Ava sat up so fast the room spun. "Sorry, Dad. I'll be there in forty."

"Thirty and not a minute later. I'm serious, Ava."

She could tell by the annoyed tone in his voice that having the privilege of being the boss's daughter wouldn't help her if she disobeyed. "Yes, sir," she said before hanging up, throwing the covers off, and sprinting to the bathroom.

After a quick shower, applying moisturizer and arranging her shoulder-length curls into the semblance of a bun, Ava went to her walk-in closet to grab the simplest outfit she could find, a navy suit with a double-breasted jacket that she didn't have to wear a blouse under, matching skinny crop pants, and a pair of white calf leather Manolo loafers. She headed back into her bedroom only to stop in the doorway at the sight of a curvaceous body outlined in her bed. She squinted trying to remember what happened the previous night and who the woman could be. The last thing she remembered was being at the bar with her best friend Travis and dancing with some Beyoncé-looking chick. She tiptoed toward the bed and saw a mass of blond curls spread across the pillow.

"Excuse me." The woman didn't even flinch. "Excuse me!" she said a little louder. This time she received a groan in response. "Um, I've gotta go, which means so do you."

Ava stepped away to finish getting dressed.

"What about the breakfast you promised me?" the woman said from behind her.

"Sorry, I've got a meeting, but you're welcome to use the shower and grab something from the fridge. My housekeeper should already be here so she can show you out."

Ava didn't mean to sound so callous, but her options were to enjoy a leisurely morning having breakfast in bed with a Beyoncé wannabe or not pissing her father off for the hundredth time. It was a no-brainer. Once she was dressed, she quickly glanced at herself in the mirror, grabbed a pair of diamond studs off her dresser, and rushed out of the bedroom without a glance back.

"Good morning, Ms. Prescott. I filled your to-go thermos with coffee and there's a whole wheat bagel with almond butter in a bag next to it," her housekeeper said as Ava passed her in the hallway.

"Sonya, you're a godsend. Would you please also ensure that my guest gets a little breakfast and finds her way out?"

Sonya shook her head with a knowing grin. "Of course. Have a nice day."

Ava stopped in the kitchen, grabbed her breakfast, and headed down the elevator to the lobby.

"Good morning, Ms. Prescott, would you like me to get you a cab?" the doorman asked.

"G'morning, Lenny. No, it'll be faster walking, thanks."

Lenny opened the door and touched the tip of his hat in parting. Ava was glad she'd chosen to walk. It was a beautiful spring day and Chicago's Willis Tower where Diamond Unlimited Wealth Management's offices were located was just a ten-minute walk from her apartment at Randolph Tower City. As she walked at a clipped pace and sipped at her coffee with a splash of vanilla just the way she liked it, Ava wondered what was so important that her father needed to meet at nine a.m. on a Monday morning. Mondays were usually her day to stroll into the office around noon to ensure that she'd recovered from whatever she'd done during the weekend. It had been an unspoken understanding between them for the past ten years as long as it didn't affect her work. Ava always made up for it by working ten- to twelve-hour days during the rest of the week and some Saturdays. When she'd seen the meeting pop up on her calendar Friday, she thought it might have been a mistake, so she didn't bother setting her alarm last night.

Ava arrived at her father's private conference room with a minute to spare. Of course, he was already there with his lap dog and chief financial officer Kyle Edwards who was sitting on her father's right in HER usual chair. Ava just smiled and headed toward the chair on her father's left. She'd let Kyle have his little power move moment, after all, he'd never have what he truly wanted, the position of CEO of Diamond Unlimited. He'd been gunning for that role since he'd joined their firm ten years ago and began sticking his nose so far up her father's ass Ava could swear there was a permanent brown ring around it. When her uncle Max, her father's brother and previous chief operating officer, retired two years ago, both Ava and Kyle were up for his vacated position, but Ava had worked too long and hard to let some brown-nosing hot shot take it from her.

The fact that her father had even been considering Kyle for the promotion pricked her pride, but she knew it was for optics. It couldn't look as if she got it because she was his daughter and heir-apparent, not that she'd received any of her jobs and promotions at the firm for that reason. Ava had literally started her career at her own family's business from the bottom as a mail room clerk right out of college and slowly moved up through the ranks like everyone else. Marcus Prescott did not play favorites or just give anyone something without making them work for it. He'd scraped, begged, borrowed, and sometimes even stole to provide for his mother, younger brother, sister, and himself after their father left them broke and homeless when he was just fourteen years old. Her father continued with that struggle as he put himself and both siblings through college and started Prescott Financial as a small brokerage firm with his brother Maxwell. By the time he was thirty, they had changed the name to Diamond Unlimited Wealth Management and were managing the investments and providing financial advice for some of Chicago's wealthiest young entrepreneurs and heirs to their own families' Fortune 500 businesses. Now, at sixty-five years old, he'd made Forbes 400 List of Richest Americans for the fifth time in the past five years, and the firm had also made the Fortune 500 list of top companies several times over the years.

Despite that, Ava's father never forgot where he started and how hard he worked to get to where he was. There was no way he was going to let his own child become one of those pampered and coddled rich kids who had everything handed to them because of who they were.

They would have to earn their privilege, money, and position just as he did. Unfortunately for Ava, she was his only child so all his hopes and dreams for the future of Diamond Unlimited were wrapped up into her. She didn't really mind because she loved what she did. She'd always had a gift for numbers and a head for business. To her father's surprise and enjoyment, she'd started many money-making ventures throughout her youth. The most profitable was a math tutoring business when she was in middle school that funded the purchase of many of her first big ticket items. Her first bike, all her electronics, and her first car were all bought with the money she made on her own. The only thing her father insisted on paying for was college. He didn't want her focusing on anything but getting her degree.

Unbeknownst to him, Ava still found ways to make a little extra cash on the side since he had her on a strict budget that covered the necessities like living and eating with no additional money for fun and entertainment. She gave financial advice, became a money lender, tutored, and held underground poker games all out of an off-campus apartment she'd rented under an alias and paid for with her own money so her father wouldn't be the wiser. She brought that same hard work and determination when she joined the firm and quickly proved to her father that she was not there to play or take handouts. Diamond Unlimited Wealth Management was just as much a part of her as it was him.

"Rough weekend?" Kyle said with a smirk.

"It was probably better than yours. Still seeing that mousy dental hygienist?" Ava said as she sat down and removed the bagel Sonya had packed for her from the bag.

"Better a mousy hygienist than partying all night and not knowing who the woman is you wake up next to," Kyle clapped back.

Remembering last night and how she woke up this morning, that hit a little too close to home. Ava gave him the finger as she took a bite of her bagel.

"Are you two finished?" her father said, trying not to look amused.

"Sorry, Dad," Ava said around a mouth full of food.

"Apologies, Marcus," Kyle said with a deferential nod.

"Good. First, Ava, explain this." Her father slid a magazine across the table to her. "Page six."

Ava set her breakfast down, licked a bit of errant almond butter off her fingers, and looked down at the publication. It was one of those gossip magazines people read while standing in line at the grocery store. She turned to page six. "Shit," she said under her breath.

FAMILY SITCOM ACTRESS SEEN IN A PASSIONATE POOLSIDE EMBRACE AT HER SANTA MONICA HIDEAWAY WITH A GORGEOUS MYSTERY WOMAN

Beneath the large print headline was a blurry picture of her and actress Selena Carlyle making out in a pool cabana. Next to that picture was an equally blurry one of her leaving Selena's house wearing a baseball cap, sunglasses, and a plain gray sweat suit.

"You can barely tell who it is." Ava slid the magazine back toward her father, sipping her now lukewarm coffee.

"If our marketing team can tell it's you then so can our clients. We have an image to uphold. Now, when you told us you were gay you promised to be discreet about your little dalliances. This isn't discreet. Nor is the parade of women coming in and out of your penthouse every weekend," her father said.

Ava frowned. "Are you spying on me?"

"No, but people talk. Especially people looking to profit off a possible scandal from your private life."

"Is there someone trying to do that?"

"The person who took those photos managed to figure out who you were and has been tailing you for several weeks taking more photos of you and Travis out partying and the women you bring home with you. Fortunately, your doorman Lenny caught him trying to sneak in the building and called the cops. When his camera was confiscated, they found the photos and the police chief called me concerned he might be a stalker. When he was questioned, he told them he was just a freelance paparazzo trying to make a buck. I promised I wouldn't press charges if he gave up his camera and computer. I paid him far more than they were worth and had them destroyed."

Ava felt embarrassed that her father had to clean up her mess that way. When she'd first come out to her parents in college her mother already had suspicions and embraced her, but her father had assumed it was just a phase. That it was normal for young people these days to experiment with their sexuality, but it wasn't the lifestyle the future CEO of Diamond Unlimited should consider permanent. Whatever she did behind closed doors was her business, but what happened in the light of day needed to be held up unblemished if they wanted people to trust them with their fortunes. Ava had been hurt by his reaction and figured he'd come around in time. After all, being gay wasn't the shameful pariah of a secret that it used to be. It wasn't until she'd brought her first serious girlfriend home to meet her parents that she realized her father's old-fashioned thinking wouldn't change. He had been pleasant enough the whole evening, but when Ava had returned home from dropping her girlfriend back off at her place, he'd told her that she would be held to a higher standard than their other employees as she was a representation of their family and the future of the business.

Ava didn't understand how her being gay represented the firm in a bad way, but it was her future and until she took over the reins, she would present herself in the way her father wished. So, she kept her romantic relationships discreet and brief. She now realized that the stress of the job since her promotion and the need to cut loose after work had caused her to be less careful than she usually was in her off hours.

Ava pushed her breakfast away and focused on her father. "I'm sorry, Dad. I'll be more discreet about what I do in my private life from now on."

He gave her a small smile and patted her hand. "I know you will." His expression turned serious again. "Now, this brings us to the other reason for this meeting. I brought you both here to discuss a merger that could benefit not only you but the firm."

"What kind of merger? I know Kyle mentioned the idea of bringing on a smaller firm to expand our portfolio, but I still think we don't need to do that. Our financial portfolio and business standing is fine without taking on another firm's debt."

Kyle gave her a look of frustration. "I hadn't suggested just any firm. It's a Black-owned brokerage firm that could use our reputation and backing to turn into something more. We could give them a chance to grow and expand the same way your father did when he started Diamond."

"That's not the type of merger I was referring to," her father said impatiently as if he were talking to two bickering children. "I'm talking about between you two. I'm going to suggest something, and I need you to both listen before responding. Can you do that?"

Ava frowned at Kyle who was frowning back at her. "What type of merger could possibly happen between us?"

Ava could admit that Kyle was great at his job, but something about his personality had rubbed her the wrong way since his second week at the firm when he'd tried to convince her father he'd be a better manager for two of her biggest clients. She wanted her father to string his ass up and kick him to the curb for trying to steal her business, but he explained it away as Kyle being overzealous in trying to impress him. Her father had sufficiently reprimanded him and there had been no further issues, but Ava still got a distrustful sneaky vibe from him when she caught him watching her sometimes.

"Ava," her father said sounding more annoyed.

She looked at him and nodded. "I'll listen."

Kyle nodded as well when her father looked over at him.

"Excellent," he sat back in his chair with his elbows on the arm rests and his fingers steepled beneath his chin the way he did when he was about to deliver a serious speech or bad news. "We have two issues here. One is Ava's predilections, which obviously are not going to change if they haven't after all this time, and the other is who will be running the firm when I decide to retire."

"Predilections!" Ava said angrily and was about to continue until her father narrowed his gaze at her. She clamped her mouth shut, matching his gaze with a twin version of her own.

Her father looked away first. "As I was saying, we have two issues which I feel can be resolved if you two can find a way to come together to present a wholesome and united front to our clients and competitors who are just waiting for Diamond to fail. All it will take is one scandal like the one that was narrowly averted with that photographer for us to lose our standing as one of the most prominent and successful Black-owned wealth management firms in the industry."

"Marcus, I'll do whatever it takes for that not to happen," Kyle said.

Ava scowled at him. "Kiss-ass," she said to herself.

"I'm glad to hear that, Kyle, because I think you and Ava should consider getting married."

"WHAT!" Ava and Kyle said in unison.

"It would be a marriage of convenience. A business arrangement to ensure that you, Ava, can avoid any such future scandal and hopefully give me some grandkids to continue our legacy. Also to have you both run the company together, as a team." Her father looked very proud of himself for his outlandish suggestion.

"Dad, you can't be serious. I'm GAY, remember? Not only am I quite capable of still having a family if I marry another woman but I'm also more than capable of running OUR family's business without a partner."

"Marcus, while I'm flattered you think I'm worthy of marrying your daughter, I don't think we would make a very good match even if she agreed with the idea. I am, however, more than happy to become a partner at the firm to work with Ava to keep it going upon your retirement." Kyle gave him one of his schmoozing smiles.

"Of course, you would. It's what you've been wanting since walking through our doors," Ava said with disgust.

The look Kyle gave her was filled with an angry intensity she'd never seen from him before, but it was quickly replaced by his usually deprecating smile when he looked back at her father.

Ava turned to her father. "May we speak in private?"

"Of course. Kyle, we'll continue this conversation later," her father said.

"Yes, sir." Kyle stood then left without giving Ava a second glance.

"Dad, why are you doing this? Are you that ashamed of me that you'd barter my future off to a man you know I don't even like?" Ava held back tears of disappointment.

Her father rolled his chair close to her and took her hands. The look on his face was the same sad look he used to give her when she was a little girl and he was trying to make her understand why she was being put on punishment for something she did. Was he punishing her for being gay? Hadn't she proven how capable and devoted she was to him and their business that she wouldn't do anything to jeopardize it? That she wanted a legacy just as he did to carry on.

"Ava, I'm doing this for you. You've given up more for this company, for my dreams, than I ever expected you to. You spend twelve hours a day here in the office and your weekends floating from one party and woman to the next. That's not the life I wanted for you."

"It's the life I chose. I love this firm just as much as you do. I wouldn't do anything to jeopardize it."

"I know, and that's the problem. What kind of LIFE will you have if I turned the reins completely over to you? What about love and a family? When was the last time you took a vacation that wasn't connected to a business trip? Also, I want grandkids to bounce on my knee before I'm too old to enjoy them. I want to know that our legacy doesn't end with you. And I'm prepared to do whatever it takes to ensure that."

Ava pulled her hands from his grasp. "You think marrying me off to Kyle and making him a partner will do that? You do remember you have to have sex to have children, don't you? I'd just as soon spend my life alone than have sex with that man, or any man for that matter. If you want to make him a partner, fine, but I won't marry him to satisfy your need for grandchildren."

He sat back in his chair with a tired sigh. "You will settle down and start a family, whether it's with Kyle or another man, you will maintain the image of a wholesome Black family behind this firm. As far as getting pregnant, I'm not so old that I don't know about artificial insemination. You and Kyle wouldn't even have to share a bedroom to do what needs to be done."

Ava couldn't believe what she was hearing. "And if I don't do this?"

"I didn't want it to come to this. I'd hoped you would come around and snap out of whatever this thing is you're going through and settle down, but it's obvious that won't happen, unless I step in. If you don't do this with Kyle or find some man who would be willing to strike up a beneficial arrangement with you, then I'll name Kyle as my sole replacement as CEO. You don't have to stay married forever, just a good five to ten years to make it believable."

Ava felt as if she'd just been gut-punched as all the air seemed to leave her body in one shaky breath. He was willing to take everything she'd spent her entire life working toward away from her just like that.

"Does Mom know what you're doing?" she asked when she was able to speak again. "She knows I'm gay and how I feel about Kyle. She'll never believe this farce."

He looked guiltily down at his hands. "No, and I'd prefer if she didn't. Let's keep this between us. You can tell her it turns out you're bisexual so when you start dating Kyle, or whoever you choose, it'll be more believable."

Ava shook her head in disbelief. "This is crazy. You can't honestly believe this will work."

"You're my daughter, you'll make it work," he said, almost too proudly. "So, what's it going to be, attempt at a normal life while running the firm with your partner in life and business or continue on your current path where you'll be working for, instead of with, Kyle Edwards?"

CHAPTER TWO

Paige stood at the entrance of her client's private jet carefully surveying their surroundings. Half of her twelve-person advance team was already on the tarmac. The others were at the villa her client rented for the week. As she walked down the steps, one of the men broke off from the group to meet her.

"Grant," she said in greeting.

"Sarge," he responded.

"I heard you had a little trouble."

Grant shrugged. "Nothing we couldn't handle. Found a few of the staff assigned to the villa had sketchy records. They've been removed."

Paige nodded. "You get the updated itinerary?"

He didn't even try to hide his annoyance. "Yeah. I think it's a bad idea. Something feels off about this one."

"I tried to warn him off the last-minute change, but he was insistent. Told me I was being paid to protect him, not to be his mother," Paige said, shaking her head.

Grant frowned. "Well, he needs a good ass-whooping from somebody's mother. I can't believe Ezekiel stuck us on this babysitting assignment while Lucas's crew got the one with the foreign dignitary in Dubai."

Paige gave him a sympathetic smile. "There'll be plenty of dignitaries in Dubai to protect in the future. Besides, isn't it nice not having to worry about bomb threats and military coups for once? We're going to be on a beautiful island in the Caribbean for an entire week watching over a spoiled Richie Rich with too much money and time on his hands. Considering the shitstorms we've been in, this is a much-needed vacation."

Grant sighed. "I guess you're right. My therapist has been telling me I need to slow down and de-stress."

Paige gave him a playful punch on the arm. "See, it's working out already."

"Yo! We doin' this or what?" someone shouted from behind her.

Grant smirked. "Vacation, huh?"

Paige rolled her eyes and turned toward their client who stood on the platform of the stairs with a cocky grin while the three buddies who had traveled with him jostled and joked behind him. Landon Scott, or L-Boogie as he liked to be called, was the son of a real estate mogul father and fashion designer mother and a wannabe rapper trying to become the next Eminem. For his twenty-first birthday his parents gifted him a week at a private villa on Mexico's Isla Mujeres with a few of his friends. His idea of a few friends was to invite over twenty people for a birthday blowout. Paige had no problem with him inviting people, it was his waiting until they were on the plane to tell her about it and refusing to give her a list of names, so there was no time to vet any of his guests. She tried explaining that her team couldn't do their job properly if he didn't cooperate, but the kid couldn't have cared less. He was just as annoyed with his father for hiring a security team to protect him, despite the kidnapping threats they had received recently.

Paige met Landon as he reached the bottom step. "Landon, I asked you to wait on the plane until I made sure everything was clear with my team. How can I keep you safe if you insist on making your own rules?"

Landon didn't look the least bit worried. "Look, every so often my father gets these threats that never result in anything but a new line item in the budget for additional security for everyone in the family. Look around, Paige, we're in paradise. Trade in that hot ass black suit for a sexy bikini and chill." He gave her a wink then headed toward the limo behind the lead car that would be taking them to the ferry transfer to the island. Paige shook her head in frustration.

This was supposed to be an easy assignment. No drama, no danger, and no death. It's what Ezekiel had promised for her last assignment as a private security contractor at Gold Standard VIP Protection, his executive protection firm. With a tired sigh, she headed toward the lead vehicle. Grant would be driving the limo with two other team members riding shotgun while the fourth member drove the lead car that she was riding in with the last two team members. As they left the airport, just for a moment, Paige had a flash of the last day of her tour of duty in Iraq five years ago. She'd been riding in the second vehicle of a three-car convoy heading back to the Marine base camp in Fallujah when the lead vehicle suddenly exploded. Her vehicle was rocked from the impact, but their driver was able to swerve off the road as debris from the explosion rained down on them. The third followed them and, as her driver radioed the base, Paige and the other soldiers exited the remaining Humvees ready to defend themselves against further attack. After several minutes with no gunfire or further explosions, Paige had ordered the soldiers from the third vehicle to cover them as she and her fellow riders moved in to check for survivors in the lead car. The sight that had greeted her still caused her such distress that she had to shake her head to rid herself of the haunting vision.

"You all right, Sarge?" Brian, the driver, asked.

Paige nodded. "I'm good, just tired."

It wasn't a complete lie. Fifteen years in the Marines, five of those as a counterintelligence specialist, two tours of duty in the Middle East, and the past five years working as a private security contractor had taken a lot out of her physically and emotionally. Before Paige even graduated high school, she knew she was going to be a Marine. Her mother had served ten years in the Army reserve before she and her brothers came along, and her father had recently retired from over forty years of service as a Marine. Her brother Randall had gone into the Navy and her brother Joshua had also chosen to follow in their father's footsteps into the Marines. Joshua's current location was classified, and Randall was stationed in Japan. They had planned to make their military service a lifelong career. Paige had considered it, but counterintelligence work wasn't as glamorous as the movies made it. It was a lonely and dangerous life. It could be weeks or months before she was able to contact family or friends, which made having a long-term romantic life almost impossible. She not only had her own safety to consider but that of her team and the people they were trying to obtain intelligence from.

When Paige retired, she'd been offered a position with the federal government as an analyst with the CIA but saw it as a civilian version of what she did in the military which she was trying to get away from. She spent two years after that in therapy to cope with all she'd seen and done and working on her uncle's ranch in Texas for peace of mind. When her old Marine captain contacted her about helping on a private security contract to protect the CEO of a financial firm during his travel to Dubai, she thought she found her niche. A job that utilized her military and counterintelligence skills without putting herself or anyone else in mortal danger. After that job, she signed on with Gold Standard VIP Protection as a freelance contractor not realizing that there were just as many dangerous contracts as there were straightforward. She spent almost as much time in the Middle East protecting some foreign dignitary or business executive as she did while she was in the military. After five years of too many close calls, she was ready to walk away from it all and retire on the ranch she bought in Oklahoma a year ago.

"Hey, Sarge," Grant's voice came through her earpiece sounding annoyed.

"Yeah."

"Richie Rich wants to stop and pick up a few things before boarding the boat."

Paige shook her head in frustration. After just one day with Landon, she was beginning to wish they had been given the Dubai job as well. "No, whatever he needs that isn't already supplied at the villa can be brought in by someone on the staff. If he argues, tell him that I said we can just as easily turn back around, and he can spend his birthday on the jet for all I care."

"Will do," Grant said happily.

Paige smiled. Grant and most of the members on her team had been on assignments with her at one point or another while she was in the Marines. She would trust any one of them with her life and felt bad that she'd dragged them along for this babysitting job, but they didn't know this was her last assignment. She wanted their time together to end on a relaxed note and planned to tell them once the assignment was over. They made it to the ferry in time to get the cars aboard and Landon and his friends settled in a mostly unoccupied section on the upper deck where Paige and her team could keep an eye without crowding them.

"I'm going to give Ezekiel a call to find out if he was able to get in touch with Landon's parents about the possible guest list for this party," Paige said

Grant nodded. "I'll sit here and pretend this glass of water is vodka which I'm going to need once this week is over."

Paige chuckled. "A bar will be our first stop as soon we drop Richie and his crew back home, I promise."

"I'm gonna hold you to that, Sarge."

Paige saluted him and stepped into the foyer for privacy.

"How's my number one contractor doing?" Ezekiel asked when he answered her call.

"About ready to throw Landon Scott overboard."

Ezekiel chuckled. "Hey, you said you wanted a no-stress last assignment. This was as low-stress as I could get you."

"I know and I appreciate it. It was fine until Landon sprung the party on me. Any luck on getting a possible guest list? According to the birthday boy, they're supposed to start arriving on Wednesday. That gives us a couple of days to try to at least get a cursory background check on them."

"His mother was able to get me a list of people that came to his New Year's Eve weekend party. She said they would most likely be the same people he invited to this shindig. I've already got our techies checking them all out. I'll send you a face book and let you know if there are any red flags."

Paige felt some relief over that news. "Great. If anyone shows up that's not on the list, we'll just have to make sure we keep an eye on them. I can't imagine there being any trouble, but better safe than sorry."

"Agreed. Have you told the team yet?" Ezekiel asked.

"No. I don't want to distract them from the job. It can wait."

"You know Grant is going to take this the hardest. He refuses to work with anyone else since you joined the company."

"I know, but I also think he'll understand more than anyone why I'm leaving."

"Yeah, you're probably right. Well, I'll get that intel to you within the hour. Call me if there are any other issues. I'll see you guys when you get back."

"Will do. Thanks, again Ezekiel. Not just for this but for everything else these past five years."

"You're more than welcome. I should be the one thanking you. It's been a pleasure working with you again."

They said their good-byes and Paige returned to the deck. Grant stood at the railing looking out over the water. Paige watched him for a moment, once again thrown back into the memory of the roadside bombing of their convoy. Grant had been in that first vehicle and lost a leg during the attack. He currently wore one of those high-tech prosthetics with the realistic silicone skin covering the entire prosthetic below the knee and the foot. You would have to look close to notice it wasn't real. He had proven himself many times over that having to wear it didn't hinder him in the least. Paige admired his tenacity and strength to get back into fighting mode and she had no hesitation with working with him. Unfortunately, it didn't stop the guilt she felt over his injury. She was supposed to be the one in the first vehicle but wanted to ride in the second with a communications specialist she'd recently started seeing, so Grant traded places with her. If she hadn't been thinking with what was in her pants, it would've been her instead of him walking around with a prosthetic leg. The guilt had been so bad that she couldn't even look at the woman after that.

Paige joined Grant and leaned on the railing beside him.

"Ezekiel said he'll have a possible guest list for us within the hour." She watched a bird soar over the island they were headed to in the distance.

"Good. I don't do surprises well and I have a feeling we're in for a big one."

"You still feeling like there's something off?"

"Yeah, I just haven't pinpointed it yet. I'll let you know when I do."

Paige nodded. She'd learned to trust Grant and his feelings during their assignments together in the military. Those feelings had gotten them out of some situations that were headed in a wrong and very dangerous direction. One was an assignment in London where they were collecting intelligence on a terrorist cell. Grant had been suspicious of their contact and decided to follow him after a meet one night. He found out the guy was playing both sides. The assignment was shut down and her team was pulled out of London just hours later.

"So, when were you planning on telling me that this is your last assignment?" Grant turned away from the Caribbean blue waters to look at her.

Paige looked at him in surprise. "How did you know?"

Grant smiled. "I didn't until you just told me."

Paige punched him in the arm. "Asshole."

"True." He gazed ahead of him again. "I don't blame you. You've been at this Secret Squirrel and protection shit a lot longer than I have. Hell, I'm thinking of retiring myself next year. Take over my father's garage, give Patrice the house in the suburbs with the white picket fence and two point five kids she's been wanting, and call it a life."

Paige smiled. "You think she's ready to have you home full-time?"

"She's pregnant." Grant's gaze was soft as he looked at Paige.

"Wow, Grant, congratulations!"

Grant's smile broadened proudly. "Thanks. It's a girl. We just found out before I left."

"I truly am happy for you. You deserve all the love and joy coming your way."

"You know you don't have to keep feeling guilty over what happened. Honestly, as devastating as losing my leg and my military career was, I think God was trying to tell me something. I was considering re-upping for another tour, Patrice was threatening to leave me if I did, and I honestly didn't care. The long stints of isolation with just the team were starting to get to me. Before our last assignment Patrice told me she felt like she was losing me. That I'd come home with this haunted look in my eyes that scared her. If the explosion hadn't happened and I didn't have Patrice supporting and taking care of me, I don't think I would've made it. I was in a dark place, and she became my lifeline, Sarge. I don't want her having to worry whether I'll make it home from an assignment every time I walk out the door, especially now that she's carrying our child. So, in a sense, losing my leg saved my life."

Paige's vision clouded with tears that she refused to let fall. She blinked them away and gazed out across the water. "It doesn't take away the guilt, but I'm glad to hear that you don't blame me."

"So, what are your plans after this?" Grant asked.

"I've been thinking of starting my own private investigation company. Something I can do from the ranch and be able to pick and choose which jobs I want to take on."

"Sounds cool. Paige Richards, Private Eye," Grant said in a dramatic television voice.

Paige chuckled. "Something like that."

"How are the renovations coming on the ranch?"

"It's move-in ready. Ezekiel has the Tech Twins doing a final sweep of the system and they'll be out by the time we get back."

"Nice. Well, feel free to give me a call if you need an extra pair of eyes for a case with a cheating spouse or embezzling executive. The less risk, the less likely my wife will kill me if I die."

"Will do."

They grinned happily at each other then turned back as the ferry neared the dock at Isla Mujeres.

Paige stood on the second-floor balcony overlooking the living room of the Villa surveying the room full of guests circulating in and out of the house and outdoor space. She did not have enough manpower for the craziness this had turned into. She'd received the face book of guests Ezekiel had put together and most of the people on that list had arrived as scheduled. It was the other fifteen who arrived just that morning that had her and her team of fourteen scrambling to wrangle the thirty-five people drinking, smoking, snorting, and doing God knows what else throughout the grounds. Her focus was guarding the room where Landon was currently occupied with two of his female guests.

"Sarge, we've got an issue down by the private dock," Tracey, her only other female team member, said over the earpiece.

"You want me to handle it?" Grant joined the conversation.

"No. I got it if you can come and keep an eye on lover boy up here."

"I'll be right there."

"Tracey, are you good until I can get down there?" she asked, giving Grant a nod as they passed on the stairs.

"Yeah, just some guy saying he has a delivery—What the fuck!"

Tracey's voice faded into a muffle and the connection was cut off. Paige was running and shoving people aside as she made her way through the crowded room.

"Brian, upstairs with Grant. Grant—"

"I'm on it," he said before she could finish telling him to get Landon to a safe place.

"Everybody else on me to the dock."

As soon as Paige managed to get clear of the crowded house, she was joined by six others as they sprinted past the pool down toward the villa's private beach and dock. A gunshot rang out and a surge of partiers that had been hanging out on the beach came running toward them.

"MOVE MOVE MOVE!" Paige shouted at them as her team drew their weapons and rounded the bend leading to the dock.

With Grant and Brian at the house, Tracey at the dock with three others, that left Paige with the remaining seven team members merging on the commotion taking place on a small charter boat where the security team was subduing three men.

"Grant," Paige said into the communication device.

"We're good, but Richie Rich is gonna have quite the headache when he wakes up."

Paige was tempted to ask what that meant, but if Grant said they were fine then it could wait until she got back to the house. They approached Tracey and her crew as they were zip-tying their attackers' hands and feet and collecting what looked to be two handguns and an AR15 rifle. It wasn't until she made sure that they were sufficiently subdued that she put her gun back into her holster.

Tracey looked annoyed but unharmed. "These clowns attempted to pull an okeydoke on us. This one"—she pointed to a man with a bloody and probably broken nose—"claimed they had a birthday delivery for Landon, but when I told him we needed to check it out before we could let him take it off the boat. He freaked out yelling about how he was going to lose his job and some other crazy shit. Just as I signaled for the guys to come aboard and check it out, the idiot tried to pull a gun on me, but I popped him in the nose before he could. Then the hatch opened, and the other two idiots jumped out with their weapons, but Locke and Drake quickly disarmed them."

"What was the gun shot?" Paige asked.

Tracey grinned in amusement. "Idiot number one tried to jump ship until I shot his hat off."

"You could've blown my head off, stupid bitch," he said angrily.

"Yeah, I could've," Tracey said with a shrug.

Paige held back a grin. "You call the local police yet?"

"Not yet. I thought you might want to have a chat with them. I'm guessing by the lack of an accent that they're American."

"Yeah, bring them to the boathouse while I check on things at the main house. I'm guessing a couple of our party goers weren't who they said they were, and this was their ride home."

"Will do, Sarge," Tracey said.

"You three with me," Paige said pointing at three of the guys who had followed her down to the dock. "The rest of you go through that boat and see what you can find."

As Paige neared the house, she realized the music had stopped and it was quiet. When they came into view guests were sitting around the pool and standing in the doorway of the house looking anxiously in their direction.

"Everything is fine, folks," she announced.

"We heard gunshots," someone shouted.

"It was the engine backfiring from a delivery boat at the dock. Nothing to be concerned about. Continue enjoying yourselves." She gave them her best smile as she strode through the crowd and headed straight upstairs.

Brian was standing outside Landon's room. He gave her a nod and opened the door. Landon sat on the bed wincing in pain with an ice pack on his head. The two women he'd been with were zip-tied just like the men at the dock and Grant stood nearby smirking in amusement. Paige directed the men who had come with her to take the women down to the boathouse. Unfortunately, with a full house of people, there was no way to be discreet about it.

"If you can, take them through the service hall and out the kitchen. There's a more shrouded path to the boathouse from there used for offloading supplies."

They nodded and did as she instructed, leaving her and Grant alone with Landon.

"Bitches tried to kill me," Landon complained while rubbing his head.

"If they wanted you dead then you would be. They were probably just trying to incapacitate you to get you out of the house." Grant had no sympathy for him.

"Do you know how they had planned to do that?" Paige asked Grant.

"The balcony. I guess they were going to lower him down from there and take him to whoever was waiting for them at the dock. Everybody good?"

"Yeah, Tracey broke somebody's nose and fired a warning shot, but the team is good. I guess they wouldn't have gotten far with the men you decided to station under the balcony."

Grant nodded. "Spidey sense for the win."

Paige smiled. "The party is over," she told Landon.

He looked up at her with a frown. "What? No!"

"Yes. I told you we couldn't protect you if you didn't cooperate. Going your own way almost got you kidnapped. Your so-called friends ain't gotta go home, but they gotta get the hell out of here and we're leaving first thing in the morning."

"You can't do that!"

"I can and I will."

Paige took her phone out of her pocket and called Ezekiel. She barely gave him a chance to say hello. "We're wrapping it up. Need you to contact the locals to pick up some trash, but give me about an hour to go through it for information."

"Will do. How's the family?" Ezekiel asked.

"Present and accounted for. We'll see you back at the house tomorrow."

After a brief parting word, she hung up.

She joined Grant who stood by the balcony. He placed an arm around her shoulder.

"Did you really think you would be able to walk away without a little excitement," he said in amusement.

Paige sighed tiredly. "A girl could hope."

This just proved she'd made the right decision. If the kidnappers had been more professional instead of the bumbling idiots they were, this could've gone sideways really quick, and Landon's guests would've been caught in the crossfire. She looked over at him sitting there pouting like the spoiled child he was and decided that once she started her private eye business, there would be no cases involving babysitting self-absorbed little heirs and heiresses.

Chapter Three

A va gazed at herself in the mirror as a seamstress made the final adjustments on her wedding dress. It was a four-thousand-dollar designer fit and flare gown in white crepe with a deep v-neckline, cap sleeves, and a deep v-back. It was simple and elegant. Under any other circumstances she would've loved the way the gown accentuated her small breasts, narrow waist, and softly rounded hips and behind that she'd inherited from her mother, but at that moment, she felt like a dressed up ungainly giraffe.

"You have the perfect frame for this gown. Your husband-to-be will be left speechless when he sees how beautiful you look," the seamstress said as she smoothed the gown over Ava's waist and hips. "Are you ready to show your family?"

Ava gave her a small smile and nodded. She lifted the hem of the dress just enough to walk without tripping since she didn't have her heels on and through the door the seamstress held open for her. Her mother, her father's sister Joan, her mother's sister Charise, and her best friend and man of honor Travis all sat outside the dressing room waiting for her to perform her happy bride routine. As soon as she came into view of them gasps of delight filled the room. Her mother's eyes filled with tears as she gave her a toothy smile. Ava tried to return the smile, but her heart just wasn't in it. She stepped onto the pedestal and did a little turn.

"It looks even better now than it did when you first tried it on. I know I said you should've gotten a more dramatic and detailed gown, but now that I see the final look, I must admit this was the perfect choice for you. You make a beautiful bride." Her mother stepped up onto the pedestal beside her and wrapped an arm around her waist as they both gazed at her reflection in the mirror.

Ava felt tears she'd been holding back burn her eyes and despair clog her throat. "Thank you," she managed to squeeze past the lump.

Her mother's bright smile dimmed, and her brow furrowed in worry. "You don't like it?"

"Oh, no, I love the dress. It's perfect." Ava tried to sound happier than she was.

"Then what's wrong? You don't look like a woman about to walk down the aisle to marry the man of her dreams in a week."

Ava wanted to scream and cry that this was all a farce. She didn't want to get married, especially to Kyle Edwards who she had developed even more of a dislike for over the past eighteen months of their fake romance. On paper and in the public eye, they were perfect for each other and madly in love. The fear of completely losing her family's legacy to a man who didn't truly appreciate the sacrifices that that legacy was built on pushed Ava to hone acting skills she hadn't used since her theater days in college. Ironically, that was where she'd first met Selena, the actress she had an on-again, off-again affair with for the past twelve years and who she'd been photographed with that started the mess she was in now. She couldn't tell her mother any of that because she would talk her out of continuing with the charade and probably ream her father another asshole for browbeating her into it.

"Just pre-wedding jitters, I guess." Ava broadened her smile to appear happier.

Her mother knew her too well. "Uh-huh," she said skeptically. "We'll talk later." She gave Ava's waist a quick squeeze and gave her a peck on the cheek before stepping down to allow Ava's aunts to fawn over her.

An hour later, she sat across from Travis at their favorite brunch spot. Normally she couldn't get enough of enjoying the restaurant's spectacular view of the jewel-like sparkling water of Lake Michigan, but even that couldn't breach the fog of despair clouding her heart.

"Are you sure you want to go through with this?" Travis asked.

Ava picked at her roasted chicken and Brussels sprout hash, which was usually her favorite dish, but she currently had no appetite for. "I don't have much of a choice, do I? It's either go through with this fiasco or walk away from everything I've worked my ass off for all these years."

"Is going through with it so bad? I mean Kyle is a self-absorbed, conniving prick but he's a fine-azz self-absorbed, conniving prick. At least your father isn't trying to marry you off to Conrad in accounting."

Ava had to smile at that. Conrad was nerdy, socially awkward and didn't have an athletic bone in his body, but he was funny and sweet. He'd been crushing on Ava since they'd started in the mailroom together all those years ago and was devastated when he found out she was gay, but they'd remained friends. He and Travis were the only ones who knew the real reason behind her surprising romance with Kyle and he'd even offered himself up so that she wouldn't have to marry a man she couldn't stand. Ava had thanked him and politely turned him down. She didn't think his fiancée would've been too keen on the idea.

"I could've dealt with Conrad as a fake husband, he doesn't seem to have a deceitful bone in his body, but there's something about Kyle I just don't trust. At least this way I can keep a better eye on him if we're living in the same house." Ava gave a shudder at just the thought of sharing her space with Kyle.

Travis gave her a sympathetic smile. "My offer still stands. If I have to marry a woman for appearances, I couldn't imagine anyone better than you."

Paige reached across the table and took his hand. "Aw, thanks, but I wouldn't do that to you. It wouldn't be fair to pull you back into the closet with me. Besides, I need you to keep digging for anything you can find on Kyle. If anyone can find what I need to oust him for the schemer that I think he is, it's you."

Ava had met Travis at college when she'd inquired with the tech geeks on campus about who was the best hacker among them. Travis had been sent her way and made his introduction by hacking into her computer and uploading dozens of selfies of himself on her main screen. A normal person would've been angry, but considering he'd managed to get through the security her father's best IT guys had put on her personal laptop she was impressed. She'd hired him to hack into the personal cell phone and computer of a male professor who had been rumored to be sexually harassing Black females on campus, one of which she had been dating. The administration had pretty much ignored the complaints. With Travis's assistance she exposed the man by blasting screenshots through social media of the inappropriate text messages and emails that he'd been sending making sure not to reveal who they'd been sent to. They'd been best friends ever since.

"Other than the juvie record I managed to dig up, Kyle is cleaner than Mr. Clean, but I'll keep looking," he promised.

"Thank you."

Travis shrugged. "What's the point in having a professional hacker as a best friend if you can't use him to dig up dirt on your archenemy?"

Ava chuckled. "Have I told you how much I love you?"

Travis gave her a cocky grin. "No need to. Who wouldn't love me?"

Ava had promised her mother she would come over for dinner that evening and was considering canceling with the excuse that she wasn't feeling well. She knew her mother wanted to continue the conversation she'd started at the bridal boutique about Ava's obvious lack of enthusiasm over her wedding. She wished she could avoid it, but her mother would probably just show up on her doorstep if she didn't show up for dinner. Once Lynn Prescott locked on to there being something wrong with someone she loved, she didn't let up until she found out what it was. She could have you confessing to something you'd just thought about doing by the time she finished interrogating you.

Ava stopped by a liquor store to pick up a bottle of her mother's favorite tequila on her way to their penthouse apartment at the luxury high-rise Coast at Lakeshore East located right on the Chicago River. It was their home when they stayed in the city, but their main residence was the home Ava had grown up in the Chicago suburb of Forest Glen. Since the wedding was just a week away and taking place at a venue in the city, her parents had been staying at their penthouse for the past two weeks so that her mother could personally make sure all the arrangements were perfect for her only child's big day. In the elevator on the way up to the apartment she tried to quell her nervous energy, or her mother would definitely know something was wrong.

Ava had been the only child who had survived to full-term after a decade of her parents going through infertility issues and treatments. They were considering using a surrogate when her mother had found out she was pregnant with Ava. She spent most of the pregnancy on bed rest and Ava arrived four weeks prematurely but was healthy and thriving within a matter of weeks. Her mother always said she'd been a fighter, not letting anyone push her around or make her cow to their wishes.

"I guess that isn't completely true," Ava said to herself as the elevator pinged for the top floor.

Ava took a deep breath to steady her nerves then used her key to enter her parents' private domain. The penthouse had an open concept layout so she could see her mother across the expansive space stirring something in a pot on the stove. She turned, smiling happily at Ava's entrance.

"Hey there, Buttercup," her mother said, calling Ava by the childhood nickname she'd been given because it symbolized new beginnings and joy, which was what her parents had believed Ava's birth symbolized for their lives.

"Hey, Mom." Ava made her way across the room and planted a loud kiss on her mother's cheek. "Brought you a little present." She handed her mother the bottle of Roca Patron Reposado Tequila she'd stopped to pick up.

Her mother looked at the bottle with a smile of delight. "I was just telling your father we needed to get a few more bottles to replace the ones we finished off at my birthday party. Thank you." Ava received a kiss on her cheek in return.

"What smells so good?" Ava peeked into the pot her mother had been stirring.

"Just marinara for the pasta. Would you mind grabbing a bottle of that sauvignon you brought back from California?" her mother asked.

"Sure."

Ava walked across the kitchen to a wine pantry where her father meticulously categorized and labeled the wine by country and type. She searched for and found the four bottles she brought back during a business trip to Diamond Unlimited's West Coast office. Ava and Selena had spent the weekend prior to that scandalized photo of them at a bed-and-breakfast in Napa Valley. Her parents thought she'd gone there by herself for a short sabbatical, but she and Selena had barely left the room until their last morning when they had spent the day at a nearby winery. She'd bought a case of cabernet sauvignon and had it shipped to her parents. Ava smiled wistfully as she thought about that weekend and how she'd tried to convince Selena that they could make a serious relationship work if they just tried. But Selena wasn't willing to leave her life in Los Angeles and Ava wasn't willing to leave the company in the hands of someone other than a Prescott once her father retired. The irony of that now in the face of what was going on didn't go unnoticed. Ava sighed in frustration and went back to join her mother who was just finishing setting up their dinner at the smaller dining table in the kitchen.

"Here you go." Ava gave her mother the bottle.

Once they were settled with dinner on their plates and their wine glasses filled, Ava's mother took a long sip of hers then cleared her throat. "So, why are you marrying a man you don't love?"

Ava should've known her mother wouldn't waste time getting to the point. "What makes you think I don't love him?" She looked down at her plate and concentrated on twirling spaghetti around her fork.

"Ava, look at me."

Ava hesitated for only a moment before she laid her fork down, folded her hands in her lap, and met her mother's piercing hazel eyes.

"What's going on? Does your father have anything to do with this sudden trip to the altar with a man you couldn't stand just days before you suddenly started dating after spending the past fifteen years dating only women?"

"This was my decision. I told you, Kyle and I hadn't gotten along because we were too busy competing at work to become friends. Then when we spent that weekend in New York stuck at the hotel during a nor'easter we got to know each other and found we had a lot in common. Our friendship and mutual respect turned into more and here we are."

It didn't sound any more believable now than it did when she'd first repeated the story that she and Kyle had come up with eighteen months ago. She could see in her mother's eyes that she still found it hard to believe.

"Bullshit," she said, confirming the look.

"Mom, I'm getting married in a matter of days. Does it matter? It's too late to turn back now." Ava took a large sip of her wine.

"It's never too late. You insisted on a small, intimate wedding with just close family and friends so it's not like we broke the bank to pay for the three-hundred-person extravaganza your father wanted, so I don't care about the money. What I do care about is my daughter being pressured to do something she doesn't want to do that could affect the rest of her life and happiness. Now, I know your father has something to do with this because he is way too excited to be giving his baby girl away. If you don't tell me then I'm going to ask him."

Ava's mother sat back in her chair with her arms crossed and a determined gleam in her eyes. She knew that look well. She would have to tell her the truth sooner or later because her mother would not give up, even if it meant badgering her father into admitting all.

"If I tell you, you have to promise me you won't get mad at Dad. He meant well."

Ava's mother gave an unladylike snort. "I'll make no such promises. Now talk."

Ava decided full-out honesty with her mother was best. It's what kept their relationship so close. When it came to serious matters, they'd always been open and honest with each other. Sure, it had led to some pretty heated arguments and days of not speaking to each other when she was a teenager, but Ava's mother's relationship with her own mother was toxic. She'd promised herself that she wouldn't be that way with her children. Ava took another sip of wine and then told her mother everything. Including the paparazzi photographer that started it all. She listened with a quiet intensity that always unnerved Ava. She continued to sit quietly several minutes after Ava finished. She knew not to say anything. It was her mother's way of processing something she wasn't thrilled to hear.

"So, your father basically blackmailed you into marrying Kyle in order to save the wholesome family appearance behind the firm."

"I guess you could call it that." Ava was wary of the calm before the storm she knew was about to erupt.

Her mother pushed her chair back, stood, picked up her water glass, and went to the sink. She poured the water out, opened the bottle of tequila Ava bought her and filled the glass. When she raised the glass to her lips and drank the contents down as if it were still water, Ava watched her worriedly.

"Mom?"

"I'm going to kill him," she said calmly, then refilled her glass and came back to sit at the table.

"I don't think prison orange is your color."

"I hear they have a nice khaki in some facilities."

There was a tense moment of silence before her mother looked at her, gave her a quick smile, then frowned again. "He's gone too far this time, Ava. That damn company almost destroyed this marriage once. Now he's using it to manipulate your life. I won't let him do that."

"Mom, you know what the business means to him. It represents his life's struggles and achievements. If it fails, if there's anything that puts it in a negative light, then he's failed. I don't like that he found it necessary to blackmail me and it hurts that he believes being true to myself makes me unqualified to take over when the time comes, but I understand why he did it."

Like him, at the time, she was willing to do whatever needed to be done to maintain the Prescott Legacy which was why she'd agreed to the arranged marriage. Ava's mother laid her hand palm up on the table. Ava laid her hand in her mother's.

"Are you truly going to go through with this? I can't simply sit by and watch you throw your life away like that," her mother said angrily.

Ava's father chose just that moment to walk in. "Well, would you look at that. My two favorite girls."

Ava looked from her mother's livid expression to her father's happy grin and wanted to run for the hills. Instead, she turned her cheek up for the kiss he was bending to give her. "Hey, Dad."

He went to her mother, bent to give her a kiss as well but was rebuffed when she stood and carried her glass over to the counter and refilled it. Ava's mother could hold her own against the alcohol, but she feared for how her father was about to fair against his angry and slightly inebriated wife.

"You've got a lot of nerve, Marcus Emmanuel Prescott," her mother said.

Her father looked at her mother, then Ava and back in confusion. "What did I do?"

"What did I do?" Ava's mother mocked him. "You did what you promised me you'd never do again. You put the reputation of that damn company before your own family's happiness."

Ava's father walked over, looked at the bottle of tequila, and corked it. "Lynn, honey, I think you've had enough. Whatever it is I did, I'm sorry."

She snatched the bottle from him. "Are you?"

"Dad, she knows about the arrangement," Ava admitted.

Her father looked disappointed but also relieved. "Surprised it took this long for her to find out." He sat in his mother's vacated seat and took a sip of her wine. "I did what I thought was best for Ava and the company."

"Bullshit. You did what you thought was best for YOU and the company. We're calling this wedding off. I won't allow Ava to be shoved back into the closet to marry that self-absorbed prick in order to satisfy a bunch of old rich White dudes' delicate sensibilities," Ava's mother commanded.

Ava held back a smile. Her mother may be able to hold her alcohol, but it loosened her tongue. All she needed was one more glass and she was close to dropping the F-bomb any minute.

Ava's father sighed. "Lynn, can we please sit down and discuss this like reasonable adults?"

"No because you're the one not being reasonable. Marcus, this is our daughter's life you're playing with, not some financial portfolio. You can't just sell her off like some unwanted stock." Ava's mother sat on the other side of her, the glass of tequila forgotten on the counter. "What would ever make you think this was a good idea?"

"Lynn, you, of all people, know the blood, sweat, and tears I put into this company in order to build the legacy my father denied us. I won't let a scandal kill our business, see it turned over to a board of directors or run by someone other than a Prescott, or someone of my choosing. This was the most efficient and sensible solution. It doesn't have to be long-term, just long enough to secure our standing once Ava steps up to take the plate. Besides, Ava agreed to it."

"Of course, she did, after you threatened to take away the one thing that matters even more than her own happiness. That was beyond manipulative even for you. I'm so disappointed in you."

Ava sat between her parents looking at her mother's heartbroken expression and her father's look of regret and felt compelled to find a way to make them both happy. If she went through with the marriage, her father would get what he wanted, and, in a way, so would she, but she'd also sacrifice her own freedom and happiness in the process. If she called it off like her mother wanted, she'd have her freedom, but she would sacrifice her dream and allow her father to turn the company over to a man she didn't trust. She wanted to tell her father about her doubts about Kyle, but he would think she was trying to get out of the marriage and would also want proof, which she didn't have. A juvenile record didn't prove anything since her father also had one. He saw himself in Kyle, as well as probably the son he never had, which was why he was so blind to what Ava's instincts, the same ones she'd inherited from him, were telling her.

"Mom, this is my decision. Despite how he went about it, Dad isn't forcing me to do anything. It's about the optics and a business arrangement that I chose to agree to. This company, our legacy, is worth any sacrifice I need to make." She reached over and took her mother's hand. "Please try and understand. Both Kyle and I agreed that it would only be for five years. After that, we can go our separate ways and live the life of our choosing."

"And the children you're planning to have? What will happen to them when you two end your arrangement? Will they have to pay the price for this foolishness?" her mother asked bitterly.

Ava hadn't thought about this being a trigger for her mother's own issues as a child of a very public and nasty divorce. Honestly, she and Kyle hadn't even discussed children yet. They had been too busy trying to maintain the appearance of the happy power couple to talk about anything past the wedding except for the agreed upon dissolving of the marriage in five years.

"I guess that's something you'll have to discuss at the meeting to draw up your agreement with Bernie in the morning," her father said.

"Is that all marriage is to you, Marcus? A contract? Forty years together and this is what giving away our daughter on what should be the happiest day of her life has come to?" Tears slid down her mother's cheeks.

Ava's heart was breaking for her mother and making her doubt the sense of this plan. She looked at her father. He looked just as unsure, something she'd never seen in the confident man she'd known her whole life.

He moved to sit in the chair beside her mother and took her hand. "Lynn, you are the love of my life and have been from the moment I met you. You made me want to be a better man and showed me how to love. You and Ava are my world, I would never do anything to hurt you."

"Then don't go through with this." Ava's mother gazed over at her and offered her hand. Ava took it. "Don't let that damn business break this family again." Her mother looked back at her father. "There's still time to call it off. There's no reason why Kyle can't still be made a partner and Ava still can't have a family of her own in her own way. The day Ava was born you promised that you would always be here to love and protect her. That nothing would ever come before your family. This is the second time you've broken that promise. I love you with all my heart, Marcus, but I won't sit by and wait for a third."

Ava's father looked surprised. "Are you threatening me?"

"No. I'm telling you what will happen if you persist on this path." She turned back to Ava. "I won't stand by and watch you walk the same path your father has, putting this legacy you two speak so proudly of before your own happiness. If you decide to go through with this wedding, I won't be there. I have loved and supported you no matter what was going on in your life, but I can't support this." She released both their hands, stood, and left the room.

Ava gazed over at her father who stared in the direction her mother had gone. He looked so small and vulnerable. Like her mother was the one that gave him strength and when she left the room, she'd taken all of it with her.

"Dad?"

It took him a moment meet her gaze. "She's right. I'm an ass."

"She didn't say that."

Sighing heavily, he reached for the glass of wine her mother had left behind. "Not in those exact words but that's what she meant." He looked at her. "I knew I was going too far suggesting this idiotic plan, but when your uncle Max retired, and Maxwell Jr. showed no interest in stepping up and taking a leadership role beside you as a partner I got scared. I didn't want to solely burden you with keeping Diamond going and Kyle showed such promise and interest in the company that I thought he'd be the only person outside the family I could trust with helping you. Then this ridiculous idea for a marriage arrangement came to me and somehow seemed like the perfect solution to truly keeping it all within the family. Max knew your and Kyle's relationship was all a charade from the beginning and guessed I was probably behind it. He told me it was wrong, but you had agreed to it, and I'd already gotten it in my head that it could work so I didn't put a stop to it like I should have."

"The only reason I agreed is because you threatened to take the company from me. You know I love Diamond just as much as you do and would do anything to keep her. You even had me believing this was for the best, but lately I've wanted to march in your office and tell you I'm done. If this is the only way for you to see that I'm more than capable of stepping into your shoes, then I don't want it. But then I think of Diamond being put in Kyle's hands and having to work for him and tamp all of that down and just keep trudging ahead." It felt good admitting that to her father.

"I would never have given Kyle full reign if you hadn't agreed to the arrangement," her father admitted quietly, looking like a child caught in a lie.

Ava wasn't sure she'd heard him correctly. "Are you serious?" Marcus Prescott was known to be a shrewd poker player. Ava had seen him in action and had learned from the best, but she was hurt that he'd deal and bluff such a shitty hand with her. "How could you?" She felt the pinprick of tears coming and let them fall. She wanted her father to see how hurt she was.

He moved the wineglass aside and reached for her hand. Ava shook her head and put her hand in her lap. He looked disappointed and she didn't care in the least.

"Buttercup, I'm sorry. I was blinded by the fear of losing everything we both worked for. Then when that photographer showed up ready to bring you down with that story, I thought that I had to protect you. This plan was supposed to keep the company, and you, safe."

Sadly, Ava could see what her father was trying to do and knew he meant well, but it still hurt like hell that he played her. "You could've just talked to me. We could've figured out another way that wouldn't involve having to marry me off to a man I don't like or trust. All this did was make me think you don't trust me to run Diamond because of my sexuality."

"That's not true at all. You've more than earned the right to take over once I retire. I just didn't want you having to do it alone and make the same mistakes I did. For so many years, I was so focused on the business that I wasn't there for you and your mother like I should've been. I was being truthful when I told you I didn't want that life for you and honestly believed this would help. Your sexuality has nothing to do with any of this. I may not agree with it, but I love you and I don't ever want you to think I don't accept you for the beautiful, intelligent, strong woman that you are, and I'll prove it to you right now." He pulled his phone from his inside jacket pocket and made a call. "Hello, Kyle, are you busy? Can you come by the penthouse? Excellent. I'll see you then." He hung up and laid his phone on the table.

"What are you doing?" Ava asked.

He gave her a tentative smile. "What I should've done months ago. Calling this whole thing off. Now, in the interim, I need to go do some serious groveling to get your mother to forgive me."

CHAPTER FOUR

An hour later, Ava's parents had made up and were sitting with her in the formal dining room when Kyle arrived. Her father went to greet him as she and her mother waited.

"Do you think he'll take this well?" her mother asked.

Ava shrugged. "Hard to say. Kyle is a tough read and judging by how believable we've been as a couple all this time he's just as good at acting as I am. The distrust I have for him is more from what he did early on and just a vibe I get in general. I can't imagine him not at least being relieved since he'll still have his status at the company and won't have to be married to someone he doesn't like just as much as they don't like him."

When Kyle and her father entered, he didn't seem surprised to see Ava there, which she found curious considering she didn't hear her father tell him she would be there. Maybe she was reading too much into it. After all, it was her parents' house, they were supposed to be getting married in a matter of days and her parents were footing the bill. It made sense that they might want to discuss final logistics with the bride and groom.

Kyle placed a kiss on Ava's mother's cheek. "Good evening, Lynn. You're looking lovely as usual."

Ava discovered that her mother wasn't a fan of Kyle's either but had kept her opinion to herself until tonight. She told Ava he was just too perfect and too charming for his own good, but she accepted the kiss and compliment with a pleasant smile. "Thank you, Kyle. Can I get you something to drink?"

"A seltzer would be great, if it's not a problem."

"Not a problem at all." Her mother went to the mini fridge in the corner to retrieve a bottle of seltzer, then grabbed a glass off the credenza and placed it on the table in front of Kyle before retaking her seat beside Ava.

Ava's father sat at the head of the table with her and her mother sitting on his right and Kyle sitting alone on his left.

Kyle poured his seltzer in the glass and took a sip. "So, are we here to discuss the final wedding details?"

"I guess you could say that," Ava's father answered. "We're going to call it off. I had no right into pressuring you and Ava into doing this. You'll still retain your projected seat as a partner as you've earned it. You're free to return to your life as it was before my egomaniacal scheming interrupted it."

"You're calling the wedding off? Just like that. Like I have no say in it." Kyle glared angrily at her father and then Ava. "Is this your doing?"

Ava was confused by his anger. "I thought you'd be relieved. You wanted to get married about as much as I did. It was a business transaction you will still reap the benefits of without having to tie us to each other for the next five years."

Kyle glared at her for a moment longer then schooled his face back into its usual amenable expression like sliding a mask on. It was a little disturbing. "My apologies, I was just surprised. I mean the wedding is just days away. Won't our canceling cause a bit of a scandal. It may not look good for the optics."

Ava's father waved dismissively. "I'm sure we can come up with a reasonable story to satisfy the gossipmongers."

"I have an idea. Instead of calling it off completely, we can postpone it. Say Marcus wasn't satisfied with the pre-nuptial agreement you were supposed to finalize tomorrow and wants to put the wedding off for a bit. That way it won't be either Ava's or Kyle's fault." Her mother quirked a brow at her father. "After all, you got them in this mess, you should be the one to take the fall for them to get out of it."

Ava's father grinned in amusement. "Sounds like a sound plan. Then, over time, your romance fizzles out and you're both free to move on with your lives. Are you two in agreement?"

Ava nodded. "I am."

Everyone looked expectantly at Kyle. Ava could see a slight tic in his cheek and his smile didn't reach the angry glare in his eyes as he looked at her. "Sounds good to me."

Ava's father sighed in relief. "Excellent. I'll have my assistant start emailing and calling the guests first thing Monday morning. Kyle, would you like to contact the few people you had on the list, or would you be fine with Lori doing it?"

"I'd prefer to reach out to them myself if you don't mind. Ava, if it's no trouble, I'd also like to pick up the few items in the morning that I'd already brought over to your place. No need to prolong the inevitable."

"That's fine. I have an appointment, but I'll let Sonya know you'll be coming by. Dad, do you have anything else?"

"No. I think we're good. Kyle, why don't we meet on Monday at eight to discuss next steps in your move to partnership. I hope you'll accept my apology for this fiasco," her father said.

"Of course, Marcus. I completely understand and agree this is all for the best."

There's the ass-kisser she recognized and despised, Ava thought. They all stood as Kyle got up to leave. Her father walked him out.

"That went well," Ava's mother said.

"Almost too well. Did you see his face?"

Ava's mother shuddered. "I'm glad I'm not the only that caught that. It was like watching someone morph into another person."

Ava gazed toward the doorway. "That's what I was thinking. I've seen it happen several times since this whole thing began. I'll turn to find him staring at me with this dark look of almost hatred then it quickly changes back to that creepy smile. How does Dad not see it?"

"I don't know, but even he couldn't have missed it this time. Watch your back at the office, Ava. I don't trust him not to throw a figurative knife in it after tonight. I think Kyle may have had his own agenda for agreeing to your father's scheme and it was just shot to hell."

Ava thought the same thing but hoped they were wrong.

As Ava and Travis sat in the café of the fitness center where they worked out enjoying protein smoothies after their Saturday morning session, she filled him in on the wedding update.

"I can't say I'm not relieved. I mean, I was going to look great in that burgundy tux, but I would've rather been wearing it for your real wedding."

Ava smiled. "You did look GQ cover worthy in it." Then she frowned as she gazed wistfully down at her cup. "You know, I hadn't really thought about marriage or a family of my own until this craziness began. Now I'm wondering if I wasted too much time for it to happen."

"Of course not. You're only thirty-five which is when many women nowadays are starting families because they choose to focus on their career first. Unless there are medical issues, you've got a good five more years to pop out a kid or two."

"Medically I'm fine. After my mother's infertility issues, I make sure to have regular checkups with a specialist to ensure everything is in working order, so I'm not worried about that. It's the amount of time it will probably take to meet someone and hold on to an actual relationship without getting bored that has me worried. You know how I am."

Travis chuckled. "Yeah. You're worse than me. I've at least had a few that could've gone the distance if I didn't feel the need to hack into their online life at the slightest whiff of infidelity. Other than Selena, you haven't made it past a month with a woman. Speaking of Selena, since the wedding is called off, will you be hitting her up?"

"This all just happened yesterday, and I have to play it cool for a while until my romance with Kyle *fizzles* out," she said using air quotes.

"Tell me again why you two never made it a permanent thing? You were all hot and heavy in college. She was even the first girl you brought home to meet your parents. What happened?"

"You know what happened. She was trying to get her acting career off the ground and moved to California. I had my responsibilities here. Nothing's changed and we like what we have. Well, we did until Marriage-gate." Ava smirked.

"Now that that's over, you still want me to keep digging?"

"Yes. Either way, I want Kyle out. The fact that my mother also gets the same vibe that I do from him cements it. I just need my father to take off the blinders and see it as well."

Travis nodded. "I agree. I've got one more source I can hit up before I've hit a wall. I'm meeting up with him on Monday. Hopefully, he'll be able to get us something by the end of the week."

"That would be great. I want to have something to put on my father's desk before he has partnership papers drawn up for Kyle."

"You know I got your back, no matter what."

Ava returned to her apartment looking forward to a rare full day home alone since she and Kyle began their fake relationship. They were either meeting for breakfast, spending the day together doing some outdoor activity or having dinners out. They had even begun spending the afternoons or evenings together at her apartment when they didn't want to be bothered with public shows because Kyle lived in a studio apartment with no room for them to keep their distance. She had the guest room set up for him to use as an office while she would work in hers, barely speaking a word to each other in passing. As much as she despised having to give the appearance of the happy couple in public, Ava began to prefer that to having Kyle in her space with his secretive brooding glances and distrustful vibe. She did cut the line at overnights which Kyle was just as averse to doing. Now that the wedding wasn't happening, she would be getting her place and her life back to herself and she planned on celebrating with a hot shower and strolling around the apartment in her underwear.

She entered, left her sneakers by the door, and headed straight to her room. As she entered the hallway leading to the bedrooms, she heard a male voice. Kyle was still here? She'd gotten a text from Sonya a half hour ago saying that Kyle had arrived at the apartment not long after Ava had left for the gym and that she was leaving to do the grocery shopping. That meant Kyle had been there for a good two hours. He hadn't brought that much stuff, just enough to fit into one box, so there was no need for him to still be there. Annoyed, Ava headed toward the guest room. Since their fake relationship was over there was no need to for her to continue with her nice, agreeable fiancé guise.

She reached for the doorknob and stopped as she heard, "The Prescott bitch could be back any minute, we don't have much time to talk."

Ava wasn't the type of person to purposely eavesdrop on someone's conversation, but since he was in her home calling out her name, eavesdropping was called for. She stepped aside and listened.

"Yeah, we're going to need to move forward with the backup plan. Everything's in place here." Kyle was quiet for a moment, obviously listening to whoever he was speaking with on the phone.

"Okay, meet me at the usual spot in an hour…I don't give a fuck about what you had planned. This needs to go down as quickly as possible. This shit has gone on long enough. I want it over."

Ava was shocked by Kyle cursing. He barely said hell the entire time she'd known him, yet he just spewed some pretty good foulness in a small amount of time.

"Hold on, I have another call…yeah, what's up? What the fuck do you mean you lost her? You had one fucking job!" Kyle said something under his breath that Ava couldn't hear. "I'm back. I gotta go. The dipshit you recommended to tail Ava lost her. She could be on her way back here any minute—"

Ava didn't stick around to hear the rest of what was said. She quickly tiptoed her way back to the door, grabbed her shoes tip-toed out into the hallway all the while trying to process the fact that Kyle was having her followed. That's why he hadn't been surprised to see her at her parents' the other night. She'd left the gym out of the café entrance around the corner from the main entrance which was probably how Kyle's guy lost her. She slipped her sneakers back on and took her keys back out to go into the apartment. Just before she turned the key, the door opened, and Kyle stood in the doorway holding a box under his arm looking genuinely surprised to see her this time.

"Oh, hey, sorry, I thought I'd be gone by the time you got back to make this less awkward," he said.

Ava pasted on a pleasant smile. "No problem. You find everything okay?"

Kyle gazed down at the box then back at her. "Yes. I guess this is it. Back to just being co-workers."

"Yeah. What a relief, right?"

"Yeah, big time. Well, I'll see you on Monday."

Ava stepped aside to allow him to pass. "Bright and early."

Kyle's smile wavered as he quickly walked past her out of the apartment. Ava re-entered and turned every lock and bolt on the door. She even started to put the chain on until she remembered that Sonya would be back soon from the grocery store. She went to her bedroom and sat on the bed in an angry daze. Listening to Kyle on the phone, knowing he'd been having her followed for God knows how long, and his fake pleasantries as he was leaving had Ava seeing red. She pulled her phone out of her pants pocket and was just about to call Travis when she remembered something Kyle said, *"Everything is in place here."* He had been in her apartment, alone, a lot longer than he should have been to collect his box of possessions. She gazed around her room expecting to see the red light from a hidden camera somewhere, or even something placed in her room that she hadn't put there herself. She'd watched enough *Dateline* series to know that cameras could be hidden in anything. Now paranoid, she rushed from her room, grabbed her keys from the foyer, and left the apartment. As she nervously waited for the elevator, she kept peeking toward the emergency exit door waiting for Kyle to come walking through ready to do her harm. When the elevator finally arrived, Ava stepped on and pressed the door close button until her finger ached. She called Travis as soon as the doors closed.

"Hey, didn't I just see you?"

"I need you to come over." Ava told him what happened and what she'd overheard. "I think he might've planted hidden cameras in my apartment. I mean he's had me followed, Travis, anything is possible." She knew she sounded like a crazy person, but she couldn't help it.

"Okay, I need to stop at my place and pick up a few things and I'll be there as soon as I can."

"I'll wait for you in the coffee shop in the lobby. Unless Sonya gets back before you get here, I'm not going back up there alone."

"That's probably a good idea. I'll text you when I'm on my way. Just breathe, Ava. It's probably nothing." He didn't sound too convincing to her.

"Okay. But please hurry."

After they hung up, she considered calling her father, but she didn't want to worry him until she had something to show him. Just as she reached the lobby she ran into Sonya.

"Oh, hey, are you heading back out?" Sonya asked.

"Uh, no, I'm waiting for a delivery. Here, why don't I take the groceries and you take the rest of the day off, with pay, of course. I'm going to be home all day and there's no need for you to stay with me underfoot making a mess as soon as you clean one up." Ava hoped she looked as calm and collected as she attempted to sound.

Sonya cocked her head to the side with a curious gaze. "Are you sure? Is everything all right?"

Ava broadened her smile. "Everything is fine." She reached for the handles of the two shopping bags Sonya carried.

"Go enjoy the day with that handsome husband of yours." Okay, maybe she laid it on a little too thick there, but she was in panic mode. She didn't want to put Sonya in harm's way until Travis was able to find out if there was anything to worry about.

Sonya looked as if she would argue then released the bags. "Okay but call me if you need me."

"I will. I'll see you on Monday."

Sonya nodded and turned to leave. Ava watched her until she was out of sight and breathed a sigh of relief. She carried the bags with her to a coffee shop with access from the building's lobby, ordered a vanilla latte, and found a corner booth to huddle in until Travis texted her an hour later that he had arrived. She grabbed the grocery bags and met him in the lobby.

Travis gazed curiously down at the bags in her hand. "You go shopping while you were waiting?"

"No, I ran into Sonya as she returned from the grocery store, and I thought it best to send her home for the day."

"Did you happen to check and see what she got? Looks like something is melting." He pointed to a growing puddle from something dripping from one of the recyclable grocery bags.

"Dammit, it's probably the ice cream I asked her to get. I was really looking forward to enjoying that after dinner tonight."

Travis looked amused. Ava was annoyed. Her nice relaxing day at home had been far from relaxing so far. She let the lobby concierge know about the mess then turned and headed for the elevator with Travis in tow. When they got up to her apartment, she realized she hadn't closed the door all the way in her rush to leave. She looked worriedly back at Travis.

"I'm sure it's fine, but I'll go in first, just in case."

"No, it's my apartment and I didn't take all that Krav Maga training for fun."

Travis grinned in amusement. "Okay, Wonder Woman."

Ava rolled her eyes and handed Travis the shopping bags. Then she slowly pushed the door open, grabbed an umbrella out of the stand beside the door, and held it at her side as she exited the foyer of her apartment into the main space. Like her parents' penthouse, she could see the entire living room, dining area, den, and kitchen from the entryway. It appeared to be empty. She sighed with relief. She'd never had to use any of her self-defense training outside of the dojo, and despite the high degree of belt she'd achieved, she didn't feel very confident in using it on someone in real life.

"Is the coast clear?" Travis said from the foyer.

"It's clear." Ava tossed the umbrella on the sofa and grabbed the bags from him. "Let me see if I can salvage the groceries while you do what you need to do."

Travis tossed his backpack on a stool at the counter and took out two small electronic devises that looked like digital meters and slowly began walking through the apartment.

"Hey, Ava," Travis called not even a moment after he'd begun his check.

He was standing by the coffee table in front of the sofa. She tossed the container of softened ice cream in the freezer and joined him.

"Remember that guy I said was flirting with me during our kickboxing class?" he said, pointing toward a pen on the table and showing her how one of the meters lit up as it got closer to it.

Ava's eyes widened in shock. "Yes, what about him?"

She went to grab the pen, but Travis stopped her and headed for the hallway leading to the bedrooms. Ava followed him. He continued talking as he did so.

"Well, I was right, he was flirting with me. He caught up with me as I was leaving today and asked me out."

Ava nervously played along. "So, what did you say?"

"What do you think?"

"I'm going to assume you said yes. When are you going out?"

There seemed to be nothing in the guest rooms or bathroom, but they'd barely stepped into her bedroom before the meter lit up as they neared her dresser. It seemed the charging station for her electronic devices was setting it off.

"We're doing brunch tomorrow." Travis signaled for her to unplug it.

Ava did and he ran the meter over it, still getting a signal. He pointed to the bathroom. She carried it there. Travis opened the toilet and pointed. Ava scoffed for a moment before Travis quirked a questioning brow. She'd just bought the station a month ago, now she was going to have to replace it. With a sigh she dropped it into the toilet with a watery plop. The meter light flickered then petered out.

"I'm going to check the den since that's where you work sometimes. It seems Mr. Kyle spared no expenses in making sure the listening devices he'd planted wouldn't be noticeable."

Despite her paranoia, Ava honestly hadn't expected Travis to find anything. MAYBE a hidden camera but not bugs planted everywhere, including her most sacred of spaces, her bedroom. She didn't know what he expected to hear in there but just the thought of him listening to whatever happened made her shiver with disgust.

"That pen is even a listening device? Where would you get stuff like that? Especially something that looks exactly like the charging station which I just bought."

"The same place I can get stuff like this." Travis held up the meters. "One is to detect hidden cameras. The other is to detect listening devices. There are all sorts of sites online you can get gear like this, but you have to pay a pretty penny to get them custom like he obviously did with your charging station, so it looked exactly like the one you already had. All he had to do was replace it."

Ava shook her head in disbelief. "This is crazy."

"Sit tight while I check the den. I'll also disable the pen."

Ava followed him out of the bathroom then sat on her bed as he did a quick search of the entire room, including her closet before he left her alone to finish his check. She was too anxious to sit and got up to pace back and forth by the bed. Travis returned shortly after with two pens instead of just the one they'd discovered on the coffee table. He'd taken them apart and laid the pieces on the bed.

"Are you sure that's it?" Ava asked worriedly.

"Yes. I did another go around in the living room, kitchen, and guest bathroom on my way back here. Fortunately, there were no cameras, but this here is just as frightening. You can't listen to this from a distance. He'd have to come back and pick them up to download the recordings."

"Wait, you're saying that he more than likely planted these and had planned to come back? How? There would be no reason to since we're no longer *together*."

"Did you give him a key, and did he return it today?"

Ava sat dejectedly on the bed, her heart beating frantically in fear. "Yes and no, he didn't."

Travis sat beside her and took her hand. "My guess is that he probably planned to make a copy, return the original one to you and probably send someone back here while you're at work or something. At least, that's what I'd do."

Ava looked at him as if he'd lost his mind.

"What? It's the truth."

Ava flopped back on the bed, covering her face. "I can't believe this. What could he have possibly expected to gain from this?"

Travis laid on his side facing her. "Information to bribe you?"

Ava hadn't thought of that, but it brought another thought to mind. She turned her head and looked at Travis. "The paparazzi guy that got the pictures of Selena and me had to have been tipped off somehow. All these years of sneaking around, making sure we took every precaution possible not to be caught in any compromising situations, even barely speaking to each other when we've attended the same event or fundraiser, yet somehow that guy was conveniently at the right spot at the right time to catch us, and despite the very grainy pics he took, knew it was me and where to find me."

"There's no telling how long he's had you followed. What are you going to do? I'm sure this is enough proof to give to your father."

Ava sighed tiredly. "You would think so, but I have no proof Kyle even planted this stuff. It could've been Sonya for all I know."

Travis chuckled. "Sonya still has a flip phone. Do you really think she would know where to find technology like this and how to use it? Besides, she wouldn't need a listening device to blackmail you with the discreet company you keep. All she would need are a few pictures snapped on her little phone and she'd be rich for life."

"Wow, thanks. That makes me feel much better," Ava said sarcastically.

"I'm just saying, your father can't be so blinded by golden boy's shine that he can dismiss what's happening."

"I guess you're right. I'll take these into the office on Monday and show him. It needs to be while Kyle isn't around. I swear he must know when my father and I are meeting one-on-one because he shows up nearly every time with a different financial report that needs his immediate attention. You think he has my father's office bugged also? Should we go by their apartment and check like you just did mine?"

"The office is a possibility but unless Kyle has been left alone in your parents' apartment for an extended time, I doubt he'd have the bandwidth to set anything like this up there."

Ava felt a sense of relief at that. "Maybe I can convince Dad to bring Uncle Zeke in to check things out at the office, just to be safe."

"Probably a good idea."

They lay there quietly for a moment before Travis sat up, pulling her up with him. "I don't know about you, but all this Secret Squirrel stuff has made me hungry. Why don't you go shower and change so we can go out and celebrate your newfound freedom? Nothing crazy. I'm craving a fried bologna sandwich and root beer float from Au Cheval and I know how much you love their chocolate martini shots. Then we can come home, break out your partially melted ice cream, and binge on some trash TV."

Ava smiled. "You know, for a gay guy, you sure know the way to a woman's heart."

Travis gave her a smug grin. "What can I say, my years as a former ladies' man come in handy every now and then."

Ava was awakened by an incessant buzzing and vibrating near her head. She sleepily blinked her eyes open to find she'd laid her phone right next to her pillow instead of on her nightstand where she usually placed it at night. After several chocolate martini shots at the restaurant then a few glasses of wine while they spent the rest of the day binging on trashy reality TV shows, Travis had talked her into calling Selena. He'd fallen asleep on the sofa and Ava had gone to her room and called her. They'd talked for hours, making up for not keeping in touch after Ava told her she was marrying Kyle and why. Selena had been disappointed with Ava for giving in to the fake marriage and hadn't called or answered Ava's calls since then. Ava hadn't realized how much she'd missed her until they spoke.

She gazed down at her phone and noticed it was two in the morning as MOM flashed on the screen.

"Mom? Is everything okay?"

"Ava, there's been an accident, your father's been hurt. We're at AMITA Hospital." Although Ava's mother sounded calm, she could hear a tremor in her voice as if she were barely keeping it together.

Ava sprang out of bed and hurried to her dresser. "I'll be right there. Is anyone else there with you?"

"Max is here."

"Okay, good. I'll see you soon."

They said good-bye as she grabbed a pair of sweatpants and a T-shirt. She didn't even put socks on as she slipped her feet into a pair of casual sneakers and ran out of her room. She gave Travis a shake and he gazed up at her in confusion.

"Wow, I didn't even realize I fell asleep. What time is it?" He rubbed his eyes sleepily.

"It's after two in the morning. I've gotta go. Dad's been in an accident."

Travis sat up, now wide awake. "What?"

"Yeah. Mom just called, they're at the hospital."

"Okay, I'll take you."

"Thank you." Ava was relieved. She didn't think she was in a good frame of mind to drive and there was no telling how long it would be to get a car this late.

The hospital was close to their family home in Forest Glen, a half hour drive from her place. The ride felt like the longest half hour of Ava's life. She did something she couldn't remember the last time doing, she prayed, silently begging, and making all sorts of deals with God for her father to be all right. Travis dropped Ava off at the hospital entrance so she wouldn't have to wait for him to find parking. When she was directed where to go, she practically ran through the halls. When she caught sight of her mother, she did run, and her mother almost collapsed within Ava's arms. Her body trembled as she cried and Ava held her tightly, giving her this moment and holding back the questions bursting to be asked.

With a shuddering sigh, Ava's mother shifted partially from her embrace and wiped her eyes and nose with a balled-up tissue. "I'm sorry. It was just such a relief to see you and know that you're all right."

"I'm fine. How are you? How's Dad? What happened?" Ava hadn't meant to throw it all at her at once. "I'm sorry, I didn't mean to bombard you like that."

Her mother gave her a sad smile. "It's okay, honey. I'm better now that you're here. Your father was shot, he's in surgery right now. We don't know exactly what happened. Uncle Max is down the hall speaking to the police."

Ava's heart felt like it had stopped for a moment. "He was shot? Where was he when it happened?"

"He'd left some papers at the house and went to pick them up late this afternoon since we had planned to spend the day out on the boat tomorrow…or I guess I should say today," her mother said, looking confused.

Ava led her over to a chair and held her hand as they sat down. Her mother shook her head as if to rid herself of the confusion and continued. "I was spending the afternoon and evening with Joan, so I wasn't aware that your father hadn't come home until I got home around eleven. He'd been gone since four and said he'd be back long before I would be home. He hadn't called or texted me to let me know he was going to be late, which isn't like him. I called his cell and the house phone and got voice mail on both. I didn't think to panic because he also told me that he may stop by Max's while he was out that way and they probably lost track of time. You know how they can be when they get together."

Ava smiled and nodded. Her father and Uncle Max were very close and when they got together, they acted like two mischievous silly teenagers, despite both being in their sixties. It was even worse when her father's best friend Ezekiel, Uncle Zeke as Ava called him, joined them.

"I waited another hour and still had no response to my text or voice mail messages, so I called Max. He hadn't spoken to your father since he arrived at the house. They had tentatively planned to meet up for drinks if your father didn't decide to just come back to the city. When Max didn't hear back from him, he assumed your father came back here, that's when we both knew something was wrong. Max decided to go by the house and when he got there your father's car was still in the driveway, but the house was dark. He used his spare key to get in and not long after found your father laying in a pool of blood in the study." Ava's mother's voice broke for a moment. "He'd been shot in the head. The doctors said the bullet had entered his right frontal lobe then traveled through and exited at an angle that caused relatively mild damage compared to if it had entered at angle that hit his brainstem, which could've been fatal.

He has some brain swelling which they're trying to alleviate now." She began crying again.

Ava pulled her into her arms and held her as she tried to think of a reasonable explanation of what may have happened. Uncle Max and Travis entered the waiting area together.

Uncle Max gave her a soft smile. "I found this guy wandering the halls, so I figured he was with you."

Ava's mother gazed up at them. "Travis, I didn't know you were here."

Travis leaned over and gave Ava's mother a kiss on the cheek. "I was already at Ava's place and thought it best not to let her drive under the circumstances. Max filled me in. If there's anything I can do, please don't hesitate to ask."

Ava's mother took Travis's hand and gave him a smile of appreciation. "Thank you so much."

Ava met her uncle's worried gaze. "Mom told me the gist of what she knows. What do you know and what are the police saying and doing about it?"

Max gazed around the waiting room suspiciously then looked back at her. "Why don't we go someplace more private to talk."

Ava glanced around the room. There were several other people there but no one she recognized or that looked suspicious. She also trusted her uncle's judgment and if he didn't think this was a good place to talk then it wasn't. She nodded and followed him to another, smaller waiting area around the corner that was currently unoccupied.

"Uncle Max, what's going on?"

With a tired sigh, her uncle ran his hands through his locs that lay just past his shoulders. "After looking at the home security video on your father's phone, the police are saying it was a home invasion and your father may have been shot trying to stop it."

"I take it you don't believe that."

"No. First, other than what was in your father's safe in his office and his wallet, there was nothing else stolen. All your mother's jewelry, your father's watches, and anything else in the house worth something was still there. Second, according to the video, your father let them in."

"He knew them?"

"That's the only thing I can think of. They arrived in a moving truck and were dressed in overalls, work boots and baseball caps worn low over their faces. They also made sure to avoid looking in the direction of the doorbell camera and even blocking it at one point."

Ava remembered her mother telling her there had been a rash of burglaries in the area last year with fake utility workers scamming their way into homes, but the police had quickly caught the men and things had been quiet. It was the reason her parents had upgraded to the doorbell security system. "And Mom didn't know about Dad expecting any deliveries or having something picked up that would require movers?"

"No, but he was obviously expecting someone because you can hear the conversation even though the camera was blocked. It didn't take long for Marcus to realize they weren't the delivery guys he was expecting and when he tried to shut the door on them one of them tells him he has a gun. I'm assuming that's when he let them in. After that, the only person that can tell us what happened is Marcus."

Ava found this all so crazy. She sat down and kept racking her brain about who and why someone would want to hurt her father. Her heart skipped a beat. "No. There's no way he would do something like this," she said out loud to herself.

Max sat beside her. "Ava," he said expectantly.

"How much do you know about Kyle Edwards?"

Her uncle looked confused for a moment then his expression turned serious. "Not enough, apparently. You think he may be responsible for this?"

"I don't know. It could just be coincidence, but I don't believe that."

Ava told Max of her suspicions about Kyle before they even began their fake relationship, what she'd overheard during his phone conversation at her apartment, and the listening devices Travis found. Her uncle's expression became a mask of fury as she spoke. When she finished, he took out his phone and made a call.

"Yo, Easy, it's Max we're calling in that favor."

Ava looked worriedly at her uncle as he explained the situation to Ezekiel Frost, her father's best friend. If Max was calling him, then it was more serious than she imagined.

"Uncle Max, do you really believe Kyle would do something like this?"

Max frowned. "Baby girl, I've learned not to put anything past anyone. We're all capable of doing something no one would expect if we felt forced to do so. To be honest, there was always something about

Kyle that gave me pause, but your father sees himself in the boy and can't seem to look at anything past that. We did a thorough background check and didn't find anything except a bit of trouble he got into while he was in high school, but that just made your father more enamored of him because of his own troubled past."

Ava nodded. She knew that was why her father had chosen Kyle for his crazy marriage plan. "What I don't understand is why would Kyle want to hurt Dad after everything he's done for him?"

"That's what we need Ezekiel to find out. Do you think we could pull Travis in on this? His tech skills partnered with Ezekiel's guys could go a long way to finding answers."

Ava smiled tentatively. "Travis has been looking into Kyle for some time now. Before Mom reamed Dad a new one about his plan and got him to change his mind, I had Travis trying to find anything that I could use to prove to Dad that Kyle couldn't be trusted. We found the same information you did."

Max sighed tiredly. "Ezekiel will be here tomorrow so we'll see what he can do before we jump to any conclusions."

Ava nodded in agreement. She was hoping their suspicions were wrong. Unfortunately, until her father could tell them what happened, it was all they had to go on.

CHAPTER FIVE

It had been almost a month since Ava's father was shot, and he was still in a coma. The surgery had gone well but he hadn't woken up. The doctors said it was probably for the best so that he could heal. Ava, her mother, her aunts, and Uncle Max had all taken turns sitting with him, talking to him, reading to him, anything that would stimulate him into waking up. Kyle had attempted to visit, but the hospital rule of family members only saved Ava from having to tell him she didn't want him anywhere near her father. Ezekiel had also assigned security outside her father's room just in case someone decided to finish what was started. Even with Ezekiel and Travis working together, they still hadn't found a connection to Kyle and the attack on her father. For Kyle's part, he seemed devastated by the news when she and Max told him in a meeting the next day. To Ava's surprise, there had been actual tears in his eyes, but they soon dissipated at the news that her uncle would be stepping in as acting CEO until further notice.

Ava used what happened to her father to explain bringing in Ezekiel and his security team for the tightened and new security protocols they had quickly implemented to hopefully catch Kyle, or anyone within the firm that could be connected to the situation. Everyone was working in overdrive to ensure Diamond Unlimited's clients that the firm and their accounts were still in good hands. Ava had also come up with the idea of using the situation to change the narrative of their postponed wedding. No one would fault them for putting it off under the circumstances. This way it was no one's fault and both she and Kyle saved face, which seemed to satisfy Kyle.

Ava never mentioned the listening devices she'd found in her apartment and neither Ezekiel nor Travis could trace it back to him. They were purchased online and shipped to a P.O. Box under the name Corrine Jones. Ezekiel had assigned some people to watch the post office where it was located, but no one had come to collect anything from it. In the meantime, they had to treat Kyle as if it were business as usual. Ezekiel told her that if he was behind her father's accident, they didn't want to tip him off by treating him differently or acting suspicious. Ava was beginning to believe that maybe they had been wrong about Kyle and that her father's accident really could've been the result of an attempted robbery. The police believed that accidently shooting her father may have scared the thieves off and that's why they hadn't gone for any other valuables in the house. There were still no leads, but they hadn't closed the investigation which gave her family some relief. Ezekiel's team had combed through the doorbell video so many times they had it memorized and couldn't find anything different than what the police had found. At this point Ava just wanted her father to wake up and for all of this to be done with.

She sat by her father's bedside talking to him about the one subject she knew he loved to talk about just as much as she did…work.

Her mother walked into the room. "I swear, if that man wakes up from you reading him financial statements and not from me telling him how much I love and miss him I'm going to put him back into a coma."

Ava chuckled. "Since the numbers are looking good there's nothing for him to wake up and complain about so I doubt that will do it. Did you eat anything?"

Ava's mother shrugged. "I had some soup. I wasn't really hungry."

Ava looked her over. Her mother had always been slim with just the right amount of curves, but she'd lost weight in the past month from the stress of worry and not eating. She'd also been spending her days sitting at her father's bedside instead of keeping busy with work, the charities she volunteered for, and her usually active fitness routine. Her mother looked tired all the time and Ava worried that she might end up in a hospital bed right next to her father if she continued this way.

"Mom, you're wasting away. You know Dad wouldn't want you doing this to yourself. Why don't I take tomorrow off and sit with him while you take a day just to decompress and rest?"

Ava's mom shook her head. "No, I need to be here in case there's a change."

Seeing the stubborn gleam in her mother's eyes, Ava knew it wouldn't do any good to argue. "Okay, well, I'll take the day off anyway to keep you company."

Her mother smiled. "I'd like that. Your uncle just got here. He looks a little harried but won't tell me what's wrong. He wants to talk to you."

"Oh, okay." Ava stood and gave her mother a hug and kiss on the cheek. "I'll see you in the morning. Try to get some rest tonight."

"I will." Ava didn't believe her but there was nothing she could do.

Her parents' love for each other ran deep and they were lost without each other. She remembered how miserable her father was during their separation. Her mother had the same lost look now that he had then. She wondered if she would ever be that close to someone. Ava exited the room to find Max pacing in the waiting area.

"Hey, Unc."

"Hey, baby girl, Easy is waiting at my house with Travis. We need to talk to you." There was a look in his eyes Ava had never seen before. Something had scared her uncle.

"Okay, I'll meet you there."

"No, leave your car here, you can ride over with me. We'll pick it up later."

"Uncle Max, what's going on? You're scaring me."

He gave her a smile that she guessed was supposed to reassure her, but since it looked forced it only made her more nervous.

"We'll explain everything when we get to the house."

"Okay." Ava left the hospital with him wondering what happened that could've possibly spooked her no-nonsense adventure seeking uncle so much that he was checking the rearview mirror every few minutes during the twenty-minute drive to the house.

When they arrived, Ava noticed two dark-suited men standing at the front door as if they were security at an exclusive night club. Max pulled into the garage and didn't turn the car off until the door closed completely. She followed him into the house where Ezekiel and Travis were waiting for them in the kitchen sitting at the counter. They both looked relieved when they saw her. Travis even stood and pulled her into a hug, which worried her further.

"Okay, you guys are freaking me out right now. Start talking," Ava demanded.

Her uncle spoke first. "Things have been quiet since we've upped security at the office and Ezekiel put some guys on Marcus's room. We also haven't been able to find anything that would connect Kyle to your apartment being bugged or your father's shooting, so we were beginning to think that the two incidents weren't connected and that your father's accident was just what the police believe, a home invasion gone wrong. But then this came to the office this afternoon. Your assistant opened it and brought it directly to Ezekiel as he instructed both of our assistants to do if they received anything suspicious."

Ava took the envelope he offered to her. It was a plain white envelope with just her name printed in all caps on the front. She opened it and read the two-line message.

WATCH YOUR BACK.

YOU'RE IN DANGER.

Ava really was scared now. "This came today?"

"We think it might've come over the weekend. It's just that your assistant hadn't opened it until this afternoon after you'd already left for the hospital," Ezekiel clarified.

"And you couldn't call to let me know?"

"I've had a tail on you for a week now just to be safe so there was no need to freak you out until we were able to investigate it further. There's no return address or postage which meant it came from within the office, but it was with a bundle of regular mail so it's someone who has access to the mailroom. When we questioned the mailroom staff there was one person missing, a Lawrence Friedman. Do you know him?"

Ava racked her brain trying to place the name with the faces of the mailroom and operations staff she knew. As chief operating officer, she made it a point to try to get to know everyone from the executives on down to the coffee kiosk guy. She believed everyone was critical to making sure the firm ran smoothly. "I think so. He's new. Was referred by Cathy Booker in accounting. He's her sister-in-law's nephew."

Ezekiel and her Uncle Max exchanged a look.

"You think it was him?"

"Once again, we don't have a direct connection. All we know is he went to lunch on Friday and didn't return to finish out his shift. We can talk to Cathy in the morning. In the interim, I'm going to suggest an idea and I need you to hear me out before shooting it down."

Ava looked at Ezekiel warily. "That sounds a lot like what my father said before he suggested the fake relationship with Kyle. We see how that turned out."

Ezekiel chuckled. "There'll be no arranged marriages involved. I think you may need to go underground for a bit until we can figure all this out. My resources are being stretched thin trying to keep you all safe and investigate what's going on. I've pulled my entire team from any future assignments to focus solely on this. Since you've become a target, getting you out of the picture could cause whoever this is to slip up."

"What do you mean go underground?" Ava asked.

Travis slid a manila envelope across the counter to her. Ava hesitantly opened it, surprised to see a passport and a New York driver's license with her picture as well as a social security card, none of which were under her name.

Travis grinned. "Never thought you'd see that name again, huh?"

"What is this?" Ava gazed in confusion at the name Travis had created a fake identification for her that she'd used while she was in college for all her side hustles.

"Your new identity," Ezekiel explained.

"My new identity? No, I'm not leaving. Dad is still in a coma, Mom needs me, and I need to be here to make sure Diamond stays in Prescott hands."

Her uncle turned her to face him. "Baby girl, I know it's going to be difficult for you to let go and walk away but it's only for a little while. We need to make sure you're safe. Your father would want it this way."

Ava shook her head and tossed the fake identification on the counter. "No. I need to be here to help you all, to make sure Dad is okay, and if not—" She couldn't even imagine him not being okay. "I need to help Mom deal with whatever comes after that."

"Ava, somebody tried to kill your father, and I didn't want to tell you this, but I was also attacked last week."

Ava looked at her uncle in shock. "What?"

"I had been working late at the office and stopped at that sandwich place down the street. When I came out, some fool shoved a gun in my side and tried to get me into a van. Fortunately, a cop pulled up for his own dinner break and the guy took off in one direction while the van went in another," Max explained, looking shaken just talking about it.

"Oh, Uncle Max, I'm so glad you're all right." Despite him towering over her, Ava pulled him into a hug, then turned to Ezekiel. "That's why you put a tail on me."

Ezekiel nodded. "There's one on your mother as well. But, like I said, I'm starting to stretch my resources too thin, and we all decided that keeping you safe is the priority. The best way to do that is to make you disappear."

"How do you plan to explain me leaving while my father isn't out of the woods. While we're still trying to convince our clients that Diamond is still as strong as ever and has their best interest at heart despite what's going on?" The thought of leaving her family, the firm, and her life behind frightened Ava more than the threat of staying did.

"We're going to announce that Diamond is considering a possible merger with an unnamed European wealth management firm to open an international office in London. It's something your father and I toyed with some time ago but never followed through on it. It'll be the perfect cover, and who better to send than the future CEO of the company to oversee the talks and the search for locations and keep you out of town for an extended period," Max explained.

Ezekiel picked it up from there. "But you won't be in London. You're going to disappear some place under your new identity. You decide where that will be as long as it's not where Diamond might have an office, or where you'll have more chance at being recognized. We don't want you to tell any of us where you're going, and your only contact will be with Travis until we know everything is secure."

Travis picked up a backpack that had been sitting beside his stool and plopped it in front of Ava. "There's a laptop and cell phone in there. The safeguards I put up on them should keep most other hackers out. I say most because I know guys that work for the government who could make me look like an amateur, but since the government isn't going to be after you, then you'll be fine. I programmed my number in there for you just so you can occasionally let me know you're alive and kicking. Keep it simple. If there's an emergency or a change in your father's status, then I'll text 911 to let you know to call."

Ava's head was spinning. "This is crazy. You all are acting like I'm leaving right now."

Ezekiel gave her a sheepish grin. "I actually wanted you to leave tonight, but Max convinced me that in order for the fake trip to London to work it has to be planned as if it were a normal business trip."

"As soon as we're done here, I'll send out a meeting request for first thing in the morning with the executive team, which of course will include Kyle, to announce how this opportunity came up again and I wanted to move quickly on it since it was something Marcus wanted which is why you need to leave that afternoon," Max said.

"After you finish up at the office, you're going to head home to pack. I'm going to meet you at your apartment with one of my female agents who matches your height and build and will be dressed to resemble you as much as possible. She's going to get in a car heading to O'Hare Airport and I'm going to be waiting in the garage to take you to Midway. From there you'll be on your own and free to fly wherever you choose, just be sure not to use your own credit or bank accounts to purchase your ticket," Ezekiel said.

"Oh yeah, almost forgot." Travis took a bank card from his wallet. "I noticed you still had your Lacey Crain bank account, so I added some additional funds to the stash you still had in there and got you a new card. I didn't think it would be a good idea to transfer anything from your regular bank account because it could be traced to the stash account."

"How did you manage that without me there?" Ava asked.

Travis cocked his head toward Ezekiel. "We tested your body double. Worked like a charm."

Ava shook her head in disbelief. "I have to sit down."

She sat on a stool and looked at each of the men as if she didn't recognize them. They had managed to create a whole new life for her in a matter of hours without her even knowing. It was fascinating and frightening. "What if I said no to this craziness?"

Her uncle took her hands in his. "We're not going to force you to do anything you don't want to do. Ezekiel said it was a suggestion and he meant it. We just wanted to make sure that if you went along with it that everything would be ready for you, but the choice truly is yours."

As much as she didn't want to admit it, Ava knew that if Ezekiel thought she needed to go underground then she needed to go underground. There were few men that her father trusted not only with his secrets, but his life and Ezekiel Frost was at the top of that list. If her father could trust him then so could she.

"I'll do it but only because you said it wouldn't have to be for long. I won't abandon my family or the business, I don't care who's threatening me or why," Ava said adamantly.

Ezekiel nodded. "Understood."

The next morning, sitting in the boardroom with the entire executive team helping her uncle weave lies about an international deal that would never happen made Ava a little sick to her stomach. She noticed Kyle watching her and Max like a hyena trying to detect weakness in its prey.

"I don't mean to play the devil's advocate, but why hasn't Marcus mentioned this deal before? I don't recall ever seeing anything in the financial records regarding it. Also, why the need to move so quickly on it?" Kyle asked. Ava wanted to slap the smug expression off Kyle's face but managed to sit calmly and smile as she let Max handle him.

Max gave Kyle an amused grin. "Kyle, as much as you like to think so, not everything in this company revolves around what you know. This was something my brother and I had discussed doing long before peach fuzz was even growing above your lip. We never found the right firm to work with until now, and I'd like to be able to gift my brother with a done deal when he finally rejoins us."

Kyle managed to keep smiling as he shot daggers at Max with his eyes. "As CFO I think it would be prudent for me to join Ava on this venture just to make sure the financials will benefit us in the end."

"This is just an exploratory getting to know you, the area and market. I think Ava will be able to handle both the business and financial discussions just fine. After all, she was our top financial earner her entire career before becoming COO," Max said.

"If there are any questions or issues that I'm not able to answer I'll be sure to set up a call with you." Ava hoped that would appease him.

Kyle gazed at her skeptically but nodded.

Uncle Max gazed around the table. "Any more questions?" When no one else spoke up he clapped his hands and stood. "Excellent. Ava, MJ, and Kyle, I want to meet with you before Ava hits the road. Everyone else, feel free to chill here for a bit and enjoy the breakfast."

Ava, her cousin Maxwell Jr., and Kyle followed Max to her father's office. They discussed MJ taking over as acting COO in Ava's absence and her uncle even put together a feasibility report for the fake deal for Kyle to look over. It amazed Ava how well her uncle had planned all this on such short notice. The tiredness she saw in his face showed that he must've been up all night working on the report and what he was going to tell everyone. She felt guilty that it was all for her sake. Not long after, MJ left leaving Ava, her uncle, and Kyle alone.

"You have something you want to say, Kyle?" Max asked impatiently.

Kyle gazed down at the report in front of him. "I just think this is awfully sudden. Marcus never mentioned anything like this to me. Even when I brought up a similar idea last year."

Max grinned knowingly. "I'm fully aware of the idea you brought up to him and as he told you at the time, it wasn't the right company. The company we're currently vetting is one that we've worked with in the past on international accounts. I'm choosing to keep their name anonymous for now because I don't want to take the chance of this information leaking. Now, considering I am still an active partner with this company, despite having retired, and you haven't been made a partner yet, I don't see why Marcus would feel the need to fill you in on every idea he and I discuss. I appreciate your diligence and concern, but we got this. When it's time to include you in the financial side, we'll circle back. Does that work for you?"

A muscle twitched in Kyle's jaw despite the agreeable smile he gave Max. "Yes, thank you. I'll look the report over and provide any feedback I think will be helpful."

Max sat back in his chair and returned Kyle's smile. "You do that."

Kyle stood, gave Ava one last wary look, then left.

Max's smile turned down into a frown. "That boy is wearing my patience thin. He's gotta have his hand in every pot, even when it's not necessary. Your father gave him way too much leeway."

"This is why I don't think it's a good idea for me to leave. I have experience handling Kyle. I know MJ is capable of filling in for me, but he may not know how to handle Kyle," Ava said worriedly.

Her uncle quirked a brow. "You know as well as I do that MJ can hold his own. He just chooses to stay low-key for his own peace of mind. Besides, he's got me to back him up. Now, are you all set with your travel plans?"

"Yes. Everything is confirmed."

"Excellent." He stood and opened his arms. Ava stepped into them and sighed contentedly at the warm embrace. "You be safe. If you get the slightest whiff of something wrong you call Travis and I'll send the jet for you," Max whispered.

"Okay." Ava closed her eyes against the tears threatening to fall. She hadn't even been able to say good-bye to her mother. Ezekiel thought it was best that she didn't know about Ava leaving until after she'd already departed. She had written a note and planned to give it to Ezekiel to give to her mother when he told her. She couldn't believe the situation had come to such drastic actions. Despite believing it had to be Kyle, they still had no leads as to who was behind it all. But that begged the question, if it was him trying to hurt her family, why?

After leaving her uncle, Paige went to her office to meet with her assistant regarding the last-minute travel arrangements that Ava had arranged herself and how to assist MJ once he assumed the COO duties. Her assistant was used to her being so self-sufficient, so it wasn't a surprise that everything had been taken care of. She also met with MJ and her team to officially hand over the mantle. Before leaving her office, she collected her laptop, some files, and anything else she would normally take on a business trip. Ava played her part well. If anyone working in the office was behind what was going on with her family, there would be no need to be suspicious about what she was doing. Especially since opportunities could come up at a moment's notice in their business.

Ava arrived at her apartment building and was greeted by a young woman waiting in the lobby for her.

She offered Ava her hand. "Hi, Ms. Prescott, I'm Tracey. Ezekiel sent me."

This must be her body double. "A pleasure to meet you."

Ava shook her hand as she looked her over. Their build and complexion were very similar apart from Tracey's slightly more generous bust. Nothing that an oversized shirt couldn't hide which wouldn't be a problem since Ava tended to dress more casually with loose-fitting clothing while traveling. Especially for long trips. She didn't see any resemblance in their faces, but if Ezekiel thought this could work, she wouldn't question it. They went up to her apartment.

"So, how does this work?" Ava asked.

"I need your travel itinerary, driver's license, and credit card. I'll be taking the entire trip in your place, including checking into the hotel. If, by chance, the person, or people behind what's going on can get a tail on who's supposed to be you by the time I arrive in London then I'll lose them at the hotel. The focus will be off you which should give you plenty of time to be safely on your way to wherever you're going. I'll leave the hotel undisguised and fly back," Tracey explained.

The depth to which they were taking all this had Ava feeling as if she were trapped in a mystery novel.

Tracey gave her an understanding smile. "I know this is a lot thrown at you very quickly, but sometimes that's the best way. Too much planning can lead to just as many mistakes as planning on the fly. Now, let's get me ready to become you."

In just under an hour, with the help of a wig Tracey had brought that matched Ava's hair, colored contact lenses to match her eye color, some great makeup, and sunglasses it was almost like looking in the mirror as she stood across from Tracey dressed in Ava's jeans, long sleeve, loose-fitting tunic and slip-on loafers. For her incognito look, Ava had bundled her hair up into a hair tie and stuffed it under a baseball cap, she scrubbed what little makeup she wore off, and wore a plain white button-down shirt, jeans, and sneakers. Tracey also gave her a pair of black contact lenses to hide her natural eye color and recommended that Ava only pack clothes like what she currently wore in a weekender bag to last for a week. She could buy whatever else she needed when she arrived at her destination. For her part in posing as Ava, Tracey asked her to pack one of her larger suitcases with clothes she wouldn't mind too much being left behind in London so that Tracey wouldn't be traveling with an empty suitcase which obviously would look suspicious to airport security.

Once all that was complete, they were ready to leave. Ava looked around her apartment dejectedly. She was being driven from her home by some mystery assailant and didn't know when she would be able to come back. It pissed her off and made her more determined to figure out who was behind it. She didn't know how she would be able to do that while she was gone but she knew she was leaving things in good hands with Travis and Ezekiel working together. Ava laid an envelope on the kitchen counter for her housekeeper with a letter explaining she would be gone for an extended period and that since she wasn't sure when she would return, Sonya wouldn't be needed in a full-time capacity. Ava asked if she could just keep an eye on the apartment occasionally and promised she would continue receiving her full-time salary while she was away.

Included with the letter was a bonus check in an amount comparable to six months of pay. Ava and Tracey left the apartment together then Ava locked the door behind her.

She took a deep breath and turned to Tracey. "I guess this is it."

Tracey placed a comforting hand on her shoulder. "If Ezekiel thinks you can handle this then you're stronger than you think. Good luck, Ms. Prescott. Hopefully, we'll meet again under better circumstances. Maybe even go for a drink." She gave Ava a flirtatious smile.

Ava returned it. "Maybe."

They parted ways with Tracey heading to the elevator and Ava taking the stairs down to the garage. Seeing as she was on the top floor, it was a lengthy walk and gave her time to calm her nerves. When she reached her destination Ezekiel waited by a standard inconspicuous sedan with windows tinted just enough not to be able to clearly see who was in the car. She'd walked to the office this morning and given Ezekiel her garage key fob so that he could enter without having to notify the building security.

"You ready?" Ezekiel reached for her bag and opened the back door for her.

"As ready as I can be."

He gave her an encouraging smile. "I remember a certain little pony-tailed girl who used to love hearing about Uncle Zeke's adventures and wished she could have some of her own. Well, here's your chance."

Ava chuckled. "I don't think this was quite what I meant, but I get what you're saying and appreciate the effort."

Ezekiel smiled and placed an affectionate kiss on her cheek before she got in the car.

CHAPTER SIX

Paige closed her eyes and let Zorro take the lead as she let the wind whip through the locks of twists in her hair. The feel of the stallion's powerful muscles rippling beneath her and the speed at which he ran gave her an unfettered sense of freedom. She trusted Zorro completely. She'd helped bring the Morgan horse into the world when his mother had a difficult time delivering him at her uncle's ranch. She'd been there when he'd taken his first wobbly steps and had cared for him during the years between her military discharge and starting her security contracting gig. When she returned home from assignments it was to her uncle's ranch and Zorro. He was her balm after particularly rough jobs and the only one who'd ever seen her vulnerable and weak during some of her worst PTSD episodes. She'd even slept in his stall every night for a week once when the thought of sleeping alone in bed sent her into a deep depression. Zorro was the closest thing Paige had to a life partner. It was why her uncle gifted her the horse when she left his ranch to move to her own.

She felt Zorro slowing down, opened her eyes, and found that they were drawing close to the stables. He stopped just outside, allowed Paige to dismount, and headed straight for his stall where Willie, her ranch manager, was exiting after freshening up Zorro's hay and restocking his feed.

"Hey, Willie," Paige said as she entered the stables, grabbing a towel and brush hanging on the inside wall.

"Hey, Paige. Z looks happy. You must've let him lead." Willie patted Zorro's behind as he entered his stall.

"Yeah, he wasn't too happy that I'd been gone so long and gave me a hard time when I tried to get the saddle on him. When I gave up and just tossed the blanket across his back and hopped on, he knew he'd get his way." Paige followed Zorro, gave him a minute to get situated, then rubbed him down with the towel and the brush shortly after. "You forgive me, buddy?" she said, rubbing the white Z-shaped marking on his forehead.

Zorro huffed and pushed his head into her hand. Paige smiled, changed the rubbing to scratching and the horse bowed his head contentedly.

"I'll get Farrah and Jackie settled and head out for the evening unless you need me for anything else," Willie said.

"No, I think we're good. Thanks, Willie. See you in the morning."

Willie nodded and walked across the way to the stalls of two other stable occupants, Welsh ponies Farrah and Jackie that Paige had inherited from the previous owner of the ranch when he retired to Florida to be closer to his grandchildren. They weren't the only tenants that she'd inherited. There was Brutus, a huge, midnight black Angus bull that had been saved from the slaughterhouse; Hershey, a chocolate brown retired show pig; and Lucy and Ethel, two Nubian dairy goats. Not counting the two nameless cats that came and went as they pleased, it was an eclectic group of livestock. Paige didn't mind becoming their new caretaker. They were all good company if you didn't mind the smells or that all your conversations were one-sided.

After brushing Zorro down and grabbing a few carrots for him from the refrigerator in the tack room, Paige left him to finish up paperwork she'd delayed doing long enough. She hopped in the golf cart she sometimes used to get around the property and headed to the main house. Her ranch was set a half mile back from the main road on twenty-one acres of land with a breathtaking view of nearby mountaintops, surrounded by trees, and two ponds. On the property was her one-story five-bedroom, five-and-a-half-bath ranch-style home, along with a three-car garage, workshop, barn, storm shelter, animal pen, and horse corral.

When she arrived at the main house, she punched in the code in the keypad lock to enter and waited for the locks to click into place before she walked away from the door. Paige had knocked down the original three-story, three-bedroom, one-bath farmhouse that hadn't been updated since the previous owner's wife passed away twenty years ago.

The home that now stood in its place was close to six thousand square feet, with all the modern amenities, but Paige insisted on keeping the country charm of the original house. Her décor was warm, charming, and comfortable with eclectic touches of accessories she'd collected from her international travels. The modern touches were hidden or made to blend in with the style. Her widescreen television had the appearance of a large beautifully framed mirror above the fireplace. Her audio system was hidden in an antique armoire with small surround sound speakers mounted in the corners of the room. Even her kitchen appliances blended in with cabinet style fronts matching the regular cabinets.

There were other hidden amenities, like the high-tech security system Ezekiel's Tech Twins installed that had cameras throughout the entire property. The electronic key system to get into the house, which could be switched to a regular key entry if she chose to. The security room with all the alarms and camera feeds located just off the kitchen with a secret entrance from the pantry. The weapons room located in the workshop also accessible through a secret entrance. The safe room located behind a bookshelf in her office. The smaller weapons cabinet located behind the armoire in her bedroom. There were also various smaller caches of weapons hidden in various places throughout most of the house. Her beautiful, quiet, secluded, sanctuary was a secret fortress that even had an underground escape system that led to all the outer buildings. Paige knew it was a lot, but her previous life led to dangerous enemies, and having those kinds of enemies led to paranoia. She'd rather be safe than sorry.

As soon as she sat down and booted up her laptop, her phone buzzed in her pocket. Ezekiel's name appeared on the screen.

"Hey. It's been a while," Paige greeted him.

"Hey, Paige. Yeah, it's been a little crazy lately which is why I'm calling you. I need a favor."

"If it involves me coming back, I'm going to have to say sorry, but no."

Paige's life since she'd left the private security game had been pretty peaceful. She started her private investigative business a year and half ago and loved it. She could pick and choose the jobs she wanted which meant steering clear of anything that looked to be the slightest bit dangerous or had her away from home for more than a few weeks. She'd come to treasure her quiet life on the ranch.

Ezekiel chuckled. "I know better than to ask you that. This is a favor for an old friend. She needs to locate her daughter who left but didn't tell anyone where she was going."

"Okay, a lost and found. I can handle that. Send me the info."

"Will do. These are good people and I want them taken care of by the best, which is why I called you."

Paige smiled. "Don't go making me blush now. Thanks for the referral."

"My pleasure. Talk to you soon."

This was the first time Paige and Ezekiel had spoken in months. He recently started getting more government contracts and was busier than ever. The only other person she'd kept in regular touch with from the team was Grant who had finally settled down with his wife in their suburban Atlanta home with a genuine white picket fence and were expecting their second child. He was happily running his father's garage with his brother but would call Paige to see if there was anything he could assist her with whenever he got the itch for something different. Over the past year, Ezekiel had thrown a few missing person cases, or what she called lost and found jobs, her way. Paige's phone buzzed again. She looked to find an email from Ezekiel with the contact information for the client he'd referred. She called and after a brief overview of what the client needed, Paige booked a flight to Chicago departing the following day. She hated leaving so soon after she'd just returned home, but considering the situation, there wasn't much time to waste. Hopefully it wouldn't take more than a couple of weeks to complete the job.

Ava rubbed her burning eyes with a tired sigh. She'd just spent an hour looking over the account books for her boss to make sure the past week's numbers were in order. She reached up to attempt to rub a kink out of her neck from having her head bent at an angle for so long.

"You know, it would be a lot easier if you just let me do that," a male voice said seductively.

Ava pasted on a flirtatious smile and gazed up to find Leo Drake, owner of Red Velvet Cabaret, leaning casually against the doorway with his hands in his pockets and feet crossed at the ankles as he watched her. "As I keep telling you, Leo, I don't mix business with pleasure. But if I ever decide to, you'll be the first person I call." She stood and placed the account book back in his desk drawer.

"As far as I can tell, you don't seem to mix pleasure with anything. I have yet to see you out drinking or partying somewhere in the year you've been here. You are too gorgeous to be wasting your youth away." He looked her over from head to toe and back up again, stopping his gaze at the low-cut cleavage of her uniform.

"I'm just not the party girl type." She strode from behind the desk toward the doorway. He blocked it so she halted a few steps from him.

"Then what type are you, Lacey Crain?" His gaze met hers, full of genuine curiosity.

Ava kept her smile in place. "The type that needs to get the bar set before she gets in trouble with her boss."

Leo chuckled. "I think the boss will understand." He stood there a moment longer with a wistful look before he shifted aside to let her pass. Before she cleared the doorway, he gently grasped her hand. "You know being so mysterious makes you even sexier," he said before releasing her to be on her way.

Ava sighed with relief when she reached the bar. Leo straddled the line of flirtatious and sexual harassment, but she knew it was all talk. His love life was full with his wife, Robin, and their partner in business and love, Kenny. They were all madly in love with each other but played the outlandish flirts because it gave some spice to their polyamorous relationship to watch each other do so. Leo managed the lounge, Robin did the marketing and promotions, and Kenny oversaw the talent and entertainment. Ava, or Lacey as they knew her, had been hired last year as a bartender then took over the lounge's bookkeeping when their accountant was fired after Leo started finding discrepancies in the records from the till and what he recorded in the ledgers. She mentioned that she'd done some accounting in the past, they gave her a thirty-day trial run, liked her work, and added the additional duties as well as upped her salary. She still got to keep her tips from bartending, so she wasn't doing bad.

Not that Ava needed the money. She still had quite a bit in the account Travis had added funds to before she left Chicago. She couldn't believe it had been a year and Travis and Ezekiel still hadn't found any dirt on Kyle that would finally give her the leverage to come back home and boot his ass right out Diamond Unlimited's doors and into a prison cell. She kept up with what was going on back home through her brief monthly calls with Travis. There had been a worrisome update shortly after she'd left. The new mailroom employee who had not shown up to work the day the warning note was sent to Ava hadn't returned and couldn't seem to be found. Cathy, the woman who referred him for the job, also became a no-show the day after she was questioned about her supposed nephew by marriage's whereabouts. From that point on she and Travis mostly communicated back and forth about the Kyle situation through brief encrypted emails. It all felt very James Bondish but it was necessary.

There was good news about six months ago when Travis reported that her father had awoken from the coma and there didn't seem to be any permanent brain damage, but they wouldn't know for sure until he began rehabilitation. Ava had cried with relief. He was currently still going through physical therapy, but the doctors determined that other than memory loss surrounding the day he was shot, he would fully recover. A month ago, she took a chance and called him the day before his birthday.

"Hello," his voice came commandingly across the line. She missed the sound of it.

"Hey, Dad. Happy birthday."

"Hey, Buttercup! Thank you. How are you?"

"I'm good now that I hear your voice. How are you?"

"Fine. Your mother just finished fussing at me for sneaking out of the rehab place and going for a walk. I made it three blocks before having to call somebody to come get me. Told me I needed to slow down and not push my body into doing anything before it's ready."

Marcus Prescott didn't know the meaning of relaxation. "She's probably right. You need to be listening to her and the doctors."

"Who knows more about my body and what it needs than I do. I'm sick of being treated like a child. I'm a grown ass man, dammit," he said petulantly.

Ava laughed. "You're right, you are a grown ass man. One that was shot in the head, survived, and needs to listen to his doctors to get fully recovered so we can get back to business as usual when I come home."

It was quiet for a moment. "We'll see. When are you coming home? I miss my baby girl," he said softly.

Ava wiped away tears. "I can be on the next—"

"Yes, I see. Well, hold off on sending the information until I confirm exactly what we need," her father interrupted, his tone business-like.

"Dad, is there someone there?"

"Yes."

"Is it Kyle? Is there something wrong?"

"Yes, it could be but we're still investigating the numbers. Give me a call back in a week and we'll see where we stand."

"Dad, I'm coming home tomorrow." Ava felt a sense of panic at her father's attempts to hide who he was speaking with.

"No, hold off. There's probably nothing to be concerned about, but it's better to be safe than sorry when it comes to the numbers. You know how it is."

"Okay, if you need to reach me, contact Travis. I love you."

"Same to you. Bye." He abruptly ended the call.

Ava had contacted Travis immediately after and told him about the call. He'd promised to check in with her father that evening. When he got back to her later that night it was through email with a message from her father saying to stay wherever she was until Travis told her it was safe to come home and don't try to contact him directly again. She'd been worried sick ever since, but she'd done as he asked. She kept up her charade in New Orleans and didn't try to reach out to her father again. The fact that he didn't want Kyle to know he was speaking to her made her realize that he must have accepted the possibility that his golden boy wasn't as shiny as he'd believed. Travis had told Ava that when they informed her father several weeks after waking from his coma about their suspicions of Kyle being behind Ava's apartment being bugged, her being followed, and his shooting, he had refused to believe it. It took a long and private conversation with Ezekiel for him to finally see what the rest of them did.

Travis told Ava her father had been visibly hurt and angry when he'd set up a meeting with him, Ezekiel, and Max to figure out next steps, but he was also just as determined to do whatever it took to trip Kyle up.

As far as they all knew, Kyle's parents had passed away when he was a teenager, they hadn't been close with their own families, so he'd been placed in the foster care system, fortunate enough to stay with one family until he turned eighteen. His academic records were spotless, he rarely got into trouble and was a good student graduating from high school with honors. He paid his own way through college with scholarships and work-study programs, received a degree in business, and worked at some of the top financial services and brokerage firms until he landed at Diamond. He'd never been married, never had children, rarely drank, even in social settings. He was tall, dark, handsome, charming, a perfect gentleman and probably a walking wet dream for many straight women out there. He was too perfect, which meant there was something dark and ugly in his past that he'd managed to find a way to hide even from experts like Travis and Ezekiel. For his part in the plan, her father decided to use his close relationship with Kyle to learn what he could. He had Kyle added to his visitors list and saw him two to three times a week to discuss business or for her father to use that time to try to get to know Kyle personally. Now that he had finally opened his eyes to the situation, her father had begun seeing what he missed. Ava hoped he was able to learn information no one else had managed to dig up so she could go home soon.

Ava finished her inventory then set up her mixers and garnishes at the bar before going to the dressing room to finish putting on her uniform which consisted of the vintage style men's vest that she currently wore and the remaining items hanging in her locker, a pair of tuxedo hot pants, black stockings with a seam down the back, and black high-heeled booties. The final piece was a black bobbed flapper wig. Once she was dressed, she stood in front of the mirror at one of the performer's dressing tables applying her makeup. She finished just as the other performers began arriving. She liked having the peace and quiet of the dressing room before the frenzied chattering and squealing began when it was full. There were four burlesque performers, two drag queens, and a revolving door of jazz and blues artists depending on the night.

"Lacey, child, if I'd been born with that svelte little body and cute booty of yours, I'd probably have a man by now," one of the queens said with a pouty frown.

Ava smiled. "Carmella, you're more woman than me. I wish I had your height and curves. Any man who doesn't appreciate the beauty you are is a fool. You just wait, the right man for you is out there."

"Well, child, if you see him, please send him my way, but only if he can afford the lifestyle for which I've been accustomed," Carmella said, grinning as she patted the faux jewels hanging from her ears and lying on the pillow of her generous bosom.

"I'll make sure I do. Good luck tonight, ladies and gents."

Ava blew them all kisses and left them to their tittering and laughter. She joined Alan, the other bartender, dressed in black tuxedo pants with suspenders over his bare, muscled torso, behind the bar.

"Hey Lacey, are we still on for brunch in the morning?" Alan asked. "Bruce is back in town and wants to join us."

"Of course we are, and I'd love it if he did. I guess that's still going well."

"Honey, I am not messing this one up. He's fine as hell, has a good paying job, and has more pipe than the Roto-Rooter man," Alan said with a shiver of delight.

Ava shook her head. "I did not need to know that last part, but I'm glad you're happy. You deserve it."

"Yes, I do. After that Vincent debacle I was afraid I'd never find another good man."

Ava quirked a brow. "Another? Vincent was a con man and a thief who almost took you for everything you had."

Alan's face darkened with a blush. "Yes, well, other than that, he was a good man. He treated me like gold."

"With your money," Ava reminded him.

Alan waved dismissively. "Enough about my love life. When are you going to let me fix you up? I know several bois who'd love a gorgeous little thing like you."

"I told you I'm not interested in meeting anyone. I'm quite happy being solo."

"Bullshit. I see you looking at some of the women that come in here like you're a starving kid in a candy store watching a carousel of sweets go by. You practically drool."

Ava chuckled. "Looking and touching are two different things. I'm fine."

"If you say so." Alan continued to look doubtful but didn't say anything else.

They readied the bar for the night in companiable silence. Ava did her best to keep her personal life as private as possible. She'd made a few friends since she'd been in New Orleans, Alan was the first and the one she'd grown closest to, or as close as she allowed herself to get without revealing anything other than the past she'd created for Lacey Crain. She was from New York, moved to New Orleans after a bad breakup, and wasn't close with her family. Ava thought that was more than enough information, especially since she hadn't planned on being here much longer. Despite what her father said, she planned to go back home in a couple of weeks unless she heard from him through Travis before then. She hadn't liked the way their phone call had ended and worried that he was getting mixed up in more trouble. Ava had considered calling Uncle Max but didn't think it would be smart to reach out to too many people while she was trying to remain hidden.

Her musings were interrupted by the DJ doing his sound check with one of her favorite Nina Simone songs, "My Baby Just Cares for Me." Alan squealed, grabbed her hand, and pulled her into his arms. It was one of his favorites as well. They danced behind the bar singing loudly and happily. For just a little while, Ava could imagine what her life would've been like if she hadn't been born into the money and pressure of the life she was currently hiding from.

CHAPTER SEVEN

Paige arrived at the lobby of the luxury high-rise where her prospective client lived and stopped at the concierge desk. "Good afternoon, I'm Paige Richards. I believe Mrs. Prescott is expecting me."

"Yes. Just take the elevator to the Penthouse. I'll let them know you're on your way up."

"Thank you." She held on to her neutral facial expression until the elevator doors closed then rolled her eyes with a sigh. She hoped this wouldn't turn out to be another Landon Scott episode. If so, she'd leave whoever it was that they were asking her to look for right where they were and go home.

Once the elevator arrived at its destination, the doors opened and Paige was greeted by two familiar faces, Doug and Gene, the biggest and most highly trained guards from Ezekiel's security crew.

Paige smiled. "Hey, fellas. It's good to see you again."

Their only acknowledgements were a twitch in their lips that was considered a smile from them and a nod. "Sarge," they said in unison as Doug raised his hand and gave a curt knock on the door.

A few moments later it opened, and to Paige's surprise, she was greeted by Lynn Prescott herself instead of a maid or houseman. She offered Paige her hand and a warm smile. "Ms. Richards, thank you so much for coming on such short notice."

If it weren't for the heavy streaks of silver in her hair pulled back into an intricate twist, Paige would have never guessed her client was a woman of seventy. Her golden honey complexion was flawless with barely a wrinkle except for the laugh lines around her mouth and eyes. Judging by how the fitted sleeveless dress she wore showed off arms that Michelle Obama would envy and hugged her svelte figure, she took very good care of herself.

Paige accepted her hand and was impressed by her firm handshake instead of the limp fingertip shake she received from most women of Lynn Prescott's status. "You're very welcome, and please call me Paige."

Lynn nodded. "Please call me Lynn. Come in." She stepped aside to allow Paige to enter.

The apartment had just as much square footage as her entire house, but it was warmly and comfortably furnished. Not like the mausoleums she'd been in with ridiculously wealthy clients before. Lynn led her toward what looked like a formal dining room where two men waited. Paige recognized Maxwell Prescott from the background she'd done on the Prescott family after her initial call with Mrs. Prescott regarding her runaway daughter, but not the other gentlemen. Maxwell Prescott reminded her of a college professor with his salt-and-pepper beard and loc style hair, wearing a tweed jacket with leather patches on the elbow, a denim shirt, khaki vest, jeans, and loafers. Paige assumed the third guest was probably their attorney as he looked like a slick, smooth talker with his shiny bald head, neatly trimmed goatee, and expensive looking tailored suit. They stood at Lynn's and Paige's entrance.

Lynn made the introductions. "I'd like you to meet my brother-in-law Max and Ava's best friend, Travis."

Paige shook both their hands then everyone took a seat. "You didn't give me much detail on the phone."

"I thought it best if we spoke in person. May I get you something to drink before we begin?" Lynn offered.

Paige could tell she was nervous and stalling. "I'll take a seltzer if you have it."

Lynn nodded, then stood and retrieved a bottle from a mini fridge and a glass. Paige thanked her and took her time opening and pouring her water in the glass as she gazed from Lynn to Maxwell to Travis. They all had excellent poker faces, but Paige was a trained professional who picked up on subtle cues most wouldn't, like the bead of sweat on Maxwell's upper lip or the way Travis's bicep flinched as he clenched and unclenched his fist under the table.

"Lynn, judging by the security outside, I'm sure it's safe for you to speak openly. I can't help you if you aren't honest with me about what I could be getting into taking your case," Paige said.

Lynn bit her bottom lip then gazed at Max and Travis.

"If Easy sent her then we should trust that he knows what she can handle," Max said.

Travis nodded in agreement. Lynn took a deep breath and brought her gaze back to Paige. Her eyes sparkled with oncoming tears.

"Someone tried to kill my husband and threatened our daughter," Lynn said softly.

Max reached over and gently grasped her hand. She squeezed his in return, blinked the unshed tears away, and explained what was really going on.

"How's your husband doing?" Paige had seen the damage a bullet could do to a person's head at just the right angle. It wasn't a pretty sight, especially once the person's helmet was removed. She mentally shook off the gory memory.

Lynn gave her a small smile. "He's doing well and wants his baby girl home."

"What did the police say?" Paige asked.

"That it was a home invasion. His laptop was still on his desk, his wall safe was filled with cash, jewelry, and a gun, all of which were the only items taken from the house. There were documents I assume were from the safe strewn about the floor, but if they had taken any of them, I wouldn't know as I didn't know what he kept in there. They think the shooting was accidental as there were signs of a struggle. They investigated it as a robbery and nothing more. I'm no police detective, but even I think there's more to it than a botched robbery," Lynn said angrily.

Paige agreed but she wouldn't say anything yet. She needed more information. "That's why the security."

Max nodded. "With police writing off Marcus's shooting as a robbery we thought it best to bring in private help to handle the investigation ourselves. The Prescotts take care of our own."

Paige wasn't surprised to hear that from Max. She'd done some research on the Prescott family as well as downloaded Marcus Prescott's biography *The Making of a Man* which she'd read halfway through on her flight here. In the book as well as articles she'd found online from various business magazines, he was very up-front about his juvenile criminal past to support his family after his father abandoned them and his determination to do whatever it took to keep his brother from making the same mistakes. Unlike his studious, business-oriented older brother, Maxwell Prescott became a thrill-seeking party boy for several years before he finally settled down, going into business with his brother, getting married and having five kids, two of which joined the family business while the other three were making their own names in their chosen fields.

Even Lynn Prescott's past was dirt-free. She was the youngest daughter of a well-respected judge in Michigan and an estate planning attorney. Lynn chose a career in education and was a middle school teacher when she met and married Marcus. She was now on the board of a local charter school. She'd also done her research on her runaway heiress, Ava Prescott, but there wasn't much written about her publicly and the few pictures Paige found were the professional photos with her family or attending one of the many charitable events the Prescotts supported. Ava was gorgeous and although she didn't know her, Paige could imagine her being the spoiled little princess most of these heiresses tended to be. The Prescotts might look like the picture-perfect family on the outside, but there had to be some skeletons in their closet for them to be pretty much hunted like this.

"Is there anything else I need to know? Was Marcus involved in anything illegal or mixed up with the wrong people? Could your daughter have been kidnapped rather than run away?" Paige asked.

Lynn looked offended by the questions. "You sound like the police. Marcus is a good man. He left that life behind him many years ago. His and Diamond Unlimited's reputation means everything to him, and he'd never do anything to jeopardize it. People are so quick to kick a Black man of his status down because they can't imagine he worked hard for it on his own and honestly."

"My apologies. I didn't mean to offend I just need to make sure I'm not missing anything. What about your daughter's disappearance, could it be connected to these attempts on your family?"

Lynn and Travis exchanged a look, then Travis slid a folded piece of paper across the table toward Paige.

"That's the information you'll need to find Ava. Her disappearance is connected but not in the way you think," Travis said.

Paige unfolded the paper and saw the name Lacey Crain, a phone number, and an address. She looked back up at Travis and he nodded in response to her unasked question.

"So, if you all have known where she was all this time why call me?"

"Because we don't want to chance anyone following and thought it would be safer if she had a secure escort home that couldn't be traced back to any of Ezekiel's people. Travis can fill you in further," Lynn explained.

"What do you do again?" Paige asked.

Travis smiled. "I didn't say."

Paige quirked a brow in amusement.

"You know, I did a background check on you and you're pretty badass. A Marine counterintelligence specialist offered a sweet analyst position with the CIA and turned it down to work as a VIP private security contractor and now a private eye. Pretty cool." He took a swig from a bottle of soda he'd been nursing.

Paige took a swig of water from hers, watching Travis curiously. "You seem to know quite a bit about me, and I know nothing about you other than you're Ava's best friend and your name is Travis, if that's your real name."

Travis chuckled. "It's the name on my birth certificate and I am Ava's best friend. As a matter of fact, I'm the one who helped her disappear," he said proudly.

Paige understood now. "You're a professional hacker."

Travis nodded. "They call us ethical hackers now. They even offer Certified Ethical Hacker training. Going legit with a six-figure salary for what I spent years doing in a dark windowless room for fun has been a game-changer."

"I'm assuming you used your pre-professional skills to get Ava her new identity."

Travis shrugged. "I made sure she was able to disappear so well that it would take me twice as long to find her as it did to make her disappear."

Travis explained what he did to help Ava avoid being digitally tracked and how he destroyed any trace on his end of what he'd done so that the information couldn't be found if anyone happened to get past his own protocols.

"What happened to make her leave?"

Travis gazed over at Lynn as if asking for permission to answer.

"She might as well know everything," Lynn answered his unasked question.

Travis turned back to her. "It started when Marcus pushed her to marry Kyle Edwards, the firm's CFO and Marcus's golden boy. It was supposed to be a marriage on paper only to maintain the conservative image of the company."

"Did he not trust her to find a husband on her own?"

"Ava is gay. She came out to all of us back in college, but her father doesn't think it would be a good look for the face of the firm. He's a stickler for optics, especially being a Black man running a wealth management company in a mostly White, good ol' boy, world."

"That's crazy. She couldn't just say no?" Paige directed her question to Lynn.

She looked annoyed and embarrassed. "Unfortunately, Marcus didn't include me in his ridiculous idea. If he had, maybe I would've been able to talk some sense into him sooner and we wouldn't be in this situation."

Travis continued. "Marcus threatened to make Kyle his successor when he stepped down if she didn't go through with it. Ava loves that firm more than she loves herself and worked her ass off to prove to her father that it would be good in her hands. She even kept her personal life on the down low. She was very careful not to do anything that would put her, her family, or the firm in a bad light. But she slipped up, and although the crisis was averted, her father used it to push her into what he wanted her to do. In his warped, old-fashioned thinking, he claimed he just wanted her to be able to have a life and family and not be so focused on maintaining their legacy that she lost sight of living like he did."

Paige shook her head. "If she'd been his son there wouldn't even have been a discussion about her ability to take over."

"Exactly. But Ava would do anything to preserve the Prescott family legacy, so she agreed to the marriage despite her dislike and distrust of Kyle. She always felt he was too perfect and too eager to be within Marcus's good graces. We had hoped to find something on him to prove to Marcus that he wasn't all that he appeared, but we barely found anything that would help her case," Travis said in annoyance. "Fortunately, Lynn found out about the fake relationship and it being Marcus's idea and managed to talk some sense into him and Ava and they called the wedding off. Ava had thought Kyle would've been happy with that, but he wasn't."

"Do you all believe that he's behind these threats?"

Max picked up the explanation from there. "Yes, but we can't prove it. Everything we have so far is circumstantial. Marcus has stipulations in the event he either becomes too incapacitated to run the company or, God forbid, dies before he's officially named his successor. If I'm still around then I take over and make the decision of who the successor is. If I'm not, then it would automatically be Ava. If, for some crazy reason, Ava chooses not to take over then the decision goes to the board of directors who Kyle has managed to charm."

"So, if you and Marcus are out of the picture and Ava doesn't stake her claim, Kyle could be the one to take over at the board's recommendation."

"Exactly."

"And Ava is aware of this?"

Travis frowned. "Yes. We keep our update calls to once a month, and I try not to email her too often just in case someone does manage to get past my firewalls. Marcus thinks it's time for her to come home so we'll have a better chance of protecting her."

"There's one thing I don't think you all have considered." Paige looked at the group before her wishing she hadn't realized what she was about to tell him. It just made this job a lot more complicated.

"What's that?" Lynn asked.

"If I find Ava and convince her to come back, which I doubt won't be too hard considering recent developments, her life is in even more danger because she's right back in the lion's den."

They all had the same look. As if they were balloons that had suddenly lost air.

CHAPTER EIGHT

It had been several weeks since Ava had spoken to her father. She figured he would've sent word about coming home by now. She gazed down at her phone. She had two hours before closing time. Maybe she could step away for a quick break once the next performance started and call Travis. She knew it wasn't time for their monthly call, but she'd been worried about her father, and it had intensified in the past week.

"Hi, can I get a seltzer with lime?"

Ava looked up at a very attractive woman with eyes the color of rich mahogany and a sexy crooked smile. It took a moment for the woman's drink request to register. "Seltzer with lime, got it." She quickly made the drink and set the glass on a napkin in front of her. "Would you like to start a tab?"

"No, thank you, I'm not staying long." The woman placed a ten-dollar bill on the bar. "I'm in town on business. I passed this place earlier and was curious. I've never been to a burlesque show."

"Really? Well, this is the best show in town. The next act should be hitting the stage in a few minutes." Ava turned to the register to get the woman her change.

"Keep the change," she said as Ava offered her a five-dollar bill.

"Thanks." Another customer waved her down. "If you'll excuse me."

The woman nodded, her smile tempting Ava in ways she'd avoided in the year she'd been in New Orleans. The lights dimmed and the MC announced the next performer.

Ava joined Alan on the opposite end of the bar. "I've gotta make a quick trip to the little girls' room."

He gave her a thumbs-up and Ava left him to handle the other customers. She went to Leo's office instead of the bathroom for privacy and was hitting the speed dial for Travis's number before the door closed. Ava sighed with disappointment as her call went to voice mail. She considered calling her father but knew he probably wouldn't answer since he told her not to call him directly again. She shoved her phone back into her pocket and went back out to the bar. She noticed the businesswoman had taken a seat at the bar sipping at her seltzer and watching the show.

Ava took a moment to check her out. She could tell when she took the woman's drink order that she might have Ava by a couple of inches right now but was probably a good four inches taller than Ava's five-four height without her heels. At first glance, her layered, shoulder length hair looked to be in locs, but at closer inspection Ava noticed the texture of twists. Her profile was sleek and angular, her neck long and graceful, and her shoulders broad but not in a masculine way. She wore a blue blazer and pink oxford shirt. She picked up her drink and took a sip, her sexy lips wrapping around the straw and causing a twinge of desire in Ava. The woman's fingers held the glass lightly and were long with neatly trimmed manicured nails. There was something about the way she watched the performer so intently that made Ava want her to look at her that way.

"Girl, if you look any harder, she may burst into flames," Alan whispered near her ear.

Ava jumped. She was so caught up in the woman she hadn't even heard him approach. "Shut up," she said, then returned to her end of the bar.

A moment later, the woman set her empty glass on the bar.

"Would you like another?" Ava asked.

She seemed to think about it. "Maybe one more."

Ava made her another seltzer and lime and switched out her empty glass for a new one.

"Thanks. You were right, it's a good show," she said.

"The best one is at midnight. Lexi is the star attraction on Friday nights. She does a fantastic feather fan dance to the jazz song "New Orleans Bump." You won't want to miss it," Ava suggested.

"Well, with that glowing recommendation and the fact that I don't have any meetings tomorrow, maybe I will start a tab." She gave Ava a wink.

Ava felt her face flush hotly. She took the credit card the woman offered and started a tab with her second seltzer. She also peeked at the name on the card, Paige Richards. Because of Lexi's popularity, the crowd began to pick up in anticipation of her midnight show. Ava couldn't chat with Paige further as drink orders from waitresses and customers directly coming to the bar took up a good half hour of her time. Now and then she would gaze over in Paige's direction to find her still there, nursing that seltzer and watching the crowd. She caught Paige watching her a few times and Ava would give her a shy smile in return. Something about Paige's intense stare made her feel nervous and turned on at the same time. When things slowed down, Ava made her way back over to Paige. She noticed Paige's drink was getting low, so she made her another.

"Are you sure I can't get you anything stronger, Paige?" Ava asked.

Paige quirked a brow in amusement. "No, I'm good."

"Not a drinker?"

"Yes, but not while I'm traveling and working. With my job I need to keep a clear head for the unexpected."

"Ah, I see. I better stock up on some more limes then."

Paige grinned. "I would appreciate that and your name as well since you know mine."

Ava grabbed several limes from a bin under the bar. "It's Lacey," she said, quickly slicing the fruit to replenish her garnish tray.

The lights dimmed and the crowd roared excitedly as the MC began his introduction for Lexi.

"I guess the show is about to begin," Paige said.

"Yes, I think you'll be glad you stayed for it."

Paige gave her that sexy grin. "I think I'd much rather go someplace quiet and talk to you."

Ava almost dropped the glass she was drying. "I think you'll find Lexi's performance much more interesting than talking to me."

"I beg to differ, but I guess I'll have to watch the show in order to find out." Paige gave her another wink and turned in her chair to face the stage.

Ava turned away to straighten the liquor bottles on the shelf behind her even though they didn't need it. Her face wasn't the only thing flushed from Paige's flirting. She never spent this much time talking to a customer, even if she knew them. If her end of the bar slowed down, she would go to the other end to help Alan if he needed it or help the waitresses clear their tables. But something about Paige had her feeling flirty and aching for a physical contact she'd been avoiding. Since she didn't know when she would be picking up and leaving to go home over the past year, she chose not to get involved in any type of intimate relationship casually or romantically. The less people she had to keep lying to and the less ties she had to cut when she eventually did leave the better. But Paige was different. She was only in town for business which meant if she was seriously flirting, Ava could have a little fun without worrying about what to say or do the day after.

When she turned back around Lexi was beginning her performance and for only the second time since she began working at the club, Ava allowed herself to truly see the sensuality of it. When she looked in Paige's direction, their gazes met, and Ava became momentarily lost in the dark depths of Paige's eyes before another customer stepped into view asking for a drink.

Paige had the sudden urge to shove the guy that had stepped in front of her back in the direction he'd come from. She directed her attention back toward the stage but had lost interest in the sexy performance. Now that she had a second to think clearly, she was thankful for the guy cutting off her view of Ava. In the beginning, her flirting was innocent. Just a way to get Ava to talk, but the realization that the actual smiling, flirting Ava was much more beautiful and sexier than the serious businesswoman in the news articles made her flirting more genuine. Paige reminded herself that she was there for a job, not to sleep with the target.

She arrived in town the night before and had been surveilling Ava's movements to determine the best way to approach without spooking her. When she first saw Ava walking out of her apartment, she almost didn't recognize her. Paige had been impressed with the changes Ava had made in her appearance. Her long natural black curls were gone, with a platinum blonde close shaven cropped hairstyle in its place, the simple classic jewelry she wore in all the photos was replaced with chunky Bohemian-style earrings and necklace, and in place of her designer business suits was a batik print maxi dress and sandals. She wore very little, if any makeup, displaying a natural beauty that attracted Paige in an unexpected way considering she was usually attracted to women who looked as high maintenance as they were.

Paige was thrown for another loop when she entered the club and spotted a woman behind the bar who resembled Ava but couldn't be her as she wore a full face of makeup and had a black bobbed hairstyle. It wasn't until she overheard the other bartender call her Lacey that she realized it was Ava. She was like a chameleon, blending into whatever environment she was in. Paige glanced back at Ava as she assisted another customer. Seeing her in such vastly different looks was kind of sexy. She could picture sensual nights of role play with Ava in a different look each night.

Ava looked up and their gazes connected just at that moment. As if she knew what Paige had been thinking, Ava blushed and looked shyly away. Paige liked that she had that effect on Ava considering what she'd learned about her from Travis. He said Ava was a bold, confident, and independent woman who didn't shy away from much and wasn't easily intimidated. Paige wondered, if that was the case then why didn't she stand up to her father when he tried to marry her off. Then she remembered how intimidated she was by her own father, even after all her military experience and training. From what she learned of Marcus Prescott, she could imagine the two prideful and life-hardened men getting along well. A bullet to the head hadn't even stopped Marcus.

Lexi's performance ended with much fanfare and then all the other night's performers came out for a final bow and an announcement for last call for the bar was made. Paige waited until most of the customers had closed out their tabs before she closed out hers. It seemed Ava had the same plan in mind as she asked her fellow bartender if he could handle the rest while she took care of one last customer. He grinned knowingly at her and leaned over to whisper something that made Ava give him a playful shove before she made her way over to Paige.

Ava laid the little tray with Paige's bill and credit card in front of her. "I'm assuming you've had your fill of seltzer for the night?"

Paige smiled. "I think so." She signed the receipt and picked up her credit card.

Ava took the tray and placed the receipt in the register. "How did you like your first burlesque show?"

"It was entertaining. I may have to come back again before I leave."

"You should. If you're still here, Thursdays are our drag shows. The best—"

"In town," Paige finished for her.

Ava chuckled. "Exactly. Well, I better finish closing. It was nice to meet you, Paige."

"So, Lacey, what are you doing for the rest of the night?"

Ava seemed surprised by the question. "Uh, I guess go home and go to bed."

"Do you live far?"

"No, on Dumaine, near the waterfront."

"Do you have a ride?"

"It's just a few blocks. I usually walk."

"This late by yourself? Is that safe?"

Ava smiled. "Thank you for your concern, but I'll be fine."

"I'm sure you will, but I'd feel better if I could walk you home, or at least get you a cab."

"She'd love it if you walked her home," Ava's shirtless partner said with a grin.

"Excuse me?" Ava said in annoyance.

"Girl, let the woman walk you home. I've always hated the thought of you walking home alone in these streets in the wee hours of the morning. Especially walking past Jackson Square," he said.

Ava quirked a brow. "Alan, I've been walking those same streets for a year now and you never said anything."

"Because I know how stubborn you are. I can close out. You let this very attractive woman walk you home."

Ava looked as if she would argue, but stopped when Alan stood to his full, Paige guessed, six-foot height, crossed his arms, and gave her a stern expression. Ava sighed and turned back to Paige.

"If you don't mind waiting, I just have to change my clothes."

Paige smiled because she didn't look too disappointed at having given in. "No problem. I'll be right here."

"Thank you." Ava walked from behind the bar and disappeared down a hall where Paige assumed the dressing room was.

Paige looked down at her watch. This was going a lot smoother than she thought. She considered just coming straight at Ava with the truth of who she was and why she was there, but her gut was telling her it was best to do it where there were less people and Ava felt comfortable. Besides, while they were at her apartment Ava could pack, and they could be on the private jet Max had arranged that brought Paige there and would bring both her and Ava back within a couple of hours.

As Ava changed back into her regular clothes and washed the makeup from her face, she wondered what she was doing letting a woman she'd just met walk her home. Alan had been the only person she'd trusted enough to know where she lived. She didn't even have mail delivered to the address. It was delivered to a post office box she set up as soon as she'd settled in. She was letting Paige's charm and attractiveness whittle away at her self-imposed celibacy. Before her fake relationship with Kyle, she hadn't let a weekend go by without sharing a few hours or a whole night tangled in another woman's arms, so it had been over two years since she'd been intimate with anyone. It made curbing her desire, especially working at a burlesque club, difficult but getting to know the dancers as acquaintances took away the sexuality of their performances for her. She also didn't go anywhere at night but work and home so there was very little opportunity for temptation at a bar or just cruising Bourbon Street. Her flirtation with Paige was the first time she'd allowed herself to even consider being intimate with anyone in all that time.

Ava gazed at her reflection in the mirror, which still surprised her sometimes. She ran her hand over her dyed shorn hair. Her hair had been her pride and joy, and although she loved the freedom her shorter hair provided, she missed the versatility of longer hair. She also missed her closet full of designer clothes and shoes. She'd left with an overnight bag filled with enough nondescript casual clothing to get her through a week until she figured out where she was going. She'd originally thought about South Beach or Key West, places she hadn't visited since her college spring break years but thought it best to go someplace her family didn't know she'd gone before and that was New Orleans. She'd only been here once with Selena one spring break. She loved the city and hoped to come back some day but never did. She knew she would have to become anonymous, to find a way to blend into a city with so many groups of people and not look like herself so she found the nearest barber shop and had them lop off her curls then she picked up hair color at a drug store on the way back to her hotel and dyed her hair. The final touch for creating Lacey Crain was a new, nondescript wardrobe.

Ava gazed at herself for a moment longer then turned away and finished gathering her things. She was Lacey Crain. There was no way Paige knew her as anyone but that, so she could afford to indulge in a little fun after all this time without worrying about being found out. Especially since Paige would more than likely be gone in a few days and Ava would never see her again. She said good night to all the performers and headed back out to meet Paige. As she entered the main part of the club, she spotted Paige talking to Leo and was able to see her fully. Because of the dim lighting, Ava hadn't noticed that Paige's blazer was a beautiful royal blue sporting a fully lined colorful floral interior. She also wore matching royal blue tapered pants and a funky pair of blue paisley sneakers. She laughed at something Leo said and the husky sound stroked over Ava like velvet.

"You need a napkin to wipe that drool about to fall?" Alan said.

Ava couldn't even be mad at him because she was drooling. "See you tomorrow." She walked toward Paige and Leo.

"There she is," Leo said. "This fine young lady tells me she's waiting for you. Should I be jealous?"

"Unless she's trying to steal Robin from you, I think you'll be fine. Good night, Leo." Ava gave him a brotherly kiss on the cheek then turned to Paige. "Ready whenever you are."

Paige gave her that crooked smile and a slight bow. "After you."

Ava led her out of the club and turned right out into Bourbon Street which was full of revelers.

Paige stepped up to walk beside her. "Your boss and co-workers are very protective of you."

"What did they say?" Ava asked in exasperation.

"Alan tried finding out what hotel I was staying at in case anything happened to you and Leo told me they had me on camera if you didn't show up for work tomorrow."

Ava covered her face in embarrassment. "I can't believe they did that. I mean they were overprotective in the beginning when they found out I was here alone, insisting on having the bouncers take turns walking me home, but I eventually convinced them I could take care of myself."

"How'd you do that?"

"I told them I held a brown belt in Krav Maga. They didn't believe me, so I had to prove it by demonstrating on the bouncers. I didn't hurt them too much. Just enough that they knew I could take care of myself, if needed."

"I'm impressed. Why didn't you continue to black belt?"

"Life got too busy. I'll get back to it one of these days."

"Have you been in New Orleans long?" Paige asked.

"Long enough." Ava avoided giving a specific answer. "How long will you be here?"

"Hopefully I can wrap my business up quickly and be out in a couple of days."

"Have you had time to do some sightseeing?"

Ava didn't want to ask too many personal questions because they would lead to her being asked questions she didn't want to answer. She'd told her lie enough to almost believe it herself sometimes, but she was also sick of having to do it. It was safer to keep the conversation light.

"Not really but I've been to New Orleans a few times, so I've seen all the touristy stuff."

"Ah, but it's the non-touristy stuff that makes it more interesting. To get to know the real New Orleans you need to go where the locals go."

"Oh really? Are you offering to be my tour guide?" Paige bumped Ava with her shoulder.

Ava gave her a shy smile and quickly looked away. She wasn't used to feeling so bashful around a woman. She liked being the one in control, the one making women blush and giggle girlishly while she charmed and seduced them. It threw many women off because of her femme appearance. They didn't expect her to be the aggressor, but she was Marcus Prescott's daughter. He didn't raise her to be sweet and demure which was why she rarely dated masculine-presenting women. It turned into a power struggle she didn't have the patience or desire to deal with. But it was different with Paige. She wasn't masculine or feminine presenting. She seemed to be a tempting combination of both that intrigued Ava and made her react much differently. For once she didn't mind not being the aggressor.

"Maybe if you're still in town on Tuesday or Wednesday. Those are my nights off." What was wrong with her? She shouldn't be offering to make any plans, whether they were for tomorrow or a week from now, she may not be here herself.

"I'd like that," Paige said.

They strolled together in silence until they were within view of Ava's apartment building.

"Well, this is me, just up ahead. Thank you for escorting me home." Ava was suddenly nervous. Other than Alan, this was the first person she'd brought anywhere near her personal domain since moving in.

"Thank you for allowing me to, even though you could probably kick my ass Miss Brown Belt in Krav Maga," Paige teased her.

Ava smiled in amusement. "I'm glad you didn't give me a reason to."

Losing herself in Paige's dark eyes, Ava found she didn't want to walk away. She didn't want to spend another night alone. "W-Would you like to come up for a quick drink. I have seltzer but no limes."

Paige frowned thoughtfully. "I don't know. No limes could be a deal breaker."

"Oh, well, if that's the case—"

"But I think I can live without them," she quickly said.

"Okay then." Ava ignored the little voice in her head that had kept her distant from anyone who tried to get close.

They walked to the second-floor landing where her apartment was located, and she stopped. "That's strange."

"What?"

"Since I get home so late, I have my lights on a timer to come on at eight o'clock so that I don't come home to a dark apartment. They're not on." Ava moved toward her door but was stopped by Paige's hand on her shoulder.

"Wait, do you mind if I go in first?" Paige asked

Ava looked worriedly toward her apartment door. It didn't appear to be open or unlocked. "Maybe I accidently switched the timer off and don't remember."

"Do you really believe that may be the case?"

Ava shook her head and handed Paige her key.

"Get behind me," Paige said, moving toward the door.

Ava did as she was asked and watched as Paige moved toward the door and lay her ear against it.

"What—"

Paige held a finger to her lips and Ava clamped her own shut. When she took a step back from the door, reached under the back of her blazer, and pulled a small handgun out of a holster attached to her belt, Ava's heart began beating frantically in her chest and she practically merged with the brick wall. Who the hell did she bring to her home?

CHAPTER NINE

As they entered Ava's apartment, Paige had allowed herself, just for a moment, to enjoy the flirting and forgot the reason she was here. She'd done something she never did with a target, she let her guard down to enjoy just being in the company of a beautiful woman. Ava's concern about her lights not being on was like a slap in the face to wake her ass up and remember who she was. Not the charming flirt she'd been portraying to make Ava feel at ease, but the serious, analytical soldier that she quickly became in the face of a threat.

"Ava, I need you to step away from the window and over to my right closer to your neighbor's window," Paige said quietly, realizing too late that she had used Ava's real name.

There was a moment of hesitation before Ava did as she had asked. Once she felt Ava was out of possible danger, Paige released the safety on her gun, unlocked the apartment door, turned the knob, pushed the door open and stepped aside against the outer wall with her gun pointed low just to wound, if needed. She listened for any noise that would give away that there was someone inside, breathing, whispering, shuffling, but it was silent until a cat suddenly appeared in the doorway with an annoyed *meow*.

"It's only Gray Beard, don't shoot him!"

Ava rushed from behind Paige into the doorway.

"AVA, NO!" Paige reached out to stop her but kept her gun raised toward the doorway with her other hand because she knew Ava hadn't seen that the cat didn't just stroll but was pushed into the doorway.

"Drop the gun or I shoot her." A lean shadow appeared in the light from the balcony as a man stepped into the doorway with a gun pointed toward Ava.

Ava gasped and took a step back. Paige gave the man a quick, assessing perusal. He was about six feet, slim, with a fit build. His stance, the way he was also assessing her and the way he held his weapon showed he had some training. She quickly went over all the scenarios in her head of how she could take the guy the down, but all of them still put Ava in harm's way. She lowered her gun, clicked the safety back in place.

"Uh-uh, I said drop it," he said with a knowing grin.

Keeping her eyes on the man, Paige bent and lay her gun on the ground then slowly straightened with her hand raised to show it was empty.

"Now, both of you inside. Don't try anything stupid and no one gets hurt."

Paige looked over at Ava who gazed wide-eyed at the gun pointed at her. She grasped her hand to get her attention. When Ava's frightened gaze met hers, she gave her hand a squeeze. "Just breathe."

Ava released a shaky breath.

Paige gave her a nod. "Good, c'mon." She led her into the apartment.

"Close the door," the man told Paige.

Paige shut the door as they stepped in. Gray Beard protested with another annoyed meow at the door being closed in his face.

"What do you want?" Ava asked. "I don't have much worth stealing, but you can take whatever you find."

"He's not here to rob you," Paige said.

If Ava wasn't so frightened, maybe she would've noticed the fresh lineup of the guy's hair, how the black of his T-shirt and running pants were barely faded, and the expensive brand of his running shoes. He was dressed to blend in and be inconspicuous, like someone out for an evening stroll, not out to rob or complete a hit on a certain heiress.

Ava looked from him to Paige. "What's going on? How did you know my name? Who are you guys?"

Paige was glad to see anger was replacing Ava's fear. Fear made you freeze as your brain tried to figure out how to react to the stress of the situation. Anger made for clearer thinking and Paige needed Ava to be thinking clearly when she saw an opportunity to make a move.

"I'm not here to hurt you. Your mother sent me," Paige explained.

Surprise then understanding came into Ava's eyes.

"I'm gonna need you two to stop talking." He reached into his pocket, pulled out a large zip tie and offered it to Ava. "Does the princess know how to use these?" he asked sarcastically. Ava gave him a look that told him what he could do with the zip tie before she snatched it from him. He smiled in amusement. "Put it on her."

Ava looked hesitantly down at the tie then up at Paige.

Paige put her wrists together and lifted them for Ava. "It's all right."

Ava put the tie around Paige's wrist.

"Now, you stay where you are while Veronica Mars there has a seat," he said.

"Ouch, Veronica Mars? Really? You couldn't have at least chosen Christie Love or Foxy Brown?" Paige said in mock offense.

Ava's apartment was a small studio, so Paige only took a few steps to the sofa nearby. As she did, she gazed at the coffee table to see if there was something she could use as a weapon even with her hands bound. Unfortunately, financial magazines wouldn't hurt anything but a fly. As it turned out Paige didn't have anything to worry about. Their assailant took his eyes off Ava to look at Paige and with surprising speed Ava lifted her hands, grabbed the barrel of the gun with her left hand, shifted it to her right, used her right hand to block his wrist from moving, moved in with her shoulder pressing against his arm and twisted the gun toward his thumb to cause him to release it. He was able to get a shot off, but it went wide, and the bullet went into the wall by the door. Ava stepped back staring in shock at the gun now in her hand and Paige was off the sofa, barreling into the gunman, and slamming him into the wall. His head bounced off it, dazing but not knocking him out.

"Ava, hit him on the temple with the butt of the gun!" Paige yelled as she used all her strength to keep him down while he was dazed. She could only pray that Ava had recovered from the shock of having unarmed the man that she heard and followed through with Paige's command.

Paige heard Ava rushing toward them, saw only her feet as she dug her shoulder in the man's sternum and heard the *thunk* of the gun hopefully hitting the spot she'd directed Ava. Paige knew it worked when she felt his heavy body go limp. She scrambled out of the way before he fell on her and gazed up at Ava who looked at the unconscious man in shock before she dropped the gun and wiped her hands on her shirt as if she'd touched something distasteful.

Paige stood up but kept her distance. "Ava," she said, trying to get her attention but Ava continued staring at the man.

"Did I kill him?" she asked fearfully.

"No, you just knocked him out, but we need to get out of here. It may be late but I'm sure one of your neighbors still heard the gunshot and have probably called the police."

Ava looked at her in confusion. "Then shouldn't we stay to talk to them? To tell them what happened?"

"Under normal circumstances I'd say yes, but if we do then you'll have to tell them who you really are and possibly expose yourself to even more danger."

Ava gazed back at the man slumped along the wall, then at Paige and nodded.

Paige almost sighed aloud with relief. She raised her arms above her head, brought them down while pulling her wrists apart as she used the momentum to break the zip tie against her torso.

"I thought that only worked in the movies," Ava said in amazement.

Paige smiled. "Surprised they didn't show that little trick in Krav Maga. I was quite impressed when you disarmed him."

Ava shook her head. "I can't believe I actually did it."

"Is there a back way out of the complex? We don't know if he has someone waiting in a car out front." Paige wanted to kick herself for not noticing anyone when they arrived. She wouldn't let a distraction like that happen again.

"Yes, there's an alleyway behind the building. Go left out the door and down the back stairway."

"Great, let's go."

Paige rushed to the door but stopped and peered out the window beside it before opening it slowly. She poked her head out just enough to be able to check both directions of the balcony for any other assailants. Seeing that the way was clear, and noticing Gray Beard was also nowhere in sight, she signaled for Ava to follow and hurried out the door. The lights were on in both apartments next to Ava's, which meant they probably heard the gunshot and called the police. The sound of sirens in the distance proved her correct. After grabbing the gun she'd dropped, they rushed down the back stairway into a courtyard and out a gate to the alleyway Ava had mentioned.

"Which way? Preferably away from where the police will most likely stop," Paige said.

"They'll come in from the main courtyard on Dumaine. This will take us to Chartres. But where are we going from there?"

Paige was thinking they could head back to her hotel, but the fact that the guy had called her Veronica Mars told her that he knew who she was, that she was a private investigator and probably where she was staying. That could only mean one thing, they had been compromised. For all she knew, she had led them right to Ava.

"Is there anyone you trust or know of a place where we can go until I can get us safely out of town?"

"Alan," Ava said without hesitation. "He has a townhouse just past Bourbon at Dumaine and Dauphine, about four blocks from here."

"Okay, let's go." Paige began walking in the direction Ava recommended.

"Wait, you need to tell me what's going on before we involve anyone else in this craziness. You said my mother sent you, why? Travis knew how to reach me so why didn't he just contact me?"

Paige sighed. "Ava, I can explain everything, but not right now. The sirens are close, our mystery gunman, or possibly a partner, could already be looking for us, and we need to get someplace where I can think straight and get us out of town quickly."

"To go where? Home?"

Paige didn't need this right now. Ava had seemed like a sensible woman just moments ago, but her current hysterics and questions were not helping. "Am I the one that put a gun in your face and threatened to shoot you?" she asked.

"No."

"Have I given you any reason not to trust me?"

"Other than acting like you didn't know who I was, no." Ava sounded just as annoyed as Paige was feeling.

Paige ignored the comment. "Then trust me when I say we need to get out of here. NOW!"

There was just enough light for her to see Ava give her an angry glare before walking past her toward the street. Paige followed wondering how she always ended up in situations like this. She seemed to draw danger to her like a bee to pollen and she was sick of it.

❖

Ava's mind raced between confusion, anger, and fear as Paige insisted on taking a less direct route to Alan's in case someone was following them. The thought that there could be a second gunman had her practically running until Paige made her slow down and not look so harried so they wouldn't draw unnecessary attention. Not even an hour ago she was imagining a very different, and more pleasurable, end to her night. Now here she was ducking and hiding through the streets of New Orleans with a woman she barely knew but was putting her trust in to hide from an unseen predator out to kill her. She was glad they were moving because when she eventually stopped and had time to think about what just happened, she'd probably lose her mind.

Ava still couldn't believe that Krav Maga move she'd done to disarm the guy actually worked. She'd done it plenty of times in training with a fake rubber gun but never thought she'd ever have to use it in real life. The problem was, despite knowing how to shoot, once she had control of the gun, she couldn't bring herself to use it on a real person. Targets at a range were one thing, harming an actual person was much more intimidating. When Ava mentioned that they had arrived at Alan's place, Paige pulled her into the doorway of an antique shop across the street, something she'd been doing as they took their zigzag route there and peeked around the wall to make sure they weren't being followed.

After a few minutes, Paige stepped out onto the sidewalk. "Okay, it's safe."

Because it was mostly a residential area of the French Quarter, the streets were quiet as the galleries, stores and restaurants had been closed for hours now. Ava hurried across the street and pressed the buzzer. She probably should've called first, but she'd left both of her phones, the one that Travis had given her and the inexpensive everyday phone she'd bought in case Leo or anyone at work needed to get in touch with her, at the apartment when she'd dropped her bag. She rang the buzzer again, holding it down a little longer than necessary. A few minutes later she heard someone stomping down a staircase and the curtain on the door shifted as Alan peeked out.

"Alan, we need your help," Ava said in response to his obvious confusion at seeing her on his doorstep in the wee hours of the morning.

There was the sound of locks clicking and a chain being removed before the door opened to reveal Alan with his blond hair mussed and wearing nothing but a pair of silk pajama pants.

He looked from Ava to Paige and back again. "Lacey, what's going on?"

"It's hard to explain but we need a place to stay for the night and you're the only person I can trust," Ava told him.

"Of course, come in." He stepped aside to allow them to enter.

Ava had been to his house many times, so she went up the stairs to the first floor living space of his three-story town home, straight to the kitchen, grabbed a bottle from his liquor cabinet and poured herself a glass of vodka. It burned like hell as she drank it straight down, but she didn't care, it had been a rough hour or so.

Alan shifted his gaze between her and Paige, who stood warily peeking out the window like a nosy neighbor. "Okay, what has you so freaked out that you're on my doorstep in the middle of the night drinking vodka, which you hate, like it's water and looking like you've seen a ghost."

"I think you better sit down. This is going to take a minute." Ava left her glass on the counter and moved to sit on the sofa.

Alan looked toward the stairway then followed her.

"Bruce is here?"

Alan smiled and nodded.

"I'm sorry, I didn't mean to interrupt. I know you guys don't get much time together because of his traveling."

Alan took her hand. "Honey, please, you know I'm always here for you. Besides, he's asleep. I had barely made it in the door from work before he was undressing me." He smirked.

Ava gave his hand a squeeze. "Thanks for letting us in."

Alan looked at her in concern. "What, no snappy comeback? Okay, now I know something is seriously wrong."

"I'm not who you think I am." Ava told him everything, including how they ended up on his doorstep.

He sat looking stunned. "And why aren't you talking to the police?"

"Because whoever is after her isn't going to stop until they get what they want," Paige answered from her post by the window.

"You still haven't told me why my mother sent you instead of contacting me herself."

Paige leaned against the wall and ran her hands through her hair looking frustrated and tired. Ava wanted to have sympathy for her having to get mixed up in this mess, but the fact that her family wasn't there or hadn't contacted her since they obviously knew where she was had her more worried about them.

"Your family, particularly your father, thinks you'd be safer at home where they can keep an eye on you while whoever is behind the danger on you all still hasn't been discovered. They believe that since the attempts on your father and uncle were unsuccessful that you're going to be the focus of whatever your mystery stalker has planned, which was proven tonight. I was hired to find you and bring you home," Paige explained.

Ava's heart felt as if it had dropped into her stomach. As it slowly made its way back up, so did the vodka she drank. She ran to the kitchen sink and emptied what little contents were in her stomach. She hadn't eaten since she'd left for work, so she drank too much alcohol too fast on a practically empty stomach. She felt a hand gently rubbing circles on her back and saw Alan's bare feet beside her. She reached up, turned on the faucet and rinsed the sink and her mouth then stood.

"Sorry, I didn't think I'd make it to the bathroom," she said.

"No worries. That's not the first time that sink has witnessed such degradation."

Ava gave him a weak smile. She looked over at Paige still standing by the window but watching her worriedly.

"Is my family all right? Travis?"

"Your family is being protected by one of the top security firms out there."

"Uncle Zeke."

Paige looked at her in confusion. "Uncle Zeke? Ezekiel Frost is your uncle?"

"Not biologically. He and my father go way back to their criminal youth in the Cabrini-Green housing complex. When my father's family moved there, he was a bit of a nerd and got picked on. Uncle Zeke stepped in one day to protect him, and they'd been best friends since. Ezekiel's mother was a drug addict, and his father wasn't around so he practically lived with the Prescotts. After high school my father went off to college and Uncle Zeke joined the Marines. When he retired from the military, Dad helped him start his security firm. Uncle Zeke has spent every major holiday with us for as long as I can remember. He's the one who insisted

I needed to take Krav Maga and learn to use a gun. When are we going home?"

"I need to make a call," Paige said, looking around the room and heading to Alan's reading room.

"She's awfully intense. It's sexy," Alan said.

Ava shook her head. "I come ringing your doorbell after a harrowing escape from possible death and you somehow find something sexy about it."

"Uh, hello, do you know who I am?" Alan chuckled then wrapped an arm around her waist and placed a kiss on her temple. "You know sex and humor is my coping mechanism. I'm glad you're safe and that you trusted me enough to come to me with the truth." He turned her around to face him. "Ava Prescott, what a great rich girl name. I like it much better than Lacey Crain which always recalled some frilly froth of a girl from a romance novel."

Ava smiled. "Probably because that's pretty much where I got the name from. The first name from one character and the last name from another from two romance novels I read back in college."

"It all makes so much sense now. The mystery of your past, why you haven't had any friends or family visit since you've been here, why you haven't even gone on a date or made any more friends besides me. Not that I'm complaining. I love having you all to myself, but it must have been so lonely the past year."

Ava shrugged. "I did what I had to do. I just wish I had stayed rather than run. Instead, I left my family to face the threat alone." Tears blurred Ava's vision.

"Aw, honey." Alan pulled her into his arms as she cried.

"What a touching scene," a male voice said sarcastically.

Ava and Alan turned to look in the direction of the stairs. Alan's boyfriend, Bruce, stood there dressed in jeans and a T-shirt, holding a belt, and pointing a gun in their direction.

"Bruce? What are doing with that?" Alan asked in confusion.

Ava was tired of having guns pointed at her. She looked at Alan then stepped out of his embrace. "Alan, please tell me you're not also involved in this."

Alan didn't take his eyes from Bruce as he shook his head. "Honey, I swear, I have nothing to do with this."

Ava could see he was just as shocked as she was about Bruce holding a gun on them. She also realized that Alan couldn't be involved as he'd been working at the club at least two years before she'd come to New Orleans. Bruce, on the other hand, showed up just a few months ago when Alan met him at a nightclub. He said he was from Baton Rouge and worked as a regional manager for a major grocery store chain to explain why he traveled so much. He was an average-looking guy, nothing distinct about him, but was very sweet and seemed to genuinely care for Alan. When Ava met Bruce, he never asked anything personal about her other than where she was from and what brought her to New Orleans so there didn't seem to be anything suspicious about him. Looking at him now holding the gun with a dark smirk as if he enjoyed scaring the hell out of people, Ava assumed that was the point.

Bruce moved slowly toward them. "I've been waiting months to be done with this shit. Tonight, was supposed to be my last night with this charade, but obviously somebody fucked up somewhere or you wouldn't be here," he said to Ava. "Imagine my surprise when I wake up and hear you two down here chatting when you're supposed to be on your way back to Chicago."

Alan began to walk toward Bruce. "I don't understand. How do you know about Ava?"

Bruce pointed the gun at Alan. "Don't take another step. It's been fun, Alan, but you were just a means to an end. The easiest way to get to Ava without making her suspicious. They needed eyes on the situation before they could make their move and you were my in."

"You told me you never met anyone that made you as happy as I do, that you loved me. We were talking about you moving in here. I introduced you to my family, for Christ's sake! Was all that a lie?"

Bruce shrugged, looking coldly at Alan. "I did what I needed to do to get the job done."

"You fucking asshole!" Alan's voice broke with emotion.

Ava reached for Alan's hand. She couldn't stand the pain of heartbreak on his face. He grasped her hand tightly and stepped back to stand beside her. Bruce pointed the gun back on her.

"I don't know how you were able to avoid the guys sent to your place, but it doesn't matter because you're here now and I guess I have to clean up their mess." He tossed the belt on the kitchen island. "Ms.

Prescott, I'd appreciate it if you would use this to bind Alan's hands behind his back. He's quite familiar with the position." Bruce gave Alan a cruel smile.

Ava wished she was close enough to do to Bruce what she'd done to the guy in her apartment except this time she wouldn't feel bad about it. She reached for the belt and saw Paige stealthily moving toward Bruce.

CHAPTER TEN

Paige had been completely thrown finding out that Ezekiel was close to the Prescotts. Although he'd been her commanding officer during her first three years in counterintelligence, the job didn't leave room for personal connections, but he had been a father figure to her during those years away when she could barely stay in touch with her own father. Hearing Ava talk about Captain Ezekiel Frost as her Uncle Zeke with such affection was weird because Ezekiel wasn't a "bounce a kid on his knee" type of guy.

She called him. "There was a problem with the pickup location."

"What's the status of the package."

"A little wear and tear but undamaged."

There was a moment of silence on the other end before she heard Ezekiel clear his throat. "Do you think it's wise to complete the delivery."

"No. Probably best to store it in a safe location until the route is clear."

"Send me the info so I can send more personnel."

"I think it's best if I handle the storage and delivery solo. The less hands on the package the better."

"I trust your judgment."

"Good to know and don't worry, I'll handle the package with extreme care. I'll contact you once we reach the storage facility."

"Thank you," Ezekiel said softly before hanging up.

Paige gazed through the glass door of the room at Ava and Alan talking in the kitchen. Ava wasn't going to like not being able to go home, but Paige saw no other way to keep her safe from whatever was happening there. She geared herself up for breaking the news to Ava and headed toward the door when she noticed a third voice and saw Alan and Ava looking nervously in the direction of the second set of stairs she remembered seeing. She recalled Ava mentioning someone named Bruce being there and the smile on Alan's face. She assumed Bruce was Alan's boyfriend, but if that was the case then why would they look so frightened.

Paige removed her shoes then looked around the room for something to use as a weapon because she really didn't want to use her gun. She picked up a trophy shaped like a cocktail mixer on a heavy marble base and quietly stepped toward the door. She had left it slightly ajar when she entered and listened as Bruce revealed his connection to Ava. When he mentioned he'd been watching her for months Paige felt some relief in knowing that she hadn't led them there. She also concluded that they weren't trying to kill Ava. That theory was confirmed when Bruce said Ava should've been on her way to Chicago by now if things had gone according to plan.

Bruce stepped into view and Paige focused on what he was doing instead of what he was saying. He obviously didn't know she was there, or he wouldn't have so much focus on just Ava and Alan, so she had the advantage. She opened the door just enough to slip through and slowly made her way up behind Bruce briefly making eye contact with Ava who thankfully didn't give her away. He was maybe a couple of inches taller than her, skinny with no obvious muscle, but she'd seen some unathletic people do some damage with the right training, so she wasn't taking any chances. She aimed her blow to the base of his skull but didn't put all her weight into it as she could cause a serious spinal cord injury, or worse, kill him. She was not trying to be up for murder charges when all this was over. The base of the trophy connected with his head and as he fell, he looked back at Paige in bewilderment. His gun fell out of his hand when he hit the floor and Paige kicked it away.

"Give me the belt," she told Ava.

Ava slid it back across the counter to her. Paige flipped Bruce over, bound his wrists, stood, then grabbed a small knife from the butcher block on the counter to put a hole in the belt to tighten it. "Alan, do you have another belt and some zip ties?" He didn't respond right away, just stared down at Bruce's prone body with angry tears.

"Alan." Ava touched his cheek to get his attention. He looked at her as if seeing her for the first time. "We need another belt and zip ties. Do you have that?"

Alan nodded woodenly. "I'll get the belt. The zip ties are in the pantry." He headed for the stairs then stopped and gazed back at Bruce with a frown before continuing.

Ava disappeared around a corner where Paige assumed the pantry was located and came back with a variety pack container of zip ties.

"Thank you. Are you all right?" Paige asked.

"I'll be all right when I get home."

Paige didn't say a word. She grabbed a thicker zip tie and looped it through the hole she'd made and the belt buckle to make sure it stayed in place in case Bruce regained consciousness and tried to get out of his bindings. Alan returned with another belt and Paige did the same thing with his ankles.

"What now?" Alan said.

"Could you bring me his cell phone and wallet?" Paige asked.

Alan nodded and headed back upstairs.

Paige grabbed a dish towel hanging from a drawer on the island, picked up the trophy and wiped it down before returning it to its original location and retrieving her shoes.

"Why did you do that?" Ava asked.

"My prints were all over it. Once we leave, there can't be any evidence we were here."

"What do you mean? We can't leave Alan here alone with Bruce. There's no telling what he'll do to him."

Alan returned. "I'll be fine. I'll call the police and tell them he attacked me." He handed Paige a cell phone and wallet and set an overnight bag on the island. "This is also his."

Paige pressed the button and found it had a thumb print lock. She stooped and used Bruce's thumb to unlock the phone. She went to his photo gallery and found picture after picture of Ava at work, running errands, outside her apartment. She checked his text messages where there were communications between him, and two contacts labeled G and S instead of names. The messages consisted of status updates on Ava, meeting times and places, and instructions on how to handle Alan when all of this was over. It seemed G thought Alan was expendable, but Bruce thought he could extricate himself from the relationship without hurting him. Paige looked at the unconscious man on the floor. Guess he had a conscious after all, she thought. She removed the sim card, wiped the phone down with the dishtowel and dropped it in a pocket in the overnight bag. She checked his wallet and found credit cards and ID for Bruce Johnson and a twenty-dollar bill but nothing else. Going through his overnight bag was a different story. There were four passports. One for Bruce Johnson and the others under three different aliases. Paige took a picture of them, wiped them down and dropped them back in the bag. She finished by wiping the handles of the bag down as well just to be safe.

Paige turned to find both Ava and Alan gazing at her expectantly. "Alan, it's completely up to you what you'd like to do, but there are two options. One is to do what you suggested, call the police claiming that you were attacked. The only problem with that is trying to explain your relationship with Bruce and why he would attack you after you'd been dating for so long."

Alan seemed to think about that. "What's the other option?"

"I can call some people to discreetly pick him up and take him somewhere for questioning. Maybe we can find out who he's reporting to."

Alan ran his hand through his hair and sighed. "Will they hurt him?"

Paige could see he was on the fence because he still cared about what Bruce had represented despite the truth.

"No. Once they're finished questioning him they'll drop him someplace inconvenient without any communication to keep him from warning anyone if they were able to extract any helpful information."

"Okay. After Vincent, I would rather not have to deal with the embarrassment of the police or anyone else knowing how I appear to be a target for catfishing criminals."

"Do you have some place you can go for the rest of the night?" Paige asked.

"My nana is around the corner. I have a key to her place; I'll just go there. I do that sometimes when I don't want to be home alone after work, so she won't be suspicious if I just show up."

"Okay, good. Grab whatever you'll need for a couple of days. There will be two separate crews, one to collect Bruce and one who will come through to do a sweep of your place to make sure he didn't hide anything while he was here and wipe it down for useful prints. If your neighbors ask, you hired an exterminating service for a rodent issue. That'll keep them from being too nosy."

Alan nodded then turned to Ava with a sad smile. "I guess this was our last night together. At least we went out with a bang. I feel like I'm living in an action movie."

Ava chuckled. "I know the feeling. We'll see each other again when all of this is over, I promise." She pulled him into an embrace. "What do you want me to tell Leo? He's going to be devastated."

"You can tell him I had a family emergency and had to fly back home. At least it won't be a lie. Oh, and if you can, please go check on Gray Beard. He was scared off by all the commotion, but I know he probably didn't go far since he's very much an indoor cat."

"I will. Call me when you're safe, if you can." He gave her one last hug then turned to Paige. "Keep her safe. She's precious cargo."

Paige gave him a smile. "I will. I have one more favor to ask. Do you have a car we can borrow? I'll have it returned to you in a few days."

"Of course. There's a black Mercedes parked out front. The keys are by the door."

"Thank you." Paige offered her hand for a handshake.

Alan smiled. "Girl, please, we're practically family now." He pulled her into a tight hug before walking away.

While Alan went upstairs, Paige went back into the other room to make two calls. One was to Ezekiel again to request an exterminating service using humane traps to let him know to keep Bruce, or whatever his real name was, alive. By the time she finished her calls Ava and Alan were saying good-bye once more, then she and Ava were alone.

"The crew will be here in the next fifteen minutes, so we better get going. We also have a long drive ahead of us. You think Alan has a few bottles of water and snacks he won't miss?"

Ava didn't say anything. She just turned and went back to the pantry and came out a few minutes later with one of those reusable shopping bags filled with items. Paige double-checked to make sure Bruce still had a pulse and that his bindings were tight but not cutting off his circulation then grabbed the dishtowel off the counter and the car keys hanging by the stairway. When they got downstairs, she used the towel to open the door just enough to poke her head through and check the street. She'd heard Bruce say there had been two people at Ava's and just wanted to make sure there was no one lying in wait for them. The street was quiet.

She hit the button on the key fob and a car parked one door down beeped in response.

"Okay, let's go, but be casual," she said as she walked out then held the door open for Ava.

They calmly strolled to the car and got in. Paige drove around for several blocks to make sure they weren't being followed before she headed to I-10, the highway leading out of town. It wasn't until then that she typed their destination into the car's GPS system.

"I thought we were going home," Ava said.

"That's not the safest place to be at the moment."

"I don't care if it's the safest place to be. It's where my family is which is where I should be," Ava said angrily.

"Ava, we are not going through this again. Someone is targeting your family to do them harm. Your mother hired me to find you and keep you safe so that's exactly what I'm going to do. Taking you home would be the opposite of that."

"I'll pay you double what she's paying if you take me back to Chicago."

"You rich folks crack me up. You always think it's about the money. We're not going back to Chicago right now."

"Don't you understand! This is all my fault! I left my family to deal with Kyle alone and I need to go back and fix it before it's too late." There was desperation in Ava's tone.

Paige pulled off to the shoulder of the road then turned to Ava. Tears were streaming from her beautiful amber eyes, and she looked so lost Paige was ready to give in to what she was asking but she knew she couldn't, and she had to make Ava understand why.

"Ava, none of this is your fault. You didn't create the greed of the person more than likely behind this and you leaving was probably the smartest thing you could've done. There's no telling what would've happened to you if Kyle Edwards is responsible for your father being in the hospital, the attempt on your uncle's life, and your attempted kidnapping. With the protection surrounding your family back home, you're the main target now so you going back will not only put them in further danger but also the people Ezekiel has protecting them. Do you want that?"

Ava wiped her tears with the hem of her T-shirt. "But I need to go back to make sure my parents are safe. I need to help figure out if it really is Kyle and what we need to do to stop him."

"Ezekiel, your uncle Max, and Travis are handling all of that. Let them do what they need to do without the added burden of worrying about trying to keep you safe. They've asked me to do that, and I can't if you continue to fight me about it. Can you please just work with me?"

Ava appeared to think about what she was saying. Paige waited anxiously for her reply.

Ava looked miserable. "If they all trust you then I guess I can."

Paige held back a sigh of relief. "Thank you." She pulled back out onto the road.

Three hours later, after a brief rest stop, Paige heard Ava's breathing slow to a relaxed, even rhythm and knew she'd finally fallen asleep. She felt some sense of relief that Ava was comfortable enough to do so considering what was going on, but she also couldn't let her own guard down. She was still beating herself up for doing so earlier. If Paige had been doing her job rather than thinking with her crotch, then she would've noticed any suspicious people sitting in a car outside Ava's building. She would've been on alert so the guy in the apartment wouldn't have gotten the jump on them. She could've warned Ava right then what was going on and had her stay hidden somewhere as she did a sweep of the building. Not only did that not happen but Ava ended up saving their asses by disarming the guy and knocking him out. Paige gazed over at Ava who had curled up in the seat facing her. Her face was softened, making her look even younger than she already did, her long lashes brushed her cheeks, and her lips were moist and slightly parted as she breathed softly. She looked peaceful and beautiful, and Paige could imagine waking up to gazing at that face each day and starting it off with tasting those full, soft lips. Ava shifted, snapping Paige out of the fantasy she was building in her head. She jerked her head back around and glued her gaze to the road. All they would need now was to crash because she was distracted by thoughts that would never happen.

Ava slept until they arrived just outside of Atlanta. "How long did I sleep?"

Paige tried not to look at her stretching like a leisurely cat. "We're just about a half hour from our destination so pretty much the entire trip."

"I wanted to at least offer to help with driving. I'm sure you're even more tired than I was."

"No, I'm fine. I'm used to pulling all-nighters and long hauls. I'll sleep when we get there. If I can get everything squared away, we should be able to leave by tomorrow morning."

"Leave? I thought this was our final stop."

"No, this is just a layover to replace a few things I left back in New Orleans and arrange for our transportation for the rest of our travel."

"Oh." Ava sounded disappointed and Paige didn't blame her. "Will I be able to call home sometime today?"

Paige hesitated. She knew Ava wouldn't be happy with the answer to that question either. "I don't think that's a good idea. We need to make sure we have a secure line before we do that and that won't be until we reach our destination tomorrow."

"Tomorrow! I agreed to not going home right now, not to not having any contact with my family."

"I'll see what I can do but I won't make any promises."

The daggers Ava shot Paige when she gazed over at her looked deadlier than the ones she'd left in her bag at the hotel in New Orleans. Ava didn't speak to her the remainder of their drive. She pulled up to an auto repair shop then picked up her phone and sent a text. She got an immediate response and pulled the car around to the back of the garage. Grant stood outside with that Cheshire grin he'd developed since retiring and becoming a family man.

"Grab whatever you're taking with you because we're leaving the car here," Paige told Ava then got out and walked to Grant.

"What's up, Sarge!" he said happily as he pulled her into a bear hug that practically lifted her off the ground.

"What's up, Grant. How's the family?"

"They're all good. Patrice is ready to pop. She's due any day now. Another girl," he said proudly.

Paige chuckled. "You poor man, a house full of women."

"Hey, ain't nothing wrong with being the only king of the castle."

Ava joined them wearing Paige's blazer and carrying the shopping bag they'd taken from Alan's place which now only held the empty water bottles and packages of the snacks they had brought.

"Ava, I'd like you to meet an old friend of mine, Grant Baxter. Grant, this is Ava Prescott."

Grant offered Ava his hand. "Nice to meet you, Ms. Prescott. Sorry to hear about the trouble following you, but if there's anyone worth safely putting your life in their hands, it's Paige."

Ava accepted his hand and smiled. "That's good to know. Thank you."

"Did you get my shopping list?" Paige asked.

"Yes. Everything is bagged and ready to go. Your transportation is also set, so we'll just load the groceries directly while you guys get some rest. Patrice has the guest room all set up and plans on cooking up a mini feast tonight."

"Thanks. She doesn't have to go to all that trouble," Paige said.

Grant chuckled. "Yeah, I'll let you tell her that. At this point in her pregnancy, I just let my wife do whatever she wants to make her happy. Cooking makes her happy."

Paige smiled. "Got it. Here are the keys to the car. I already put gas in it even though I know you're returning it on a flatbed, but it's the least I could've done for the guy."

Grant nodded. "Okay, cool. Let me just drop these in the office and we can head out to the house. Bertha is in her usual spot." He turned and went into the back door of the garage.

"You look like you're about to fall out any second," Ava said.

Paige felt like she was. The adrenaline and caffeine from the coffee she bought when they stopped were wearing off.

"I'm fine. Nothing a couple of hours of sleep won't cure. Let's wait for Grant in the truck." Paige led Ava to Grant's truck, Bertha, the twin sister of her own truck, Betty.

It was a Diamond Black Dodge Ram 2500 Laramie with all the bells and whistles offered as well as a few custom additions that rivaled that of the car used for the president of the United States. Both of their trucks were equipped with run-flat tires, night vision gear, bulletproof windows and doors, and a bomb-proof plated undercarriage. Not that they would ever encounter driving over a bomb, but Paige figured that was for Grant's own peace of mind after what he'd experienced in Iraq.

"I take it this is Bertha," Ava said.

"Yep. You prefer to sit in the front or back. It's just a quick ten-minute ride to Grant's house."

"I'll take the back then. I'm sure you two probably have some things to talk about." Ava opened the door to the crew cab, stepped up onto the running board and into the truck as gracefully as if she were stepping into a limousine.

Paige held back a smirk. Ava was not the stereotypical pampered princess she'd made her out to be. Yes, she argued with Paige at every turn about wanting to go home, but she'd been holding her own when the situation called for it instead of cowering in fear. Judging by the bare minimum of luxuries in her small studio apartment, Ava also didn't seem to have an issue with giving up the luxurious life she was used to. That would come in handy when they arrived at the ranch because her home was built for comfort and safety, not to be a show piece for *Architectural Digest*. Then a surprising thought came to Paige. This would be the first time she'd ever brought any woman to her home that she wasn't related to or already friends with. The thought of Ava being in her space, her inner sanctum, made her more nervous than if she'd been walking into any of the dangerous situations she'd encountered until now.

CHAPTER ELEVEN

A va sat in the back seat of the huge pickup watching Paige and Grant talking. They looked so serious and at one point, both turned their gazes on her. Their outward appearances were nothing alike. Paige had a slim, athletic, build, was still wearing her dress pants with her shirt still neatly tucked in and the holster with her gun shifted from the back of her belt to her side, and stood about five eight. While Grant, dressed in camo pants, work boots, and a black T-shirt, was a giant of a man standing well over six feet with the broad barreled chest and shoulders of someone who took his weightlifting seriously. The only similarity was the identical intense, dark and dangerous looks in their gazes that told her they had shared more than a friendship in their past. Ava didn't know who she should be more afraid of, the people chasing her or the ones protecting her. She pulled Paige's blazer tighter around her to stave off the sudden chill she got and was relieved when they turned away to finish their conversation.

A moment later, they were climbing into the truck and were off with a surprisingly quiet start of the motor. With a beast of a truck like this owned by a big manly man in the South like Grant, Ava expected it to sound like something revving up on a NASCAR track.

"So, Ava, I hear you're a financial wizard. Maybe, before you guys take off tomorrow, you can give me some advice on the best way to invest a little nest egg I have set aside for my baby girls. I have a financial planner but I'm not seeing the growth in my investments I know is possible," Grant said.

"Uh, sure, yes, I'd be happy to."

It was such a normal request during a very surreal situation Ava wasn't sure how else to respond. Judging by the look on Paige's face, she found it amusing. Ava just shook her head and gazed out the window wishing this past year had all been a weird dream that she'd soon wake up from in her bed at her penthouse in Chicago. That wasn't the case as they pulled into the driveway of a picturesque ivy-covered Tudor-style home surrounded by a white picket fence. It looked like something straight out of one of those family television series, especially when an adorable pig-tailed toddler burst out of the front door and came running down the walkway toward the truck dressed in pink from her hair ribbons to her frilly lace-trimmed dress down to her pink sneakers that lit up as she ran. Grant had barely turned the engine off before he was hopping out of the truck and running toward the little girl. It was then that Ava noticed a limp to his gait. He swept the girl up, threw her at least a foot in the air, and caught her smoothly before wrapping his arms around her. Seeing the sweet moment and the joy on the little girl's face made her ache for her own father and similar moments they had shared when he'd come home after a long business trip.

"Are you okay?" Paige asked.

Ava wiped away a tear. "I'm fine."

She opened the door and climbed out of the cab. Paige exited shortly after and headed toward Grant.

"Auntie Paige!" the little girl said excitedly trying to wiggle out of Grant's arms.

"Okay, okay," he said, laughing as he set her back down to run into Paige's waiting arms.

"Hey, Supergirl."

Paige lifted her up and the little girl spread her arms while Paige twirled her around as if she were flying. She squealed with delight and Ava was in awe of how Paige's features softened with an expression of pure joy. Her attraction to Paige that she'd been trying to ignore reared its head at the tender moment. She felt the ache of having a wife and family of her own that she'd put on the back burner to focus on the family business grip her heart in a gentle reminder that it was still there.

"Lily, would you like to say hi to my friend Ava?" Paige said, pulling Ava out of her thoughts.

"Hiiii!" Lily said with a happy wave and sweet smile.

Ava gave her a wave and smile in return. "Hi, Lily. I love your sneakers."

"Dada bought them," she said, reaching for Grant who took her from Paige and swung her around onto his back.

Ava smiled at how, despite her girlie attire, he didn't treat her like a delicate princess. Her father had been the same way with her. He'd told her that if she wanted to be successful in a man's world she would need to be just as tough as them.

"Let's go see what Mama is up to," Grant said, leading them into the house.

Paige stepped aside to allow Ava to go first. Ava gave her a smile and received a sexy one in return. It seemed no matter how Paige smiled, Ava thought it was sexy. She needed to nip whatever these feelings were in the bud. Paige was here to protect her, not curb any desire she still felt after how close they'd come to giving in to their flirtatious foreplay before the ambush at her apartment. Then an unpleasant thought came to her. Would Paige have gone through with sleeping with her before revealing who she really was and why she was there? The very thought of Paige doing such a thing was like throwing cold water over a growing flame. Ava gazed back at her with a frown.

Paige looked at her in confusion. "What?"

"Nothing," Ava said angrily, turning away.

"Patty Cake, we're home!" Grant shouted as he squatted to allow Lily to climb off his back.

They all followed her into a family room that opened to a dining area and kitchen where a petite and very pregnant woman was setting up a tray with glassware and plates.

Lily bounced on her toes pulling on her mother's pant leg. "Mama, Mama, Dada's home. Can I have a cookie now?"

Grant laughed. "So that's why you were so happy to see me. The promise of cookies." He went to his wife and planted a loud kiss on her cheek.

Patrice smiled lovingly down at Lily. "You may have one cookie if you can carefully carry the plate over to the table."

Lily's bouncing stopped as she nodded at her mother's request. Patrice carefully placed a plate of cookies in her outstretched hands and Lily's brow furrowed in intense concentration as she carefully made her way toward the coffee table. She was just the right height to slide the plate from her hands onto the table, setting them in the middle and rearranging the cookies that had shifted during transport. With a satisfied nod, she gave her mother a wide-eyed gaze of anticipation.

Patrice gave her a proud smile. "Excellent job. You may have one cookie. Take a napkin and have a seat at your play table. Daddy will bring you some milk." She turned a happy smile toward Paige and waddled from behind the counter to be pulled into a hug. "It's good to see you."

"It's good to see you too." Paige separated them just enough to place her hands on Patrice's protruding belly. "I think this one is going to take after her daddy."

"You're not kidding. The doctor says she'll be at least an eight-pounder," Patrice said with a pained expression.

"Good Lord, woman. I'm assuming this one won't be the natural home birth Miss Lily was?"

"Unfortunately, not. The doctor thinks we may have to do a C-section. She's just too big."

Grant came up behind her and placed his hands on her shoulders. She stood just to his chest. "I'll be right there, holding her hand and making sure the doctor doesn't mess up."

Patrice rolled her eyes in exasperation. "He means he'll be there to intimidate the poor man. He becomes flustered every time Grant comes to an appointment with me. Anyway, where are my manners?" She directed her attention to Ava. "You must be Ava. Grant told me what's going on. You'll be perfectly safe here, especially with Frick and Frack watching over you, so please make yourself at home. I made some refreshments, the guest room is all set for you guys, and, Paige, your jump bag is in there as well."

"Thank you. I'm so sorry to be putting you to all this trouble," Ava said.

Patrice waved a hand dismissively. "Paige is family and whatever she needs, we're here. Now, there's nothing like a brown butter chocolate chip cookie and some lemonade to take some of your worries away."

Patrice had been right. Sitting down, enjoying her melt-in-your-mouth cookies, lemonade with just the right amount of tart and sweet, and listening to some very entertaining stories about Grant and Paige's time in the military, with the interjection of feedback from a very bright and precocious three-year-old, made life seem almost normal for a little while. When Patrice noticed that Paige could barely keep her eyes open, she insisted Ava and Paige go upstairs to rest. Grant showed them to the guest room.

"Sorry you have to share a room, but since the baby will be sharing Lily's room with her, we moved her castle and toys into the other guest room. It's now become Lily's Kingdom," he said, grinning in amusement. "I'll bring in the air mattress before you guys turn in tonight."

"No need. Ava can take the bed and I'll just do the sofa," Paige offered.

"Okay, but if you change your mind, just let me know. There are fresh towels in the bathroom. I'll be in my workshop out back when you're ready to go over plans for tomorrow."

"Thanks, Grant. I really appreciate the hospitality," Paige said.

"I'd like to thank you as well," Ava said.

Grant smiled. "You know I got you no matter what," he said to Paige then turned to Ava. "As long as you're still willing to give free financial advice, we're even."

Ava smiled. "It's a deal."

Grant nodded and left the room, closing the door behind him.

"Why don't you use the bathroom first," Ava offered, seeing how tired Paige was.

"You sure?"

"Yes, besides, I have no clothes to change into, so I'll probably have to wash what I have on while I'm in there. Do you think Grant has a shirt I can borrow to at least sleep in?"

"I probably have something you can wear." Paige picked up a duffel bag propped against the wall near the bathroom and tossed it on the bed. She rummaged through and pulled out a pair of jeans, a blue plaid button-down shirt, a sports bra, and a pair of women's boxer briefs. "I always keep a jump bag at places I visit frequently with several days of clothes, a first aid kit, and a tool utility kit. These should work for you until we get to our destination tomorrow. Sorry I don't have anything more feminine in the undergarment department."

Ava accepted the clothes. "This is fine. Probably much better attire for being on the run than Victoria's Secret."

"Yeah, probably, but not as sexy."

"I don't know. Depends on who's wearing it." Her face grew hot, she hadn't meant for that to sound flirtatious.

Paige grinned in amusement. "Well, let me go jump in the shower so I can try and get at least a couple of hours of sleep in."

"Okay."

Ava watched her go into the bathroom, sat on the end of the bed, and stared at the closed door for several minutes completely confused by her conflicting feelings. On the one hand she was glad Paige had been there the night of the attack because there was no telling where she would be right now. On the other she was still annoyed at the deceitful way Paige had approached her. She'd let her guard down in the hopes of finally having some intimacy in her life again. It was difficult to stay angry at Paige remembering how hot she looked when she took charge the way she had at her apartment and then at Alan's with Bruce. She felt like she was living her own personal *Bodyguard* movie, but unlike Whitney Houston, she couldn't sing to save her life. Then the sweet moments with Lily, the tender way she treated Patrice, the warmth of her friendship with Grant, all wrapped up into the intriguing package of Paige. Ava flopped back onto the bed wishing, once again, that this was all a crazy dream she'd wake up from any moment.

She didn't realize she'd drifted off to sleep until Paige woke her with a gentle shake, calling her name. Ava noticed she'd fallen asleep with Paige's clothes still gripped in her arms as if she were embracing a lover. She quickly sat up.

"The bathroom is all yours," Paige said.

"Oh, thanks."

Paige was dressed in a pair of tan khakis and a military green short sleeve fitted T-shirt that emphasized her toned torso and arms with *United States Marines est. 1775* emblazoned across her chest, the American flag on one sleeve and *Grunt Style This We'll Defend* with two rifles crossed in the middle of the phrase on the other. Her hair appeared to be damp, and Ava could smell coconut oil, probably from hair moisturizer. It never smelled so intoxicating before. Ava lowered her head and rushed into the bathroom to escape the feelings overwhelming her. She showered and dressed quickly, using a dab of the moisturizer she'd noticed sitting on the counter in her own hair before looking at herself in the mirror. The jeans were a little roomier than she was used to, and she had to roll a cuff into the bottom since Paige was several inches taller than her. The briefs were surprisingly comfortable, and she was seriously considering investing in several pairs when she got home. The shirt was a little long, but she didn't mind. It was made with soft and light cotton.

Ava smiled as she realized this was the comfiest and most casual that she'd dressed since college. Even her sweat suits had designer brand labels, and she couldn't remember the last time she hadn't worn a pair of heels with jeans. Even with trying to stay discreet while she was in New Orleans, she still managed to make her discount store bohemian style look high fashion. Ava also realized that it would probably be weeks before she would be able to go home to her own space and wardrobe closet bigger than this bedroom. With a sigh of resignation, she grabbed her clothing which was now ripe and needed a good washing and walked back into the bedroom to find Paige already asleep on the sofa. She couldn't blame her after the past night. She looked so peaceful, and Ava could picture herself lying beside Paige and being the first person to see her beautiful intense dark eyes first thing in the morning. Ava yawned tiredly. Despite her nap in the car, she was still tired as well. She folded her clothes at the foot of the bed and since she was used to sleeping barely clothed, if at all, she took the jeans off and didn't bother with getting under the covers as she lay down and promptly fell asleep.

Paige awoke with a start, breathing heavily and momentarily confused by her surroundings. When she saw Ava asleep on the bed everything came back to her in a rush. She closed her eyes and took several deep breaths to calm her racing heart and wipe away the nightmare she'd been in the throes of. Looking at her watch, she noted that she'd slept what was left of the morning away. It was almost two o'clock in the afternoon and her stomach grumbled at not being fed a proper meal in almost twenty-four hours. She stretched then put her sneakers on and went over to the bed. She gazed down at Ava lying spread-eagle on her stomach looking incredibly sexy as her shirt had risen and gathered around her waist giving a generous view of the briefs that were molded to her rounded bottom and showed off her shapely legs. Paige's eyes were glued to the sight until Ava whimpered in her sleep. Paige gazed up to find her frowning and her brows furrowed fretfully. She was tempted to wake her, but Ava settled down a moment later.

Paige decided to let her sleep. The rest would be good for her after what they'd gone through and what was ahead of them. She expected the rest of their trip to run smoothly, but she'd learned through the years that letting your guard down too soon could get you hurt or killed. She wouldn't feel comfortable enough to do that until they reached her ranch. She quietly left the room and headed downstairs.

"In here," Paige heard Grant say before she hit the bottom step.

She went in the direction she heard his voice which was his office just to the left of the staircase. "Hey. Where are the ladies?"

"Taking a nap. How'd you sleep?"

"As well as can be expected under the circumstances."

Grant gave her a look of understanding. "Yeah, I can imagine what the past hours triggered."

Paige nodded. "This is so not what I signed up for." She flopped tiredly into a chair in front of his desk.

"You ought to know by now that you and danger seem to have a special bond. I can count on one hand the number of times we DIDN'T end up being shot at or come pretty damn close to our cover being blown during assignments. Even after joining Ezekiel's team, we had to play superhero and get assets out of some tight spots more than what the original job called for."

Paige frowned. "I'm tired, Grant. I just want a quiet life doing something with as little risk as possible. I was doing that until this job. I should've known better after I met with the Prescotts and was given the truth of what was going on. Two attempts on two men's lives should have been enough of a warning to walk away, yet I still took the job because Ezekiel asked me to."

"You could always take her home and leave it to him and his team to protect her."

Paige had considered that, but instinct was telling her that would be a bad idea.

"Yeah, I didn't think so," Grant said, as if reading her thoughts. He opened a drawer in his desk and handed her a cell phone. "Per your request. Now, what's your plan."

"Thanks. We'll fly into Bethesda instead of Tulsa to stay under the radar as much as possible then hole up at the ranch until Ezekiel gives me the all-clear."

"I can't think of a better place for you to hole up. If you weren't so far out in the boonies, I'd be your next-door neighbor."

Paige smiled. "Too much country for this city boy?"

Grant grunted. "I think that's too much country for a country boy."

Paige chuckled. "I was the same way when I first moved there, but after a tough assignment you can't beat the peace and quiet, the open land, the sky peppered with more stars than you could ever dream, and the sunrise over the mountains."

"Your own little piece of heaven."

"Exactly."

They both turned at the creak of the floorboard as Ava appeared in the doorway. "I couldn't help but overhear. So, we're headed to your home?"

Grant stood. "Why don't I go get Lily's snack ready. She and Patrice should be up from their nap soon."

He left Ava and Paige alone in the office. Ava sat in the seat next to Paige.

"Yes, it's the best place I can think of to keep you off the grid," Paige explained.

Ava quirked a brow. "Please tell me you're not one of those doomsday preppers living in some fortress in the woods."

Paige held back a grin. "Not quite. More like a fortress in the plains of Oklahoma."

Ava gazed at her as if she were trying to figure out if Paige was serious or not. Then shrugged. "As long as you have running water, Wi-Fi, and I'll be able to call home, I'll be fine."

"You can call home now if you like." Paige picked up the phone Grant had given her and handed it to Ava. "Make your call short, no longer than ten minutes."

"Or what, the phone will self-destruct?" Ava said humorously.

"Are you willing to risk finding out?" Paige gave Ava a wink and left the room.

As much as she tried to fight it, Ava enjoyed the playfulness between her and Paige. When she wasn't being the serious ex-military superwoman, Paige was charming. Ava looked down at the phone and thought through what she wanted to say when she called her mom and how she could condense it all into a ten-minute conversation. With a heavy sigh, she dialed her mother's cell not wanting to take a chance calling the house.

"Hello?" her mother answered.

Ava almost cried at the sound of her voice. "Mom, it's me."

"Ava? Oh my God! How are you? Where are you? Are you someplace safe?"

"Mom, I don't have long to talk. I'm safe. How are you? How's Dad?"

"I understand. I'm good. Your father is doing well. The doctors are pleasantly surprised that there wasn't any other damage than the minor memory loss. Guess your father having a hard head has finally paid off."

Ava chuckled, wiping tears of relief from her eyes. "Guess so. Please tell him I love him and that I'm sorry I'm not there."

"You have nothing to apologize for. There's no telling what would've happened to you if you stayed. You did the right thing. I'll give your father your message when I go back to the rehab facility. I needed to come home and grab a few of his things. You know how vain he is."

"Probably where I get it from. Travis and Uncle Max are good?"

"Yes. Max has contracted Travis to restructure Diamond's entire IT system after a recent breach. I won't go into details, but the issue you and your father were concerned about should be ending soon."

Ava collapsed back into the chair with relief. That meant it wouldn't be much longer before she could go home. "That's good to hear. You all please stay safe. I'll try and call you again soon. I love you."

"I love you too, Buttercup."

Ava had never been so happy to hear that nickname. After saying a final good-bye, she gave herself a few minutes to give in to the tears of joy from hearing her mother's voice. Then she grabbed some tissue from a box on Grant's desk and cleaned her face as best she could without a mirror handy. She left the office and followed the sound of laughter in the family room. Grant was sitting on the floor with Lily as she painted his nails with an expression of focused concentration. It was the sweetest moment she'd ever seen. He held up a hand to show Ava.

"What do you think?" he asked with a happy grin.

Each finger was painted surprisingly neat for a three-year-old in a different color looking like a rainbow on his big hand. "Perfect," she said, chuckling.

Ava walked toward the kitchen to find Paige seasoning a platter with a huge sirloin steak and several salmon steaks. Patrice was mixing a pasta salad. She laid the phone in front of Paige.

"Thank you."

Paige nodded. "You're welcome. Is everything okay?"

"Yes. My father's recovering well. My mother said they're making headway on the situation, and it could be over soon."

"That's all good to hear." The look on Paige's face seemed doubtful. Ava ignored it. She probably just didn't want to get Ava's hopes up. "Is there anything I can help with?"

"How handy are you in the kitchen?" Patrice asked.

"When it comes to dinner, I can do enough not to starve, but I'm great at breakfast and salads," Ava said proudly.

Paige looked amused.

"Great, Paige is manning the grill, I'm just about finished with my contribution since I've been commanded by Sergeant Bossy here to sit down and relax, so just grab whatever salad fixings you like out of the fridge and go to town. There are some salad bowls in the cabinet down there." Patrice pointed toward a lower cabinet in the island then covered the pasta salad and put it in the fridge before joining her family in Lily's makeshift spa.

Ava did as Patrice suggested and went into their refrigerator and took out three different types of lettuce, cherry tomatoes, peppers, carrots, cucumbers, and mushrooms. She grabbed a cutting board propped next to the butcher block of knives where she also took a knife for cutting up the vegetables. Finally, she took a bowl from the cabinet Patrice had pointed out.

"You look like you know what you're doing," Paige said.

"I told you breakfast, and salads are my specialty."

"Why just those two?"

"While I was in college, salads were the cheapest and quickest meal that pretty much covered all the food groups when I didn't have time to cook because my school workload was crazy. Breakfast is sort of my way of showing my appreciation to a lady who may have stayed over. The better the night, the better the breakfast." Ava focused her attention on her task so that Paige wouldn't see the blush she felt creep hotly into her cheeks.

"Wow, okay. On that note, I'm going to put these on the grill."

Ava's face grew warmer at the amusement in Paige's tone. She could've just said breakfast was her favorite meal of the day. There was no need to reveal that particular truth. She didn't even look up as Paige exited. She let the calming effect of slicing the vegetables then tossing and mixing them up in the bowl relax her. An everyday task that made her feel, for just a moment, like everything was normal. Like she was visiting with friends and helping with dinner like she did at home or with Alan in New Orleans. When the colorful combination was complete, she snapped the top that came with the bowl in place and placed it in the refrigerator next to the pasta salad. When Ava gazed up at the Baxter family, she was completely charmed by the site of Patrice sitting on a makeshift cushion throne while Lily combed her hair and Grant expertly painted her nails. Not wanting to disturb the family's moment, she chose to join Paige outside.

"Salad duty complete?" Paige asked.

"Yes. Patrice is getting a queenly makeover from Grant and Lily. I didn't want to interrupt, so I figured I'd come keep you company, unless you prefer to be alone. I'm sure I can find something to do."

"No, you're fine. I probably spend far too much time alone as it is. At least that's what Grant, Patrice, and my family are always telling me." Paige gave her a cynical smile.

"Sounds like my family and Travis."

"Is that why your father tried to marry you off? He was concerned you would spend the rest of your life alone?" Paige brushed marinade on the steaks, closed the lid, walked a few steps to a sitting area, and sat in a lounge chair.

Ava followed, then sat across from her on the sofa with her legs folded beneath her. "Yes and no. He didn't want me to regret not focusing on having a life as well as the business. My parents married just as Diamond Unlimited began its growth, so he spent more time at the office than he did at home. My mother spent a lot of time alone dealing with her infertility issues and miscarriages that happened before I came along. I don't think I even spent more than one day a week with my father until I was like six or seven years old, and that's only because my parents were separated, and I stayed with him on the weekends. Almost losing the love of his life and the prospect of only seeing me on weekends and holidays made him realize what he was missing."

Ava remembered several times during her weekend visits when she would overhear her father crying on the phone with her mother. She'd never told him about that because she knew he hated anyone seeing him as being vulnerable. "Like him, the business means everything to me, and he saw me heading in the same direction. He wanted me to have a family, to give him grandchildren to dote on and be a legacy for the Prescott fortune."

"He didn't think you could do that with a woman?"

"Yes, but you have to understand my father's position. Financial companies like ours are few and far between. Diamond Unlimited is a Black-owned, self-made, multi-million-dollar company catering to clientele that, back in the day, would much rather have my father shining their shoes than handling their money. There aren't many that still think that way but enough to keep my father on his toes about how we represent ourselves. Being gay may not hold the shame it once did, but it's still something frowned upon by the ones that could make or break Diamond's reputation. My father and Uncle Max made sure that despite their questionable past, they represented Diamond as a business run by a wholesome family."

Paige shook her head. "And a gay family doesn't represent wholesomeness."

Ava sighed. "Look, I'm not saying I agree with my father, but I do understand what he was trying to do, even though I didn't go through with it in the end."

"But you would have if your mother hadn't intervened," Paige pointed out.

"I thought I was doing what was best for the company and to prove to my father that I was just as dedicated to it and our legacy as he was."

Ava frowned. Thinking about it now, she realized the mistake in her logic and the reasoning behind it. Her father claimed he wanted her to have a life. To not lose herself in the business, yet that's exactly what marrying Kyle would've done. She had been ready to give up her freedom, put herself back in the closet, and spend the next five to ten years with a man she couldn't stand all to be able to take her rightful place in her father's seat once he retired.

"Look, I didn't mean to get you upset. I was just curious. You come off to me as being an intelligent, strong-willed, independent woman who wouldn't let anyone force her into compromising herself or her goals, so it surprises me that you would have given in to your father's farfetched agenda to get you married off without a fight."

Ava knew Paige didn't mean anything by her comment and was just stating what she believed. But, seeing it from another's perspective, Ava could understand why it would surprise anyone that she'd almost gone through with the marriage. But it didn't make the words sting any less, especially since she already felt her actions had led to where they were now.

"It wasn't far-fetched. He thought he was doing what was best for me. Besides, you don't know me or my family well enough to judge us," she said defensively.

Paige shrugged. "You're right, I don't. My apologies if I offended you." She pulled her phone out of her pocket.

They both sat silently, Ava pouting and stewing in her own guilt and Paige focused on her phone. There was nothing purposely sexy about what she was doing, but Ava found the way the twists in her hair fell forward and partially hid her face from view, the way she bit her bottom lip in concentration, the way her long, slender fingers held the phone as her thumbs typed furiously disconcertingly sexy. It took Ava a moment to realize Paige's fingers had stopped moving over the keyboard and she gazed up to find her watching her with curious amusement. Ava looked away and stood.

"I'm going to get a glass of water. Would you like something?" she asked as she headed toward the house.

"I'll take one as well. Thanks."

Ava didn't even bother looking back as Paige would've seen the darkened blush that heated her face, and she didn't want her to know how she affected her. They were probably only going to be together for a few more weeks before this would all be over, and she could go back to her regular life. A life filled with long, stressful days and lonely nights but at least it was her life to control.

CHAPTER TWELVE

The next morning, they were up at six heading to a local airfield. Despite not having any issues while they were at Grant's, Paige was relieved to be heading home. She didn't feel comfortable possibly putting his family in harm's way since there was no confirmation who was behind what was going on and how they were able to track Ava down in the first place. With all the safeguards Travis had put in place, they obviously had someone who was equally as good as him and Ezekiel's tech team. They arrived on the tarmac to find a Cessna passenger airplane waiting for them. As they exited Grant's truck, a woman whose height and build almost rivaled his dressed in stained khaki-colored mechanic overalls, a beat-up baseball cap with curly strands of ginger hair escaping, and Converse sneakers jogged out of the hangar toward them.

"Wait, is that Bobby?" Paige asked Grant.

"The one and only."

"Sarge!" Bobby grinned broadly, her blue eyes sparkling merrily as she grabbed Paige, picked her up, and swung her around before setting her back on her feet. "It's good to see you!"

Paige laughed at Bobby's enthusiasm. No matter what situation they were in, she'd always managed to keep her smile and jovial attitude as she flew them in and out of missions and dangerous locales with skills many male pilots envied. Despite her smile, Bobby struggled with personal demons after ten years in the service. Her mother and son managed to keep her from disappearing into the same dark place Paige and Grant had once teetered on the edge of.

"It's good to see you too, Bobby." Paige felt Bobby's hardened biceps. "Looks like you've been in the gym just as much as Grant."

Bobby shrugged. "I try. I don't really have an excuse not to be since I own the place. Keeps me sane."

Paige gave her a skeptical look. "When have you ever been sane?"

Bobby laughed heartily. "Maybe when I was ten. At least that's what my mother tells me."

Paige, Grant, and Bobby laughed.

"How is Grace? And Little Bobby?" Paige asked.

"Momma is good. She's in Cancun with her new boyfriend," Bobby said with an eyeroll. "Little Bobby isn't so little anymore. Only sixteen and he's almost as big as me. He's looking at colleges already. Trying to get a football scholarship with dreams of being in the NFL."

"Well, I'm happy for them both. I see you got a new ride there. Are you going to be our pilot?"

"Yeah, she is a beauty. Just got her last month. A Cessna TTx. She's got a twin-turbocharge, six-cylinder, fuel injected, 310 horsepower engine that cruises at a max 235 knots, a Garmin G2000 avionics powered flight deck and a custom-fit interior." Bobby looked as if she was describing a lover.

Paige grinned. "I'm guessing that all means she'll get us from point A to point B with speed and comfort?"

Bobby's freckled cheeks turned a rosy red. "Pretty much. So, is this the precious cargo Grant mentioned?" Bobby said, looking at Ava.

"Yes. Bobby, this is Ava. Ava, our pilot, Bobby."

Ava offered Bobby her hand in greeting. "It's a pleasure to meet you, Bobby. Thank you for taking the time to fly us to our destination."

Bobby accepted Ava's hand and gave her a big smile. "You're very welcome. Whenever Sarge calls, I'm here." She turned back to Paige. "We finished loading your shopping bag just before you pulled up and she's gassed up and ready to go. I just need to change and lock up so we can hit the skies."

"Cool. We'll wait here," Paige said.

Bobby jogged back to the hangar and Paige turned to Grant.

"I owe you big time for all this, Grant."

Grant shook his head. "It's the least I can do. You've put your ass on the line for our team on one too many occasions. We owe you far more than you owe us."

Paige felt a lump of emotion in her throat. Her former counterintelligence team always made it seem as if she'd saved them, but it was them that had saved her in the end. Grant opened his arms and she walked into them, allowing him to envelop her in his bear-like embrace. It was like a cocoon that made her feel safe and grounded. When they separated, he nodded in understanding.

"Don't hesitate to call if you need backup for anything," he said.

"I won't. Take care of those precious girls of yours and be sure to call me when Rose makes her appearance."

Grant smiled proudly. "I will."

He turned to Ava and held his arms open. Paige almost laughed aloud at the momentary look of confusion on her face before she smiled and accepted his embrace.

"Thanks again for the financial advice and referral. I'll be kicking our advisor to the curb as soon as I get back. You take care of yourself, Ava Prescott. Give 'em hell when you get back home and if you need backup as well, I'm just a phone call away."

"Thank you, Grant, for that and your hospitality. Please give Patrice my best and tell Lily I look forward to spending some time in her spa after this is all over."

Grant gave her a smile of appreciation. "I will."

Bobby joined them a short time later having traded her overalls for cutoff denim shorts and a low-cut V-neck T-shirt that showed off the generous bust that had been hidden under the baggy overalls. She'd kept the Converse on but gotten rid of the baseball cap to allow her long, thick ginger curls to flow down her back. Grant whistled in appreciation.

"You practically live in those overalls, so I forget what you're hiding under there. If I wasn't so in love with my wife…" Grant gave Bobby a wink, making her blush again.

"Too bad there aren't any single men out there who appreciate a big girl like me. Guess I'll have to wait for Patrice to get sick of you before I find one." Bobby punched him in the arm and Grant chuckled.

They said good-bye once more then boarded the plane with Paige sitting in the front passenger seat next to Bobby while Ava sat in the single passenger seat behind them. As soon as they were cleared for takeoff they were on their way. Paige felt most of the tension and stress leave her shoulders as they went airborne. In just a couple of hours they would be landing at the airfield in Bethesda, Oklahoma, and she would finally be home with a guest in tow. She gazed back at Ava and gave her the "okay" sign. Ava nodded with a smile in return. Paige faced forward again wondering if she was making a mistake. There were plenty of safe houses in Ezekiel's inventory where they could've gone, but for some reason she felt as if none of them would give them the protection they needed like her ranch would. She didn't know what was coming, but her instincts were telling her this was not going to be over as soon as Ava was expecting it to be. Something dangerous was coming their way and Paige would much rather face it on her own turf.

As if she knew they needed something to keep their minds off what was happening, Bobby chattered happily away about her gym ownership venture, the interesting clients she'd shuttled in her plane, and her family with interjections from Paige every now and then. Since she didn't ask anything about why they had needed a last-minute, early morning, undercover flight to Oklahoma, Paige assumed Grant hadn't given Bobby any details for the reason behind it. The less people knew the better. Halfway through their flight, Paige gazed back to find Ava asleep. It had been a crazy couple of days. If she wasn't so anxious about getting home, she'd probably be asleep as well.

Even in sleep, Ava was beautiful. Paige could picture rolling over and watching her sleep. Waiting for the moment she would awaken and lay her amber eyes on Paige with a sleepy smile. Her heart ached with just the thought of such a moment coming to fruition. With a wistful sigh, she turned away from Ava and found Bobby grinning knowingly.

Paige held back her own grin. "Eyes on the skies, Walker."

"When whatever this is ends, I want details. Been a long time since I saw anything close to that look on your face."

"I don't know what you're talking about." Paige feigned ignorance.

Bobby chuckled. "Yeah, okay."

Ava woke up just as they were beginning their descent. She was surprised she'd fallen asleep. Usually, she was wide-awake during flights, whether they were commercial or on a private jet, but that was probably because she was also working. With nothing but blue skies and fluffy white clouds to look at and Bobby's expert flying, she'd fallen right to sleep. She gazed out the window and saw nothing but open plains, forests, and mountain ranges in the distance. As they descended closer, the land was dotted with farms, fields, and a scattering of housing developments and shopping centers. She thought Patrice had been kidding when she told Ava that Paige pretty much lived in the middle of nowhere.

"Don't worry, you'll have all the modern amenities despite the remote location," Paige said as if reading her thoughts.

Ava gave her a noncommittal smile and turned her gaze back to the window. The landing was as smooth as the flight had been. Paige's home could be a literal castle, but it still wouldn't be where Ava wanted to be, which was her own home with the ability to be with her family and working to ensure that Diamond stayed in Prescott hands. Until then, she couldn't relax. She would just take things day-by-day with the hopes that this would be over soon.

Once they landed, Bobby taxied the plane into a hangar where a man with a deep bronze complexion and regal features looking like he belonged on the cover of a western clothing catalogue smiled and waved at them. He was dressed in a cowboy hat, western-style flannel shirt, and jeans with just the right amount of baggy around weathered cowboy boots. He even wore a gun belt with pistols sticking out of the holsters on either hip. He stood next to a pickup truck that was the exact replica of Grant's.

"I hope you'll come by the house and visit for a bit before you head back," Paige said to Bobby after they deboarded.

"Maybe next time. I'm going to fuel up and head back. Little Bobby…I mean Robert," she said with an eyeroll, "has a game tonight and I'm on concession stand duty."

Paige chuckled. "Trying to find his own identity, huh?"

"Yeah. I told him you don't see me trying to get people to call me Roberta, and I'm a grown-ass woman. When did teenagers get so formal? Pretty soon he'll have me calling him Mr. Walker."

"Well, drop me a text when you land and give him my best," Paige said.

"Will do." Bobby turned to Ava, offering her hand. "I hope you had a pleasant flight."

Ava accepted it with a smile. "I did. Thank you again. Have a safe flight back."

Bobby nodded then headed toward the hangar office. Paige grabbed her jump bag and a second duffel bag that had already been stored behind the back seat when they boarded and swung one over each shoulder.

"Can I carry something?" Ava asked, trying not to look at the muscles flexing and shifting in Paige's arms and back.

Paige shut the plane door and turned to her with an appreciative smile. "No, thanks. Just carrying them to the truck so I'll be fine."

"I take it Grant hooked you up with that beast?"

"Yep. That's Betty, Bertha's twin in every way."

"Hey, Paige," the bronze cowboy greeted them when they got to the truck. Up close, Ava noticed a thick braid hanging down to his midback and the fancy six-shooters in his holster.

"Hey, Junior. Thanks for picking Betty up for me. I hope it didn't put you out too much."

"No, not at all. Pops dropped me off at Tulsa and Trinity is waiting for me out front." He handed her a set of keys. "She runs so smooth it was pure pleasure driving her."

Paige set the bags in a storage box located in the bed of the pickup. "Are we good with the other stuff?"

"Yeah, I gave the descriptions you sent to just a few of my most trusted guys as well as distributed it to the reservation police, without giving too many details. They've got better eyes and ears on the street than the sheriff's office and will know who's coming in and out of the area before anyone."

"Great. Ava, this is William Acothley, the deputy to the sheriff in these parts and son of my ranch manager, Willie."

Ava offered her hand. "Nice to meet you, William."

He took her hand and gave her a flirtatious smile. "The pleasure is all mine and, please, call me Junior."

"All right, Junior."

Junior held her hand a little longer than necessary before slowly releasing it.

"Thanks again, Junior," Paige said pointedly.

"You're welcome." Junior gazed at Paige briefly before turning back to Ava with a grin and tipping his hat at her before walking toward the office.

Paige watched him with a shake of her head. "Sorry about that. Junior considers himself a ladies' man, which his current girlfriend, Trinity, is unsuccessfully trying to curb."

"Well, I wouldn't blame him for thinking that way. He's ruggedly good-looking. I'm sure there are plenty of women that like that."

"I guess. His father is Cherokee and Black, and his mother is Nigerian and British."

Ava looked at Paige in confusion. "How did they manage to meet?"

"Willie served in the Marines with my father. He was stationed in London. Adele, his wife, worked on the base. They met, fell in love, had three strapping boys, moved back here after Willie retired, and the rest is history."

Ava chuckled. "Such a romantic story."

Paige smiled. "Sorry, you want the fairy-tale version, you'll have to ask Adele yourself when we get to the ranch."

Paige opened the passenger door for Ava and held out a hand to assist her up the high running board. Ava gave her a smile. "Thank you."

Paige nodded, made sure Ava was settled, then shut the door. Ava wasn't used to such treatment from another woman. Men did it all the time, but since she was always the one that initiated anything with a woman, she also ended up being the one with the chivalrous manners. Spending her entire career competing in a predominantly male business world had made Ava a bit aggressive with the need to be in control which spilled into her private life, no longer leaving any room for the soft and demure Ava she was in college. Since the moment they'd met, Paige had her feeling soft, shy, and feminine. It was weird but she was also beginning to like letting someone else be in control. If Paige had been a man, it would be a different story, but she wasn't and that's what made it more appealing.

Paige climbed in, started the truck, and turned to Ava with a smile. "Next and last stop on our adventure, Two Ponds Ranch, I hope you won't be too disappointed in the accommodations."

Ava chuckled. "I'm sure they'll be just fine."

A moment later, they were pulling out of the hangar and were on their way.

"The ranch is only a short fifteen minutes from here. You'll be comfortable and settled in before lunch."

"I thought we were stopping in town on the way. As much as I appreciate the availability and comfort of your clothes, I would much rather have clothing of my own to get me through the next couple of weeks or so."

"I thought it might be best to limit exposing you to too many people. This is a small town and news travels fast. If whoever is after you manages to track us down, I'd rather not make it easy for them to be led here by an unwitting comment from someone in town. I connected your mother and Adele who picked up some things for you already."

"Thank you."

Although she appreciated the surprising courtesy, Ava couldn't imagine what she was going to end up wearing. When she realized they would be leaving town without any of her belongings and Patrice mentioned they would be coming out to the middle of the western frontier, she wasn't expecting to find any major department stores, but she had been hoping there would be a cute little dress shop where she could pick her own clothing. With an inward sigh, Ava reminded herself that she could be in the hands of men who meant to do her harm instead of under the safe custody of a former marine sergeant who was, judging by the way Grant and Bobby gushed over her, obviously well-respected by her former team members and who had been nothing but attentive and courteous to her needs despite the tantrums she had thrown. Ava gazed out at the rolling hills in the distance, then inhaled a deep breath of fresh air from the open window. It smelled clean and refreshing, a far cry from the city air she was so used to.

Ava set her elbow on the window and propped her chin in her hand as she gazed out at the scenery. "It's beautiful out here. Seems so peaceful."

"It is. It's why I moved here. Willie talked about this place all the time before he came back for good, so I had to come see what the big deal was for myself. Hearing about it and seeing it are two widely different things. No words could do this part of the country justice. I see what brought our ancestors to this area once they were freed. The idyllic peace, the majestic open land, who wouldn't want to start a new life here after living through the pain and violence of slavery," Paige said wistfully.

"When my mother was a schoolteacher, she advocated for Black History and Black Literature classes in the district she worked for. She helped to come up with a curriculum about slavery in America, the accomplishments of Black people in American history, the settlements of Black towns, and the works of Black artists and writers. Of course, by the time I started school such curriculums began disappearing, so she taught me everything I know. We'd even spent a summer traveling to locations where historic Black towns once existed and ones that still did at that time. I wish I had found time to go back."

"Sounds like a pretty cool summer vacation. Maybe while you're here we can visit the towns that still remain in Oklahoma."

Ava turned to Paige. "Really?"

Paige shrugged. "Why not? Willie has a ton of records on the towns in the Tulsa area. He wanted to show his wife what Black people had achieved after slavery."

Ava shook her head in amazement. "You have an eclectic group of friends."

"Since I'm not all that interesting I like to keep interesting people around me." Paige gave her a wink and teasing smile.

As her face heated with a blush, Ava turned to look back out the window. "You are far from uninteresting, Paige Richards."

"That's nice to hear you say. Let me know if you feel that way in a week of living on my ranch. I live a very quiet and boring life when I'm not saving heiresses from dangerous kidnappers."

Ava smiled. "After the past couple of days, I'll take quiet and boring for a little while."

Paige snorted. "I'm going to remind you of that in a few weeks."

Ava didn't plan to still be here longer than a few weeks. She was going to insist on being taken home even if she had to get a taxi to the airport herself if Paige refused to take her.

"Well, here we are." Paige pulled off the main road.

Ava didn't see anything for some time but soon spotted a tall wrought iron gate with an equally tall brick wall on either side mounted with wrought iron spikes. When they pulled up to the gate, Paige leaned out the window and punched a code into a security keypad, and the gates slid smoothly open. She also spotted a camera above the keypad and mounted on the brick wall on both sides of the gate. Seeing the gate had her remembering Grant's comments about Paige's home being a fortress. Ava wasn't sure what to expect her home to look like, but it wasn't the soft butter yellow ranch home with a huge gabled window above the double front door, arched windows along the front and side of the house that faced the road anchored by white shutters, a wraparound porch with clusters of wicker furniture seating areas and a porch swing, a beautifully manicured lawn, and trees lining the entire perimeter past the gate. It looked more like an idyllic suburban home than fortress. Connected to the house by a covered walkway was a detached three-car garage with what looked to be an office or living space above it. Past the house, she could see the sparkle of sunlight on water and a barn. Farther on looked to be forest framed by the mountains in the distance. Paige said it was peaceful and she was right. Ava heard nothing but birds chirping happily in the trees.

Paige pulled up in front of the house. "Not quite what you expected, huh?"

"Truthfully, not at all. Well, maybe the barn and the security entrance, but it all looks so…normal."

Paige laughed. "I'll take that as a compliment."

Ava's face grew hot. "I didn't mean you aren't normal. I just thought it would look like some cold, modern, high-tech house. This looks so warm and welcoming."

"The best fortresses are the ones that don't look like fortresses. The enemy will underestimate you, giving you the advantage when the attack happens."

If Paige wasn't smiling when she said it, that analogy would've made Ava very nervous about the people after her. She hoped they had been able to lose them when they left New Orleans.

"Like you with your Krav Maga ass-kicking self." Paige gave her a wink before turning to climb out of the truck.

Instead of Ava's face burning with a blush from Paige's compliment and sexy grin, her body reacted this time with a pleasant warmth. Like she'd just sat by a cozy fire.

"Stop it!" she reprimanded herself then turned to open the door only to have it opened for her by Paige. Ava took Paige's offered hand of assistance. "Thank you."

"You're welcome."

Their bodies were mere inches from each other, their gazes held in a shared look that said far more than words, and Ava wanted so much to close the distance between them, to press her lips to Paige's. The moment was interrupted by the bleating of an animal. Paige blinked as if awaking from a trance and quickly released Ava's hand. They both turned to find two goats staring expectantly at Paige. She stepped away from the truck toward the goats and knelt in front of them.

"Hello, ladies. Couldn't wait for me to come see you, huh?" She scratched both behind an ear as they gazed up at her adoringly. "I hope you've been good while I was gone."

"They're close to becoming goat stew if they don't stay out of my garden," a feminine voice said with a soft British accent.

The goats' ears pricked up, they gave a combined bleat and took off down a path leading around the house. Ava assumed they were not too keen on becoming tonight's dinner. She looked at the person who they obviously feared but not enough to stop going in her garden and met the friendly smile and bright eyes of an ageless and beautiful mahogany-skinned woman. She looked to be at least an inch taller than Paige as they embraced, but her regal stance, and intricately tied head wrap made her seem even taller.

"It's good to see you, Adele. How was your trip to London?" Paige said as she stepped back but still held the woman at a distance.

"It was good, everyone is healthy and happy and looking forward to coming here for the holidays. Are you sure you want to have my crazy family all up in your house?"

Paige chuckled. "I'm very sure. I'll be in Texas with mine and there's plenty of space here for you all to spread out and enjoy yourselves."

Adele shrugged. "Can't say I didn't warn you." She turned to Ava. "So, this is our runaway heiress. Come here, let me look at you."

Ava smiled and did as she was asked.

"Ava, meet Adele, my Godsend of a housekeeper and the real queen of this domain. Adele, meet Ava Prescott," Paige said.

Ava offered her hand to Adele. "It's nice to meet you, Adele."

Adele looked at her hand in offense then spread her arms. "Child, once you've received an invite into this house, you're considered family and family doesn't shake hands."

Ava entered her embrace and was enveloped by the sharp but pleasant scent of lemongrass. Adele's warm hug made Ava think of her mother and almost brought tears to her eyes. She managed to hold them back and took a deep, shuddering breath to ease the homesickness threatening to overwhelm her. By the time Adele released her she had a pleasant smile pasted back on.

"I know you've had a long trip. I made lunch, but it can keep until you two get settled and freshen up," Adele said.

"Let me just grab my stuff from the truck and I'll be right in. In the meantime, why don't you show Ava her room. I'll give her the grand tour after lunch."

Adele nodded and looped her arm through Ava's as she led her into the house. After being amazed by the welcoming exterior she'd decided she wouldn't have any expectations of the inside of the house, but she was still pleasantly surprised to find the interior warm, charming, and comfortable. The windows allowed the sunshine to flow in and brighten the open layout without the need for artificial lights. It was a brief look before Adele led her down a hallway leading toward other rooms.

"Since Paige wants to give you a tour, I'll just tell you this is where all the guest rooms are. Paige's room and office are on the other side. There are four guest rooms. I put you in the biggest since I was told you're going to be here a while. It's at the end of the hall here."

Adele stopped at a set of double doors, released Ava's arm, and opened both doors wide as she entered. Ava followed her in and was awed by the size and grandeur of the room.

"This was supposed to be the master suite, but Paige isn't too keen on sleeping in such a big open space, so she took the smaller guest suite on the other side," Adele explained.

Ava found that to be an interesting quirk, but she wouldn't complain. Sitting in the center of the room was a huge four-poster bed anchored by matching nightstands and a padded bench at the end of the bed. On the right side of the room was a comfortable seating area in front of a fireplace with a large, framed mirror above it and floor to ceiling picture windows on either side. The left side of the room had a reading nook and a door on each side.

Adele led her to one. "This is the bathroom."

She opened the door for Ava to enter first. There was a claw-foot soaking tub in front of a floor to ceiling frosted window, a separate spa shower, and a double vanity.

"This panel," Adele indicated a digital screen just inside the door, "controls the heated floors, the privacy frost on the window, and the sound system."

Ava looked at her in confusion. "The privacy frost?"

Adele grinned and touched the screen where different labeled buttons popped up. She chose the window button, pressed *Clear*, and pointed toward the window. Ava watched as the frosted glass slowly faded, giving her a breathtaking view of the bordering woods and mountains.

"The sunset is gorgeous here. You can soak in the tub with a glass of wine and just enjoy the view. There's security fencing and sensors around the entire property so you never have to worry about Peeping Toms," Adele said.

"I'll keep that in mind."

"One last thing." Adele left the bathroom and Ava followed.

They went to the door on the other side of the reading nook. It was a walk-in closet just as big as the one she had at her place. It was mostly empty except for one section of shelves filled with stacks of neatly folded jeans and sweaters on the top three and shoes on the bottom three consisting of a pair of running shoes, hiking shoes, two pairs of serviceable but cute sandals, two pairs of casual sneakers, and a pair of cowboy boots. Next to the shelves hung half a dozen plaid shirts like the one she borrowed from Paige, a couple of denim jackets, and, to her delight, several dresses in differing designs but all like the style she wore while she was in New Orleans.

"There are under garments and pajamas in the drawers here."

Adele opened a drawer in the island in the center of the closet. Ava smiled at the Victoria's Secret labels on the underwear and bras, all her correct size.

"How did you guys do all this so quickly?"

"After Paige called me, she connected me to your mother, then I went into Tulsa yesterday with one of Willie's nieces and picked out what I could from information both Paige and your mother gave me. The dresses I wasn't sure about since it wasn't the style your mother described you liked, but I based the choices on a picture Paige sent to me of you in New Orleans."

Ava was a little thrown by the idea of Paige taking pictures of her without her knowing. "Oh, okay. I changed my style to help with not being recognized." She ran her hand over her shortened hair. "Cut my hair as well. Still trying to decide if I should let it grow back."

Adele cocked her head to the side with a thoughtful expression then nodded. "I think it brings more focus to those stunning eyes of yours."

Ava smiled. "Thank you. Thank you also for this." She spread her arms to indicate the clothes.

"My pleasure. I'll let you get settled. Come on out for lunch whenever you're ready." Adele turned to leave then stopped and gazed back at Ava with a very serious expression. "Paige has never brought anyone here that wasn't family or in her very small circle of friends. She's also never brought her work past those front gates so if she brought you here to protect you then she considers the threat against you very serious. I understand that you're probably a very independent and self-sufficient woman who's used to being in charge, but I love that girl like she's my own child so please don't do anything that would put her life at risk or jeopardize the peace she's worked so hard to maintain or you will have to answer to me." The look Adele gave her told Ava she meant what she said.

"Understood."

Adele's jovial smile returned. "Good. Please know that Paige will protect you like you're one of her own...if you let her." With that she left Ava alone to ponder the seriousness of her situation.

Chapter Thirteen

Paige threw both her jump bag and the duffel that had been loaded on the plane before they left onto her bed. Out of habit she did a perimeter check of the room, ensuring the windows in the bedroom and bathroom hadn't been tampered with, that the hidden door in her walk-in closet was still secure, and that the cache of weapons in the footlocker in the back of her closet still had all but the weapons she'd taken when she left almost three weeks ago. Satisfied with her inspection, she went back out, grabbed the duffel bag, and brought it back into the closet. She unzipped it and smiled. Grant had managed to replace everything she'd left in New Orleans with the same brand and style. The cleanup crew that took care of Alan's apartment also swept clean her hotel room. They would ship her luggage back to her, but the weapons would have to go in a stash somewhere in Ezekiel's inventory until she could personally retrieve them again. She pulled out a leather-wrapped bundle of throwing knives and placed them into the footlocker. Next was the Sig Sauer and the Smith and Wesson M&P handguns which she placed in the lockbox built into the bottom of the footlocker, then two boxes of ammo and a shoulder holster. Once everything was put away, she secured the footlocker again and stashed the duffel on a shelf until she could return it to Grant.

Before walking out of the closet, she grabbed a pair of denims, a work shirt, cowboy boots, and hat and tossed them on her bed on the way to the bathroom for a shower. Her room wasn't as big and luxurious as the master suite, but it was all she needed. A comfortable bed, a fireplace, a television, a big closet, and a serviceable bathroom. Like the other bathroom, she had the heated floor, the spa shower, and the music system, but that's where the similarities ended. The window was a quarter of the size as the one in the master bath, but it was perfect for allowing in fresh air when needed and Paige wasn't a luxuriate in a bath kinda girl. If she could occasionally get a steam in her shower, then she was good to go. She also had a small monitor in the mirror that would allow her to either watch TV as she got ready or check the security cameras on the property, if needed. As much as she would've liked to relax with a steam, she had a houseguest to attend to and a moody horse to contend with that was probably going to have an attitude with her for leaving again so she quickly showered and dressed.

As she left her room, she heard laughter and followed it to the kitchen where Ava sat on a stool at the kitchen island while Adele set out their lunch. She looked relaxed and comfortable in her new wardrobe that fit her much better than Paige's baggy clothes. The jeans cupped her rounded hips nicely and the peasant top with embroidered neckline and cuffs on the three-quarter-length sleeves made her look soft and delicate. Paige was surprised to see a pair of cowboy boots sitting on the floor beside the stool.

"What are you two in here cackling about," she asked.

"Adele was telling me how she and Willie met. I can't wait to meet the Cherokee warrior who managed to literally sweep this Nigerian queen off her feet," Ava said with an amused grin.

"So, you got the fairy-tale version you wanted?" Paige asked.

"Yes, and I love it. We need more romance like that these days. Everyone is so quick to hook up and fulfill some unseen timeline for marriage and kids that no one is taking the time to date someone the good old-fashioned way."

Paige quirked a brow. "This from the woman who told me the other day that she rewards her lovers after a passionate night with breakfast."

Ava's face darkened with a blush. "I also pay for a car service to get them home safely," she said, sticking her tongue out at Paige.

"That's more than most men do," Adele said, coming to her defense.

Paige held up her hands in surrender. "I can't argue. I don't even remember the last time I had a real date."

"Not counting that girl that you spent the weekend in Tulsa with last year, I'd say you haven't had a proper date since leaving the military." Adele passed her a plate of chicken salad on a bed of lettuce with garlic toast on the side.

Paige frowned. "Geez, Adele, did you really have to put my business out there like that?"

"Considering you had no problem putting Ava's out there, yes, I did. Now, eat. I've got some gardening to do. You two can clean up." Adele headed for the back door, grabbing an apron and a gardening tool belt hanging from a peg before leaving.

Paige sat on a stool beside Ava. "As you can see, Adele has no filter."

"Yes. I think I love her already."

"I'll be sure to mention to Willie that he may have some competition for Adele's affection."

Ava chuckled. "No, please don't, especially if he still has the tomahawk that he threatened to scalp Adele's ex with."

Paige laughed out loud. "She told you about that? My father said that got Willie put in the brig for a week."

"Will I get to meet this infamous Willie soon?"

"I need to check on a few things if you'd like to tag along. I can give you the tour and you can meet Willie and a few of the other residents."

Ava looked at her curiously. "There are others living on the ranch?"

Paige grinned. "Yes. You encountered two of them when we arrived. That was Lucy and Ethel."

"The goats are named Lucy and Ethel?" Ava looked as if she didn't believe her.

"Yep, and they get into just as much trouble as their namesakes."

"Okay, then I will definitely tag along. I even have cowboy boots to feel authentically on a ranch. They're surprisingly comfortable."

"I didn't know Adele got you boots. I hadn't even thought to suggest that when we spoke about what you needed."

"Speaking of that. Adele told me you sent her a picture of me. When did you take it?"

Paige looked from Ava down at her plate. "When I first got to New Orleans and located you. I needed a picture to send back and confirm it was you since I almost didn't recognize you with your haircut."

"Oh. Well, that makes sense. So, you weren't stalking me?"

Paige smiled. "Not necessarily. I had to follow you to get your routine and figure out the best way to approach you without scaring you off."

"And you thought hiding who you really were, flirting with me, and deciding to come back to my place for…" Ava didn't finish the sentence.

Paige could feel her eyes boring into the side of her head. She met her gaze again. "I'm sorry about that. I wanted you to feel comfortable enough around me to speak freely. I had no intention of sleeping with you. I was going to tell you everything once we got to your apartment but, as you know, that didn't quite work out as planned."

"So, the flirting was all part of the job? You weren't attracted to me at all?"

Paige opened her mouth to speak then closed it again. She could tell Ava that she was just playing a part, but she'd be lying. She needed Ava to trust her and the only way to do that was to be honest.

"No, it wasn't part of the job. I found you attractive and enjoyed our flirting very much. So much so that I let it distract me from what I should've been doing which was being on guard and protecting you from danger. I'm sorry about that. It won't happen again."

Ava looked hurt before she turned away and focused on eating her food. Paige did the same, not understanding what she may have said that caused that look. They ate in silence. When Ava was finished, she carried her plate to the sink then turned and began closing the Tupperware containers Adele had stored the food in.

"After we clean up here, can I call home? You said it would be more secure for me to do that once we got here."

She sounded so sad, and Paige had a suspicion she'd caused that sadness. "Why don't I clean up while you make your call. You can use the phone in your room and although the line here is secure, I don't know if your mother's is so—"

Ava nodded. "Keep it brief. Got it."

Paige watched her walk away until she disappeared around the corner. As she cleaned up their lunch, she went over what she'd said that might've hurt Ava's feelings. "You idiot," she said to herself. She'd basically told Ava it was her fault she'd gotten distracted just before they were ambushed by the guy at her apartment and that she'd never let it happen again. Paige's social skills when it came to the intimacies of dating and romance were sorely lacking. Adele wasn't exaggerating when she'd said Paige hadn't gone on a proper date since she'd left the military. The woman Adele mentioned that she'd hooked up with in Tulsa was purely for pleasure's sake. They hadn't seen or spoken to each other since. It's not like she wanted to be alone. She just didn't think it would be fair for any woman to have to deal with her demons. They were hers alone to battle.

She gazed up in the direction Ava had gone with a smile. Ava was different than the women Paige had casually hooked up with over the years. She hadn't been looking for girlfriend material, just someone to have a good time with who shared the same mindset. Although Paige had a feeling that Ava was about the fun, casual romp, as well, she was also the type of woman that once she was serious about someone, she was in for the long haul and would stand by you ready for any battle that came your way. Paige could see it in how calmly Ava had reacted under pressure when she could have easily freaked out. She had been difficult at times, but who wouldn't be under the circumstances. In the end she came around to doing what was best. Paige could see herself with a woman like Ava which was why she couldn't let herself get caught up in what she was feeling. This was a job and Ava was here for her to protect, not date.

Paige's phone buzzed in her pocket. Seeing that she received a text from Ezekiel was like an exclamation point for what she'd just told herself.

Can you talk?

Yes.

She'd barely sent the text before he was calling. "Hey."

"Hey, are you in a secure location?" Ezekiel asked.

"Yeah, I'm at the ranch."

She heard what sounded like a sigh of relief. "Good. How's Ava?"

"She's been a trooper. I can't imagine a nonprofessional handling this situation any better. She's getting anxious about going home. She's in the other room talking to her mother. I told her to make it brief since I don't know how secure things were on your end."

"I know, I'm at the Prescott penthouse now. Travis hooked everyone up with untraceable phones, so they can talk for a little longer than usual. I wanted to give you an update on the situation here. The kid, Lawrence, from the mailroom who went missing after that warning letter was sent to Ava turned up at Max's house singing like a songbird. Just as we suspected, he was the one who left the note for Ava. It seems he was having second thoughts about the scheme his fake aunt had gotten him involved in. He's a friend of her son who's serving time for larceny theft. Cathy told him she had an easy embezzlement scam going with an insider at Diamond and brought Lawrence in as her eyes and ears. It seemed he was too good at his job after overhearing her setting up an earlier attempt to kidnap Ava. That's when he found out Kyle was Cathy's inside guy and why he sent Ava the warning letter before disappearing because he was afraid of what would happen when Cathy and Kyle found out. He also gave us a lead on Cathy that I have Tracey and Brian following up on. Unfortunately, Kyle Edwards must have gotten tipped off before we could confront him. He left a letter of resignation on Max's desk and is currently in the wind."

"So, he is the one behind all of this."

"Yes, and from what we found out from Lawrence and the information on Cathy's laptop, which we assume she was keeping as an insurance policy in case Kyle screwed her over, this isn't just about a corporate takeover or embezzling. Kyle Edwards, whose real name is Curtis Wilson, is wanted in Los Angeles for fraud and kidnapping under that name."

Paige ran her hand through her hair worriedly. "Shit."

"What's wrong?" Ava asked.

Paige hadn't even heard her come back. "Let me just finish this call and we'll head out." She attempted to give Ava a reassuring smile.

Ava nodded, and Paige left her to go to her office. "That was Ava. I'm assuming her mother didn't tell her anything because she didn't look worried."

"Probably not. Lynn doesn't know. Marcus and Max thought it best that since she's become the direct line of communication with Ava she should know as little as possible to keep Ava safe. They think if she knew Kyle was gone then she'd come home believing she needed to protect her family with no concern for her own safety."

"Are you pulling in outside help? With a record like that this has obviously gone beyond you and me protecting a client or solving a private case."

"I've got a guy in the Feds who can help. We don't want to draw too much attention because it could jeopardize Ava's safety. He can't get to any of the other Prescotts, I've got my entire team on their protection, but as long as Ava remains with you, he may get desperate. Her best chance until we can find him is with you."

"Yeah, okay. Did you guys figure out a motive yet?"

"No. That's the thing. Marcus and Max had never seen Edwards before he walked in for an interview. His credentials were obviously faked, and after questioning the guy from Alan's apartment, we know he's got connections in the criminal world that we haven't locked in on yet so it's going to take some time to sift through it all and connect the dots."

"Got it. Keep me posted."

"Will do and, Paige, you and Ava are like the daughters I never had. Please be safe and don't hesitate to call me for backup. I've got people in Tulsa."

Paige's heart swelled with emotion. "Will do." She hung up and stared at the phone for a moment before she took a deep breath to clear her head. She knew what needed to be done, she just hated having to keep Ava in the dark, but Ezekiel was right. She'd be in more danger at home, possibly jeopardizing the rest of her family. Paige wouldn't force Ava to stay if she was insistent on leaving, but the only way to avoid that confrontation altogether was not to let her know what was going on. After five years in counterintelligence partnering with some of the most dangerous people in the world to get the information she needed, handling Ava should be a piece of cake.

"You ready for that tour," Paige said as she came back into the kitchen smiling.

"Sure. Is everything okay? You seemed upset with your call."

"It's nothing. Just a delay with a part I ordered for our mower."

Ava quirked a brow. "Okay. I hope you don't mind but I raided your fridge for a bottle of water."

"No, not at all. Feel free to make yourself at home. Today you're a guest, tomorrow you're on your own." Paige gave her a wink then grabbed a bottle from the refrigerator as well.

Ava couldn't dismiss the feeling that something was wrong, but she knew Paige would tell her if there were.

"How are things at home?" Paige asked as she headed toward the back door.

Ava followed. "Dad should be home in a week. Of course, he's practically got an entire office set up in his room at the rehab center, but that's not surprising. Any news from Uncle Zeke on their progress with Kyle?"

"They may have found something, but they have to confirm whether it's relevant before they can make a move to confront him. So, would you like to walk or take the limo?" Paige indicated a golf cart hooked up to a charging station parked outside the back door.

"If you don't mind, I'd like to walk. We've spent a lot of time being transported from one location to the next. I'd like to feel the ground instead of a motor beneath my feet for a while."

Paige smiled in understanding. "Works for me. The first stop on our tour is the garden which I take no credit for."

They walked toward a greenhouse and fenced in garden where Adele knelt in the dirt pulling weeds. Above the arched entrance of the garden was a sign that read *Adele's Sanctuary*. She gazed up as they approached.

"Hey, has the tour begun?" Adele asked.

"Yep, you're our first stop," Paige said.

"Ava, I hope you like eggplant because these babies are ripe and ready to go." Adele smiled happily as she held up a large, blemish-free eggplant.

"As a matter of fact, I love eggplant," Ava told her.

Adele nodded. "Good. Also, I'm making a run to the market after I'm finished here. Is there anything you'd like that we may not have?"

"Well, if it's no trouble, I didn't see any almond milk in the fridge. I'd like that and, if they have it, some Greek yogurt. Any flavors are fine with me."

"I'm sure I can find that. A fancy new health market just opened so I'll probably be able to find everything there. Anything for you, Paige?"

"Looks like I'm out of Oreos," she said, grinning sheepishly.

Adele chuckled. "Got it."

"Double-stuffed, please," Paige said.

Adele nodded and turned back to her task. "Enjoy the tour, Ava."

"Shall we continue?" Paige asked.

She gave Paige a smile. "Yes, please."

Their next stop was the first of two ponds Paige said were on the property, hence the name Two Ponds Ranch. It wasn't very original, but she told Ava the previous owner had named it and she didn't see any reason to change it.

"When I can't sleep, sometimes I like to come down here for a swim just to clear my head and work off some energy. When the moon is full and high in the sky it's like swimming in a pool of diamonds."

"That sounds wonderfully peaceful. I do the same thing at home except I go to the pool in my building. I don't have the moonlight, but the fluorescent lights almost work the same."

Paige smiled in amusement. "You gotta work with what you got."

"Exactly."

"Well, feel free to come out here anytime."

"I may take you up on that."

They continued the tour. Ava was enjoying the easiness between them. It was the same feeling she had when Paige escorted her home the night they met. She peeked at Paige from her peripheral thinking about what she'd said earlier of being attracted to her and how it had distracted her from doing her job. She had taken it personally at first, but when she thought about it after her call with her mother, Ava realized Paige probably wasn't blaming her directly for being distracted, it was her own feelings that had distracted her. It gave Ava's ego a boost to know that she had such an effect on a woman like Paige.

Their next stop was the corral across from the barn. In the center of it was a man Ava assumed was Willie since he looked like an older and even more attractive version of Junior, and a gorgeous dappled gray horse galloping around the ring close to the wood slatted fence. Paige climbed the two bottom rungs of the fence and whistled. The horse galloped to a stop then turned in their direction and raced toward Paige. He stopped just out of reach of her outstretched hand.

"Aaaw, c'mon, Z, don't be like that. I got something special for you." Paige reached into her pocket then offered her closed fist to the horse.

He tentatively closed the distance between them and sniffed her hand then bumped it with his nose. Paige smiled happily, turned her hand over, and opened it. Three white cubes lay in her palm. The horse greedily lapped all three up and Paige scratched the Z-shaped marking on his head.

"Do you forgive me, boy?" she asked. The horse snuffed in response and pushed his head against her fingers. "Thanks. I wouldn't leave you like that so quickly unless it was important. I'd like you to meet a guest who'll be staying with us for a bit." Paige gazed back at Ava and tilted her head indicating Ava could join them. "Ava, I'd like you to meet Zorro. Zorro, this is Ava."

Paige took two more cubes of sugar from her pocket and offered them to Ava. "I didn't think to ask if you liked horses."

"I love horses but never learned to ride them," Ava admitted. She took the treats and offered her palm to Zorro just as Paige had done. "Hey, Zorro. You're quite a handsome fella. It's nice to meet you."

Zorro eyed her warily, sniffed her palm, then lapped the sugar cubes up before snubbing her for more scratches from Paige.

Paige smiled. "He'll come around. It takes him a minute to adjust to strangers since we don't get that many here."

The man strolled over. "He won't admit it, but he's missed you. He won't give the new mare the time of day."

"Zorro are you being disrespectful to the new lady of the barn?" Zorro softly whinnied in response then turned away and took off out the back of the corral to the pasture beyond like a mischievous child.

Paige shook her head. "Willie, meet Ava. Ava, this is Willie."

Ava offered her hand to Willie. "I've heard so much about you I feel like I know you already."

Willie removed his cowboy hat to reveal a shiny bald head and gave her a gap-toothed smile as he took her hand. "My wife been telling stories about me again?"

Ava smiled. "Only good ones. It's a pleasure to connect the myth with the man."

"Pleasure to meet you too, Miss Ava. If there's anything I can do for you while you're here, please don't hesitate to ask. You'll usually find me around here."

"I'll do that, thank you."

He nodded, plopped his hat back on, and turned back to Paige. "I'm assuming you want to see the newest resident."

"Yes, then, if you have a minute, I got a call about a delay for that part we ordered," Paige said.

Willie looked confused for a moment. "Oh yeah, that part. Sure, we can talk about that." He exited the corral from the gate and joined them.

Ava followed them to the barn where Lucy and Ethel, trotted out to greet them. Paige shooed them on and kept walking. The barn was big, roomy, and well-lit with six stalls and what looked like a tack room in the back. Two of the stalls on the left with signs marked *Farrah & Jackie* and *Zorro* were empty. The last one didn't have a sign yet. Across from it were three more marked *Brutus, Hershey, Lucy & Ethel*. They stopped at the stall with no sign to find a beautiful and sleek tawny brown and cream-colored mare enjoying some hay.

"She's gorgeous," Ava said.

"She is, isn't she. Hey, beautiful." Paige held her empty palm out to the mare who snubbed her and continued with her meal. She chuckled. "Uncle Reggie wasn't kidding when he said you're a siddity thing."

"Yeah, she's been like that since she arrived. Pranced in here like she owned the place and only deems you worthy of attention when she's ready. She's a gentle ride though. Adele gave her a quick run after she arrived just to stretch her legs. She's been calling her Amina ever since."

"Why Amina?" Ava asked.

"There's a story of a Nigerian queen named Aminatu who ruled over the kingdom of Zazzau. She was the first female Islamic ruler and was known to fight in battles alongside her brothers. She was known as a warrior queen. Adele said when she rode the mare, she felt the name come to her," Willie explained.

"Well, then, I guess we'll be calling you Amina from now on," Paige said.

At the sound of the name, the mare's ears perked up and she finally left her meal behind to greet Paige who smoothed her fingers through her forelock. "Nice to meet you, Amina. We'll get to know each other a little better tomorrow. Welcome to your new home."

Paige turned to Ava. "Give me a minute to talk to Willie and we'll continue the tour."

Ava nodded. "I'll be here."

Paige gave her a smile then walked out of the barn and out of sight with Willie in tow. Ava turned back to Amina.

"You really are a beauty."

Amina stuck her head out over the stall door and lowered it toward Ava. Ava smiled and tentatively reached up to rub Amina's head. The horse closed her eyes and made a noise that Ava would swear was a contented sigh. Then Amina's ears suddenly perked up and she looked toward the entrance of the barn. Ava looked in the same direction and her heart stopped at the sight of a huge bull with a shiny midnight black coat, whose massive shadow practically blocked the entire entryway, slowly walking into the barn. Ava was frozen in fear as it approached, stopping about two feet from her, eying her curiously. No longer the center of Ava's attention, Amina went back to munching on her hay.

Ava gave the horse a quick side-eyed glance, too afraid to take her full attention away from the bull or make any sudden movements. "Thanks. Some warrior queen you are."

The bull took a few more steps forward and snuffed the air around Ava, who squeaked in fright.

"Brutus! Are you scaring our guest?" Paige asked.

Ava glanced past the behemoth toward Paige who calmly strolled up and slapped him on the behind.

"Shame on you. Go to your room."

The bull let out a low "moo" in response then turned from Ava and walked into the stall marked *Brutus*. Ava let out the breath she hadn't realized she was holding and placed a hand over her racing heart.

"Sorry about that. Brutus likes to try to intimidate people, but he's just a big ole softy."

"Could've fooled me. I thought I was about to have a heart attack and have my body trampled by that beast."

Paige chuckled. "If anything, he would have licked you to death. Brutus was saved by the previous owner of the ranch from being slaughtered for steak and burgers while he was still a young and spry bull. Now he's in his prime enjoying a long cushy life here. Aren't you, big boy?" Paige went over and patted his huge head. "Make sure you show Ava the gentleman that you are while she's here." Brutus gave her low moo in response.

Ava looked at Paige as if she didn't recognize this woman who spoke to animals like she was Dr. Doolittle. There seemed to be so many facets to this interesting woman that made her more charming by the day.

She gazed back toward the entrance of the barn nervously. "Are there any other frightening beasts like him walking around that I should know about?"

Paige chuckled. "Well, there are Farrah and Jackie, our resident ponies; and Hershey the pig who are probably wandering the pasture. There are also a few cats running around here somewhere helping to keep the barn rodent-free."

As if on cue, a black-and-tan striped tabby cat strolled from Lucy and Ethel's stall, wound through Paige's legs, and into Brutus's stall to curl up on a pile of hay in the corner.

Ava held back a hysterical laugh that threatened to bubble up. "I have to say, the past few days have been the most surreal of my life. I seriously need a drink."

Paige looked at her with concern. "There are some bottles of water in the fridge in the tack room."

Ava quirked a brow. "Not quite what I had in mind."

Paige gave her a knowing smirk. "I figured. I've got several bottles back at the house that may contain more of what you're looking for. We can head back now if you like?"

"Was this the end of the tour? I assumed since the ranch is called Two Ponds there was a second pond somewhere."

"There is. Just beyond the trees past the workshop."

"Well, let's go. I'm sure the bottles will still be there when we get back."

Ava quickly headed for the entrance, wanting to get as far away from the barn as possible to avoid any other creatures wandering in and scaring the crap out of her. You could take the girl out of the city, but you couldn't take the city out of the girl. Just a few more weeks, that's all she was giving this craziness before she got the first flight out of here.

Chapter Fourteen

Riding Zorro, Paige glanced over at Ava who sat astride Amina as if she'd been riding for years instead of two weeks.

"You're getting pretty good at that."

Ava winced. "My butt would disagree."

Paige grinned. "Give it another couple of weeks and you'll be fine."

Ava snorted. "If you say so."

They arrived at the back gate of the ranch and halted the horses. Paige leaned over, tapped in the security code, and the gate slid open for them. They rode out into the forest on a well-tread horse trail that led to the mountains in the distance. Over the past two weeks of the three Ava had been on the ranch, this had become a daily trek for them during the week after lunch. After that first week Ava had decided she needed a daily routine to keep her busy. She'd told Paige that she was not a woman of leisure and sitting around reading and watching television all day was going to drive her crazy. To Paige's disbelief, Ava woke up at sunrise every day for a morning run around the ranch then spent an hour working out in the gym set up across from Paige's home office. After that she'd make breakfast for both, which Paige happily found out she was as good at it as she claimed, then spent an hour poring through financial newspapers and magazines that Adele regularly brought for her. Ava had also begun helping Adele in the garden and Paige and Willie with the animals. She was still wary of Brutus but was slowly warming to him as he followed her around like a lovesick puppy. Farrah, Jackie, and Hershey had also taken to her, and she and Amina seemed to develop a bond once they began these daily rides. Zorro was the only one who still completely ignored her. Paige figured he saw her as competition for her affection but, despite her growing attraction to Ava over the past few weeks, she assured him he had nothing to worry about.

Paige and Ava had developed an easygoing relationship that leaned more toward roommates than client and protector. Paige had managed to keep the news about Kyle disappearing from Ava but only because they didn't spend much time together outside of when Ava helped at the barn, during these rides, and during meals. They usually kept to themselves the rest of the time. Keeping such important information from Ava was starting to wear on Paige's conscious. Willie and Adele thought she should know so that she could make her own decision. Both doubted she would do what her family expected. Paige wasn't so sure. Ava was very protective of her family and Paige knew she felt guilty about leaving despite knowing it was probably for the best. She'd also noticed that Ava's mood was more somber lately which Paige chalked up to homesickness and worry about her family. She thought to cheer her up with the picnic lunch she'd packed for their ride. They arrived at a clearing along a stream about five miles from the ranch.

"This is so picturesque. I feel like we've gone back in time, we're heading west for a new life and decided to camp by the stream for the night," Ava said wistfully gazing out over the water.

Paige smiled. "Well, we are stopping for a bit but not the whole night. At least not without my shotgun."

Ava gazed around nervously. "I guess there are probably a lot of creatures out here at night that aren't of the cuddly, furry variety."

Paige dismounted Zorro and tied the reins to a tree near the stream. "There are some of those, but they usually stay hidden from the ones we wouldn't want to encounter."

Paige gazed up to find Ava awkwardly dismounting from Amina. It was the one thing about riding that she was still struggling with. She quickly jogged around Amina to catch Ava before she fell on her backside. Something that had happened several times before. She was hanging from the saddle trying to reach her toes to the ground. Paige gently grasped her waist to help her the rest of the way and Ava tumbled backward into her arms. Paige helped to steady her, and Ava quickly stepped out of her embrace, turning to face her with a shy smile.

"Thank you. I still haven't quite got the hang of that."

"At least this time you didn't get your foot caught in the stirrup." Paige grasped Amina's reins and walked her over to the tree Zorro was tied to trying to slow her racing heart and calm the flame of desire that rose at the intimate contact of having Ava in her arms.

When she turned back, she found Ava kneeling by the water patting her cheeks with a dampened kerchief. Paige grinned. Was Ava feeling that same heat from their contact? Then she shook her head. No mixing business with pleasure. The proximity of living together, something she'd never done with another woman other than living in military barracks, was causing a false sense of domesticity. At least that's what she was telling herself to keep from doing something she may come to regret. She went to Zorro and removed a rolled blanket and her saddle bags.

"I packed a small lunch for us if you're hungry," Paige said as she joined Ava.

"Really? That was nice of you."

She shrugged. "It's nothing fancy. Just a couple of sandwiches made from the leftover ham Adele made yesterday, a few of the cookies I made, and a couple bottles of lemonade." She set the bags down in the middle of the clearing to spread the blanket out.

Ava came over to help her. "It still blows my mind that you bake. And not just open up a package of refrigerated dough, throw it in the oven and bake but melt in your mouth cookies from scratch bake."

Paige grinned. "Wait until you taste my chocolate cake."

Ava's eyes widened. "Between Adele's three course dinners and you feeding my sweet tooth, I'm going to be packing on the pounds if I stay here much longer."

Paige quirked a brow. "From what I see, that's not a problem."

Ava blushed and looked down, concentrating a little too hard on spreading the corners of the blanket out. Paige secretly enjoyed moments like this, when she was able to make this strong, independent, and self-assured woman blush like a schoolgirl. She grabbed the saddle bags and unloaded their picnic lunch. She handed Ava a sandwich and lemonade then set the baggie of cookies between them to share. They ate in silence, as they always did during meals, but it wasn't an awkward silence. It was as if they could enjoy each other's company without the need for small talk or unnecessary chatter. It could've also been the peacefulness of their surroundings. The horses even seemed to enjoy it as they dipped their heads for a drink of water then nuzzled each other affectionately.

Zorro had finally accepted Amina's presence in their lives probably because she'd been completely ignoring him up until a week ago while they were loose in the pasture when he decided to show off with a few dressage moves Paige had taught him. It turned out her uncle had taught Amina a few moves before she'd come to live with them. Ava and Willie had watched in amusement as they began moving in rhythm with each other. Shortly after that they began a tentative but sweet flirtation which is exactly what Paige had been hoping for when she'd purchased Amina from her uncle.

Paige couldn't help but envy their budding romance. She was a forty-year-old woman who'd never been in love. Sure, she dated back in high school and in her early years in the military but never really managed to maintain a serious relationship. Then after she left the Marines, she was barely in any kind of emotional shape to focus on herself, let alone a romantic relationship. Now, since Ava had taken up temporary residence in her home, she wondered what she'd been missing by closing herself off to anyone who wasn't a family member or close friend.

She gazed at Ava. Her facial expression was soft but there was a sadness in her eyes as she stared off into the distance. In the beginning it was weird having a stranger in her home, but now she didn't mind sharing her space with someone, hearing off-key humming, having her stomach growl hungrily at the smells coming from the kitchen as breakfast was being prepared, and an extra pair of hands when Willie wasn't around. There was also having Ava's sweet smile greet her each morning, catching her watching Paige with a hungry gaze when it got too hot and she took her shirt off to work in a sleeveless tank top, and when they happened to brush against each other while maneuvering around the kitchen or in the barn. Those were the moments that made Paige ache not just for emotional intimacy but physical as well. And not just with anyone. She wanted Ava and it took all her restraint not to pull her into her arms during those moments and show her how much.

"So, uh, I've been meaning to ask you, how has your family handled explaining your absence for so long?" Paige asked, trying to distract herself from where her thoughts were headed.

"In the beginning they were telling everyone that I was working from a temporary office in London to get the feel of how business was done there. For the past several months they said I've been on a well-deserved sabbatical since my engagement was called off." She sounded annoyed at the last part.

"I take it you didn't like that explanation."

"No, but as usual, my father and his concern about the optics. I couldn't possibly have decided to take a sabbatical just because I needed one. It had to be as a result of some silly female emotional breakdown. Makes me seem like a lovesick twit that's run off to nurse a broken heart."

Paige chuckled. "I guess that's not quite the image you want people to have of Ava Prescott, kick-ass businesswoman."

Ava sighed. "My father seems to forget that I inherited the Prescott pride. We don't like to let anyone see us as weak or vulnerable."

Paige nodded in understanding. "Imagine coming from a family of soldiers. Weakness isn't in our vocabulary."

Ava smiled. "Yeah, I guess that's a pretty tough environment for a girl to grow up in."

"It has its good and bad. I was able to handle difficult situations like bullying from other kids or harassment from boys better than most girls. But it also kept me from making female friends as they all seemed so silly to me. If you can't tell, I was a bit of a tomboy and that was before I accepted my attraction to girls. I was more interested in sports and horses than I was going to the mall, sleepovers, and parties. I had no interest in boys and certainly wasn't going to act on my interest in girls at that young age. It wasn't until high school and joining the ROTC that I was able to find female friends with the same interests. Nothing romantic, just simple friendships."

"So, you were basically destined to go into the military."

Paige shrugged. "Not really. My parents had hoped I would take a different path especially since they had begun letting women take combat jobs. They didn't want their little girl having to experience life in combat, but I always knew going into the Marines was what I wanted to do."

"I can't imagine the things you must have witnessed or gone through. Ezekiel rarely talked about his time in the military. When he did, he always had this far-off look in his eyes."

"Yeah, being a Vietnam vet, serving in Desert Storm and Iraq, he's seen more than I could even imagine. That's why when he told me it was time for me to retire, I took his advice seriously. He saved my life because if I had served even just one more tour of duty I probably wouldn't be here today."

Ava reached over and grasped her hand. "I'm glad you listened to him. Without you I wouldn't have discovered the country girl trapped within me."

Paige gazed up at Ava's teasing smile and grinned in amusement. "I have to admit. I didn't think you'd make it this long. I figured you would've tried to hijack the golf cart and high-tailed it out of here by now."

Ava quirked a brow. "Don't think I haven't thought about it."

Paige chuckled at the image that came to her mind of Ava speeding down the highway in the ranch's golf cart. "That would've been an awesome sight to see."

Their hands remained clasped as they gazed back toward the stream.

"Ava, I know this hasn't been easy for you and I wish I could tell you how much longer this will be, but unfortunately the situation is proving to be more difficult and dangerous than anyone expected."

Ava slid her hand from Paige's and stood to take a few steps away. She wrapped her arms around herself. "I don't understand how nothing can be found on whoever is behind this. At this point, whether it's Kyle or someone else, I just want to be able to go home. I need to be able to see and talk to my parents in person and to be there to help figure all this out. I can't do that here." She turned back to Paige looking frustrated. "My mother thinks my father isn't telling her something. When she asks him about Kyle, he gives her vague answers and changes the subject. Is there anything Ezekiel may have told you that my father might not want me to know?"

Paige did her best to keep her face neutral. If she could keep major military secrets from being found out by a very determined and ruthless foreign enemy, she could do the same from a civilian like Ava despite the guilt eating away at her from doing so.

"Not that I'm aware of. I just assumed that whatever your mother fills you in on is the same thing they fill me in on."

Ava's gaze narrowed on her, and Paige felt as if she could see right through her, but she refused to flinch, blink, or do anything that would give her away.

"So, you won't have a problem with me borrowing your phone to call home? I'm assuming your cell is full of all kinds of safeguards to keep the call from being traced or anything."

Paige met the challenge in Ava's gaze with her own. It was a standoff that she was confident she would win, but she obviously underestimated Ava who hadn't budged, barely blinked, and held her hand out waiting for Paige to hand over her phone. She could just give it to her, let Ava call her mother who didn't know any more than her daughter to settle the matter, but something held Paige back from doing that. She decided something that she knew she was going to immediately regret but found she could no longer keep Ava in the dark.

Paige sighed. "Ava, why don't you sit down. There is something your mother didn't tell you because she doesn't know either."

Ava hesitantly did as Paige asked and sat back down beside her on the blanket. She had been feeling so homesick lately as well as sick with worry about how her father was handling Kyle. She knew Ezekiel and her uncle would keep him safe, but it didn't lessen her concern. She'd tried to stay busy and distracted by continuing with her workout regiment, something she had maintained even after she'd gone into hiding, and helping around the ranch. She had even been spending several hours a week ensconced in the amazing library located above the garage with floor to ceiling shelves around the entire room filled with a vast array of fiction ranging from Shakespeare classics to contemporary lesbian fiction. After college she hadn't been much of a casual reader unless it had something to do with the business and financial industry, now reading the financial magazines and newspapers Adele brought for her just made her more homesick leaving her to rediscover writers she hadn't read in years as well as finding new ones she would've never picked up before.

Ava glanced at Paige, trying to tamp down the growing fascination with this complex woman. Paige gazed down at her hands clenching and unclenching in her lap, making Ava nervous about what she was getting ready to tell her.

"What is it?" Ava asked impatiently.

She looked up at Ava with a sigh. "Kyle resigned and disappeared shortly before we got here."

"WHAT? And you're just now telling me this?" Ava stood, heading for the horses.

"Ava, wait! Where are you going?"

"Home!" Ava untied Amina's reins from the tree and pulled herself up into the saddle with surprisingly less effort than it usually took.

Paige stood and blocked her path. "Ava, rushing home without a plan wouldn't be the best decision. For all we know, Kyle could be waiting just for that to happen so that he can send people after you again. That's why your father, Max, and Ezekiel thought it was best not to tell you until they could get a lock on his whereabouts."

Ava glared angrily down at Paige. "That was a decision that I should've been allowed to make. You asked me to trust you and you've been lying to my face for weeks. I'm done. Now, kindly move out of my way. As angry as I am, I would rather not have Amina trample you."

"Ava, please, let's talk about this."

Ava urged Amina forward. She took two steps then stopped within reach of Paige who gave Ava a pleading look before stepping out of the way. Ava tapped her boot along Amina's side to send her into a gallop and left Paige behind. It wasn't until she got a half mile down the path and reached a fork when she realized she had no idea how to get back to the ranch. She refused to go back and figured Paige would be coming after her, so she waited. A few minutes later Paige arrived at the fork and angled Zorro toward the path on the left. Ava quietly rode alongside her until they reached the security gate. Paige punched in the code, and as soon as the gate slid open enough for Amina to fit through, Ava sent her into a quick gallop, not bothering to wait for Paige. When they reached the barn, it took Ava a moment to dismount without falling on her ass. Then she led Amina into her stall, gave her some fresh hay and water, and marched out of the barn. She was just climbing into the golf cart they had ridden over in together when Paige and Zorro slowly sauntered toward the barn. Ava didn't bother waiting, she took off toward the house angrily mumbling to herself about the stupid overprotectiveness of the men in her life and how she wished they would stop seeing her as a helpless little girl and realize that she could handle anything they could.

Ava pulled the cart up to the charging station, plugged it in and almost pulled the screen door off its hinges as she angrily opened it.

"That was a quick picnic. I wasn't expecting you guys back for at least another hour," Adele said as she sat on the sofa watching her soap operas and folding laundry.

"I just came back long enough to pack before I head to the airport." Ava went to her room, walked to the closet, and realized not only did she have nothing to pack her things in, but she also didn't have much to pack except for the clothes she'd been wearing the night they'd left New Orleans.

Her anger fizzled to sadness. She was tired of running and hiding as she waited for the men to handle things the way they thought was best. Tired of being ignored as if she didn't have a say in what was going on. She was also mad at herself for letting them talk her into leaving in the first place.

Adele entered the room and sat beside her. "Remember what I said on the day you arrived? Paige will do whatever she needs to do to protect you. Whatever it is she's done that's got you all riled up was probably for a good reason."

"She lied to me, Adele. She asked me to trust her, then she lied to me for weeks."

"Ava, it was for your own protection."

Ava frowned. "You knew?"

"Yes, but only because I overheard Willie telling Junior so that they could keep an eye out for anyone suspicious coming around."

"Great, so everyone knew but me. I've been going around here like I'm on some extended ranch vacation while everyone around me was making decisions about my life without including me." Ava knew she sounded like a petulant child, but she was so frustrated.

"We're all trying to do the same thing your family and friends at home are trying to do, keep you safe. Now, if you want to leave, no one will stop you, but before you do, consider what going home will mean not only for yourself but those you care about. It's obvious this Kyle has no qualms about hurting anyone to get what he wants, and you waltzing back out into the open could lead to a situation beyond anyone's control except his. Paige was hired to keep you safe. You may not agree with her methods, but you have to agree with the results considering where you could've been the night of your attempted kidnapping and where you are now."

Ava's shoulders slumped in defeat. "I know you're right. I just wish she would've told me. I probably would've decided to stay, but I wasn't given the opportunity to make that decision."

"You're right, and I'm sorry about that."

Ava gazed up to find Paige leaning against the doorframe. "I'm sorry for stranding you like that."

Paige shrugged. "As you know, I don't mind the walk. Can we talk?"

Ava nodded.

Adele gave her hand a squeeze and stood. "I have to help set up the women's auxiliary craft tent for the carnival this evening so I'm going to finish the laundry and head out. There's a Crockpot of beef stew cooking on the counter for dinner. It should be ready in a couple of hours." She left them alone.

Ava stood and went past Paige toward the seating area of her bedroom. She sat on the sofa with her legs folded beneath her hugging one of the throw pillows. Paige joined her but kept her distance.

"I didn't like keeping you in the dark about such a major turn of events, but I didn't know you well enough then to judge whether you'd try to leave like your family and Ezekiel worried that you would. I've been in the job of protecting people for so long it's difficult for me to see the person and their feelings outside of the threat," Paige explained.

Ava gave her a tentative smile. "I understand. I probably would've threatened to leave, but once I had time to consider the consequences, I wouldn't have followed through with it. I know my family is afraid for me, but that doesn't make it right for them to treat me like a child who needs to be kept in the dark to keep from harm. This is my life, and I should have a say in how I want to handle it."

"You're right and like Adele said, no one is going to force you to stay if you don't want to."

"But you think I should."

Paige chewed thoughtfully on her bottom lip before responding. "I think you should give it another week or two. If Kyle doesn't surface or they don't get a lead on him by then, I'll personally escort you home."

"That sounds reasonable." Ava admitted to herself that as much as she wanted to go home, she didn't want to go all half-cocked without a plan and possibly jeopardize her or her family's and friends' safety.

Paige looked relieved. "In the interim, as big as this ranch is we both could use a few hours away from it. How would you like to go to the town's annual carnival tonight?"

"Are you sure? I thought you wanted to limit who knows I'm here."

Paige shrugged. "It's been a month; I think we can venture out for one night. It's usually the locals and the surrounding towns. We could disappear in the crowd, stay for a couple of hours, and dip out. If you like, I can let you borrow one of my wigs."

Ava looked at Paige in disbelief. "Wait, you have wigs?"

Paige looked amused. "Yes. They're left over from my counterintelligence days. There aren't a lot. Maybe six or seven. They're in a trunk I haven't opened since I moved here."

Ava chuckled. "I think if we remained friends for the rest of our lives, at eighty years old, I would still be finding out new and interesting things about you."

"I hear being mysterious is sexy." Paige gave her a wink.

"I won't argue that."

The heat from Paige's gaze lit the flicker of desire Ava had been managing to subdue into a roaring flame. The ding from a notification on Paige's phone broke the spell.

Paige blinked rapidly and looked down at her phone. "Sorry, I need to take care of this."

"Okay. I need to call my mother and let her know what you told me. She's not going to be so happy about the men conspiring to keep us in the dark. They may wish they were here instead of me after she finishes with them."

Paige grinned. "I can imagine. When you're finished, come by my room and we'll see what I have to help you go unnoticed."

"Okay." Ava watched Paige leave, enjoying the sight of her tight behind and muscular thighs outlined by the jeans she wore. It was a sight she enjoyed far more than she should whenever they worked together in the barn. She shook her head and got up to call her mother. She just had to get through two more weeks without giving in to the urge to pull Paige into a pile of hay to make love.

Chapter Fifteen

Paige went to her room as she called Grant who had been the one to text her as she was talking to Ava.

"Hey, Grant, what's up? The family good?"

"Hey, yeah, we're all good. All the girls are napping. Our little Rose Bud is wearing everybody out. She seems to not only have inherited her father's size but his habit of being a night owl."

Paige smiled. "I'm assuming that means you've got the overnight shift."

Grant chuckled. "Yeah, but while it helps Patrice get some rest, Lily's fascination with her new baby sister is wearing off since they share a room."

"As a big sister, I can totally relate. Hopefully she'll be sleeping through the night soon which should get her back in Lily's good graces. I know how my goddaughter needs her beauty sleep."

"Definitely. As much as I love talking about my girls, I called about something else. The pest your cleanup crew cleared out just showed up as a John Doe in the Florida Everglades. A sketch has been all over the news down here."

Paige ran her hand through her hair. "Shit. I guess we better send someone to check on our friend in New Orleans."

"Already done. He's devastated but safe. I've got someone keeping an eye on him just in case any further pests show up."

Paige's shoulders drooped in relief. "Thanks, Grant."

"No problem. I'll keep you updated if there's any further news. Take care and tell our financial wizard that Lily and Rose are already set for college."

Paige smiled. "Will do. Give everyone my love."

Paige tossed her phone on the bed, lay back, and threw her arm over her eyes with a heavy sigh. She felt herself drifting off to sleep when a knock on her door jolted her awake. She uncovered her eyes and looked over to find Ava standing in the doorway.

"I'm sorry, did I wake you?"

Paige sat up. "No, was just resting my eyes."

Ava grinned. "Said by every grandmother when they were caught napping."

"Aw, man, so you're calling me old now?"

Ava gave her a wide-eyed innocent look. "Well, you are five years my senior."

"Well then, I guess I better be in bed by eight which means no carnival for you, young lady."

"Okay, okay, I take it back. You're not old, just well-seasoned." Ava gave her a wink.

Paige laughed. "I guess I'll take that. C'mon, let's find you a suitable disguise for our excursion."

Paige led Ava to her closet, knelt, and pulled a steamer trunk out to the middle of the floor. Ave knelt beside her as she opened it. Inside were several neatly folded camouflage uniforms, hats, military green socks and T-shirts, and half a dozen silk bags. She grabbed the bags by the drawstrings, closed the trunk, and laid them on top of the lid.

"These are the wigs."

Ava opened one of the bags and pulled out a short, pixie cut black wig. "I assume your hair was a lot shorter than it is now since I don't know how you would've fit it all up under this even with a good wig cap."

"Yeah. I pretty much kept a low maintenance fade during my military career."

Ava fluffed the wig up then held it up on her hand as she looked Paige over then smiled. "Let me guess. This was the wig you used to keep them distracted by thoughts of how to seduce you while you were seducing secrets from them."

Paige quirked a brow and smiled. "That was pretty close."

Ava nodded. "Yeah, I can see that." She stood and slipped the wig over her freshly cut hair courtesy of Adele, then went over to the full-length mirror to finger comb the hair into place. She did a little turn in front of Paige then posed with her chin lying on her hands. "What do you think?"

Paige thought Ava was sexy with her shortened hair, but the wig, her bright wide eyes, pursed lips and fluttering lashes had her looking like a real-life Black Betty Boop. Paige could almost picture her in a short black dress singing *boop a doop'ed.*

"I like it."

Ava smiled and turned back to the mirror. "I guess we have our wig."

"Are you sure you don't want to look through the others. That's the shortest. The rest are shoulder-length or longer."

"No. Since my hair used to be longer, I think anything close to that length will look too much like me. This is good." Ava removed the wig and turned back to Paige. "You wouldn't happen to have any makeup?"

"As a matter of fact, I do." Paige lifted the bags of wigs and re-opened the trunk. After placing the wigs back, she tucked the trunk back into its nook, stood and pulled a small carry case down from a shelf and handed it to Ava.

Ava looked at the case curiously as she set it on the island in the middle of the closet, flipped up the clasps, and opened the lid staring wide-eyed at the multilevel make up kit inside.

"This looks like the kit Ezekiel's agent had when she came over to pose as me when they were sneaking me out of my apartment."

"That must have been Tracey. She's one of the best disguises and makeup artists in the game. I'm good but don't even come close to her skill set."

Ava lifted a prosthetic nose from one of the tiers looking at it in fascination. "This is just plain freaky."

Paige chuckled. "I don't think you'll need to go that far, but maybe one of these might be best." She opened a drawer in the case where several clear plastic contact lens cases were neatly lined up. "Your eyes are a noticeably unique color. If you don't mind wearing contacts, you're welcome to use any of these. I replace them with fresh pairs every six months just in case I need them while working a case."

"I feel like a little girl getting to play dress-up."

Her face lit up happily and Paige's heart felt as if it would burst in her chest at being the indirect cause of that happiness after the past few weeks of seeing her so down. Ava chose a pair of dark brown contacts, opened and searched through the second drawer and chose a pair of non-prescription wire-rimmed glasses.

She laid her collection of disguise materials out and smiled. "Okay, I think I'm good."

Paige nodded. "Some good choices. Minimal but still effective."

"So, what time are we heading out?"

"The carnival opens for business at four, but I figured we could head over around six. Give time for the crowd to build so that we're not so conspicuous but also allow us a few hours to stay before they close down at eleven."

Ava looked confused. "It's only for one night?"

"No, it goes through the weekend all day Friday, Saturday, and Sunday. I like to go opening night when the local tribes participate in the opening ceremonies and while all the prizes are still fresh at the game booths." She grinned.

"Ah, I see. Well, just to warn you, if there are any of those games with the water guns blowing up balloons, I'm quite the marksman," Ava said confidently.

Paige quirked a brow. "Really? Is that a challenge?"

Ava collected her disguise. "Guess you'll have to see." She gave Paige a mischievous grin over her shoulder as she left.

Ava looked at her reflection in the mirror and didn't recognize the sexy librarian-looking woman that stared back. She'd disguised herself before when she and Travis had gone out to a club or bar that she didn't think it would be wise to be recognized in, but that had only been with a wig and bolder makeup than she normally wore. But with the wig, contacts, and glasses she'd borrowed from Paige's spy kit, it was like she was a whole other person. She had also borrowed some makeup but decided that she didn't need it. What she wore was more than enough to throw her own family off if they happened to walk by. She finished the look with a beige long sleeve, full-length, floral print peasant dress, a denim jacket, and a dressier pair of cowboy boots Adele had given her because they were too small. Ava gave her wig one last pat and practically skipped from the room because she was so excited to be going out.

She found Paige standing in front of the mirror in the foyer adjusting the braided leather straps of a bolo tie with a beautiful oval turquoise stone set in sterling silver hanging from the collar of a crisp white western style shirt. Her shirt was tucked into a pair of dark denims held up by a black leather belt with a similar, larger turquoise stone as the one on her bolo set in a silver buckle. Like Ava, Paige wore a nicer pair of boots than the ones she usually wore around the ranch. She looked sexy as hell, and Ava could imagine sitting astride Zorro within the circle of Paige's arms as they rode off into the sunset like the ending of those old western movies. She could also imagine slowly undressing her from that outfit including kneeling at her feet and sliding her boots off like some old-world concubine. That image had her body temperature rising quite a bit.

"Don't you clean up nice." She hoped Paige didn't hear the tremor of desire in her voice.

"Thanks." Paige turned, and her eyes widened in shock. "Wow, if I didn't know any better, I'd swear you weren't you."

"I know, right? It was rather disconcerting looking in the mirror and not even recognizing myself. Like I'm my own long-lost twin or something."

Paige cocked her head to the side and looked Ava over. "Yeah, I could see that. Like one of those soap operas Adele watches where the same actress plays both twins but just with a wig and glasses."

Ava laughed. "The fact that you could describe such a storyline just told me you've obviously watched those shows as well."

Paige gave her that charmingly crooked grin of hers. "Hey, when you're trying to escape the heaviness of your memories you sometimes need something as ridiculously unreal as those shows to lose yourself in occasionally. Ready to go?"

Ava noticed that Paige would nonchalantly say things like that as if it were no big deal that she dealt with PTSD. It always made her want to pull Paige into her arms and just hold her until the far-off look that came into her eyes went away but knew that would be too intrusive for the relationship they had, so she just ignored it. "Yep, whenever you are."

"Great, let me just grab my hat and we can go." Paige walked over to the sofa to pick up a black Stetson hat with a black leather and silver hatband.

Okay, now that just wasn't fair, Ava thought. Here she was looking much mousier than she ever had and Paige was looking like she just stepped out of a western fashion ad. She was tempted to go back and at least put on a bolder color lipstick but decided this wasn't the time to let her vanity get the best of her. She was supposed to be looking inconspicuous to blend in so her inner diva would have to take a back seat for now.

"All right, let's hit the road," Paige said.

Ava followed her out of the house and waited as Paige punched in the code to seal the house up tight then followed her toward the garage. Paige's second vehicle, a two-tone turquoise and white 1968 Chevrolet C10, sat in the driveway.

"Oh, wow, must definitely be a special occasion if you're breaking out the classic," Ava teased her. She hadn't seen the truck leave the garage other than to get a quick shine before Paige put her right back.

Paige grinned. "Sometimes I enter her in the car show they have the first night of the carnival, but tonight I just thought you might like to arrive in style for your much-needed night out." She opened the passenger door for Ava and offered her hand to assist her up into the truck.

"I'm honored." Ava took her hand and felt a small shock.

It could've been static, but the heat in Paige's eyes as she looked at her had her feeling like it was something more. Their gazes held for a moment before Ava was the first to shyly look away and climb into the truck. Paige hopped in, started the engine, which revved up just as smooth as Betty did, and soon they were off. Ava was told the main part of town was just fifteen minutes from the ranch, but she hadn't been outside the security gates since they arrived, so she hadn't actually seen it. They rode along quietly for a few minutes with country music playing softly from the radio. Ava hadn't been a fan of it until Paige introduced her to music by African American country artists Mickey Guyton, Kane Brown, Jimmie Allen, and Darius Rucker who she remembered from Hootie and the Blowfish but had completely forgotten he'd gone over to country.

She smiled to herself. When she finally did go home, Travis wouldn't know what to make of this version of her. Close shaven head, not a designer label in sight in her wardrobe, wearing cowboy boots almost every day, mucking out stalls and listening to country. As much as she missed the fast pace of her life in Chicago, she was growing fond of the quiet little paradise Paige had set up for herself. Ava couldn't remember when she wasn't on the move, working, wheeling, and dealing. Even in New Orleans where she spent more time at the bar than she did at her apartment because she had begun helping the performers set up their own small investment accounts. But here, out in the middle of nowhere in Mounds, Oklahoma, there were no meetings, business trips, or financial reports to review. Just farm animals to feed, woods and mountain ranges to explore, and sexy fiction to read.

"You're so quiet over there. Penny for your thoughts?" Paige said.

"Just thinking how I can see what you love so much about this place. It's wildly beautiful and peaceful."

"That's true but you've also been fortunate enough to be here during the fall season which is the best time of year. Summer is usually scorching, and when it isn't hot it's raining more often than not and also a pretty active time for tornadoes."

Ava frowned. "What are winters like?"

"December isn't bad with average temperature around forty degrees, but January and February can be brutal. At night the temps can dip below freezing."

"Oh, so not much different than Chicago. That lake effect is no joke." Ava shivered just thinking about it.

Paige chuckled. "Yeah, I can imagine, but cold on the open plains is a much different beast. Hopefully, you probably won't have to be here to experience it."

"Fingers crossed." Why did the thought of leaving not bring Ava as much anticipation as it did when she first arrived?

She glanced over at Paige whose fingers were tapping the steering wheel along with the song on the radio. Her posture and profile, which up until a little over a week ago always seemed to be at ready attention, was now relaxed. She was still as cautious as ever, making sure the entire house was locked up tight every night, checking the cameras in her hidden security room every morning before breakfast and every night before bed, and spending quite a bit of the morning riding the perimeter of the property with Zorro to check the security fencing. But in between and after those times, she was easier going. Joking around with Willie and Adele, teasing her whenever she squealed at a mouse or did something to remind them of her city girl ways, and breaking out the various number of board games she had which they recently began playing each night before bed. It gave them time to talk, and Paige seemed more receptive to sharing stories about her life before the military and her early years after joining.

It turned out they had similar backgrounds as daddy's girls wanting to follow in their footsteps and doing whatever it took to make them proud. Both their fathers were practically raised on the streets with absentee fathers and did whatever was necessary to keep food on the table and help their family escape a life of poverty. Paige's father chose a career in the military and now ran a successful landscaping business. Ava's father chose college and a career in the finance industry and built a multi-million-dollar wealth management firm. Both were prideful, decisive men who raised their daughters to be the same to ready them for a world that wouldn't treat them fair because they were Women of Color having to compete in a world run by men who would look down on them for that reason alone. Paige and Ava were both taught that where Men of Color had to work twice as hard to achieve what most White men barely lifted a finger to do, Women of Color had to work three times as hard. Ava also discovered that despite both their fathers' determination to ready their daughters for such a world, they themselves had a habit of continuing to treat them like their sweet baby girls that they had to protect no matter how strong they proved to be.

All of this led to some very competitive games that often ended in a draw to be continued another night. The only game that Paige destroyed Ava in was chess which she always seemed to be three moves ahead. The same went for Ava when they played Monopoly. Since neither enjoyed losing so epically, they rarely played either game. Despite her worry about what was going on at home, Ava was genuinely enjoying her time here with Paige, Willie, and Adele. Mostly with Paige, which she would only admit to herself. She knew her mother was picking up on that during their weekly calls, but she never mentioned it. When Ava brought up Paige in their conversation, her mother would say something like, "*So, you and Paige seemed to be getting along well*" or "*You seem to really like it there,*" all with a mother's knowing tone in her voice.

"Just a few more weeks and we'll go our separate ways back to our regularly scheduled lives," Ava said to herself but not sounding very convinced even in her own head.

Paige could practically feel Ava's eyes on her each time she glanced her way. It took quite a bit of willpower to keep her eyes glued to the road and not allow herself to get lost in Ava's bright eyes. Well, they were dark for now due to the contact lenses, but this was an internal battle Paige found herself fighting daily. She truly enjoyed Ava's company. So much that she came up with their nightly game nights to spend as much time with her alone as possible. During the day they were either with Willie or Adele, surrounded by her menagerie of animals, or in separate buildings as Ava began spending more time in the library. Their one-on-one time had been narrowed down to their daily rides on Zorro and Amina, dinner, and maybe watching about an hour of TV together before they both headed to their rooms around eight o'clock. Because they seemed to be together most of the day working around the ranch, Paige found she missed Ava's presence during the times they were apart.

While in the library one afternoon a little over a week ago, Ava had come across a box of board games Paige had forgotten she owned. Ava mentioned how much she enjoyed how her family would get together once a week for Sunday dinner and game night before she left for college. Knowing how much Ava missed her family after a year of not seeing them and wanting an excuse to spend more time with her, Paige had brought the box of games down to the house and initiated their own personal game nights. She found herself opening to Ava in ways she hadn't with any other woman about her family and childhood. She also found that she liked knowing how similar her and Ava's upbringings were. Despite the metaphorical silver spoon Ava had grown up with, she didn't come off as one of those entitled Richie Riches that Paige had dealt far too often with in her line of business. Ava was down-to-earth, not afraid to get her hands dirty or be embarrassed and carried herself with a sexy confidence that could be considered conceit to someone who didn't know any more than that about her. It was all such an appealing package that Paige found more difficult to ignore with each passing day.

She hoped getting away from the ranch for a few hours would cool her growing feelings as well as distract Ava from her homesickness. They arrived at the town proper of Mounds, Oklahoma, fifteen minutes later. Traffic in the main thoroughfare was almost at a standstill with all the pedestrian traffic crossing back and forth. Paige inched along for three blocks when she decided they would be better off walking the remaining four to the carnival grounds.

"I think I'm just going to park at the Dollar General if you don't mind walking a few blocks. At this rate, we'll end up spending half our time trying to get to Veteran's Memorial Park where the carnival is being held than we will enjoying it," Paige said.

"I don't mind at all. It'll give me a chance to see the town."

"Excellent."

Paige pulled into a Dollar General parking lot that had already begun filling up with others who must have had the same idea. She waved at familiar faces as she drove around looking for a place to park and managed to snatch one of the few remaining spots. She grabbed her hat from the space between her and Ava, hopped out of the truck, and jogged around to find Ava already opening the door to get out.

Paige simply grasped the handle and offered Ava her hand. Ava smiled appreciatively and laid her hand in Paige's. Despite all the work she'd been doing around the ranch, Ava's hands were still as soft and smooth as they had been when she arrived. It probably didn't hurt that, unlike Paige, she wore work gloves while she worked and carried around a small bottle of hand cream Adele had picked up for her. She used it every time she washed her hands, so they were never dry and cracked. Paige gazed down at her own hands and ran her thumbs over the calluses on her palms, then turned them over to find them cracked and dry. While she was home, she usually didn't bother with constant moisturizing because it would just be washed off shortly after, but now she felt a little self-conscious.

"Everything okay?" Ava asked.

Paige gazed up to find Ava watching her curiously. "Uh, yeah, give me a sec."

She reached into the passenger side, opened the glovebox and grabbed a travel size bottle of hand lotion she kept there. After all, she wasn't a complete Neanderthal. She kept lip balm and hand lotion in the glove compartments of both trucks just in case. After rubbing in a large dollop of lotion, she tossed the bottle back into the box and locked the truck up.

"Ready?" she asked Ava.

"Any time you are."

"Great."

Paige led her from the parking lot and into the mass of people walking up the street. She felt Ava's hand slip into hers and she gazed over to find her looking around nervously.

"We can go back if you like," Paige offered. She'd forgotten how crowded the first night of the festival could be.

Ava gave her a tentative smile. "No. I'm fine. It's just been a while since I've been someplace so crowded. It never bothered me before but ever since..." She left the rest unsaid.

"I understand. Maybe this wasn't such a good idea. Why don't we go back home?"

Ava grasped her hand tighter. "No, please, I'll be fine. I just got a little nervous." She gave her a reassuring smile.

Paige glanced around at the people moving along the road with them. "Okay, but the minute you start feeling uncomfortable or nervous again, tell me and we'll leave immediately."

Ava nodded. "Will do. Now, tell me how a town this small has so many churches? We passed two coming into town, about to pass a third next to the Dollar General and I see two more up ahead."

Paige chuckled. "Mounds may be small, but it has a very diverse community. There are six churches in total in the town proper and about three or four more in a few of the neighboring towns. Mounds is considered a commuting town with most of the residents working in Tulsa and Sapulpa"

"Wow. That's a lot of churches. Are you a member of any of them? How do they feel about your sexuality?"

"No. As long as I mind my business, they mind theirs. Folks here aren't as backwards as people like to believe small towns like this are. It also doesn't hurt that I live outside of town, so they don't see me regularly."

"But you seem to know so many people."

"Even with a population of a little over two thousand, there aren't that many of our folks around, especially ones that own a piece of land the size I have so the few times I do come into town I'm fairly recognizable."

"That makes sense."

"They're good folks. Of course, like every town, big or small, there are a few bad apples in the bunch but they usually stay out of my way. My association with Willie's family, who are well-respected here, and my active participation with the Veteran's Association, who are aware of my background, helps to keep the vermin at bay."

"In other words, no one in their right mind is going to step up to you if they know what's good for them."

Paige grinned. "Pretty much."

They arrived at the park where a fairground was set up with several rows of booths, a few carnival rides and a Ferris wheel. She released Ava's hand to take her wallet out of her pocket and immediately missed the soft warmth of her grasp.

"Evening, Paige. I haven't seen you around town lately," said the young woman she handed a ten-dollar bill to for two tickets.

"Evening, Raven. Yeah, I've been busy at the ranch. I'll probably be dropping by the bank sometime next week."

"Maybe you'll finally take me up on that cup of coffee I keep offering," she said flirtatiously, completely ignoring Ava's presence as she handed her one ticket and a five back.

Paige offered the money back to Raven with a smile. "I needed two tickets."

Raven gazed over at Ava, her eyes widening in surprise as if she'd just noticed her. "Oh, my apologies. Is this one of your family members here for a visit?"

"Something like that. Be sure to give your mother my best." Paige took the second ticket, handed it to Ava, then placed her hand on Ava's back to lead her through the gate.

"Someone's got a crush," Ava said teasingly.

"Believe me when I say I did nothing to encourage it. Raven works at the bank, which her mother manages. She happened to be the one to assist me when I moved here and opened an account with them. I made a nice bit of money contracting with Ezekiel, so the sum was fairly large to start. I've also been regularly adding to my retirement fund so I'm doing okay, but the average household income in this town is around forty thousand annually, so a lot of people are under the impression I'm some wealthy recluse, and Raven, who has access to see what's in my accounts, has practically volunteered to be my sugar baby."

Ava laughed. "Wow. No wonder she gave me the cold shoulder. I assume you don't regularly bring dates to town."

Paige quirked a brow. "You do recall the discussion we had with Adele about my nonexistent love life. Unfortunately, Raven isn't the only one, she's just the most open about her attraction. I've been propositioned by several closeted single women and more curious married women than I care to count."

"Do I need to watch my back while I'm here? I don't want any jealous wannabes mistaking me for someone trying to steal you away from them." Ava jokingly gazed around as if looking for danger.

Paige laughed. "I think you'll be fine. Maybe seeing us together will make them think I'm finally taken and leave me alone."

"Why, Paige Richards, are you asking me to pretend to be your girlfriend for the evening?"

Paige gazed at her thoughtfully. "You know, that might not be a bad idea," she said, only half joking.

Ava grinned mischievously. "Hey, if I can spend over a year faking a relationship with a man that I couldn't stand I think I can spend an evening faking one with an attractive and charming woman such as yourself."

Ava grasped her hand again and Paige's grew warm at her touch.

"Now, let's find the nearest water cannon game so that I can kick your ass as promised," Ava said, heading toward the first row of carnival games.

CHAPTER SIXTEEN

A va didn't know what had come over her to agree to pretend to be Paige's girlfriend. Maybe it was her growing attraction, how safe she felt under Paige's watchful gaze, how protective Paige had been when Ava had become anxious from the mass of people surrounding them, or a combination of all the above. Whatever it was, her body grew warm, and her stomach fluttered at the idea. As they strolled along the fairway, Ava enjoyed the feel of Paige's callused palms against her own, the gentle strength of her grip keeping Ava by her side as they maneuvered through the crowd, and the clean scent of fabric softener and whatever soap or cologne Paige wore surrounding them. Paige made Ava feel soft and vulnerable. Feelings almost foreign to Ava, but she found she liked it because she knew she'd always be protected by Paige, at least physically. She didn't know what shape her heart was going to be in after all this, but Ava decided right then and there to just go with it. She could only guess that Paige had similar feelings or was at least physically attracted to her from the way she would catch her looking at her sometimes. She had also admitted that she'd been attracted to Ava when she met her in New Orleans which she hoped hadn't faded in the past weeks.

"Here we are. One water cannon game for milady," Paige said with a bow and flourishing sweep of her hand toward a booth nearby.

Ava gave a curtsy. "Prepare to be trounced, good sir."

Paige gave her that sexy grin she'd come to adore. "We shall see."

Five rounds later they were tied, having been beaten by a grade school sharpshooter in the last round.

"Should we call it a draw, or would you like to go another round?" Paige asked, hefting her winnings, a stuffed bull that just so happened to resemble Brutus and an adorable teddy bear sporting the full attire of an old west gunslinger including two tiny pistols in its holster.

Ava noticed all the other guns were claimed and there were several kids standing nearby looking as if they were waiting for their chance. "No, I'd rather not get shown up again by any more elementary schoolers."

Paige chuckled. "Yeah, most of the kids around here had a hunting rifle in their hands as soon as they learned to walk."

Ava hefted her own winnings under her arms, a female gunslinging teddy bear and a lipstick- and tutu-wearing pig. "That doesn't surprise me. Besides, I don't think I can carry another stuffed animal."

Paige quirked a brow. "That's assuming you would've won."

Ava grinned. "Oh sure, talk shit after I decide not to play again. I think we're going to need to settle this at the ranch's range."

"Fine by me. I need to log some range time in anyway. Out-shooting you will be good practice." Paige gave her a look of sexy confidence.

"Conceit isn't a good look for you."

"Not conceit. Just stating fact."

Ava shook her head. "Okay, Annie Oakley, I'm craving something fried. Can we take a trip down the food fairway?"

"Of course, but I want to make a stop on the way."

They strolled over to the next lane where booths were set up for vendors selling arts and crafts, clothing, and homemade custom items like soaps, candles, and jewelry. Ava made a mental note to stop at some of the booths before they left. Fortunately, Travis had been able to transfer her bank account under Lacey Crain to her mother who then transferred the amount from that account to Paige for Ava's use. Ava made sure to keep track of what she was spending so that it stayed within the limits of what was in her account so as not to have to owe Paige anything when she finally went back home. They stopped at a booth that was twice the size of the others with tables set up and filled with adults and children making crafts. Ava spotted Adele, waved, and was momentarily confused by the lack of recognition in her face until she noticed Paige beside her and gazed back at her with widened eyes. That was when Ava remembered she was in disguise. She hadn't passed anything that would show her reflection, so she had completely forgotten that she was probably unrecognizable.

"Well, I'll be damned," Adele said as she walked over to greet them. "From a distance you couldn't pay me to believe this was you. Even up close I'm hard-pressed to say it is. You still look fabulous but more like your own sister or cousin."

"It was weird looking at myself in the mirror. I honestly forgot what I looked like until I saw you didn't recognize me."

"It's good to see that you two found a way to get off that ranch for a little while."

"I figured just because I'm a homebody it doesn't mean everyone is, and I think we both earned a night out." Paige gave Ava a soft smile.

Ava felt the traitorous heat of the blush that still occurred when Paige looked at her. She shyly turned away and met Adele's knowing grin.

"So, did you come by to craft or just to blow my mind with this." She waved a hand in front of Ava.

"Stopped by to say hi and to see if you have an extra bag I can buy." Paige lifted her stuffed animals for Adele to see.

"Child, please. You don't need to buy a bag." Adele turned to a woman sitting at a table hand-painting a floral design on a canvas shopping bag. "Fiona, would you hand me the bag I painted yesterday?"

The woman nodded, turned to open a plastic bin, then reached in and handed Adele a bag. Adele offered it to Paige. Ava gazed down and gasped at the painted scene. Two white wolves lay side-by-side in the grass next to a lake gazing up at a starry moonlit sky, its brightness reflected on ripples of water in the lake. Snowcapped mountains lay in the distance like fingertips reaching for the stars. It was beautifully captured, like a picture in a frame.

"You painted this?" Ava asked in wonder.

Adele smiled. "Yes. Painting has always been a passion of mine since my mother gave me my first fingerpaints. I was planning to give this to you to remember me by when you leave, but seeing as you all have a handful to cart around while you're here you might as well take it now."

Ava's heart felt full at Adele's kindness since she'd invaded their quiet lives. "It's so beautiful. Thank you."

Paige placed her stuffed animals in the bag, then Ava took the bag and did the same with hers, pulling the straps up to her shoulder to carry.

"I can carry it," Paige offered.

Ava smiled happily. "No, I'm good. Thank you again, Adele."

Adele nodded. "I'll see you late tomorrow morning. Don't forget, you promised to help me in the garden," she reminded Ava.

"I didn't forget. See you tomorrow."

To Ava's surprise, Paige took her hand again before they even left Adele's booth. A quick glance at Adele told Ava she wasn't the least bit surprised. They strolled quietly along toward the food fairway then passed several food trucks before stopping at a truck with signage for The Fryer Tuck where the delicious smell of bacon filled the air.

"I know you wanted something fried so I'm going to recommend a few items that are a huge hit at the Oklahoma State Fair. It's the bacon-wrapped corn, if you feel adventurous, the rattlesnake sausage corn dog, and then finish it off with the deep-fried cookie dough sundae. If that won't appease your fried food craving, nothing will."

"Okay, I can get with the bacon-wrapped corn and the deep-fried sundae, but I'll have to pass on the rattlesnake corn dog." Ava wrinkled her nose in distaste.

Paige grinned in amusement. "How about a regular corn dog then."

"That I can do."

"Great. In the meantime, why don't you grab us a table?"

Ava nodded then headed toward an open area set up a few steps away with dozens of picnic tables. Out of caution, Ava found one along the perimeter that kept her in sight of Paige with the ability for a quick escape if needed. She'd lived cautiously while in New Orleans and the habit stuck with her. Paige must have had the same mindset because when Ava looked toward her Paige was watching her while she also kept her head on a swivel as she waited for their order. It took some time as there had been several orders ahead of theirs, but when Paige finally joined her, Ava's stomach growled hungrily. She rarely ate this way but when she did her stomach happily agreed to it.

Paige set the tray of food on the table. "Give me just a sec. I have one more thing to grab." She jogged back to the truck and returned with two bottles of beer. "You can't have all this without a beer to wash it down."

Ava took a bottle, dripping with condensation, from her. "I couldn't agree more."

Paige separated the food onto two paper plates and slid one over to Ava.

Ava gazed down at the red checkered paper-wrapped corn dog warily. "You better not be trying to trick me with a snake dog."

"I wouldn't do that, but I did get one for myself in case you wanted to try it." She waved her blue checkered paper-wrapped corn dog while licking her lips.

Ava had to look away, but not because of the snake dog. It was the things happening in her lower body as Paige licked her lips. "Thanks, but no thanks. Enjoy."

Ava started with the bacon-wrapped corn, taking a bite, and moaning happily at the crunch of the crispy bacon and fresh corn, and the combination of the salty and sweet of both. "Whoever thought of this deserves a culinary award." She took several more bites before trying the corn dog after dipping it into the sides of ketchup and mustard. "Wow. Why does the food that's so bad for you always taste so good?"

She looked up to find Paige watching her with amusement.

"What? Is there something on my face?" Ava grabbed a napkin.

"No, I'm just enjoying watching you enjoy your food. You're not like any heiress I've ever met."

Ava smiled shyly as she wiped her greasy fingertips. "Is that good or bad?"

"Oh, definitely good." Paige dipped her corn dog in her mustard and took a bite, chewing thoughtfully.

"How is it?"

"A little gamier than I'm used to but good."

Ava smiled. "Do you eat rattlesnake often?"

"Sometimes you have to make do with what's available. My father used to take us camping, but of course he couldn't just do the pop-up tents with the open fire and freshly caught fish frying in the pan. He had to turn it into a survival exercise. We would arrive at the sight at the crack of dawn, set up snare traps to catch our food, then were given the old-style military pup tents and were timed on how fast we could set them up. Once that was finished, we had to dig a foot-deep trench around the tent, find spots to dig our individual latrine holes, and finally collect firewood before we were sent back out to check our traps."

"What if you didn't catch anything?"

"My mother always packed bags of trail mix for emergencies and my father kept packs of MREs for just such occasions."

"And if you caught something, did you have to kill and clean it yourself?"

Paige nodded. "By the time I was ten I could skin and prep a rabbit or squirrel better than both my brothers and my father. Ironically, the one thing I never got the hang of preparing was snake. It always came out too chewy when I made it so whenever I caught one my older brother would cook it."

"Wow. I will never complain about my childhood again." Ava had only eaten half the corn and corn dog, but she really wanted to try the fried sundae before it was a melted mess.

She unwrapped it to pretty much find an ice cream sandwich that had just begun to soften up but was still firm enough to eat. She took a bite and moaned.

"It wasn't bad," Paige continued. "We actually enjoyed it. Especially when my mother would join us and put all of us to shame with her skills. Looks like we may have to get a few more of those fried sundaes to take home."

Ava smiled unashamedly. "As you've no doubt noticed. I'm not one of those women who's afraid to enjoy food."

Paige smirked. "I like a woman who can eat. Like I said, you're not like any heiress I know."

"Do you know a lot?"

Paige rolled her eyes. "More than I care to. Working private security puts you into contact with people who can obviously afford to have private security. I've encountered far too many spoiled rich kids with no regard to anyone's well-being but their own and who wouldn't even think about picking up a shovel let alone mucking out a stall."

"I grew up around many kids like that. Spoiled rich kids become spoiled rich adults who treat anyone they deem unworthy of their status like the help. Especially ones with the old, generational wealth. Many of which probably wouldn't give my family the time of day because of my father's background if we weren't so good at what we do. They don't realize my father's past is what made him the shrewd businessman he is today."

"I read his biography. What he did, pulling his family out of poverty and creating such a successful business is something to be admired. What's even more admirable is that he didn't forget where he came from. The programs he started, the scholarships he's given, the young people he's helped reach their own success when they could've been just as easily forgotten and left in the system is commendable."

Ava smiled, feeling a sense of pride on her father's behalf. "It is and I love him for that and for not allowing me to become one of those entitled kids that expected to have everything handed to them. He made me work for it just as he did the kids he mentored. He taught me that I'm no better than the people cleaning our home and one obnoxious mistake away from sharing a box with the homeless we pass on the street. So, yes, I enjoy the benefits of my wealth, but I also know that it's not the end all, be all of my life."

Paige's brows furrowed in thought as she gazed at Ava before shaking her head and looking down at her watch. "We better get going if we don't want to miss the opening night ceremony."

As Ava gathered the remnants of her food, she wondered what she'd said that had Paige looking at her so intensely. As if she were trying to come to a decision that she wasn't sure she would like.

They finished the evening watching the opening night ceremony where the mayor welcomed the townspeople as well as those visiting from the surrounding towns, the high school's band and choir serenaded the crowd with a few songs, and the local Cherokee and Muscogee tribes performed traditional welcome songs and dances. Ava had the pleasant surprise of recognizing Willie and Junior amongst the Cherokee dancers. Paige pointed out his other sons as well. After the ceremony, Ava asked to stop by a few of the vendors booths before they left for a little shopping. Paige stood quietly outside the booths watching her and wondering when her feelings had gotten so out of control. As Ava spoke about her father and her own philosophy about her wealth, Paige realized Ava was everything in a life partner she never knew she wanted. But it didn't matter what Paige wanted because she couldn't have her.

Ava would most likely be leaving soon. Although Paige had a feeling that Ava was attracted to her, that didn't mean she had developed feelings beyond sexual desire, and if by some chance Ava did feel what Paige was feeling, they were from two very different worlds thousands of miles apart. She was pretty sure Ava would be just as disagreeable about leaving her family and their business to live on a secluded ranch in Oklahoma as Paige would be leaving her quiet ranch life behind to live in the hectic city of Chicago. Paige had worked too hard to carve out this plot of peace. If she ever decided to settle down, she would hope the woman would be satisfied with what she had here. Ava might seem fine with it, but Paige was no fool. She knew that Ava was just passing the time until she could return to her life in the Windy City.

Ava allowed the woman running the jewelry booth to clasp a necklace around her neck as she gazed at herself in the mirror with a slight frown. Paige could guess it was probably because she once again forgot she wore a disguise until she looked at her reflection. Paige had sort of liked the disguise at first, but now she couldn't wait for them to get back to the house so that Ava could remove the whole get-up and Paige could go back to losing herself in her bright amber eyes and wonder if the waves in her shorn hair were as soft as they looked. Ava held matching earrings up to her ears then smiled and nodded at the vendor as she handed them back to her as well as the necklace. As the set was being wrapped and placed in a bag, Paige entered the booth.

"Are you getting the set?" she asked Ava.

"Yes. I like them, but I think they'll look even better when I'm able to try them on without all of this." She subtly indicated her disguise.

Paige handed the vendor her bank card. "I agree. I think the citrine will complement your eyes."

Ava gave her a shy smile. "Thank you."

"Is there any other vendor you'd like to stop by?"

"No, I think I've done enough damage. The handstitched scarf for my mother, the opal cuff links for my father, the flask for Uncle Max, and the handstitched leather vest for Travis covers everyone."

"It's a good thing we got the shopping bag from Adele for the walk back to the truck."

"This is nothing compared to my annual Christmas shopping when I also get gifts for my cousins, their kids, the security and maintenance staff for my building, my assistant, and my housekeeper and her family. I look like a bag lady walking to my car at the mall."

"You mean you don't have a personal shopper that takes care of all that for you?" Paige teased her.

Ava playfully bumped her with her shoulder since they were holding hands. They seemed to automatically reach for them after only a few hours of their pretending to date. As they headed toward the entrance,

Paige noticed Raven was still manning the ticket table and happened to turn around just as she and Ava reached the gate. She looked from Paige to their clasped hands then back again with an angry glare. Paige simply smiled and kept walking. She and Ava chatted about their evening as they walked back to the truck.

When they arrived home, Paige pulled up at the front door so Ava wouldn't have far to walk. She gazed over at Ava who gave her a soft smile.

"I had fun tonight. Thank you," Ava said.

"I did to, and it was my pleasure. I think it was a night we both deserved."

"I agree. I'm so appreciative I'll even wait as you open my door." Ava gave her a teasing grin.

Paige smiled. "How kind of you." She got out and went around to the passenger side to open the door for Ava. "Madam." She gave a flourishing bow.

After Paige opened the door, Ava entered and stood in the middle of the living room looking around. "It's funny. After a full day of manual labor then walking around the carnival, I expected to be sleepy but I'm wide awake."

"Me too."

Ava turned to Paige. "Didn't you say you liked to go for a swim at the pond when you couldn't sleep?"

"Yes, but it might be a little too chilly for that tonight."

Ava waved dismissively. "Not at all. It's a balmy sixty. Perfect pond dipping weather."

Paige chuckled. "You go pond dipping often?"

"No, but we do have a lake house I sometimes escape to when I want to get out of the city and work. I've gone for a swim on chillier nights than this."

Ava dropping the fact that her family had a lake house like it was commonplace was a reminder to Paige of how different their lives were, which was why a relationship between them wouldn't work. Paige had everything she needed right here at the ranch. She didn't need separate homes, grand trips around the world, or a garage full of expensive sports cars. Her life was about simplicity and the mundane day-to-day without any major surprises. She'd seen enough of the world, good and bad, and had enough surprises to last her a lifetime.

She shrugged. "We can go but don't say I didn't warn you. Do you need a bathing suit?"

Ava grinned mischievously as she headed toward the back door. Paige quirked a brow, grabbed two blankets that were folded neatly on the sofa, and followed her. Ava had barely made it past the tall evergreen bushes that surrounded the lake before she was pulling off her shoes and shedding her clothes. Paige was frozen in place as she watched Ava strip down to a lacy bra and a pair of matching boy shorts that barely covered her lush ass cheeks, then run, laughing, into the water. Her laughter quickly turned to squeals as she delved farther into its undoubtedly cool depth. Paige had to give her credit though, she continued going until she was submerged chest-deep. Paige walked to the water's edge still holding the blankets.

"Are you just going to stand there or join me?" Ava asked as she treaded water. "It's cold when you first get in but fine once you're submerged."

Paige knew that. She'd swam in the pond plenty of times in weather like this nude and in a bathing suit. Just not with a practically naked woman that she also had the hots for.

"C'mon, Paige. The water's fine." Paige had a feeling she knew what Adam felt like when Eve offered him the forbidden fruit.

Ava gave her a sexy pout then backstroked farther out. Paige gazed up at the moon shining brightly in the sky then down at its reflection on the subtle undulations made by Ava's swimming. She seriously needed to stop overthinking everything.

"It's just a swim," she said to herself. Which was probably like Adam saying, "It's just a bite."

She laid the blankets farther up on the embankment then removed and neatly folded her clothes on top of them, leaving her dressed in her Jungle Boogie print Culprit brand underwear and matching sports bra. It wasn't as sexy as Victoria's Secret, but at least they matched. She stepped into the water until she had to tread to stay above and watched Ava swim toward the opposite bank then expertly navigated a turn heading back in her direction. She stopped a few feet in front of Paige.

"I see why you would want to come out here to clear your mind before sleep. Like pretty much everything else around here, it's beautiful and peaceful," Ava said.

"Yes, it is. During the winter it also makes a great ice-skating rink."

"You ice skate?"

Paige smiled. "Don't look so surprised. They have skating rinks in Texas you know."

Ava flicked water on her. "I know. I just don't meet many Black women who ice skate. Roller skating, on the other hand, I can get with."

"I learned so that I could impress a girl I liked who was a figure skater."

"Ah, I see. Did it work?"

"Sort of. Her family was ultra conservative, so they weren't too keen on their daughter hanging out with a very tomboyish Black girl and she wasn't too keen on her parents knowing she liked girls. Fortunately, it turned out I liked skating and got good enough to join a girls' community hockey league. Played from middle school until I graduated high school."

"What happened to the girl?"

Paige grinned in amusement. "Last I heard she was in a marriage with two men and a woman living in an artists' commune in Arizona."

"Wow. Good thing you managed to avoid that drama."

"Yeah, I guess so."

They were both quiet for a moment with Ava gazing up at the sky and Paige looking at her wondering what it would be like to share evenings like this with her on a regular basis.

CHAPTER SEVENTEEN

Ava could practically feel Paige's heated gaze on her. She tore her own from the smattering of stars above to meet Paige's eyes.

"What are you thinking about?"

Paige hesitated before answering, then smiled. "You."

"What about me?"

"I'm wondering if I should give in to the urge to kiss you."

Ava's heartbeat quickened. "What's keeping you from doing it?"

"The possibility of making this arrangement more complicated."

Ava swam past Paige to where she could stand in the water then reached a hand toward her. Paige swam close enough to take it and allowed Ava to pull her forward until they stood mere inches from each other.

"I thought it might be best to be on solid ground in case you decided to give in to the urge so that neither of us drowns."

Paige grinned in amusement then gently grasped Ava's face with both hands and tilted it back before lowering her head to press her lips to Ava's. Paige ran the tip of her tongue over Ava's lips before coaxing them open for her to explore and taste further. Ava had been chilled when she'd stepped out of the water, but now she felt an internal heat spread from where their lips met throughout her body. She moaned under Paige's slow, sensual assault of lips, tongue, and then teeth nipping and grazing at hers. Ava wrapped her arms around Paige's waist, pressing her body to Paige's only for the heat within her to intensify at the skin-to-skin contact. It had been over two years since she'd been intimate with another woman. Now she felt like a starved woman being treated to a gourmet meal. She wanted to take it slow, to savor the moment, but her hunger had been unleashed and there was no turning back now.

She returned the kiss hungrily, forcing Paige to either stop or match Ava's passion. Ava almost sighed in relief when Paige gave just as much as she was being given. Ava whimpered when Paige's lips left hers to travel along her jawline, down her neck to her shoulder where she slid Ava's bra strap from her shoulder and replaced it with warm kisses before moving toward her cleavage. Ava gripped her tightly as she felt the wet lace material of her bra slide away from her breasts. Her nipples hardened almost painfully from exposure to the cool air, her arousal, or a combination of both, but it didn't matter when one was enveloped within the warmth of Paige's lips. Ava cried out passionately as she felt every nerve ending in her body come alive with need.

The cool air hit her exposed breast again as Paige shifted and whispered in her ear, "Why don't we take this back to the house?"

Ava shook her head. She felt so sensitive and throbbed so hard between her legs that she'd probably have an orgasm from walking. "Didn't you bring some blankets?"

Paige gave her that sexy grin she so loved and wrapped her arm around Ava's waist to lead her out of the water and up the embankment. Ava was relieved that she did because she was almost weak with desire and didn't know if she would've managed it on her own without falling on her face in the grass. Paige set her pile of neatly folded clothes next to the scattered pile of Ava's then spread both blankets out in the grass. She knelt and offered Ava a hand. Ava took it and knelt before her.

"Are you sure about this?" Paige asked.

"Yes," Ava said without hesitation.

Paige didn't even wait for her to second-guess herself as she grasped Ava's face again for another soul-stirring kiss. In the back of Ava's mind, she thought it interesting how Paige doing that made her feel all soft and gooey inside. Like taking Ava's face in her hands showed she was in control, and it turned Ava on further. She shifted to lay down on the blanket, bringing Paige with her. Paige dipped her head to take Ava's nipple in her mouth while her fingers tweaked and teased her other nipple. She moaned passionately, arching her back when Paige switched her hands and lips on her nipples. Ava's breaths came in frantic pants and her hips thrust at the air. Paige abandoned her teasing nipple play to slide her fingers down her abdomen and into the waist band of her panties. When her warm callused palms met the bare flesh beneath, Ava almost came right then and there. Her body shook with need, but she held on, not wanting to rush the moment no matter how much she ached to come. Then Paige's long finger slid over her pebble hard clit and dipped between her swollen lips, and she couldn't hold back her orgasm any more than she could physically hold back a breaking dam. Ava opened her mouth to cry out, but it was captured by Paige's covering hers for a kiss that made her orgasm feel as if it would never end.

When it finally subsided, she lay trembling from the aftershock and almost came again as Paige slowly withdrew her finger. She slid her hand from Ava's panties then reached over for the second blanket to cover them. Once she was finished, she lay on her side with her head propped on her hand smiling curiously at Ava.

"What?" Ava asked, suddenly feeling shy.

"Nothing. You're very sensitive."

Ava chewed on her bottom lip. "I haven't been intimate with anyone since my fake relationship with Kyle began."

Paige's eyes widened in surprise. "Really?"

Ava nodded, looking away from Paige and up at the night sky.

"Wow. So that was the first time you—"

"Yeah."

"Wow," Paige repeated.

A moment later, she was sitting up and reaching for her clothes.

Ava gazed up at her in confusion.

Paige stood and offered her a hand. "You might want to put some clothes on before we head back in view of the house cameras."

Ava did as Paige suggested but was still confused. Did she say something wrong? Had Paige been waiting for her to reciprocate, and she was too out of it to react quicker? She slipped her arms back into her bra and pulled her dress over her head. She didn't bother putting on her shoes and jacket, just held them in her arms as she waited for Paige to gather the blankets.

"Ready?" Paige asked.

"Uh, yeah, sure."

She nodded and headed for the entrance to the clearing. Too confused and slightly embarrassed to say anything, Ava just followed her. In the short walk to the house her confusion and embarrassment turned to anger. She'd never been ashamed by her boldness when it came to expressing herself sexually. If she found herself attracted to a woman and the feeling was mutual, what was the point in prolonging the inevitable with silly flirtatious games and awkward dinner dates. She believed in enjoying the moment when the moment arose. If they decided to see each other again, great, if they didn't, at least they a had mutually beneficial experience. Paige's abrupt ending of what Ava thought was going to be the start of a very beneficial experience for them both had her feeling like she'd read the whole situation wrong. But how could she have? Paige was the one who initiated it with admitting she wanted to kiss her. Ava just gave her what she wanted. She didn't force Paige to take things to the next level so there was no reason for her to feel bad about it.

Paige opened the back door and stepped aside to let Ava enter. She barely crossed the threshold before she angrily turned to Paige.

"I will not allow you to make me feel bad for what just happened. You wanted it just as much as I did so it's too late to suddenly regret it and act like it didn't happen."

Paige looked at her in confusion. "Whoa, what are you talking about? I don't regret anything."

"Then why are we in here instead of out there continuing what we started?"

A look of comprehension came across Paige's face. "I didn't think it would be right for you to be rolling around in the grass for your first sexual experience after two years of celibacy." She set the blankets on a stool at the kitchen island, then took Ava's shoes and jacket from her to place on top before taking her hand. "I thought a bed would be much more comfortable."

"Oh." Ava's face heated with embarrassment.

Paige gave her a sensual grin, leading her down the hallway toward her bedroom. Ava had been in Paige's bedroom earlier, but it was very brief, and she hadn't really looked around. It wasn't as large as the room she was using, but the décor and furnishings were warm and comfortable. The neatly made, four-poster, king-sized bed was the first thing seen upon entering the room and there was a smaller version of the fireplace and sitting area from Ava's room in this one. On the other side was the door to the walk-in closet she'd been in earlier and a bathroom.

Paige stopped near the bed and turned to her. "Did you really think I was the type of woman to leave things unfinished?"

She grasped the skirt of Ava's dress, slowly lifting it up her legs.

"No, but I could've been wrong." Ava trembled as Paige's fingertips brushed along her skin.

"Let's get you out of these wet clothes. Wouldn't want you to catch a chill."

"No, wouldn't want that," Ava said despite her body temperature rising as Paige's fingers continued their soft teasing along her hips and waist as she raised the dress higher.

Ava raised her arms so that Paige could completely remove her dress. She then tossed it onto the bench at the foot of her bed. Ava reached up to remove her bra, but Paige placed her hand over hers and shook her head.

"I respectfully acknowledge that you're a strong, independent woman who's used to being in control, but you're in my house which means I'm the one in control," she said in a low, sexy tone of voice that gave Ava shivers of anticipation.

Ava lowered her arms to her sides while Paige unclasped the front closure of her bra and slid the straps down her arms, then sent it sailing off to join her dress. Paige softly brushed her lips across Ava's before placing delicate kisses on her chin, down the column of her throat, and the space between her breasts, then kneeling to make her way down her abdomen until she met the lace barrier of Ava's panties. Ava's breath was coming out in pants then hitched when Paige began sliding the briefs down her hips.

"Hold on to me and lift your foot."

Ava placed a steadying hand on Paige's shoulder and lifted one foot then the other so that her panties could be removed to join the rest of her clothing. She barely placed her foot back on the floor when she felt Paige's warm breath on her belly before she pressed her lips against Ava's navel and began her ascent.

Paige didn't know how she'd managed to have such self-control considering how her body was screaming at her to speed things up to the part where she got her release. But there was something vulnerable about Ava having not been with another woman in such a long time. Even after she'd gone into hiding, she'd avoided intimacy, something

Paige understood since there would be long jaunts while she was on assignment in the military where she did the same thing to keep from getting too close to someone who would discover her identity. Ava was now trusting Paige enough to let her in when she hadn't done that with anyone else and Paige wasn't going to take that lightly. She could feel Ava's legs shaking as she gripped her hips to steady her while she gave her the most intimate of kisses. Ava whimpered and tangled her fingers in Paige's hair as she dipped her tongue between Ava's feminine lips. Paige moaned in pleasure from Ava's sweet, tangy taste combined with the fresh pond water and the sharp, clean scent that she recognized as the perfume Ava had begun wearing that drove her to distraction when they worked closely together.

Paige lost herself in the taste and scent that was Ava and wanted… no…needed more. She needed Ava laid out for her to fully enjoy. Hesitantly, she slowed her intimate kiss and gazed up at Ava whose eyes were closed, mouth was slightly agape, and chest was quickly rising and falling with her excited breathing. Paige felt like a slave kneeling at the feet of a goddess.

"Lie down," she commanded.

Ava's eyes slowly blinked open, and her gaze was soft and dreamy as she looked down at Paige and nodded before taking a wobbly step toward the bed. She sat then scooted herself up to lay back on the pillows. Paige stood in wonder for a moment finding it hard to believe that she not only had this fabulous woman in her bed but that she wasn't going to have to battle with who would be on top. Paige enjoyed receiving just as much as she did giving, but for a woman like Ava to allow herself to be soft and willing to concede control was like a mental aphrodisiac. She undressed quickly, leaving her clothes in a messy pile on the floor, something her neat freak mentality never did, and joined Ava on the bed.

She knelt at Ava's feet and ran her hands up her legs. "Where was I?"

Ava gave her a sexy smile and spread her legs. Paige settled between them, holding Ava's gaze as she lowered herself until she was able to continue what she'd begun. Ava's orgasm didn't come as quickly as it did at the pond, but it was close and much stronger than the last. Paige lapped up the flow hungrily as Ava's fingers tangled in her hair again, gripping her head tightly.

"OH FUUUU…" Ava called out, the exclamation turning into a silent scream as if she seemed to lose the ability to speak.

Ava was still shuddering with aftershocks when she pulled at Paige's shoulders. Paige joined her at the top of the bed but quickly found herself flat on her back with Ava straddling her hips and lowering her head toward hers. Ava kissed her greedily, as if the taste of herself on Paige's lips sent her into a frenzy. Paige barely had time to breathe before Ava was licking, nipping, and kissing her way down her body. She moaned loudly when Ava took one of her nipples into her mouth and rolled it around her tongue as she sucked. Paige's nipples were like an extension of her clit. Anything done to them seemed to travel along a direct route of pleasure sensors to that little pebble between her legs. Her hips moved as if they had a mind of their own as she ached to be touched down there. Ava must have read her mind because she released the other nipple that she had been teasing to slide her hand down Paige's body and met with the hardened nub. She dipped her finger into Paige's wetness then brought it back up to circle around her clit slowly at first then building a steady momentum as she tightened her circle. But just when Paige felt herself reaching the peak of pleasure, Ava would slow down and widen the circle again.

Paige's pleasure sensors were firing on full power when Ava decided to take her kisses to a more intimate level. Then she showed off her multitasking skills as her tongue delved in, out, and around Paige's pussy, while she teased and tweaked her clit with one hand and her nipple with the other. Paige's body was humming, or maybe it was her, she didn't know or care as the pleasure built to a crescendo and exploded in fireworks throughout her body. As Ava gentled then slowed her touch to a halt, Paige's body felt bereft despite the tremors she was still experiencing from her orgasm. Then Ava slid up to cover Paige's body with her own and lowered her head to share a kiss filled with their mingled taste. A fierce desire for and possessiveness of Ava rose within her. Paige had never felt such intense emotions like that for anyone and didn't know what to do with them except to shove them deep down in an imaginary box to open and analyze later. For now, she enjoyed the feeling of Ava shifting to cuddle at her side, her head resting in the crook of her neck as she traced random shapes on Paige's chest.

"What are you thinking about?" Paige asked.

"Why it took so long for this to happen."

"Because I was trying to keep it professional."

Ava lifted her head, looking at Paige curiously. "You've never mixed business with pleasure?"

"Once."

An image of a truck exploding and body parts and blood everywhere bombarded Paige's mind. She squeezed her eyes shut, breathed in for a silent count of four, held it for a count of seven, then let it out for a count of eight. When she opened her eyes Ava's gaze had softened with concern.

"I didn't mean to bring up bad memories."

Paige lifted her head to press a quick kiss to Ava's lips. "It's okay. What about you? Have you ever mixed business with pleasure?"

Ava gazed at her for another moment then smiled. "Probably more often than I should have. Fortunately, it hasn't backfired on me." She laid her head back onto Paige's shoulder.

Paige appreciated her for not pushing. She didn't want to ruin this by going to that dark place. "Were you seeing anyone before your arrangement with Kyle?"

Ava didn't answer right away.

"You don't have to answer that. I was just curious."

"I don't mind answering. I was just trying to figure out how to explain it. I wasn't seeing anyone seriously, but there was a woman who I spent time with often."

Paige chuckled. "So, you had a girlfriend."

"We didn't label the relationship. She lives in California, I'm in Chicago. We'd get together whenever our schedules allowed and that's it."

"Selena Carlyle?"

"Yes."

Paige could tell by the sadness in Ava's voice that there was more to their relationship than she was admitting, but she would return the favor and not push her to discuss it further. They lay quietly for a moment until Ava's stomach grumbled loudly.

"Don't tell me that after the fried feast we had that you're hungry again," Paige said.

"Well, technically, I didn't finish my feast because I wanted to make sure I tried everything so…"

Paige laughed. "Let me see what late night snack I can scrounge up. I'll be right back."

Paige hated having to leave the warmth and softness of Ava's body, but she was feeling a bit peckish herself. She grabbed an undershirt and underwear from the closet.

"Feel free to grab something to put on if you like, but I won't complain if you're still lying there in all your natural glory when I get back." She gave Ava a wink before leaving.

Ava enjoyed the view of Paige's taut butt outlined by her boxer briefs until she disappeared out the door then lay back with a dreamy sigh. That was the best sex she ever had and all because she allowed herself to just let go and not control and analyze every move or caress, which was what she tended to do every time she had sex, except with Selena. Although now that she thought about it, Selena always gave over control in the bedroom. She had to be such a badass all day to get the respect she deserved that most women in Hollywood were denied that by the time she got home she just wanted to decompress and allow herself to be submissive. They had even ventured into some soft bondage role-playing the last time they had been together, but not even that gave Ava the intense orgasms she'd just experienced with Paige. She now understood what Selena was probably feeling.

Ava frowned. She hadn't spoken to Selena since the wedding had been called off. Travis had promised to contact her to let her know what was going on. Since Ava didn't have the phone that she used before leaving Chicago she didn't have Selena's number which meant she would have to ask Travis for it, so she hadn't asked about Selena to avoid the temptation to call her. To be honest with herself, the real reason was because living a life so different from what she'd run away from made her disconnect from things in her real life that weren't of vital importance to her. Her focus had been her family and staying under the radar. Selena hadn't crossed her mind as often as she would've thought considering their relationship had been the longest romantic relationship Ava ever had with a woman, despite its on-again, off-again status.

Ava was surprised at the lack of guilt she felt at the realization, but it was obvious from what she had seen in the various celebrity news stories over the past year that Selena had moved on with her life. She and her male costar from a film she was currently working on had been linked together for the past six months. Photos and video of them holding hands, kissing, and canoodling on set or in a car had brought on pangs of jealousy in the beginning, but after a few weeks, jealousy turned to relief. Selena looked happy and that's all that mattered. If she and Ava had decided to make their relationship exclusive maybe there wouldn't have been a need for her father to ask for the fake relationship with Kyle. Then again, since Kyle was more than likely responsible for the attempts on her family's lives there was no telling how Selena would have been hurt because of her connection to Ava. In the end, everything worked out for the best.

Ava shook the sadness away and hopped out of bed to find something to put on. She considered putting her dress back on, but it was still damp from her wet undergarments, so she did as Paige suggested and rummaged through her dresser for a T-shirt. She couldn't find anything big enough to cover her enough not to have to wear underwear, so she chose one of Paige's soft cotton flannel shirts. It was just what she was looking for. The hem hit just at mid-thigh, and she rolled the long sleeves up to her elbow. Just as she exited the closet, Paige entered carrying a tray.

She stopped and smiled at Ava appreciatively. "That shirt has never looked so good."

Ava did a little turn. "I could put a fancy rodeo belt around the waist, grab one of your cowboy hats and some boots and it'll be a hit for all those cowgirl bedroom fantasies."

Paige chuckled as she walked toward the sitting area. She placed the tray on the coffee table then went to the fireplace. Ava took a seat on the sofa, folding her legs under her and watching as Paige got a nice fire going. When Paige joined her, she sat on the floor and picked up two water bottles from the tray, offering one to Ava. There was also a bowl of fresh berries, a plate with slices of the pound cake Paige had made the other day, and a bowl of whipped cream.

"I thought this might be a good option for a light late-night snack." Paige handed her an empty bowl.

Ava took the bowl then slid off the sofa onto the floor with Paige. "Your pound cake is so good I would've been fine with just that, but I'm not going to say no to berries and whipped cream."

They both placed a slice of the pound cake in their bowls with a scoop of berries and dollops of whipped cream.

Ava took a bite and sighed with pleasure. Paige had made her own whipped cream spiked with brandy. With the moist pound cake and fresh berries, it was almost as good as sex. Almost.

"It's nice to see someone besides Adele and her house full of men enjoy my baking. I always think they're just being nice when they tell me how much they like it."

There was a hint of insecurity in Paige's tone, which surprised Ava. She always seemed so self-assured.

"I seriously doubt they were just being nice. Your baking is banging. You should've opened a bakery instead of a detective agency."

"Nah, then I wouldn't enjoy it so much." She reached up to wipe something away from Ava's cheek with her thumb then licked it off her finger.

Ava's clit throbbed in response. Paige smiled as if she knew the affect that she had on her. She took both of their bowls, placed them on the table, scooped whipped cream onto her fingertip, and offered it to Ava. Ava met her challenging gaze, leaned forward, and wrapped her lips around Paige's finger, circled it with her tongue until all the whipped cream was gone and continued sucking on her finger for a moment longer. That was the beginning of a sticky but very enjoyable hour of play in front of the fireplace before they climbed into bed and Ava fell contentedly asleep wrapped in Paige's arms.

CHAPTER EIGHTEEN

Paige had been watching Ava sleep and listening to her adorably soft snores for the past half hour. She could count on one hand how many times she'd spent an entire night with a woman, let alone looking forward to being there when she woke up. She liked the idea of being the first person Ava laid eyes on upon awakening. To be the first to wish her a good morning. Paige knew, at that moment, that she was well and truly hooked by Ava Prescott and she had no idea what to do about it. Paige had never felt such strong feelings for any of the women she'd dated previously. The longest romantic relationship she ever had was a year with a girl she dated her last year in high school. Paige had received a Dear Jane letter from her just a few weeks into boot camp. At the time, it was the most devastating feeling she could imagine. At least until she did her first tour in Iraq. Her schoolgirl heartbreak felt more like a splinter compared to the stake wedged in her heart after watching fellow soldiers die in combat.

Ava smiled softly in her sleep. Paige wondered if she dreamt of her, then laughed at herself for such a sappy thought. Then Ava sleepily blinked her eyes open.

"Good morning," she said with a happy grin.

Paige's heart skipped a beat. "Good morning. How'd you sleep?"

Ava stretched. "Best sleep I've had in a long while." She shifted forward to give Paige a soft kiss. "Thank you."

Paige scooted close enough to press her body against Ava's. "My pleasure. So, did I earn one of your famous morning-after breakfasts?"

Ava reached over and grasped a handful of Paige's behind. "Oh, definitely. I'm talking veggie omelet, crispy bacon, pancakes, and fresh fruit."

"Well damn, in that case, let's go!" Paige flung the covers off their nude bodies, rolled over on top of Ava, planted a loud kiss on her lips, and scrambled out of bed.

Ava squealed and pulled the covers back over her leaving just her wide amber eyes peeking above them. "What's the rush?"

"Let's see, it's already seven, I'm sure Lucy and Ethel have probably gotten their stall open and are probably on their way to Adele's garden, and I need to go into town to run some errands."

Ava tossed the covers back off with a sigh. "If it weren't for fear that Adele really would turn them into goat stew if they destroyed her garden, I would lie here for another hour." She got up and went to the end of the bed to pick up her clothes.

Paige rushed up and grabbed her from behind before she could reach the door. "Where are you going?"

"To shower."

Paige grasped Ava's hips and kissed the nape of her neck. "My shower is big enough for two."

Ava arched her back to press her behind to Paige's pelvis. "I think it would be best to go back to my room. If I stay here to shower, then we won't leave for some time."

Paige sighed regretfully. "I guess you're right. I'll see you in the kitchen."

She gave Ava's butt a slap then walked to the bathroom, looking over her shoulder, and giving Ava a wink before closing the door. Paige gazed at her reflection in the mirror. Apart from the goofy grin that she couldn't seem to wipe away, she looked the same. There was no glow of love that the romantics said you got when you've met THE ONE. Just the grin, the lightness in her heart, and the goose bumps that appeared when she thought about the taste and touch of Ava.

"You are well and truly fucked," Paige said to herself. With a smile still in place, she went over to turn on the shower. "Alexa, play 'Lay It On Me' by Mickey Guyton."

She sang along to the country ballad that Ava always insisted on having Alexa repeat whenever it played. Although she acted annoyed when it happened, Paige secretly loved the song. After her night with Ava, the song seemed to hit her heart a little deeper than usual and she sang along as she showered. It was about a woman telling her lover that she would love them no matter what they're going through. That she would take all the good, bad, and imperfections so that she could show them that they were worth it. She asked that they trust her and lay all their burdens on her.

Paige had a feeling that despite Ava's tough girl exterior that she wanted to find a love and settle down just as much as she did, but they were also both too afraid to put themselves out there. Most of Paige's fear had to do with burdening someone with the darkness she carried that frightened even her at times. She would love to be able to trust enough to lay it on someone, but for now she would take whatever this was that she and Ava had started and hope that it didn't blow up in her face.

After her shower, Ava stood smiling dreamily at her reflection in the bathroom mirror. Last night was not what she had expected. It wasn't just the mind-blowing sex but how the whole evening with Paige affected her physically and emotionally. The feelings Ava had been attempting to shove aside the past couple of weeks now refused to be ignored. Their evening at the carnival, making out at the pond, then spending practically the entire night in a haze of pleasure that more than made up for Ava's years of celibacy had her feeling like a horny teenager experiencing love for the first time. She turned on the bathroom sound system from the keypad by the door to a music streaming service and chose to play what had become her new favorite song, "Lay It On Me" by Mickey Guyton. She lip-synced the song as she sat on a stool moisturizing her body with a green tea scented lotion that Paige had mentioned she liked the scent of one day last week. It was from a gift basket by one of her favorite luxury brands that her mother had sent to Adele to give to her.

Ava wondered if Paige was doing anything special that she knew would draw her attention, although if she thought about it, all Paige had to do lately was be in the same room with her and Ava got distracted. Watching the ripple of muscle in Paige's forearms when she tossed hay bales, the way her ass looked in jeans, the adorable way she spoke to the animals as if they were humans, and how sexy she looked riding Zorro. It all sent Ava's pulse racing and her face heating with a blush whenever Paige happened to catch her staring like she was a starved child looking through the window of a sweet shop. Now her heart seemed to be in the mix, and she was feeling emotions she'd never felt before and liked it.

The idea of sharing a life like this with Paige would have sent her running for the hills three weeks ago, but now it had become very appealing. Waking up to have Paige looking at her the way she did this morning, working side-by-side taking care of the ranch, enjoying little outings like they did last night to come back to their own secluded little paradise was something she could get used to.

Ava went into the closet to find something to wear. Could she really turn away from the life she had worked so hard for to live on a ranch in Oklahoma to be with the woman she loved? Ava stared wide-eyed at the T-shirt she'd picked out to wear. Love? Is that what this was? Couldn't she mistakenly be confusing desire for love? Yes, she had to be. There was no way she'd fallen in love with Paige after only a few weeks together. That stuff only happened in the romances she read from Paige's library. Real life didn't work that way. It had to be due to their proximity and the amount of time they spent together that was confusing things. She had no problem admitting that she enjoyed Paige's company or that she found her interesting and fascinating but saying that it was love was a stretch. At least that's what she was going to tell herself to avoid the issue of how to deal with it when it came time for her to leave. Ava shook her head and chose to focus on now and worry about the rest later. She quickly dressed and headed for the kitchen to make breakfast as promised. When she got there the digital whiteboard on the refrigerator had a note that read, *Gone to feed the menagerie, Dr. Doolittle.*

Ava chuckled. Another thing she liked about Paige was that she was a confident woman but not so much that she couldn't take a little fun ribbing or laugh at herself sometimes. Ava gathered everything she needed and whipped up a breakfast worthy of last night's endeavors. Just as she was filling a pitcher with fresh squeezed orange juice courtesy of an electric juicer, Paige entered through the back door.

Ava almost sighed dreamily at the sight of her but caught herself. "You're just in time."

Paige leaned against the doorway to take off her boots. "Took a little longer than I expected. On the way to the barn, I noticed the gate to the garden was open and found Lucy and Ethel munching on some kale. Fortunately, I caught them before they could do much damage. I tried to clear out the evidence, but you know Adele. She knows that garden like the back of her hand."

Ava shook her head. "Those two are determined to end up in a pot. I'm telling you right now that if I smell anything that resembles a stew I'm leaving."

Paige chuckled and went to the sink to wash her hands. "I think they're safe. Adele has been threatening them since she started that garden. I think they think it's a game because they never eat more than what they did this morning."

Ava set two place settings at the kitchen island where they usually ate breakfast. "I'll take your word for it."

She filled two mugs with coffee and two glasses with the orange juice then set them next to the plates before taking a seat beside Paige. They filled their plates, reaching and moving around each other like they had been doing this forever. Paige knew to give Ava the pepper after she used it instead of setting it back on the counter and Ava knew to place a jar of jam next to Paige's plate because she knew she preferred that to syrup on her pancakes.

"How are the rest of the menagerie doing? Did I mention we're almost out of cat food?" Ava caught the way she said *we* as if she and Paige were a couple. She kept eating, hoping Paige hadn't caught it.

"They're all good, although I think Brutus was hoping to see you this morning, and I'll pick up a case of food when I go into town after breakfast."

Ava frowned. "I don't know what that beast's obsession is with me."

"Maybe he sees you as his beauty." Paige sounded amused.

"Well, he's out of luck and not my type."

"What is your type?"

Ava glanced over at Paige who picked up her mug and seemed to concentrate a little too much on sipping her coffee.

Ava looked back down at her plate with a grin. "I like women who are confident in themselves and aren't afraid to do and say what they want if it isn't to be cruel. I've also been drawn to other feminine women. I think it has to do with the fact that many of the butch and masculine-presenting women I've dated ended up butting heads over who presents as what. I think it throws them off that I present as a femme but come off as masculine in the way I treat women I date."

Paige turned in her seat to face Ava. "I don't think you come off as masculine at all. People tend to confuse a strong woman with trying to be masculine, but I don't believe that's true. I think every woman, feminine or masculine-presenting, has both traits within them. We all have moments when being soft and vulnerable is needed just as much as being hard and strong. You work in a world mostly controlled by men, so you've had to adapt, but I've also seen you soften when the situation called for it."

Ava suddenly felt shy about having been seen so easily by Paige. "What about you? I'm sure the military isn't the best place for a woman to be seen as soft and vulnerable."

Paige snorted in derision. "Definitely not. Espccially as a Marine. But, like you, I adapted when the situation called for it. Sometimes, going in with guns blazing will only aggravate a tense situation. That's when reason and a soft hand are called for. As much as I hate to admit it, sometimes a pretty face and smile are more effective weapons than a gun."

Ava cocked her head to the side as she gazed at Paige. "You do have a killer smile."

Paige gave an exaggerated frown. "Maybe I should keep it holstered. Wouldn't want to have to explain to your family that I accidently smiled you to death."

Ava slid off her stool and stood in front of Paige. "I think I can withstand your charm with only some minor bruising."

Paige grasped her around the waist and pulled her close. "Then I'll have to save all my smiles just for you." She gave her a sexy grin before lowering her head to press her lips to Ava's.

It wasn't a chaste kiss and Ava's legs felt weak from the onslaught of passion. When an alarm beeped Paige slowly ended the kiss, resting her forehead to Ava's as they both seemed to need to catch their breath.

"That was the signal for the front gate opening. I guess Willie's here," Paige said.

"Guess so." Ava hesitantly stepped out of Paige's embrace to sit back on the stool.

She thought it was funny how they both turned back to their food as if all they'd been doing was enjoying breakfast as Willie peeked in the back door before walking in.

"G'morning, ladies. I couldn't resist the smell of bacon and coffee calling to me," he said with a grin.

Ava smiled back at him. "Good morning, Willie. Help yourself, there's plenty."

"I'm pretty sure Adele fed you before you left," Paige said teasingly.

He took a small thermos from the cabinet to fill with coffee. "Yes, she did. Biscuits with gravy, as a matter of fact, but that doesn't mean I can't enjoy a little mid-morning snack." Then he filled his thermos with coffee, grabbed a few slices of bacon, gave them a nod and a wink, and headed back out the door.

"Well, I believe that's my cue to exit as well," Paige said before taking another bite of pancakes then sliding off the stool. "Want some help cleaning up before I go?"

"No, I got it."

"Okay." Paige gave her a brief kiss. "I'll see you later."

Ava couldn't hold back a happy smile. "See you later."

Paige's smile was just as broad as she walked away. Ava watched her as she grabbed her keys then gave a final wave before leaving.

Paige found she couldn't stop smiling the entire drive into town. Even when she stopped by the bank her mood was jovial which had Raven watching her suspiciously from her desk. Paige gave her a friendly wave and chose to go to a teller window rather than accept personal service from the younger woman. Once her business was finished there, she stopped at the grocery store to pick up cat food and ran into Junior.

They left together. "So, how's your houseguest? My mother sounds about ready to adopt her."

"She's good."

"Uh-huh. Judging by the grin on your face I'd say she's more than that."

Paige gave him a look of warning but found she couldn't put much threat behind it with the urge to keep smiling taking some of the heat out of it.

"Hey, I'm not criticizing. We've known each other since we were kids. It's just good to see you not looking so serious and intimidating."

"Yeah, well, she's probably leaving in a few weeks so I'm just enjoying the moment."

"Nothing wrong with that either."

Paige's phone dinged with an alarm notification. She pulled it out of her pocket and opened the app for the ranch's security system. "Shit!"

"What's wrong?"

"I need to get back to the ranch. It looks like something triggered the keypad on the west gate."

"You need backup?"

"Yes, if it's not an inconvenience."

"No, not at all. Are you sure it isn't those crazy goats of yours trying to make an escape?"

"No. The notification was for the keypad being tampered with. That's too high for them to reach and unfortunately the battery for the camera at that gate died a few days ago and I haven't gotten around to replacing it."

Normally Paige was a stickler for ensuring all the security on the ranch was in working order, but the cameras were on a motion sensor and the west gate bordered the forest, so there was a lot of animal traffic on both sides of the fence causing it to be frequently triggered, which gave that camera's battery a shorter lifespan than the others. She checked the other cameras on the property through the app and didn't see anything suspicious. They split up as Paige went to her truck and Junior jogged across the road to the municipal building where his truck was parked. Paige texted Willie to let him know about the notification and that she would meet him at the west gate. They arrived at the gate from the side road twenty minutes later. Willie waited on the other side of the fence leaning against the golf cart holding the shotgun by his side that Paige recognized from the cache she kept in the barn. He walked toward the gate and opened it for her.

"You find anything?" she asked.

"Yeah, footprints from and back into the forest leading to ATV tracks by the stream," Willie said worriedly then turned to acknowledge Junior. "Junior."

Junior gave his father a nod. "Pops."

Paige gazed up at the camera placed in a nearby tree then marched over and began climbing.

"I could get the ladder from the shed," Willie offered.

"No, it would take too long. I'm good."

She used nubs left over from the lower branches that had been cut off to help clear a path to the stream as foot- and handholds as she climbed. After pulling herself up on to the thick branch that the camera was mounted on, she opened the case and found that the camera hadn't died but the battery pack had been completely removed.

"Damn," she said to herself then placed the battery cover back and climbed down. "The battery pack was removed."

Willie frowned. "You thinking what I'm thinking?"

Paige nodded. "We've been compromised."

"You think the people looking for your friend found you?" Junior asked.

"Too many coincidences for it not to be them."

"What's your plan?" Willie asked.

"I need to look at the footage before the camera battery was stolen then spend the rest of the day shoring up our defenses. They've obviously been doing recon, or they would've hit us already. I figure we've got at least two to three days before they make their move," Paige said.

"I agree. I'll head back and check the tunnels and caches in the outer buildings to make sure everything is in working order," Willie said.

"I'll head back and reach out to my connections to find out if they've spotted anyone suspicious or new in the area," Junior said.

That gave Paige both a sense of relief and worry. Relief that she may soon have a face to watch out for and worried about the lack of manpower she had to protect Ava. She had no doubt that after saving Ava from Kyle's kidnapping plan twice, that he would be sending more than a couple of guys to finish the job.

"Great, thanks, Junior."

He gave her and Willie a nod before getting in his truck and heading back to the main road.

"I'm going to head back to the house to grab my print kit and see if I can lift any besides ours to send to Ezekiel for tracing. Let's meet back at the workshop for a debrief."

Willie nodded and climbed back into the golf cart. Paige secured the gate, deciding she would change the code for all of them once she got back to the house. She was going to have to tell Ava. There was no way she was keeping this news from her. When she arrived, the house was empty. She almost worried until she remembered that Ava was probably helping Adele in the garden. She went out back to the garden and noticed two sunhat-covered heads amongst the greenery. Ava spotted her first, giving her a sweet smile and wave. Paige returned the wave and tried putting her mouth into some semblance of a cheerful smile as she entered into the garden. Ava met her halfway with a basket full of blackberries.

"We managed to get the last batch of the season. Adele is going to show me how to make preserves. You may have to take video because no one at home is going to believe me when I tell them." Ava sounded as if she couldn't believe it herself.

She looked adorable in her floppy sunhat, gardening apron with the necessary tools sticking out of the pockets, and a pair of Crocs she must have borrowed from Adele. It took immense willpower for Paige not to pull Ava into her arms for a kiss that would make them forget, for a little while, what the outside world had in store for them. She didn't care who was behind recent events, but she would make them regret bringing stress and fear into her sanctuary.

"We need to talk," Paige said.

Ava's smile slipped away. She gazed back at Adele who was looking down at her phone with a frown. Paige guessed that Willie must have filled her in on what was happening.

Ava looked back at Paige worriedly. "What's going on?"

"It may be nothing but some troublesome assholes. The camera and security pad at the west gate were tampered with."

"You don't think it's troublesome assholes, do you? That's why you're telling me."

"No, I don't."

Ava looked around nervously. Paige hated seeing that look on her face after all these weeks. She took the basket from Ava, set it on the ground, and pulled her into an embrace. "You're safe here. I'm not going to let anything happen to you. I promise."

Ava's arms came around her and held tight. "I've trusted you this long, I'm not going to stop now."

Paige's heart felt so full at Ava's words. She separated them just enough to be able to look her in the face. "I have some things I need to check on and to call Ezekiel to fill him in, but can you meet me at the range in a half hour?"

"Of course."

"Good."

Paige gave her an encouraging smile followed by a brief kiss before hesitantly releasing her and heading back to the house. She knew she shouldn't have made Ava that promise, but she would do everything in her power to keep the woman she loved safe.

Chapter Nineteen

Ava wished she could rewind the clock to last night when she lay cuddled against Paige's side on the sofa in front of the fireplace basking in the afterglow of sex. She became angry that the sense of security and, dare she admit it, contentment she'd felt over the past few weeks had been shattered. She had hoped that with Kyle on the run it meant he had given up on his vendetta against her family. She'd racked her brain when all of this began trying to figure out what he had against them. Was it just plain old greed? Was there a connection to her family that her father wasn't aware of? What could her family have possibly done to him to make him so determined to bring them down? Whatever his reason there was no way for her to find out until this craziness came to an end.

When she finished helping Adele, Ava made her way to Paige's workshop and indoor range. Paige was already there when she arrived. She could see her in the prep room of the range through the glass door separating the workshop from the range area.

Paige smiled at her entrance. "I know last night you mentioned wanting to come here for a little friendly competition."

Ava quirked a brow. "Is this your way of distracting me from what's going on?"

"No. I figured it's been a while since you've been to the range, and this would be a good time to brush up on your skills in case something happens where I'm not around to protect you." She opened a small gun carrying case that held a Smith & Wesson .22 Caliber compact pistol. "Ezekiel mentioned he'd trained you on .22s so I thought it might be easier getting you back into the swing of things with this one."

Ava looked down at the gun then frowned at Paige. "Why would you not be around to protect me? Wasn't that what you were hired to do?" Ava could hear the panic in her voice. She was sure Paige probably did also.

Paige reached out and took her hands. "There's no need to worry. I don't plan on leaving you alone, but what if you're in the house while I'm on another part of the ranch and you find yourself needing to do whatever is necessary to protect yourself before I can get to you?"

Ava knew what she said made sense, but fear had her wanting Paige to never leave her side for as long as it took for all this to be over. She knew that wasn't possible, so she bucked up and put her big girl panties on to make the best of the situation.

"I prefer a revolver, but the pistol will be fine."

Paige grinned in amusement. "That's good to know. I have a revolver, but it's locked in the gun safe back at the house. I keep these here at the range since they're the ones I practice with the most."

She opened a second case that held an M&P Bodyguard .380. The only reason Ava recognized it was because it was the same gun Ezekiel carried.

"Ready whenever you are," Ava said.

Paige nodded, closed the cases, and carried them through the door that led to the room where four stalls and the actual range were located. She placed the gun case for Ava into one stall and the other in the stall beside it then walked to a cabinet, unlocked it, and removed two boxes of ammunition.

She went back to Ava and handed her a box of .22 caliber rounds. "I'm assuming you know how to load the gun."

Ava accepted the box. "Yes, thank you."

She laid them on the shelf next to the gun case, opened the case, took out the magazine, and loaded ten rounds. Once she was finished, she picked up the gun and slid the magazine into place before setting it on the shelf with the barrel pointing down range. She looked back at Paige who offered her a pair of ear plugs.

"Thank you."

While she put them in Paige set up a target of a male silhouette pointing a gun then sent it five feet down range and stepped aside.

"Whenever you're ready," Paige said.

Ava took her place, picked up the gun, making sure to keep it pointed down range, lined up the site with the target in the middle of the silhouette's torso, and pulled the trigger. The first shot went wide of the center bull's-eye. The second went closer. Since this wasn't her gun, she had to make an adjustment with lining up the site a little more off center than she aimed her personal gun and the third shot hit center mass. The remaining seven did the same. Once the magazine was empty, she laid the gun back on the shelf and turned to meet Paige's impressed expression.

"Nice."

"Thanks. I don't know how well I'll be able to do that shooting at a real person but hopefully I won't have to find out."

"You'd be surprised what you can do when it's either you or the person pointing a gun at you. It may not be war but it's still a matter of life or death. Your life or death."

Ava knew Paige spoke from experience, but she still had her doubts that she would be able to shoot somebody if it came down to it.

Paige shouldn't have been surprised at how great a shot Ava was considering who trained her, but the fact that she automatically knew what adjustment she needed to make was impressive. There wasn't much advice she needed to give Ava regarding stationary targets, so she turned on the moving targets at the back of the range. A paper life-size male silhouette holding a handgun slid out from the right-side wall on a track and settled down range in Ava's line of sight.

"There will be three beeps. At the third beep the target will move toward you and doesn't stop until you hit it," Paige explained. "It doesn't have to be a deadly hit, just one that would injure a normal person enough to slow them down or stop them."

"Okay." Ava looked at the target skeptically.

"Ready?"

Ava raised her gun. "Yes."

Ava's shoulders tensed after the first beep.

"Breathe, Ava. It's just a target."

Ava took a shaky breath just before the third beep ended and the target began sliding on the track toward her. That's when her nerves got the best of her. After a few jerky shots, one of which grazed the side of the silhouette, then the next two missed completely, she froze until the target slid to a stop directly in front of the stall. Ava put the gun down and stepped back. Her hands shook as she stared fearfully at the target.

"I-I can't do this." Her voice trembled.

Paige came up behind her, turned her around, and took her hands. They were ice-cold. She rubbed them with her own to warm them up.

"That's fine. Why don't you take a break while I get some practice time in. There's a beverage fridge in the outer room and snacks in the cabinet next to it."

Ava nodded wordlessly, slipped her hands from Paige's, and left the stall. Paige watched her walk through the door into the other room then stepped up, sent the target back down range, changed it from a countdown to a random start, picked up Ava's gun, and waited. A moment later the target sped toward her and was stopped before it got a foot from its starting point by the remaining seven shots landing in the stomach, chest, and between the eyes in quick succession. She then removed the magazine, made sure there were no bullets in the chamber and placed the gun and magazine back in the case. Too concerned about Ava to get some time in with her own gun, Paige placed the boxes of ammo back in the cabinet and took the gun cases out with her to the front room. Ava sat at the table looking dejectedly down at an unopened bottle of water. Paige placed the gun cases on a counter and sat in the chair beside her.

"You okay?"

Ava shrugged. "Hours spent at the gun range with Ezekiel or in Krav Maga classes and I get freaked out by a paper target coming at me." She gazed up at Paige, her eyes brimming with unshed tears. "What would have happened if you weren't there with me that night?"

Paige grasped one of her hands on top of the table. "You would have done whatever you needed to do to survive. If that meant being cooperative instead of fighting back to keep from being harmed, then that's what you do. Sometimes the best defense tactics call for a retreat so that you can regroup and come back with a better plan. Besides, you handled yourself better than most would have when you disarmed the gunman."

"If he hadn't been distracted by you that probably wouldn't have happened."

"But it did and we're here now because of you and your quick thinking." A tear slid down Ava's cheek. Paige gently wiped it away with the pad of her thumb.

"What about now. What if you aren't with me or, God forbid, you get hurt and I need to protect us? How do I do that if I'm too squeamish to shoot someone? You're a soldier at heart. I'm a negotiator. These people aren't looking to negotiate."

"Ava, I wasn't always a soldier. None of the training my father or boot camp provided could prepare me for the first time my unit came under attack while driving an escort through a village in Iraq. That first bullet that whizzes by you so close you can see it out of the corner of your eye, that moment you start seeing your fellow soldiers falling, grown men screaming for their mothers, and then someone shoves a gun in your hand and tells you to shoot or die. All I could think about was that I wasn't supposed to be there. I was just a grunt picking up an officer to escort from one base to another. My slap in the face was a bullet grazing my arm and leaving a neat little hole in my sleeve. I can honestly say I don't remember much of what happened except I was shooting at anyone who didn't have a United States military uniform on."

Paige could still recall the smoke from explosions burning her eyes, the screams of her fellow soldiers, the scent and taste of iron in the air from all the blood like it was yesterday. She felt Ava squeeze her hand and shook the scene from her head.

"What I'm trying to say is, there's nothing wrong with being scared. You've proven you have good instinct. Rely on that if you find yourself in a situation you might not feel comfortable dealing with."

Ava's tears had dried. "Thank you." She gave Paige a smile of appreciation.

"You're very welcome. Now, let's see if we can avoid you having to make such a decision by showing you the reason Grant calls the ranch a fortress."

Paige spent the next hour giving Ava the behind-the-scenes tour of the ranch with all its hidden exits, secret tunnels, and caches of weapons. She seemed most shocked by the tunnel entrance in her closet opened by a hidden button that swung the lower section of shelves holding her shoes outward to reveal a crawl space with a ladder leading into a tunnel.

"This is like something straight out of a movie," Ava said in amazement.

"If, for some reason, you're not able to get out of your room you can use the tunnel to go to my room or the barn. All the tunnel branches lead to one main tunnel into the barn." Paige explained.

"How would I know what tunnel to take?"

"Once you reach the bottom of the ladder there will be two paths. Straight ahead is the tunnel leading to my closet. To the right is the one to the barn."

Paige gazed over at Ava who was looking at the dimly lit crawl space as if something were about to jump out at her. She pressed the button to close the hidden door then offered Ava her hand. "I believe there's enough pound cake left for us to top it off with the ice cream Adele bought when she did the shopping."

Ava stared at the now closed shelving for a moment then shook her head. She gazed at Paige with fear still in her eyes but attempted a tremulous smile as she took her hand. "Top that off with the hot fudge I saw in the pantry and you've got a deal."

Just as they arrived in the kitchen, Paige's phone buzzed in her pocket. She answered the call without leaving the room, not seeing any reason to keep Ava out of the loop. "Hey, Ezekiel"

"Paige, I just got your message. I was in a remote area with little to no cell service. Has there been an update since you left it?"

"No. I've switched the cameras from motion detection to 24/7 surveillance, my contact at the sheriff's office is on alert, and we've battened down the hatches here so if any trouble comes our way, we're ready."

"That's good. I have an update of my own. We found the connection between Kyle and the Prescotts."

"Hold on, Ava should hear this."

"What's going on?" Ava asked anxiously.

"Let's go to my office. Ezekiel has some information to share."

When they arrived at her office, she put her phone on speaker. "Okay, Ezekiel."

"Hey, Uncle Zeke," Ava said.

"Hey, how's my favorite girl doing?" Ezekiel's voice was filled with affection.

"Worried and anxious to get home."

"Paige been taking good care of you?"

Ava gave Paige a soft smile. "Yes, she's my very own knight in cowboy boots."

Ezekiel's chuckle came across the line. "Well, hopefully we'll have you home soon. As I told Paige, we've found out how Kyle is connected to your family."

❖

Ava felt some sense of relief. "Hopefully you're not about to tell me he's my brother from another mother," she said, only partially joking. There was a loud guffaw of laughter in the background that she recognized immediately. "Is that Uncle Max?"

"Yes." Ezekiel sounded exasperated.

Ava grinned in amusement. Her uncle was like the annoying little brother Ezekiel never wanted. Max knew just what buttons to push with both him and her father and she could only imagine how crazy he must've been driving Ezekiel during all this.

"Hey, Uncle Max!"

"Hey, baby girl! Your mother pretty much said the same thing," he said in the background.

A tired sigh came over the line. "Can I continue?" Ezekiel said, sounding as if he were talking to Max instead of them.

Ava looked at Paige who was also grinning in amusement.

"Okay, as you know, Kyle's real name is Curtis Wilson, but that wasn't the name he was given at birth. That was Curtis William Dutton Jr.," Ezekiel said.

"Why does that name sound familiar?" Ava racked her brain but couldn't place the name.

"It was the same name as one of the original partners of the firm your father first started, Prescott Financials."

Ava nodded. "I remember Mom telling me about him when I found a picture of Dad, Uncle Max, and a man I'd never seen before standing in front of an office door with a plaque that read Prescott Financial Partners. She told me Dutton and Dad were best friends in college with similar backgrounds and goals which was why Dad brought him in as a partner. Then he was caught skimming money, but in lieu of pressing charges, Dad offered to buy him out because he and his wife were expecting a baby and he didn't want to be responsible for a child not having their father. Mom said he refused to even mention his name after that. She was surprised he still had the picture. I don't even think he remembered having it because I found it in the bottom of a box of old photos in the family room."

"Yeah, Marcus was devastated by Curtis's betrayal especially since he considered Curtis family and wouldn't have hesitated to give him money to bail him out of any financial trouble that he was in. Curtis had a penchant for gambling that he'd sworn to Marcus he had under control. Turns out he was using the money he was stealing from the company to pay off debts he'd incurred through gambling. When Marcus found out he completely cut Curtis out of his life. Curtis's life hit rock bottom shortly after that. From what my government contact was able to find out, Curtis couldn't find work in the financial field because Marcus refused to give a referral to potential employers, his wife left them when Kyle was still a toddler, and he killed himself when Kyle was just fourteen."

Knowing how serious her father was about loyalty, Ava could imagine how angry and hurt he must've been and seen what Curtis did as an unforgivable betrayal. "So, do you think Kyle blames my family and is looking for payback?"

"Could be," Ezekiel said.

Ava felt a bit of sadness over what Kyle must have gone through but not enough to forgive what he'd done to her family.

"How was he able to obtain a new identity at such a young age while in the foster care system?" Paige asked.

"The Kyle Edwards identity didn't come until after he graduated high school. It seems Curtis was a tech wizard. By his senior year he was the head of a gang of internet scammers swindling old people out of money and installing card readers on ATMs. He'd only been caught once a couple of years prior to that which is the juvie record in his background and what he'd transferred over when he stole the real Kyle Edwards' identity, a twelve-year-old killed in a drive-by. He pretty much lived a double life. Committing tech and white-collar crimes as Curtis Wilson a second alias, and living the preppy scholar as Kyle," Ezekiel explained.

"Is that how he was able to track me down in New Orleans despite all of Travis's safeguards?" Ava asked worriedly.

"I wouldn't doubt it. It's also how he's probably tracked you guys down there. It may have taken him a little longer because of Paige's safeguards put in place by my team, but there's always a way around things if you know the right people and Kyle knows the right people."

"I'm assuming in the criminal world because I can't imagine he knows any legit techs that would help him," Paige said, looking annoyed. "How were you able to find all of this out?"

"We managed to track down Cathy. She's serving time in a state prison in Alabama for jumping bail and evading a warrant. She's been

Kyle's ride-or-die in his criminal enterprises for the past ten years. He took off and left her high and dry, so she told us everything," Ezekiel said.

"A woman scorned," Max chimed in from the background.

"Anyway," Ezekiel said in annoyance again. "Unfortunately, she couldn't tell us where he might've gone, but I guess we already know if the trouble you're having has to do with him. I'm sending my guys from Tulsa your way for backup."

"No, not yet. Give me a couple of days to make sure the issues aren't coming from another source. Once I confirm that, I'll contact you and you can send whoever you like," Paige said.

"Are you sure?" Ezekiel asked.

"Yeah. If it is Kyle, Curtis, or whoever he wants to be called, I think they were just testing the system for weaknesses. Since Willie and I beefed up the security we should be fine for now. After we managed to give his guys the slip in New Orleans, I'm sure he's going to want to expand his team to avoid that again which may take a few days."

"How do you know he hasn't already done that?" Max asked, his voice no longer in the background.

"Because my contacts around town would know if a large group of strangers had come to town. Even with the carnival we have going on, it's usually locals from the surrounding towns where everybody tends to know somebody, which means new faces will be noted just in case any trouble jumps off."

"All right. I trust you know the area better than I do so I'll tell them to head your way in a couple of days whether I hear from you or not," Ezekiel said.

Paige grinned in amusement. "Yes, sir."

"You love being a hard-ass, don't you?" Ava heard Max say in amusement.

"Paige, call me if anything changes. Ava, I know you can take care of yourself, but please listen to Paige if anything goes down," Ezekiel suggested.

"I hate having to agree but the hard-ass is right. Love you, baby girl," Max said.

Ava chuckled. "I will and love you all too."

Paige said her good-bye and disconnected the call.

"So, what do we do now? Just wait?" Ava asked.

"Unfortunately, yes. We've taken all the necessary precautions with our security and defense, and I honestly don't see him making a move this soon. From what I've gathered about how he's gone about this whole thing, he likes to take his time. After all, look how long it took him to go after you. He could've had you snatched immediately but he played it out. Probably waiting for your family to be vulnerable enough to pay any price he asked for. It's the same way here, only he probably didn't expect the extent of the security I have. He's going to bide his time until he thinks he's found a chink in the armor."

It made sense to Ava, and probably would've calmed her nerves if it wasn't for the fact that he'd planned the hit on her father within a day of their wedding being canceled. But she wouldn't point that out to Paige, wanting to believe that she was right. They just needed to bide their time until he made his move and was more than likely caught before he could execute it. Paige had told her during their tour of the security measures she'd taken with the ranch that Junior had eyes all over the county, which included sheriff's officers he knew he could trust and friends and relatives from the local tribes, looking out for any non-locals or suspicious characters in the area. Kyle would need an army to get in here and a group that size would arouse suspicion in the quiet, rural town.

Paige gave her a reassuring smile. "Hopefully the ice cream hasn't melted too bad. Why don't we finish making our sundaes and watch a movie or get a nice rousing game of Scrabble going?"

Ava smiled in return. "Sounds like a plan."

Fortunately, the ice cream had been well frozen, so it was just soft enough to scoop without spraining a wrist doing so. Paige had insisted that Willie and Adele take the rest of the day off while Ava was getting the fortress tour, so it was just the two of them for the rest of the day. After their sundaes were made, they sat and watched two movies, both comedies, as Paige thought it would be good to keep the mood light, then played a few games of Scrabble. They made dinner together with Paige grilling steaks and Ava creating one of her famous salads. It wasn't until they were cleaning up after dinner that Ava realized that with everything going on they hadn't discussed what happened between them last night. They also hadn't bothered hiding their affection for one another in front of Willie and Adele, neither of whom blinked an eye at their holding hands.

"What's got your brow all furrowed in thought?" Paige asked.

Ava felt the need to talk about it. To know where they stood. She didn't regret it and assumed Paige didn't either, but you never knew what someone was really thinking.

"I was thinking about last night."

"Is that a good or bad thing?"

Ava shrugged. "I don't know. Just wondering what happens when this is all over. My life is in Chicago."

Paige quirked a brow. "It was one night. No one expects you to uproot your life no matter how good the sex was."

Ava felt her face heat with embarrassment. "Of course not. That wasn't what I meant."

Paige's face was unreadable. "Then what did you mean?"

Ava didn't quite know what she meant to say and sighed in frustration. "I appreciate you keeping me distracted since this afternoon, but I think the stress of the day is getting to me. Unless you need me for anything else, I'm going to bed."

"No, I can finish this. Good night." She returned to loading the dishwasher without another word.

Ava stood there for a moment torn between staying to try to explain and wanting to run in the other direction to avoid it. She chose the coward's way and walked, instead of ran, to her room. She had never been one to avoid an uncomfortable situation, choosing to grin and bear it rather than let it fester into something that couldn't be solved, but for some reason, the effect Paige had on her had Ava acting completely out of character. She took a long steamy shower trying not to think about Paige's offer to shower with her this morning or the fact that she would much rather have a repeat of last night than having to sleep alone tonight, but Ava didn't think Paige would be interested after her awkward attempt at discussing what was going on between them. After her shower she attempted to lie in bed and read, hoping the first of a series of mysteries by Cheryl A. Head would distract her enough not to think about the way Paige's callused palms felt grabbing her ass or the feel of rippling muscles as Ava ran her hands along Paige's back as she moved sensuously above her. Unfortunately, as much as the book distracted her mind, it didn't keep her body from craving the feel of Paige's lips as she explored Ava literally from shorn head to red polished toe.

With a sigh of frustration, she placed a page marker in the book, set it on the nightstand, and decided sleep was probably the best distraction.

She turned the lights off and tossed and turned until she found a comfortable position and practically willed herself to sleep.

Ava stood nude in the closet trying to decide what to wear for the day which shouldn't have been as difficult as it seemed to be. After all, they were just going to be mucking out stalls all morning. She finally chose a pair of jeans, a T-shirt, and was just reaching for her work boots when the shelves suddenly shifted away from her and opened to the crawl space leading to the tunnel entrance Paige had shown her yesterday. She didn't recall hitting the button that opened the entrance. Maybe Paige hadn't closed it fully when they left. She squatted to pull it closed and a shadow appeared, blocking out the light coming in through the tunnel. There was only a moment of hesitation before Ava stood and turned to run for the closet door. She had only taken a few steps when someone grabbed her ankle, causing her to trip and fall forward. The wind was knocked out of her, so she was slow to react when whoever grabbed her flipped her over and straddled her hips. She gazed up at a familiar face that she hoped she wouldn't see unless it was from behind prison glass.

"This is a dream…this is a dream…" she said over and over.

Kyle sneered down at her as he grabbed her hands, raised them above her head with one hand in a bruising grip, held a wicked looking knife against her neck with the other, and leaned into her face. "You're going to wish it was when I find you."

Ava felt the cold tip of the blade as it pushed against the tender flesh of her neck and did the only thing that she could think to do…scream.

Paige tossed and turned restlessly. There was no way she was going to get any sleep tonight. Her mind raced with ways to assess the threat they were facing, what tactics she would need to hold them off if they attacked sooner than she calculated and how stupidly she'd reacted when Ava was trying to talk about the very thing that had been running alongside worries of how best to protect her if anything jumped off. Paige hadn't blamed Ava for walking away and had considered going after her to apologize, but she was just as confused about their relationship and where it was going as Ava obviously was.

Paige threw off her covers with a sigh of frustration, got of bed, grabbed a yoga matt she kept in the bench at the end of the bed, and rolled it out on the floor. She went through five reps of a four-seven-eight breathing technique to try calming her racing mind and was just feeling herself relax and sink into the meditative moment when she heard screaming. There was no hesitation in Paige's reaction as she shot up off the floor, rushed to her nightstand to grab her gun, loaded the magazine, flipped the safety off, and quietly went over to the door to listen. She should probably check the video surveillance from her television monitor, but by the time she did all that Ava could be hurt. There was no way anyone could've gotten into the house without tripping at least one alarm, but considering what they'd learned about Kyle, she wasn't taking any chances. When she didn't hear movement outside her door, she ran to her closet, pressed the button for the hidden panel leading to the tunnel from her room and stealthily made her way to the one in Ava's closet. With her heart hammering loudly in her ears, she listened carefully before slowly opening the panel and determining that no one was in the closet. She rushed to the closet door, listened, and heard feminine crying but nothing else and noticed bright light shining under it. Paige opened the door just enough to be able to peek through and saw Ava sitting up in bed looking in wide-eyed fear toward the closet.

"Ava, it's Paige," she said, slowly opening it fully and setting her gun on a shelf just inside so as not to frighten Ava further. When she saw that Ava was alone and safe, she almost collapsed with relief.

Ava scrambled out of bed, ran toward Paige, and threw her arms around her. Paige could feel her trembling and didn't know if it was from fear, crying, or both. She just held her tightly.

"It's okay. I'm right here. You're safe," Paige murmured, wondering who she was trying to sooth more, Ava or herself.

Ava took a deep, shuddering breath and stepped out of Paige's arms. "I had a dream and I feel so stupid, but it was so real." She gazed over Paige's shoulder into the darkened closet.

Paige closed the door then led her back to the bed. "You want to talk about it?"

Ava shuddered again. "No."

"Do you want me to stay here with you?"

Ava shook her head. "I know how uncomfortable you are in this room."

Paige gave her a reassuring smile. "It's fine." She turned and crawled over to the other side of the bed, got under the covers, and held them aside for Ava.

Ava smiled and joined her. Paige pulled her protectively within the circle of her arms and Ava practically wrapped herself around her as she tucked her head in the crook of Paige's neck, wrapped her arms around her torso, and hiked a leg over hers. Paige found it interesting how she felt trapped and claustrophobic when previous lovers wanted to cuddle, but with Ava, she felt none of that. The closeness and heat of their bodies, the feel of their tangled limbs, the softness of Ava's breath on her neck, did more to relax Paige than any meditation session ever did. Within moments she was serenaded by Ava's soft snores and was drifting off to meet her in dreamland.

CHAPTER TWENTY

Paige awoke with the intense feeling that something wasn't right. She gazed over at Ava who was curled up under the covers with her back to her, so she just lay there and listened. She heard several quick successions of buzzing, letting her know someone was at the front gate. She glanced over at the clock on the nightstand which read four o'clock and her own internal alarm began ringing. In her rush to get to Ava she'd left her cell phone in her bedroom so if someone had tried to call before coming over, she wouldn't have known it. Paige eased out of the bed, grabbed the television remote, and brought the security monitors up on the screen. Gazing into the camera at the front gate was a figure dressed in dark tactical gear, everything except their eyes covered by a Balaclava face mask.

"Anybody home?" a male voice said into the intercom as he tapped the screen with his finger.

"Shit!" Paige checked the cameras at the other gates and saw similarly dressed figures at each one. "Shit shit shit!" She tossed the remote onto the sofa. "Ava!" she called loudly as she ran to the closet to retrieve the gun she'd left there.

Ava groaned but didn't wake up. Paige gave her a gentle but firm shake. "Ava! We've got company, you gotta get up…NOW!"

Ava slowly blinked her eyes open gazing at the clock in confusion. "What time is it? Who would be coming to visit at this hour?"

Paige went back into the closet, grabbed two pairs of sweatpants and a couple of T-shirts, tossing a set on the bed for Ava and keeping one for herself. "Babe, we don't have time for twenty questions. You need to get up and get dressed."

She set her gun on the nightstand and quickly put on the clothes over the boxers and sports bra she slept in. Because Ava was more petite than her, the clothes were a little snug and short but since it didn't restrict her movement, Paige didn't care. There was no way she was going to be able to fit into a pair of Ava's shoes so she would have to go barefoot. She grabbed her gun, slipped it into the pocket of her pants, and turned around to find Ava now up and nervously looking around as she put on the clothes Paige had tossed on the bed over her cami and short pajama set.

"Fortunately, they haven't breached the inner perimeter, but it probably won't be long before they do. They seem to be waiting for me to answer which means they're trying to avoid using force." Paige picked up the landline only to find there was no dial tone. Then the television screen blinked off. "They've cut off the phone and Wi-Fi."

Ava's eyes widened in fear. "What about your cell phone?"

"I left it in my room trying to get over here when I heard you scream."

Ava looked dejectedly down at her feet. "I'm sorry."

Paige walked over, placed a knuckle under Ava's chin, and raised her head to look at her. "You don't need to apologize." She placed a soft kiss on Ava's lips then gave her an encouraging smile.

"If they're trying to avoid using force let's see what we're working with." Paige took Ava's hand and led her out of the bedroom.

They went to the living room, Paige choosing not to turn any lights on as they did. She wasn't going to make it easy for them. Since the intercom by the door worked via good old fashioned electrical wiring she went there and pressed the button.

"Can I help you?" she asked in a casual tone.

"Little pig, little pig, let us in," was the taunting response.

"Look, you can play games if you want and I can just come out blasting, or we can act like adults and get to the point. Which would you prefer?" Paige said.

"Ah, there's that no bullshit sensibility the Marines are so good at. Okay, I'll get to the point. We don't want anyone to get hurt. Just bring Miss Prescott out for an even trade and we'll call it a day. No harm, no foul."

"Trade? For what?"

There was a moment of silence on the other end then Paige heard a grunt before, "Paige, don't do it!"

Paige's heart skipped a beat as she heard Willie's voice. "Willie? Are you okay? Is Adele okay?"

"I'm dandy. Nothing that some Bactine and a good shot of whisky can't take care of. Adele is pissed as hell but fine. They've got her at the house with a couple of their guys—"

"Enough!" Willie's captor cut him off and she heard another grunt. "What'll it be, Marine? Will you hand Miss Prescott over in exchange for us not splattering this old man's brains all over your front gate before we blow it open and take her anyway? I'll give you a few minutes to think it over." The line went silent.

"This is crazy!" Ava's voice filled with panic. "I'm going out there. I don't want Willie, Adele, or you hurt trying to protect me. It's not worth it."

She slipped her feet into a pair of shoes by the door and was reaching for a jacket when Paige stopped her.

"No."

Ava was on the verge of tears. "Paige, it's over. Please. I couldn't bear the thought of any of you hurt because of me. Like you said before, if they wanted me dead, they could've done that in New Orleans when they first found me. Kyle needs me alive to do whatever it is he's trying to do. You've brought me to your home and done more than enough to keep me safe, but it's no longer just about me. Me being here has brought this to your doorstep and endangered your friends. I need to stop it before something worse happens."

Paige held her grip on Ava's arm. Not enough to hurt her but just to keep her from leaving. "I can't let you do that. My job is to protect YOU."

Ava looked at her in disbelief. "You would let them hurt, possibly kill, Willie and Adele to protect me?"

"No, but what you and they don't know is that despite Willie's age, he's more than capable of protecting himself. The only reason he's here is because he let them think he was a helpless old man to lure them here for me to find out what I'm dealing with. Willie spent most of his military career since the Vietnam War in the Marines Special Forces, is a tenth-degree black belt in martial arts and has more weapons knowledge in his pinky finger than I do from my entire military career. Now, I need you to trust me. I haven't steered you wrong yet, have I?"

Ava glanced worriedly from Paige to the door and back. "No."

"Good." Paige pressed the intercom button. "You still there?"

"Yeah. Have you made your decision?" The man asked.

"Let me talk to Willie first."

"Paige," Willie's voice sounded breathless coming over the intercom which had her worried that maybe she had overestimated him being able to defend himself despite his daily workouts and still competing in annual martial arts competitions beating men half his age.

"How are you doing, Willie?"

"I could be better. You know what the doctor said about me exerting myself too much," he said weakly.

Paige smiled. Willie had just gotten a physical last week and was told he was in better shape than his sons. He was playing up the frail senior citizen routine. "This will all be over soon. I just need to know if you got this?"

"Yeah, give me a few minutes to catch my breath," Willie said.

"All right, enough of this shit. Are you coming out or do we need—"

The line went silent again.

"What's going on?" Ava asked, glancing from the intercom to the door.

"Paige," Willie's voice came over the intercom and Paige breathed a sigh of relief.

"You good?" she asked.

"Yeah, unfortunately I had to put one of them down. The other two are unconscious. They're using silencers, so the others haven't been alerted yet. I hate to leave you, but I need to get back to Adele."

"I understand. Be careful."

"I will. You do the same. I've got one of their cell phones, so I'll call Junior. I'm going to borrow the truck they left at the end of the road. I'll try and get back as soon as I can." Willie said before it went quiet again.

Paige turned to Ava. "I'm sure they were probably doing regular checks with the rest of the team, so we've got maybe five minutes before they figure out something is wrong. From this point on, Ava, I need you to follow my lead, no questions asked."

Ava nodded. "Okay."

Paige put on a pair of sneakers she kept by the door. "Let's go."

She ran to her room with Ava on her heels. Once there she headed to her closet, opened her weapons trunk, grabbed two flak jackets, and handed one to Ava who strapped it on without hesitation.

"The .38 is in the case on the bottom right. There should be ammo for it right next to it," Paige told her as she loaded the weapons slots of her jacket with her knives, her gun, and several loaded magazines.

Then she grabbed a second gun, a .45 semi-automatic, and screwed a silencer adaptor onto it before loading the magazine and placing extras into the remaining slots on her jacket. The last thing she put on were a pair of inexpensive but useful adjustable night vision goggles normally used for hunting. They weren't military grade, but they worked for what she needed and weren't bulky. She placed them on her head but not over her eyes. She wasn't going to need them until they exited the tunnels. She looked over at Ava who was grabbing a baseball cap from Paige's hat rack. The revolver was set in the jacket's holster, and she had placed several speed loaders with ammo in some of the slots. Paige felt a weird combination of impressed and turned on.

"Don't let me find out you're actually a knight and not the damsel in distress I'm supposed to be saving," she said with a wink. "Stay close."

She walked over to the tunnel entrance from her closet, pressed the button for the wall to slide away, and made sure it closed securely behind them before they got moving.

As they jogged along the dimly lit tunnel beneath the ranch, Ava's heart thumped rapidly, fear and adrenaline affecting her as if she'd just drank an espresso with a double shot of caffeine. She did her best to fight off the memory of her nightmare and the helpless feeling it brought on. She ran her fingers over the gun holstered in the jacket she wore and felt some comfort. Whether she would use it to shoot someone was another story, but at this moment she believed she could if it came down to shooting or being shot. She looked at Paige just a few steps ahead of her wondering what was going through her mind. Ava had been in a daze from the moment Paige woke her up with a tone in her voice that brooked no argument and a seriously intense look that frightened her a little. Dr. Dolittle had been replaced with G.I. Jane.

Ava thought the reality of the situation would have set in when the people out there were attempting to exchange her for Willie's life, but even that seemed unreal because it was coming from a disembodied voice through the intercom. Then it was all over within a matter of minutes and

Willie was safe and on his way to rescue his wife. Reality set in when she looked at Paige with her jacket full of weapons and ammo and a pair of neon goggles perched on her head looking like she was about to go into battle which, in a sense, she was. Her home truly had become a fortress with the enemy knocking at the gate as civilly as a neighbor asking to borrow a cup of sugar. Ava wanted to ask so many questions, but Paige had said to trust her and follow her lead so that's what she was going to do, no matter how crazy things would get.

They reached the end of the tunnel in much shorter time than it normally took them to walk to the barn, probably because they had jogged rather than gone the leisurely pace they usually took in the morning. Ava was glad she had continued her regular morning runs because Paige had kept up a quick, steady pace that didn't seem to affect her a bit but left Ava a little winded. There was an iron rung ladder that led up to a bolted steel door above them. Paige told her earlier as she was showing her all the secrets of the ranch that she and Willie regularly went around and oiled all the locks and hinges to ensure they didn't make noise if they were opened.

Paige turned to her. "I'll go up first to make sure it's clear then come back for you," she whispered, then pulled her phone out of her jacket, typed in her code to unlock it, and offered it to Ava. "Text 911 to Ezekiel and Junior. DO NOT come up until I come back."

"And if you don't?" Ava had to ask.

Paige took her face in her hands with a cocky grin and said, "I'll be back," in a bad Schwarzenegger impression before pressing her lips to Ava's for a kiss that left her more breathless than the jog did.

Ava smiled as she watched Paige climb the ladder. It slowly disappeared as she quietly slid the lock open then pushed the door up just enough to peek out of. Ava assumed the way was clear because Paige gazed back down at her, blew her a kiss then opened the door fully, with hay sprinkling down through the opening as she pulled herself up. Ava's breath hitched when the door was closed once again, and she was left standing alone in the tunnel. A blink of light caught her attention and she remembered she had Paige's phone and her instructions. There was a notification on the screen from her security app about the west gate, then another about the east gate and a third about the north gate. For a moment she debated whether she should try to go up and warn Paige or stay and wait as she asked her to do. Ignoring every fiber in her body telling her to go, she stayed put, trusting Paige could handle whatever was coming. She looked down at the phone again, opened Paige's contacts, searched for Ezekiel's name, texted 911, then did the same with Junior. It took her a moment to find his name because it was under Willie Jr. instead of just Junior. Once that was done, she stuck the phone in one of the pockets on her jacket and waited.

She tried not to pull Paige's phone out to check the time or to count the minutes ticking by in her head as she paced back and forth, gazing up at the ladder at the slightest imagined sound. Paige told her the tunnels were soundproof but that didn't stop Ava from thinking she heard footsteps or whispered voices. When the wait became unbearable Ava closed her eyes and tried willing Paige to come back. If that didn't work, she was going to kneel on the hard-packed dirt floor and start praying. Time stretched on. Ava pulled Paige's phone out and saw not only had ten minutes gone by but both Junior and Ezekiel texted back the same word: *Received*. Ava hoped that meant help was on the way because she couldn't take this anymore. She tucked the phone away again then moved to the ladder and began to climb but before she could reach the top the door swung open sending hay raining down on her head. She looked up to find Paige grinning down at her.

"Where do you think you're going?" Paige asked.

Ava was so relieved to see her she almost cried. "I didn't want to miss out on the fun."

Paige grinned and reached down to offer Ava a hand. Ava climbed the last few rungs and pulled herself through the opening with Paige's help. She was barely steady on her feet as she threw her arms around Paige's neck.

"Don't ever leave me like that again. From now on I go where you go," she whispered vehemently.

Paige's arms wrapped tightly around her waist. "You got it."

Ava gave herself a moment to allow the safety and security Paige represented to still her racing heart and calm her wracked nerves before releasing her. Paige's hand slid to her waist as she looked at Ava with such tenderness it warmed her heart.

"We need to go," Paige said softly.

Ava nodded. "You got notifications about all the gates."

"Yeah, I took care of the ones that breached the west and north gates. I would've had to backtrack to get to the east gate which is closer to the house so we're going to have to take our chances that they went to the house rather than come this way."

Ava didn't want to know how she took care of them. She just wanted this to be over.

"I've got our transportation saddled." Paige cocked her head toward Zorro and Amina standing nearby. "Since we can't get to my truck, and I don't know if there are more waiting near the main road, I figured it's best to hide out in the woods until the calvary arrives."

"Lead the way, Lone Ranger," Ava teased her.

Paige chuckled. "How many more nicknames do you have up your sleeve?"

Ava shrugged. "There's no telling. I was an only child who watched a lot of TV."

Paige shook her head and gave her a gentle nudge toward the waiting horses. It took Ava a moment to realize that they had come up in Lucy's and Ethel's stall, but the current occupants were two of the nameless cats that also called the ranch home. She gazed back to see Paige closing the door and recovering it with a pile of loose hay. She looked around the other stalls and didn't see any of the other animals.

"What happened to the menagerie?"

"There were a couple of guys heading toward the barn and I needed a distraction."

"Are they okay? The animals, not the men."

"They're fine. Brutus surprised a guy who didn't see him in the dark. He screamed, scaring Brutus and sending him charging directly at him, headbutting the guy into a wall. He must've cracked his skull from the impact because he wasn't conscious when I checked on him."

Ava frowned. "Poor Brutus."

Paige smiled in amusement. "Yeah, poor Brutus."

They mounted their horses and headed out of the barn. They passed Brutus wandering the coral who mooed at them in passing, Hershey enjoying a very early morning snack at the trough, and Farrah and Jackie asleep under a tree. She had no doubt where Lucy and Ethel probably were and hoped they didn't trash the garden too bad before they returned home. It's funny how she referenced the ranch as home. Until that moment, returning home always meant Chicago, now she just wanted to be wherever Paige was. How was it possible to develop the feelings she had for Paige in just a month? Did Paige have the same feelings? Judging by the way she was looking at Ava in the barn, she felt something. They were nearing the west gate when lights coming up the side road caught her attention. Ava's meandering thoughts quickly faded as Paige, who must have noticed them at the same time, urged Zorro into a faster pace. Ava didn't hesitate to do the same with Amina, but as fast as the horses were, they couldn't outrun a vehicle. A dark SUV reached the gate before they did and pulled up to block their escape. To Ava's surprise, Paige didn't stop. She steered Zorro to the right and Ava followed, assuming they were heading toward the north gate. Something whizzed past Ava and sprayed dirt and grass in their path.

"Next time I won't miss. I would hate to have to shoot such a beautiful animal," a feminine voice said over what sounded like a megaphone.

Paige slowed Zorro to a stop. Ava did the same with Amina, riding up along side her. It was over but not the way either of them had expected.

Paige gazed at her and Ava wanted to cry at the look of angry defeat on her face. "I won't let them take you without a fight."

Ava tried putting on a brave smile. "I won't go without one."

Paige gave her a smile and nod then urged Zorro to turn back. It took some convincing, as if he knew what going back meant, but eventually, after Paige leaned forward and cooed something in his ear, he gave in. Amina obediently followed without any coaxing from Ava. It was a slow, easy gallop back to where the SUV sat blocking the gate, joined by two men on ATVs. Spotlighted by the security light was a woman who stood about six feet with a broad, muscular build dressed in black cargo pants and shirt, dark hair pulled back into a ponytail and a long angular face that Ava thought resembled Amina's as she frowned angrily. She was leaning casually against the front of the truck, and holding what looked like a sniper rifle.

A deadly calm Paige hadn't felt since she'd left the military came over her as her fingers itched to yank her rifle from her saddle to take out as many of the intruders as she could, but that would put Ava in more danger than she probably already was.

"I was told she needed to be brought in alive, but no one said anything about uninjured." The woman shifted the gun, aiming at Ava's legs. "Hand that rifle over, nice and easy."

Paige did as she was told, keeping her eye on the woman she mentally nicknamed Rambette as she unhooked the rifle from her saddle and handed it over to one of the other fatigued dressed people nearby. Including Rambette, she counted seven people. Judging by the way they carried themselves and their figures, she counted two other women while the remaining were men. It was obvious Rambette was in charge.

"Off the horses…slowly. Once they're down, check them for any other weapons," Rambette commanded.

Paige slowly climbed off Zorro, but Ava struggled with her dismount. When she moved to help her, the barrel of a gun was pointed at her as someone began frisking her and removing all of her weapons.

"You stay right where you are." Rambette jerked her head to have someone else assist Ava.

Once Ava was on the ground, she was immediately checked for weapons as well, her gun and ammo were removed, and she was led over to Rambette. The horses were taken farther down the fence line and tied to one of the posts. Paige assessed the situation and knew there was no way she was fighting her way out of this. It was too bad real life wasn't like those movies where the hero would've fought off all seven of them to save Ava and the world. She would just have to wait until they got to wherever they were taking them and go from there. She ignored the person standing beside her pointing a gun at her head.

"Are you all right?" she asked Ava who was being handcuffed behind her back.

"I'm fine. You?" She flinched when the cuffs were tightened and gave the woman a look that probably shriveled the balls of many a man in her business.

Rambette smiled in amusement. She walked her over to one of the ATVs. "Have a seat, Princess."

Ava raised her chin defiantly and Paige couldn't help but feel pride. Rambette shrugged indifferently.

"Suit yourself." She walked away from Ava, lifting her gun toward Paige as she joined their little duo. "I wasn't told to bring you along, and out of respect for a fellow vet, I'm not going to kill you as I was instructed but I can't chance you going back to your little homestead and sending up a warning before we've gotten enough distance from here not to be tailed."

Paige smiled. "If you think distance is going to stop me from finding you, you're sorely misinformed."

Rambette smiled in amusement. "I love the confidence. Challenge accepted."

She walked away; another man came toward her carrying a needle. Paige quickly glanced at the man still holding his gun on her and knew there was no sense in fighting. Rambette said she wasn't going to kill her so the worst that could be in the needle was something to knock her out. Unless someone went against her orders and decided to poison instead of drugging her. There was only one way to find out. If she woke up, she would hunt them down and make every one of them regret turning her sanctuary into a battlefield and stealing the woman she loved. If she didn't, she'd make a deal with the devil to come back and do it anyway.

Paige felt the prick of the needle in her neck and collapsed to her knees as she began feeling woozy from whatever they had given her. She met Ava's fearful gaze as her beautiful face blurred before her. "Fellow vet or not, if Kyle Edwards hurts one hair on her head, you're both dead, Rambette," she said before she fell over and her world went dark.

Instinctively, Ava moved to run to Paige as she collapsed but was stopped by the woman who'd captured her.

"What did you give her!"

"Don't worry, Princess. She's just going to take a long nap. She may wake up with a headache but other than that she'll be fine."

Ava snatched her arm from the woman's grasp. "Stop calling me that. Let's go and get this over with."

She climbed onto the ATV as best she could with her hands bound behind her back. She'd ridden one many times while on various vacations, so she managed without an issue. Her captor climbed on behind her, wrapping an arm around her waist. Ava flinched at her touch.

"No offense, Pr—Miss Prescott, but I wouldn't want you falling off."

Ava didn't bother responding but she grudgingly did try to relax within the circle of the woman's arms. She took one last look at Paige's prone figure, then looked toward the horizon hoping the rising sun would burn away her tears as they drove away to the chorus of sirens in the distance.

CHAPTER TWENTY-ONE

A va tried to pay attention to where they were headed, but she had only left the ranch once since her arrival weeks ago, so she didn't recognize anything. They had started out going north until they reached the edge of the forest where an SUV that had gone in the opposite direction when they left the ranch now waited. Three men dressed as if they were out for a leisurely day of activity exited the SUV while she and her captors got in. The men stayed with the ATVs as they drove off. They had stayed on the main road for some time then turned off onto a dirt road heading toward the mountain range northwest of the ranch. When Paige woke up, she would be telling everyone to look out for the off-road vehicles instead of a truck. Ava had held on to the hope that Paige would find her until they switched vehicles and direction.

She looked out the window as they pulled into a farm, but there were no animals wandering around and the grounds were overgrown. For a moment she smiled to herself thinking how Lucy and Ethel would have a field day there. She already missed the ranch and its animal menagerie. It had been daybreak when they left and had driven a good hour before arriving at their destination which meant they were about an hour and a half drive from Paige's ranch. They had taken back roads, so it probably would take less than that from the nearest main road. If she somehow managed to escape she would have a long walk ahead of her, but she figured that if she headed southeast, she would eventually end up at or near the ranch enough to recognize where she was. A man walked out of the barn to open the doors so that the driver could pull the truck inside where there was a second SUV, the same make and color as the one she was in. She wondered if they bothered guarding them since they were out in the middle of nowhere. If she could get ahold of the keys she wouldn't have to worry about walking. She would need to slash the tires of the second truck so they couldn't chase her, then she'd be good. But all that would depend on if she could find a way to escape.

"If you lean forward, I can take the cuffs off you," her lead captor offered.

"I don't know why you bothered keeping them on me once we were in here. I wasn't going anywhere," Ava said with annoyance as she leaned forward.

The truck had three rows of seats. The two men, one driving, sat in the front, two women sat in the middle row, and Ava was relegated to the back row with the woman she heard Paige call Rambette, which she thought was quite fitting considering she did resemble a female Sylvester Stallone during his Rambo heyday. It was a good thing she was small because the woman's broad frame took up half the seat. Once the cuffs were off Ava circled her shoulders back and forth wincing at the pins and needles of the blood trying to circulate properly through limbs that had been held in an awkward position too long. Everyone filed out of the vehicle. Ava scooted across the seat and was offered a hand of assistance by Rambette, but promptly rebuffed her and climbed out on her own. She looked mildly offended then turned away.

"This way." She headed toward a door at the back of the barn.

Unlike Paige's, the barn was wide open with no stalls and smelled of wet hay and mildew. She followed the large woman into a windowless storage room with a cot, a card table, and a folding chair.

"I assume these are my accommodations. Not the Ritz but I guess it's doable." She was leaning on sarcasm to cover her nervousness. "Where do I relieve myself?"

Rambette gave her a knowing grin. "Someone will be outside the door. Just knock and they'll take you. Do you need to go now?"

"Yes."

Ava hated the idea that she had to get permission to go to the bathroom, but she guessed it was better than being left a bucket to do it in. Rambette…she seriously needed to find out this woman's name before she called her that to her face…turned to walk out of the room. Ava followed like the obedient little prisoner that she was. They went in the direction toward the house but before reaching it they turned left heading toward the back of the house. She saw a port-o-john and stopped.

"You can't be serious. There are lights on in the house so I'm assuming the plumbing works as well."

Rambette turned around with a quirked brow and smirk. "What, too common for you, Princess?"

Okay, she deserved that. After all it wasn't like she'd never used one before. There had been plenty of outdoor concerts where it was the port-o-john or nothing, but it was the principle of the situation. She could see if the house truly was abandoned and had no working utilities but even the barn had electricity so why was she being imprisoned in the barn and having to use the modern version of an outhouse? Then it hit her.

"He's trying to humiliate me, isn't he?"

She received a shrug in response.

"What's your name? I'd like to at least know who my jailer is."

"Remy."

Ava looked at her skeptically. "Like the drink?"

"Yep."

Ava didn't believe her, but it didn't matter. She just didn't want to piss her off by accidently calling her Rambette after she saw her frown when Paige called her that.

"Thanks, Remy," she said as she walked to the port-o-john.

It was surprisingly clean and smelled of disinfectant. Thankfully, it had toilet paper and a hand sanitizer dispenser. She removed her flak jacket and was about to take it off when she felt something hard. That's when she remembered that she still had Paige's phone tucked deep inside one of the bigger pockets. Remy had removed her gun and ammo but hadn't checked for anything else. Ava had to refrain from shouting with joy. She took care of her needs thankful for all those core and squat exercises, slathered sanitizer all over her hands and used toilet paper to open the door. She didn't know if anyone besides her was using the facility, but she wasn't taking any chances. Remy didn't even bother to make sure she followed but then where would she go? She had no idea where she was, and they had vehicles and guns. Like Remy intimated to Paige, Kyle said he wanted her alive, but he didn't say anything about uninjured. They went back to the barn, Ava checking out her surroundings along the way. Anything she could use to tell whoever she was going to contact where she was. When they returned to the storage room there was a paper plate with a sandwich and a snack bag of chips, and a bottle of water on the table.

Ava turned to Remy with a grateful smile. "Thank you."

There was a ghost of a friendly smile that softened Remy's hard angled features before it was quickly replaced by her signature stern expression. "You're welcome. I'll come get you when he's ready for you." She turned and left the room.

Ava could hear muffled conversation before the sound of a bolt lock sliding into place confirmed that she was a prisoner. She sat down at the table for her meal of turkey on white bread with mayo and plain potato chips. She preferred spicy mustard on her turkey sandwiches, but beggars couldn't be choosy. As she ate, she casually looked around the room to check for cameras. When she finished, she walked around looking for hidden ones. She wasn't surprised not to find any since they probably hadn't had time to set up a full security system, especially way out here where equipment like that wasn't readily available. She took her jacket off, opened the Velcro flap of the pocket and pulled the phone out. To her relief there was a strong signal and a twenty-five percent battery life left. She made sure it was still on silent then realized she didn't know Paige's pass code. She almost cried then thought of something else. She chose the call button which still asked for the code but also had the option for *Emergency Call*. Ava swiped that and the name and number for Grace Richards came up. She was Paige's mother. Ava had hoped she would be able to text someone so she wouldn't be heard talking, but there was no other way to contact anyone else. She went to the farthest corner of the room away from the door and called.

"Hey, honey. Two calls in one week. What's the occasion?" a teasing voice said in answer.

Ava suddenly missed her own mother and had to pull herself together before she began weeping on the phone. "Mrs. Richards, my name is Ava Prescott, you don't know me, but I need your help." She whispered into the phone hoping it was loud enough for Mrs. Richards but not anyone outside the door to hear.

"I know who you are, Ava. Why are you whispering? Has something happened to Paige?"

Ava was relieved that she didn't have to explain who she was. "I don't know how much time I have, but long story short, the man after me found us. Last time I saw Paige she had been given something to knock her out, so I don't think she's hurt but she doesn't know where they've taken me. The only reason I have her phone is because she needed me to contact some people while she took care of some of the people that had breached her security. They took my weapon and ammo but hadn't checked for anything else."

Paige heard a male chuckle. "Amateurs. Ava, this is Paige's father, Frank. Grace has you on speaker. Paige has a tracking app on her phone, so if she's conscious then she more than likely knows your location. What can you tell us about where you are? Is the security tight? Are there multiple access points?"

"Frank, she's not one of your soldiers, no need to interrogate her," Grace said, sounding amused.

Paige was right, their parents would definitely get along. "It's all right, Mrs. Richards, Paige's former boss at the private security firm is like an uncle so I'm familiar with what Mr. Richards is asking for. I'm at a farm which I believe is about an hour and a half northwest of the ranch. There is no security fencing or, as far as I could tell, security cameras. I came here with five personnel, three women and two men. There were also three men left behind with ATVs and at least two others here at the farm when we arrived. I don't know how many may be in the main house."

"Impressive. Ezekiel taught you well," Frank said.

Ava smiled from the praise.

"That should be enough to give Paige a good idea of what to expect. How much battery life does the phone have left?" Grace asked.

"It was at twenty-five percent when I called you."

"Okay. Leave it on silent. Frank is calling the house phone to see if we can reach Paige. Try to keep the phone hidden on you so she'll be able to pick up your exact location, but if you find keeping it may put you in danger, hide it somewhere in the vicinity. Stay safe, Ava," Grace said.

"I will. Thank you. I hope to have the pleasure of meeting you and Mr. Richards someday soon to thank you in person."

"Oh, you will."

They said good-bye once more then Ava's legs went weak with relief. She slid down the wall onto the floor, covered her face, and cried. All the fear, frustration, and stress of the past couple of days crashed in on her. After her tears dried, she felt extremely tired. She used the wall to help her stand then walked over to the cot. There was a folded blanket and pillow at the end of it. She tucked the phone back into the inside pocket of her jacket, took it off and placed it between her and the wall, and lay down. Ava prayed Paige would find her before she had to face-off with Kyle. Her anger and hatred of him was so strong right now that he was the only person she could see shooting without hesitation. Maybe not to kill but to seriously maim. That morbid thought comforted her as she drifted off to sleep.

❖

Paige was running through a bombed out Middle Eastern village screaming Ava's name and getting no response. She stopped and just listened, hoping to hear something or someone then she heard her name being called and ran toward the sound. She ended up on a main road where two Hummer vehicles were pulled haphazardly off the road and a third was engulfed in smoke and flames.

"PAIGE!" She heard a voice scream from the midst of the destroyed vehicle, but she couldn't get to it.

"You promised you would protect me," the voice continued to taunt her.

"I tried. There was nothing I could do," Paige cried.

Suddenly, a figure of smoke and sand rose from the flames. At first it was male, then female, then male again but missing part of his leg then female with a hole in her chest, another male with part of his head missing, continuously morphing into figure after faceless figure of all the friends, squad members, and ops team members that she'd promised to protect and lost over the span of her military career. The last figure morphed into a petite female, shifting, and forming until her bright smile and amber eyes were right there in front of Paige.

"Ava? I've been looking all over for you." She tried to pull her into an embrace, but her arms went right through her.

"You said you would protect me," Ava said.

"I will. You need to come with me. It's not safe here."

"You told me I would be safe with you, but you let them take me." Ava's smile turned down into a frown as she began to float back toward the burning wreck.

Paige tried to run after her but found her feet stuck in quicksand. She collapsed onto her knees screaming Ava's name as she was engulfed by the flames.

❖

"Paige, it's okay, you're safe," Paige heard a familiar voice say.

She awoke with a start to find Adele sitting beside the bed holding her hand. She looked at Adele then around her in confusion. Why was she in a hospital room? As the last desperate feeling from her nightmare drifted away, it all came back to her. The ranch had been breached and Ava had been taken. She tried to sit up, but the room spun around her.

Adele gently pushed her to lie back down. "Ah-ah, you're not going anywhere."

"They took Ava. I need to find her," Paige said helplessly.

"I know, honey, but you're in no shape to do anything. Junior has some people out looking and there's a crew back at the house sent by Ezekiel setting up a command post to join the search and await your orders."

Paige felt some relief hearing that, but she still needed to get out of here as soon as possible. "You and Willie are good?"

Adele smiled. "We're fine. Doc says Willie has a fractured rib, but other than that and a few bruises that he'll be bragging about for days, he'll live to tell the tale for years to come."

"They didn't hurt you?"

Adele waved dismissively. "Child, please. By the time Willie got home the two that were left behind were out cold. I asked if they wanted coffee then slipped some of Willie's sleeping meds in their cups. I called Junior who told me he'd spoken to Willie and that they were on their way to the ranch. He sent a patrol over to collect my unwelcome visitors and that was that. Being a trusting sweet old lady has its perks. People tend to underestimate you which gives you the advantage when needed."

Paige chuckled. "Have I told you how much I love you guys."

Adele patted her hand affectionately. "We love you too. You're like the daughter I always wanted."

The door opened and Junior and Willie entered, their broad shoulders and height taking up most of the space in the small room.

"Sleeping Beauty finally awakens," Junior said, grinning.

"You're lucky I can't get out of this bed without the room doing cartwheels. Glad to see you're still kicking, Willie. I couldn't live with myself if anything happened to you because of something I'm involved in."

Willie walked over to stand behind Adele, placing a hand on her shoulder. "We're just glad you weren't hurt. When Junior called to tell us that they were taking you to the hospital and Ava was nowhere to be found, I thought the worst. Doc told us you had been given a sedative. Junior found you about fifteen minutes after they got to the ranch. You've been out for about an hour."

Paige ran her hands through her hair in frustration. "An hour where Ava could've been taken anywhere in the state or country depending on Kyle's resources." She looked over at Junior. "What's the status of your search?"

"We were able to apprehend the six people you and Pops left unconscious or injured. We found three dead. The ones we questioned couldn't tell us the exact location where Kyle is holed up. All they could say was that it was a farm."

Paige sighed. "Yeah, that's helpful."

"Well, the one person left behind who could've told us was the one Pops shot." Junior looked accusingly at Willie.

Willie shrugged. "Sorry, he wouldn't stay down and would've shot me if I hadn't used his friend with a bullet proof vest as a shield. It was him or me."

"You chose wisely," Adele said, gazing up at him lovingly.

Junior shook his head with a grin. "We also managed to follow the ATV tracks north heading toward the back road to town, but then they break off into two different directions. We found several other vehicle tracks heading toward the main road, but you know once they hit 75 there's no telling where they went. I've contacted the sheriff offices in the surrounding towns to be on the lookout for Ava and gave them Kyle Edward's description. Now that you're awake, maybe we can give them more descriptions of the ones that you dealt with."

"Only one of them went without a face mask. I think she was the one in charge. With her and Kyle's description, that should be enough. If anyone has seen either one of them then we'll find Ava. In the meantime, I need to get out of here," Paige said.

Adele looked as if she would argue then shook her head. "I'll let the nurse know."

"Thanks, Adele."

"Don't go thanking me yet. Personally, I think you need to keep your ass right there for at least another hour, but I understand why you can't."

A half hour later, they were all heading back to the ranch. Paige was riding shotgun with Junior while Adele and Willie followed in their truck. When they arrived at the ranch, the front gate stood open but two men looking like Secret Service stood guard. The black suits, white shirts, black ties, and intense stares told Ava they were Ezekiel's guys. After checking their IDs and giving Paige a nod of recognition, they let them pass. As they approached the house there were two black SUVs and a familiar black pickup truck sitting in the driveway. Junior pulled up right in front of the house to let Paige out. There were two more security personnel on the porch who gave her a brief nod as she passed. She walked in to find that her home really had become a command center. Joel and Eric, leads for Ezekiel's tech team who had been deemed the "Tech Twins" were stationed at her kitchen counter with full monitors and laptops. Tracey and Brian from her old team with Ezekiel stood in the dining area unloading boxes of ammo, with several guns and a couple of rifles laid out on a sheet on the table. They all looked up at her entrance and stood to greet her with smiles and handshakes.

"Thank you all for being here," Paige said, swallowing the lump in her throat.

"We weren't going to let the boss man send just anyone," Tracey said.

"Yeah, when word got out that you were in trouble and that he was sending a crew from Tulsa we volunteered to help. Lucas is even here. He's doing a walkabout to see if the locals missed anything," Brian said.

Paige was at a momentary loss for words. For them to volunteer to want to help her find Ava blew her away. "I don't know how to thank you all."

"You could let me take those adorable ponies home for my baby girls."

Ava looked toward the kitchen to see Grant walking out of her pantry with a package of her favorite Oreo cookies grinning like the

Cheshire cat. As she moved toward him, he set the cookies on the counter and immediately enveloped her in a bear hug.

"Hey, Sarge."

"Hey, Grant."

After a moment, Paige playfully pushed him away. "What are you doing here?"

"Tracey called me, and I didn't want to miss all the fun."

"Patrice is going to kill you."

"She was the one who insisted I come. She likes Ava and you're our children's godmother. We need to keep you around."

Paige had the family she was born with and these people, the family she'd been gifted with. She loved each of them as if they were more than just brothers and sisters in arms.

"You're here one day and you've already found my snack stash." She reached in and took two cookies from the package before Grant snatched it away.

"Since I'm the one who turned you on to Double Stuffed Oreos, I would say it's OUR stash." He gave her a wink before stuffing a whole cookie into his mouth.

"I know you are not scratching up my counter with that stuff!" Adele fussed as she entered the house. She stopped directly in front of Joel and Eric with her hands on her hips glaring at them in warning. "You've got five minutes to relocate before you find all that fancy equipment on the front lawn."

They looked from the sweet-faced older woman to Paige in confusion.

Paige shrugged. "I'd do what she said. There's an empty workstation in the security room." She pointed toward the pantry.

The Tech Twins gazed back at Adele as if to argue, but she was giving them that look no Black child wants to get from their grandmother because it was usually followed by a switch to the behind.

"Yes ma'am," they said in unison and began packing up their gear for the move.

Grant grinned in amusement. "Afternoon, Miss Adele."

Adele smiled affectionately back at him. "Afternoon, Grant. How's that beautiful family of yours?"

"They're doing well."

"That's good. I hope you plan to bring them for a visit soon. Give your wife my best. Now if you'll excuse me, I've got lunch to make for a house full of people I was not expecting."

"We'll get out of your hair, ma'am," Grant said, signaling for Paige to follow him.

"And you two, there's a whole coffee table you could be doing that at instead of the dining table."

She heard Adele fussing at Tracey and Brian as she and Grant walked to the pantry to enter the security room.

"All right, what you got for me?" Paige asked.

"The twins narrowed down some possible locations based on where the tracks from the ATVs led."

Paige shook her head. "It can't be any of those. I think the ATVs were meant to draw us away from where Kyle's crew was headed. It must be some place close enough for them to drop in and out the past couple of days to stake the ranch out. Search west and north of here."

Grant nodded. "By the way, Bobby is at the airfield awaiting instructions on how she can help."

Paige looked at him in surprise. "Anybody else?"

"Nah. She flew me here and wants to help."

"She actually may be able to. Twins, once you get a lock on some possible locations give them to Grant to send to Bobby. She can do a fly-over to help us narrow our choices down to an easier search grid."

Grant nodded. "Good idea. I'll give her a heads up so she can be ready to take off as soon as possible."

She heard the house phone ring and a moment later Adele calling her name. She rarely received calls through the landline.

"You go. We got this," Grant said.

As Paige was walking out, Adele appeared in the doorway offering her the phone. "It's your father."

"Dad? Is everyone all right?"

"Hey, nugget, everyone's fine. No time for chit chat though. I have some news on Ava."

Paige was really confused now. Then he went on to explain and she had to sit down before she collapsed. Thank God she hadn't had time to ask for her phone back and that Rambette hadn't found it. While she was still on the phone with her father Paige ran to her office, opened her laptop, and turned on her phone tracker. She went back to the security room to give the location to the twins who picked up satellite images of the farm.

"We found her, Dad."

"Good," he said, sounding relieved. "You go do what you need to do. If we hear from her again, how can I reach you."

Paige gave him Grant's number until she could get ahold of a temporary phone.

"Got it. Be careful, Paige. Love you."

"Thanks, Dad. Love you too."

"I sent the coordinates to Bobby," Grant said.

"Good. As soon as she gets a lay of the land we'll go from there."

"I've got some burner phones in the truck if you need one," Eric offered.

"Yes, thank you."

He left the room and Paige began pacing. There was nothing left to do now but wait. She just hoped Ava would be okay until then.

Ava awoke a little disoriented. Then she spotted Remy sitting at the table watching her curiously. It was creepy knowing she may have been watching her sleep.

"What?" Ava asked as she sat up and tried stretching the kinks out of her neck from the uncomfortable cot.

"I'm trying to figure out how such a little bitty thing like you could cause such a big fuss? I mean, don't get me wrong, you're gorgeous AND rich, so I can see why he wants you so bad, but I lost some good people trying to acquire you and need to know why."

Ava stood to grab the bottle of water she hadn't finished. Remy never took her eyes off her.

"Why don't you ask him." She took a long drink, finishing what was left.

Remy smirked and stood. "Why don't we both? He's ready to see you."

She walked toward the door and out of the room, once again, not looking to see if Ava followed, which she did. The barn door was opened by the same man who opened it when they had arrived, with Remy whispering something to him before she left. Ava was surprised to see that night had fallen. She couldn't believe she had slept that long, but the little sleep she'd gotten the night of the festival and then the previous night before the ranch was attacked must have caught up to her. She unconsciously went to touch her jacket over the pocket where the phone was hidden, then realized she'd left it on the cot. She hoped no one would take it. Ava also worried why Paige hadn't shown up by now with the authorities in tow. It had been hours since she'd contacted the Richards. Paige should've gotten the message by now. Unless Remy had lied about what they had given Paige. Her parents weren't going to be thinking about Ava if their daughter was lying dead somewhere because of her. Until she could confirm otherwise, Ava was on her own.

Chapter Twenty-two

A va and Remy entered the house through the back door. Besides looking as if it hadn't been lived in for a very long time with peeling wallpaper, chipped paint, faded upholstery on the furniture, and layers of dust on most of the surfaces, the house was livable. She followed Remy past the living room into the kitchen where the scent of fried chicken coated the air. Kyle stood at the stove removing pieces of chicken from a pan and placing it on a large platter. On the counter of the island between them was a bowl of mashed potatoes, a bowl of green beans, and a basket of biscuits. Remy stood silently beside her practically salivating as she looked at the platter of chicken. Kyle didn't acknowledge them until he'd set the platter on the counter with the rest of the food.

"I asked you to bring her to me ten minutes ago. What took so long?" He gave Remy a hard stare.

Remy dragged her gaze from the food to look at him. "I wanted to do a quick walk around the perimeter first."

Kyle narrowed his gaze at her as if he was trying to detect the lie then sighed and looked away as he went to the refrigerator and took out a pitcher of lemonade. Once he seemed satisfied with what he had, he finally acknowledged her with that condescending smile she always hated.

"So glad you could join us for dinner, Ava."

"Enough of the games, Kyle. What do you want?"

He clucked his tongue disapprovingly. "You were always so impatient. Ready to jump without question when Daddy called. Well, Daddy isn't here and we're going to enjoy a nice dinner before we get down to business." He picked up the platter of chicken and bowl of potatoes then walked toward another doorway leading to what looked to be the dining room. "Remy, would you be so kind as to grab the rest?"

Ava watched as Remy did as she was told like an adoring lapdog, managing to balance the remaining bowls in her beefy arms. Ava gazed around the kitchen for a weapon.

"Do you have a death wish?" Remy asked.

Ava met her frown with a hard stare. "Not for my own, no."

Remy jerked her head for Ava to grab the pitcher of lemonade then had her walk into the room ahead of her. Already seated at the table were the rest of the crew that had kidnapped her. The two other women were dressed in camo pants and T-shirts while the men still wore their tactical clothing. Kyle sat at the head of the table and directed her and Remy to the other end. Remy placed the bowls she carried in the middle of the table then held the seat at the end of the table out for Ava, who placed the pitcher on the table and hesitantly took her seat. She looked around feeling like she was in some strange nightmare. It was like the weirdest family dinner ever.

Remy left and returned with two laptops. She placed one before Kyle and the other before Ava, opened it, then sat in the chair beside her. Open on the screen was a videoconferencing application.

"Since you're so eager to get things started, why don't we invite our long-distance dinner guests to join us."

Remy reached over and chose the "Join Meeting" button. First Kyle, then her image popped up on the screen followed by a third.

"Dad!" Ava couldn't believe she was looking at her father. His face looked thinner, but he looked healthy and strong, which was a big difference from the last time she saw him looking weak and frail in a hospital bed.

"Hey, Buttercup. How are you doing? Has anyone hurt you?"

"No, I'm fine, under the circumstances. How are you? Where's Mom?"

"I'm right here, honey." Her father moved over so that her mother could slide in next to him. They looked to be in his office at the house.

"And I'm fine," her father added with a small grin.

There was so much she wanted to say but knew this wasn't the time for it. Kyle must have thought so as well because suddenly the Mute symbol appeared at the bottom of her and her parents' video feed.

"Now that we've all determined we're fine let's move on to more important matters, our dinner is getting cold."

Ava could see her father's mouth moving but of course she couldn't hear what he was saying. Kyle ignored him and continued.

"In exchange for your beloved little girl I want a quarter of Diamond Unlimited's worth transferred to an offshore account, which I've emailed to you. Once I've confirmed that the money has been transferred and that you're not trying to bullshit me, I'll send you the coordinates for Ava's location."

Ava's father looked as if he were cursing Kyle out and her mother seemed to be trying to calm him down.

"Sorry, Marcus, you seem to be muted. Just nod yes or no if you agree to the terms."

Whatever her mother said seemed to take the steam right out of her father's anger. He suddenly looked tired and no longer like the youthful man he was before Kyle almost ended his life. He nodded. Kyle switched the mute off.

"I knew you'd see the sense of it. You have until nine a.m. Monday. And you can tell your little friend Travis to not even bother trying to trace this call, the email I sent, or the account. It won't do any good."

"Why are you doing this, Kyle?" Ava's father asked. "I was going to make you a partner, you would have had what you'd been wanting all along."

"You have no clue what I've wanted, only what I've made you believe. You're so blinded by your own ego that you couldn't see the truth right in front of you."

"I'm so sorry for what happened to your father, but it was not my fault," Ava's father said softly. "I'll give you the money, but please don't take any of this out on my child."

Ava's heart was breaking at the pain and vulnerability her father was expressing.

Kyle's amenable mask slipped, and something dark and angry replaced it. He looked at Ava over the top of the laptop with a cruel smile then back down at the camera. "I've changed my mind. In addition to giving me the money, you're going to announce that Ava is no longer heir apparent to the Prescott legacy. You are going to disown her publicly and legally."

"Why? She has nothing to do with this. I'll step down, I'll retire. Isn't that what you've been trying to get me to do for years now?"

"No, that would be too easy. My father's chance to provide a legacy for me was stolen by you so why should Ava be able to benefit from a legacy that I should have been a part of?"

"I can't get all of that done by nine a.m. I need more time," Ava's father said.

Kyle gave a cruel laugh. "Don't play me for a fool, Marcus. I know you've got an attorney at your beck and call at all hours of the night and day. Agree to these new terms or you won't have to disown Ava for her to lose her legacy."

He looked over at Remy who didn't look like she wanted to do whatever it was he was silently asking her to do, but she reached down, pulled her gun out of its holster, and aimed it at the side of Ava's head for her parents to see. Ava's heart felt like it stopped beating.

"NOOO!" her mother screamed.

"I AGREE!" her father yelled at the same time.

She stared at her parents' image, trying to memorize everything about them before she died. Her mother had her face buried in her father's shoulder as she openly wept. Her father also wept, repeating, "I agree...I agree..." over and over as he locked eyes with her. At that moment, all her focus and time spent on securing her place in the Prescott legacy, of dreaming of the day when she would take her place at the head of the firm's table meant nothing.

"I love you," she said to her parents.

Her mother turned back to the camera, her face tear-streaked as she tried to pull herself together. "We love you to, Buttercup. Please, Kyle, we'll do anything, please."

Ava didn't think she could despise Kyle any more than she already did until that moment when he'd broken her parents' spirit and had them begging for her life. He smiled cruelly then waved his hand and Remy withdrew the gun from Ava's head. Ava sagged with relief, and it looked as if her father did the same. Her mother had a death grip on her father's hand, her face raised to the sky whispering, "Thank you."

"Nine a.m. Monday morning, Marcus, no later or every minute you're late will cost Ava a lovely, manicured finger," he said matter-of-factly before ending the call.

With heartbreak, Ava watched her parents image disappear in a blink. She stared at the desktop screen until Remy reached over to slowly close the laptop. Ava gazed over at her, adding her to the very short list of people she despised which currently only included her and Kyle. Ava was surprised to find her looking almost as shaken by what happened as she felt.

"Well, the food's probably cold now, but everyone please feel free to eat," Kyle said, reaching for the tongs and placing several pieces of chicken on his plate as if he hadn't just threatened to kill her via video in front of her parents and his dinner guests.

Except for Ava and Remy, everyone else did the same, piling food on their plates like they hadn't had a decent meal in weeks.

"Remy, since you and our guest of honor are choosing not to eat, please take her back to her room and then begin preparations for our departure later tonight," Kyle said.

Ava couldn't have heard him correctly. "We're leaving tonight?"

"Yes. As I said to Marcus, there's no way Travis will be able to trace the call, but I'm not going to wait around to find out."

Ava was going to have to chance contacting Paige's mother again to let her know. Maybe Paige hadn't come yet because whatever firewalls Kyle had blocked the video call from being traced also blocked any other electronic devices nearby from being tracked. There was also the chance that Paige was doing what Kyle's team had done to them, lying in wait until late in the night to make their move, which could be too late if Kyle was planning to leave before then. Ava didn't wait for Remy as she stood and left the dining room. She heard a muffled curse then footsteps hurrying behind her. Remy's long stride caught up within a few steps.

"I didn't enjoy doing that," Remy said as they left the house.

"But you did it, so it doesn't matter how you felt," Ava said angrily, unsuccessfully trying to outpace her.

Remy must have caught the hint and slowed her step so that Ava could pull ahead of her. When she arrived at the storage room, Ava was relieved to see the jacket still on the cot and noticed that there were two more bottles of water on the table. Remy's thoughtfulness would've meant something if she hadn't held a gun to Ava's head in front of her parents.

"I truly am sorry, Ms. Prescott," she said softly before closing the door and locking her in.

Ava waited a few minutes before she picked up the jacket to retrieve the phone and almost cried when she saw the thin red line on the battery indicator. She had to still try and call. Just as she was about to choose the emergency call button, she heard voices and then the door being unlocked. Ava shoved the phone between the mattress and frame of the cot, praying whoever it was wouldn't stay long. The door opened and Kyle entered with a napkin covered plate. He set it on the table then took a seat in the chair.

"Came to gloat, you sadistic fuck." Ava surprised herself with her own vehemence.

Kyle smiled in amusement. "You kiss your mother with that mouth?"

"At least I have a mother to kiss." She knew that was low, but the man had a gun put to her head, so she didn't care.

His smile faltered but stayed in place. "You shouldn't talk about things you don't know shit about."

"I know that our fathers were friends at one time and that my father brought your father on as a partner in his first company, then your father thanked him by embezzling money from the company to pay off gambling debt. Your father was lucky mine had a good heart back then. He could've had your father locked up but instead he set him up with a nice cushion because he didn't want for you and your mother to have to pay for your father's lack of control. I know my father refusing to help him find a job seems unfair, but knowing what you know about my father and what Diamond Unlimited represents to him, what would you have expected him to do?"

"Did your father tell you that fairy tale? That he's the innocent one who was wronged by a friend. Well, I hate to bust your rose-colored bubble about your father but that's not what my father told me that happened. You were right about one thing; they were friends and did start Prescott Financials together. But my father said he didn't embezzle anything. Marcus wanted to bring Max in and keep the business within the family. They tried buying my father out, but he refused so Marcus set him up and threatened to turn the evidence over to the Federal Trade Commission unless he accepted the buyout. My father had no choice but to take it, but Marcus ruined his career anyway. When he couldn't find a job, my mother took what money we had left and abandoned us. To this day that bitch swears she didn't and that my father gambled it away."

The murderous look on his face made Ava thankful she wasn't his mother. She treaded cautiously seeing how the subject darkened his mood further.

"We both have seen my father's generosity extended to many of Diamond's employees without question. When Donald in marketing lost his home in a fire due to shoddy wiring by his contractor, my father covered the cost of his family's temporary housing as well as what his homeowner's insurance didn't cover. When he found out Max Jr's assistant was struggling to make ends meet while trying to pay for her mother's nursing home care, he covered the cost for a whole year so that she could get back on track with her personal finances. That's just two of the many people he's helped in and outside the company financially. That doesn't count all the interns and Diamond employees whose positions were eliminated that he's helped find jobs for at other firms when we didn't have any openings available. I'm not saying what your father said happened isn't true, I just find it difficult to believe that if my father trusted him enough to start the company with him, why he would suddenly want to push him out."

Kyle frowned. "Who knows? Greed is a powerful motivation for a man to act out of character. So is guilt. Maybe he's been trying to ease his guilt. It doesn't matter anyway. The person he should've been helping was left out in the cold to do whatever it took to take care of his family. After my mother abandoned us, my father ended up having to borrow money through illegal channels and when he couldn't pay it back, they forced him to work for them for free doing their books as payment while he struggled to keep a roof over our heads working as a janitor. I did what I could to help, but I was just a kid, not even old enough to get a crappy minimum wage job, so I ran errands for the same guys my father worked for. We did that for four years before he couldn't take it anymore and put a gun in his mouth, leaving me to not only find him, but also take on his debt. My father had taught me everything he knew about finances, so I was bumped up from errand boy to accountant. It took years to work off what my father owed," Kyle said bitterly as he stood and began pacing.

"He also told me everything that happened with Marcus and my mother. Until then I had no idea why she'd left or how we had gone from a nice house in the suburbs to a roach infested apartment in the hood. All I knew was that whatever happened had broken my father's spirit. The day of his funeral when Child Protective Services came and got me, I promised I would make Marcus Prescott pay for what he'd done to my family. He took the most important person in my life away from me," Kyle stopped directly in front of Ava, glaring contemptuously down at her. "And I plan on doing the same to him."

Ava's heart skipped a beat as the truth dawned on her. "It was never about the money or the company, was it? It's about me."

He stepped away, back over to the table, removed the napkin from the plate he'd brought in and picked up a chicken leg, studying it intently before he took a bite. He chewed thoughtfully for a moment then sat down and focused on Ava again.

"My father was good at finances, but his passion was cooking. He'd planned to open a restaurant until your father shot everything to hell." He took another bite of the chicken, smiling wistfully. "This was his recipe."

His mood shifts were all over the place. Ava felt as if she were in front of three different people. She sat quietly as he finished his chicken, tossed the bone onto the table, and wiped his hands and mouth with the napkin.

"Where was I? Oh, yes. No, this has never been about the money. It's been about finding Marcus's weakness, his kryptonite. That, dearest Ava, is you, his progeny. Once you're out of the picture, Marcus and his empire will fall like a house of cards with a good wind gust," he said gleefully.

"Do you really think disowning me will make him give up Diamond? You underestimate how much that company means to him."

"After everything I just told you, do you really believe I'm going to stop at him disowning you? I know you're smarter than that, Ava. A shrewd businesswoman like you should be able to see the full picture without someone having to spell it out for you."

Ava had seen his big picture; she had just hoped she was wrong. Kyle didn't plan on Ava ever going home. He wanted to break her father and he had a front row seat over the past ten years to find out just how to do that.

Kyle smiled knowingly. "There it is. The truth of the matter. This would've all been over with in a much less dramatic fashion if you had just gone along with the marriage. There would've been an accident shortly after the honeymoon. A car accident, an attempted robbery gone wrong, something tragic but could be easily explained away. I would be there to comfort my dear old father-in-law, suggest he take some time to mourn, then snatched Diamond right out from under him when he chose me as his heir apparent. But no, you and your mother had to fuck it all up, so here we are."

Ava shook her head, a sense of panic coming over her. "You don't need to do this. Just take the money and go. I won't say anything. I'll even convince my family not to either. You can get away with a fortune and the satisfaction of knowing what you took away from me by asking my father to disown me. Why can't that be enough? Killing me won't bring your father back."

"No, but it'll make me feel better." He moved to stand then stopped, tilting his head to the side as he looked at something beneath the cot.

Ava bent forward to look and her body ran cold. A light from Paige's phone shone brightly then blinked off. In her hurry to hide it, she must have placed the phone beneath the mattress with the screen facing down. She looked up to find Kyle coming at her so quickly she barely had time to escape before he grabbed her shirt sleeve and slammed her back down on the mattress. Ava struggled, but he grabbed her by the collar and held her down as he reached under the mattress and pulled the phone out. He kept pressing the button, but nothing seemed to be happening. Ava figured the light was from the notification about the battery dying and the phone shutting down.

"REMY!" he bellowed.

Ava was finding it difficult to breath as he pressed down on her chest. She clawed and scratched at his arm, but all he did was look down at her as if she were a pesky bug that he was sick of swatting at.

"There's no need to shout. I'm right outside the door," Ava heard Remy say.

Kyle straightened, finally releasing and giving her room to breathe. She took several gulps of air as she struggled to sit up.

Kyle stalked slowly toward Remy holding the phone up. "What is this?"

Remy looked at him in confusion. "A phone?"

His hand came up and slammed across her face so fast she stood there staring at him in shock.

"I know it's a phone, you fucking horse-faced behemoth! How the fuck did she manage to still have it after you told me that you searched her before you brought her here." His voice was deadly calm.

There was a moment of hurt in Remy's eyes before her face became a mask of controlled anger. She straightened to her full height which matched Kyle's head-to-head. "Whatever you do to me in the bedroom is fair game, but don't you EVER strike me like that outside of it or you'll wish you'd never met me. I searched for and removed the obvious threats of her gun and ammo. I didn't check every orifice and crack she has."

Ava couldn't see Kyle's face, but he'd have to be crazy not to be intimidated by Remy. Then again, he'd done a pretty good job of proving he was crazy just during their conversation moments ago. He tossed the phone at her. It bounced off her chest onto the floor as he walked around her.

"Thanks to your incompetence our timetable has moved up. We need to be ready to go within the next ten minutes," he said in parting.

Remy didn't move as she stared at the empty space in front of her, her chest heaving, and her face becoming a mottled red. "Let's go," she said between clenched teeth.

Ava hesitated. If they left now, there was no way Paige would find her in time.

Remy turned to look at her. "Do you want to get out of here or not? I don't give a shit either way because I'm done."

Ava could see that she meant it. She looked hurt and tired. "When you say out of here do you mean you're going to help me escape?"

Remy sighed with frustration. "The longer you sit there asking stupid questions the less time we have."

That's all the confirmation Ava needed. She sprung off the cot just as Remy turned to leave, retrieving Paige's phone, and stuffing it in her sweatpants pocket as she followed.

"Taking her to the john before we head out," Remy told the guard at the barn door.

He nodded and pushed the door open. Remy was just about to step through when Ava heard a *thunk* and the guard went down screaming and grabbing at his thigh where blood began pouring through his fingers. Remy stepped back behind the second door, throwing a hand across Ava's chest to hold her back as well.

"Well, I guess the cavalry is here." Remy's voice was laced with humor and a ghost of a smile appeared on her face.

"I'm glad you can find some humor in the fact that someone is shooting at us."

Remy looked over at her and quirked a brow. "Us? If I opened this door right now to reveal both of us, who do you think they'll shoot?"

Her question was answered by several more screams of pain. The guard with them that had been shot had managed to drag himself back into the barn, leaving the door open. With gritted teeth, he was strapping his belt around his wounded leg moaning and cursing in pain.

"They're here for you, so you might as well go. I imagine they've got a sniper out there somewhere who'll recognize if you're someone they need to shoot or not," Remy suggested.

That made sense to Ava. "Thank you."

Remy shrugged. "Us girls gotta stick together against the bullies of the world. And again, I really am sorry about what I did earlier. Nobody's parents should have to go through something like that."

Ava could see she was sincere but that didn't mean she was forgiving. She simply nodded and changed places with Remy so that she would be closer to the door. She eased out, with her arms raised, praying Remy was right about them being able to see who she was. Several people lay out in the open, as if they had been trying to make it to the barn when they were shot. Some were still, others were groaning in pain like the guard in the barn. One attempted to move and was stopped by the spray of dirt from a bullet shot near his head.

"Ava!" she recognized Paige's voice.

"Paige!"

"Keep walking forward!"

Ava did as she was instructed and saw a dark silhouette rise out of the tall grass several feet from the barn and began to run toward it. Something whizzed past her head, kicking up dried dirt at Paige's feet.

"Take one more step and the next one is aimed at her head. If she moves or anyone tries to shoot me, there's another aimed at your head."

Ava stopped at the sound of Kyle's shouting. After that, other than the sound of a screen door opening and slamming shut, Ava's focus was on Paige as she slowly stepped into the dim light around the perimeter of the barn. Their gazes locked and she saw fear and anger in Paige's eyes. She heard footsteps behind her then felt something pressed into her side.

"You and your little friend are getting on my last fucking nerves," Kyle said in frustration. "Tell your crew to drop their weapons and come out where me and my shooters can see them!" he shouted at Paige.

"The jig is up," Paige said.

A silhouette stood from several feet behind Paige, one stepped out from behind a storage shed nearby and another with a familiar gait and broad shoulders that Ava would recognize from anywhere walked up the path from the gate at the entrance. They stepped into the light to stand with Paige, all dressed in black cargo pants, black T-shirts and black bullet-proof vests. They resembled some elite hit squad that Ava could imagine taking on major bad guys with no problem. From the looks of it, the four of them managed to take down most of Kyle's crew.

"That's it? Just four of you did all this damage. I'm impressed."

The two other women in Kyle's crew joined them with rifles aimed at Paige and her team.

"Letty, get one of the trucks," Kyle instructed.

One of the women slung her rifle over her shoulder and jogged back toward the barn. After several minutes she still hadn't returned and there was no sound of a truck being started.

"Just give up already, Edwards," Paige said, looking bored with this whole situation.

"Or what? Obviously, despite the havoc you managed to wreak, we've still got the advantage and since I don't hear sirens or see flashing lights heading this way, you're on your own. So, why don't you just admit you're in way over your head with this whole soldier of fortune thing you got going," Kyle said.

"You invade the sanctity of my home, threaten the lives of my friends, and you don't think I'm going to make you pay for that?"

"Enough of this bullshit. Letty! What the fuck is taking so long!" he shouted.

"She's indisposed at the moment," Ava heard Remy say.

Then all hell broke loose. The second woman went down with a shot to the head, Kyle turned around holding Ava around the waist, using her as a shield as he shot at Remy who ducked back into the barn. Since he no longer had the gun pointed at her, she stomped her heel into his instep, hinged her leg back for a heel kick to his groin, slammed her head back for a head butt, grabbed the index and middle finger of the hand around her waist pulling them back to release his grip, then lifted her elbow for a strike to his throat. On his way down Ava grabbed the gun, put some distance between them, and turned pointing it at him as he knelt on the ground trying to catch his breath.

"You...bitch..." he wheezed out.

Ava looked at him, kneeling on the ground before her, and all she had to do was pull the trigger to bring all of this to an end. She knew his need for revenge was so strong that nothing was going to stop him from coming after her and her family again. He would probably get locked up for the rest of his life for all that he'd done but you never knew. Kyle could charm the rattle off a snake, there was no telling what he would do to plead his case or convince someone to take a plea deal to lessen his sentence.

He gave her a knowing smirk. "Do it."

Ava's finger hovered over the trigger. She never thought she would be capable of shooting someone until now. Seeing her father lying helpless in a coma after being shot, almost being kidnapped in New Orleans, Paige's home being overrun by his hired hands, her parents' faces as Remy held the gun to her head, all under Kyle's instruction. All she had to do was squeeze and it would all be over.

"Ava, it's not worth it," Paige said softly from behind her.

"You don't know what he's done. What he almost did." Tears of anger blurred Kyle from her vision.

"I'm sure he deserves it but not at the sacrifice of your peace of mind."

Ava knew she was right. No matter how evil he was, killing Kyle would wear on her conscience forever. She took a shaky breath and was just lowering the gun when she saw something in Kyle's hand as he moved to leap toward her. Ava didn't even realize she pulled the trigger until she saw Kyle jerk away from her. His eyes widened in shock, his mouth opened and closed like a fish, and blood began flowing from a hole in his neck as he collapsed like a rag doll at her feet. Paige's arms came around her, grasping Ava's hands and the gun.

"Let go, babe," she whispered.

Ava's hands shook as she released the gun. She couldn't tear her eyes away from Kyle's prone body and the growing pool of blood beneath him. Out of the corner of her eye she saw Paige's hand passing the gun to someone else then she was being turned away from the horrifying sight and pulled into Paige's arms.

CHAPTER TWENTY-THREE

Paige stood near the ambulance where Ava was being checked out by the paramedics, surveying the scene around her. Mounds' entire sheriff's department along with investigators from the local FBI were swarming all over the scene. Junior had allowed her team some time to "contain" the situation before calling in his guys and the feds. She'd sent her team back to the ranch to avoid having to be detained and questioned. Fortunately, the only casualty had been Kyle. Everyone else would survive with nothing more than a limp or scar to remember the night by. Lucas had even managed to sneak in the house and take out the shooters Kyle had on her and Ava without firing a shot. That's why he wasn't with the rest of them when they'd been called out. Rambette, or Remy, as Paige later found out from Ava, had surrendered after Kyle had been shot. She was saved from Paige's wrath when Ava told her that Remy was trying to help her escape when they'd shown up.

Paige glanced over at Ava who sat on the back of the truck wrapped in a blanket looking so small and vulnerable. She hated that Ava had been the one to take Kyle down. Killing someone, whether by accident or self-defense was not something you could just get over and go on with your life like nothing ever happened. Especially when you'd never been in that position before. The paramedic finished her examination and left to help tend to some of the other wounded.

Paige stepped over and sat beside Ava. "How're you doing?"

Ava shrugged. "I think I might still be in shock because I feel numb. Is that normal?"

"There's no standard reaction for stuff like this. I recommend going to talk to a therapist when you go home. The sooner the better. Something like this can eat away at you if you let it fester."

Ava turned away, looking down at her fingers as she fidgeted with the blanket. "I'll do that. Speaking of home, I need to call my parents. They've been through enough. They're probably frantic worrying if I'm okay."

"Ezekiel has been informed of what went down. He's with them so I'm sure they know you're safe, but we can call them as soon as we get back to the house so you can tell them yourself."

"Thank you." Ava gazed back up at her. "For rescuing me far too many times for one person needing to be rescued, for bringing me to your home and putting up with me all this time, and for not treating me like the rich princess everyone assumes I am."

Paige took Ava's hand. "It's been an honor and a pleasure being your knight in cowboy boots and sharing my home with you. There's nothing wrong with being a princess as long as you're a badass princess like you."

Ava gave her a sweet smile and bumped her shoulder.

"Excuse me, Ms. Prescott, I'm Agent Franklin, FBI." He showed them his badge. "We're going to need you to come to the station for a statement."

"Now? This can't wait until the morning?" Paige asked. "She's already answered your questions. Can't you see she's been through enough."

Ava gave her hand a squeeze. "It's all right, Paige. It's probably better to do it now while everything is still fresh in my mind."

"Okay, but I'm taking you and having Willie's oldest son, Tristan, meet us at the station. He's an attorney."

"Thank you…again."

Paige raised their clasped hands and placed a kiss on the back of Ava's. "You're welcome."

It was close to eleven at night by the time they got back to the ranch. The Tech Twins were asleep on the sofa bed and Paige assumed Grant, Brian, Tracey, and Lucas were in the remaining guest rooms. She set the house alarm and, out of habit, checked the perimeter cameras from her phone. The Twins had fixed and reconfigured the Wi-Fi and security pads at the perimeter gates and updated the cameras earlier that afternoon.

"Everything locked up tight?" Ava asked.

She looked like she was ready to drop any minute. "Yep. You should go to bed. You've had quite the adventure."

Ava looked worriedly toward the hall leading to her room.

"Would you like to stay with me tonight? I promise to keep my hands to myself."

She looked relieved. "Yes, I would, if it's not too much trouble. I know you're tired also."

Paige smiled and offered her hand. Ava smiled in return and placed her hand in Paige's, letting her guide her through the house to her room.

Ava felt mentally and physically drained. This had literally been the day from hell, and she just wanted it done. She'd been grateful for Paige's offer to sleep with her because she couldn't bear the thought of sleeping in that big room alone. She now understood why Paige had chosen not to use it as her master suite. She knew she would be seeing shadowy figures in every dark corner and never be able to fall asleep. Ava hoped the draining tiredness would be enough to keep her nightmares at bay. She'd been unsuccessfully trying all night to get the image of Kyle lying in a pool of his own blood out of her head, but just as she thought it was finally gone, it would pop back up bringing with it the horror that she'd been the one who shot him.

Even now, as they entered into Paige's room, Ava stopped in the doorway as she looked down to find Kyle lying on the floor at the end of Paige's bed, the pool of blood creeping closer and closer to her feet, making her back out of the room. She didn't even realize she still held Paige's hand and was tugging her along.

"Ava," Paige said.

Ava heard her but she sounded like she was far away.

"Ava!" Paige's voice sounded closer, but not enough to pull Ava away from what she was seeing.

Ava knew she had to be the one to do it, so she closed her eyes, counted to ten, then opened them to find Paige standing in front of her looking at her with concern.

"Do you still see them?" Ava asked her.

"Who?"

"All the people you…" She couldn't even finish the sentence. Paige must have understood what she was asking. "Not in detail. It's usually just shadows and sometimes includes the people I lost as well."

Ava felt her eyes burn with the tears she'd been holding back all night. "So, he'll never go away? I'm always going to be haunted by him?"

Paige took Ava's face in her hands. "Not if I can help it." She gave her a soft kiss, then steered her toward the bathroom. "I know you're tired, but I think a nice steam shower will do you some good."

Ava agreed. For some reason she felt like she had the scent of death on her. Paige had her sit on a cushioned stool then walked over and turned on her shower. After that task was completed, she helped her undress. It was then that Ava remembered that she had left the flak jacket at the farm, but Paige's phone was in her pants pocket.

Ava gave her a weak smile. "I have something for you." She handed Paige her phone. The screen had a crack, which probably happened when it bounced off Remy and landed on the ground. "Sorry about the damage. I'll pay for another one."

"Don't worry about it. I was due for an upgrade anyway. Now, you go ahead and enjoy the steam while I make you a cup of tea." Paige turned to leave but Ava grabbed her hand.

"I don't want tea. I just don't want to be alone. Stay with me."

Paige gave her a comforting smile. "Okay. I'll be right here."

"No. Come in with me." Ava pointed to the shower.

"Are you sure?"

"Yes."

As Paige undressed, Ava opened the shower door and was enveloped by warm steam. She closed her eyes, breathed deeply, and felt as if she were floating. She heard Paige enter but found she couldn't move. Paige placed her hands on Ava's waist and guided her backward until she felt her leg bump the shower bench. They sat side by side and Ava scooted over to lay her head on Paige's shoulder. Paige's arm came up around her, holding her close.

"You make me feel so secure and taken care of. No one's ever done that for me," Ava admitted.

"I've never been with anyone I felt so protective of and wanted to take care of like I do you. Especially someone so strong and independent who doesn't act like being vulnerable is a weakness."

"I never thought it was a weakness, but I was afraid to show any vulnerability. I've had to be the great Marcus Prescott's daughter for so long that I didn't know how to be me until I came here."

Paige placed a kiss on the top of her head. "You don't ever have to be anything but you when you're with me. Here or anywhere."

Ava's heart soared hearing Paige say that, but her head slowly filled with doubts. She wanted to be with Paige. To continue to be surprised by her, to laugh with her, to feel protected and safe with her, but she didn't know how it would work. Now that Kyle was gone, his threats and blackmail were no longer an issue. She could go back to her old life, but after experiencing the life she'd had here at the ranch these past weeks with Paige, her old life was no longer satisfying. She wanted more and she knew, deep down, the only place she would get that was with Paige.

"You haven't fallen asleep on me, have you?" Paige asked.

"No, just thinking."

"Anything you want to share. What's said in the steam room stays in the steam room," Paige said teasingly.

Ava smiled to herself. She loved this woman. It was hard to believe that she could honestly say that in such a short time of knowing her, but she did. What was the crazy chance that Paige felt the same way? If she did, how would they manage a relationship living thousands of miles apart? Ava had barely managed to keep her long-distance relationship with Selena going before her fake relationship with Kyle blew up her life. Although, thinking about it, as much as she cared for Selena and believed she might've been a little in love with her, Ava realized her feelings for her college sweetheart weren't even in the same ballpark as her feelings for Paige. She had to find out if Paige felt the same because she was willing to do whatever it took to explore what they could have together.

"I guess I can finally go home." Ava attempted to sound nonchalant.

"I guess so."

"Maybe, when things at home return to a sense of normalcy, I can come back and visit. That is if you aren't sick of me."

"I don't think I could ever be sick of you."

"Really?" Ava sat up so that she could look at Paige, but the steamy fog that surrounded them kept her from seeing her face clearly.

"Really." Paige grasped Ava's face and leaned in for a kiss that was steamier than the air in the shower. She followed it with a trail of kisses along her damp neck, up to her ear and whispered, "Why don't we get out of here before we turn into a couple of prunes."

"Okay," Ava agreed breathlessly.

Paige stood and turned the steam off and the fan on. Ava followed her out of the shower and accepted the large soft towel Paige offered her before taking her hand and leading her into the bedroom. To her surprise, the weariness she felt earlier was gone. The air was cool against her skin dampened and warmed by the shower, but before Ava could dry off, Paige was picking her up into her arms and carrying her over to the bed where she gently laid her down. When she joined her, Paige's touch was soft and gentle but didn't lack passion. For a little while, she made Ava forget about the past couple of days, worrying about going home, or even what tomorrow would bring. All that mattered was right here, right now, within the safety and security of Paige's arms. She brought Ava to the peak of passion and held her tightly as she free-fell over the cliff onto a cushion of sweet satisfaction.

When Ava tried to reciprocate their lovemaking, Paige stopped her. "That was all about you and helping you relax."

Ava didn't argue, just cuddled against Paige, their bodies fitting together like the last two pieces of a puzzle. She had to keep herself from asking Ava to stay so that she could continue to protect her and help her through the post-traumatic stress she was already experiencing from what happened to her tonight. She wanted to keep Ava in the safe little cocoon they had created over the past month, but she knew that couldn't happen. Ava had a whole other life Paige was sure she was anxious to return to and there was nothing she could do about it, despite how she felt about her. She would treasure this moment and whatever moments they had left before she let Ava walk out of her life. A life that obviously wasn't meant to be shared by anyone, not even someone as beautiful, funny, intelligent, and fearless as Ava Prescott.

"Paige?"

"Hm?"

"Could you ever see yourself living anyplace else but here?"

Paige didn't even have to think about it. "No. I built this place to settle down in. I have no desire to leave it."

"Oh." Ava sounded disappointed.

"Do you ever see yourself living someplace other than Chicago?"

Ava didn't answer right away. "I honestly don't know anymore. A few weeks ago, I would've said no without hesitation, but now…" Paige felt her shrug.

"What's changed?" Paige's heart felt like it had stopped beating, waiting for Ava's reply.

Ava shifted, propping her head on her hand to look at Paige. "Being here. Being with you. Before my life was turned upside down, the only thing that mattered to me were my family and Diamond Unlimited. When I was pushed to leave and began a new life in New Orleans, I felt a sense of freedom I had never experienced before. There were no pressures to prove to my father that I was worthy of filling his shoes. My biggest worry, besides Kyle finding me, was avoiding drunk customers hitting on me. Then you brought me here to what I expected to be the longest two weeks of my life out in the middle of nowhere and I became thoroughly charmed by your little slice of heaven, Willie and Adele, the menagerie, including Brutus, but don't tell him, and you."

Paige's heart stuttered to a start as she saw something in Ava's eyes that matched what she was feeling.

"I like who I am when I'm here. I like not having to be *on* and in control all the time and feeling soft and cared for. Being here…being with you…has brought out a part of me I never knew existed and I don't want to tuck her away to go back to a life that no longer fits the woman I've become."

"So, what are you saying?"

"I need to know how you feel."

Paige reached over and ran a finger along Ava's cheek. "Like everything in my life has led me to you. Up until three weeks ago, I felt as if I'd just been living day-to-day, but you've shown me that I want more in life. You've brought light into the darkness that I'd been hiding behind as an excuse to be alone. I don't want to be alone anymore, Ava, but I also don't want to be with anyone else but you."

Ava's eyes sparkled with unshed tears. She grasped Paige's hand and placed a soft kiss to each callus on her palm, then gazed at her with such deep love that it made her want to cry from joy.

"What are we going to do?" Ava asked.

Paige had a feeling that if she asked Ava to stay, she would do it, but that would be selfish. Just like Paige had to face her demons before she could move on with her life, Ava was going to have to go back home and face hers before she could do the same. She didn't want Ava to leave and knew she was taking a chance of losing her if she went back to Chicago and realized that Paige wasn't who she wanted after all, but it was what needed to happen.

"You're going to call your family tomorrow to send the jet for you as soon as possible, then you're going back home to claim your life back. Until you do that, you won't be able to move forward. When you're ready, I'll be here waiting whenever you need a little slice of heaven with your knight in cowboy boots."

Ava looked as if she would argue but Paige cut off whatever she was going to say with a kiss that left no room for anything but passion.

CHAPTER TWENTY-FOUR

Ava stood backstage watching her father officially announce his retirement to the audience of Diamond Unlimited's two hundred employees who sat before him in the audience and watched him via live stream from their offices in New York, Florida, and Los Angeles. When he announced that Ava would be stepping up as CEO, she was greeted with loud applause and a standing ovation. She thanked their employees for standing by them during the tumultuous year, promised that the change in leadership would not affect the company's structure, then announced the bonus she and her father had agreed would be a sign of good faith and appreciation. After excited applause, a buffet breakfast was served at all the Diamond offices and the employees were offered the rest of the day off to get an early start on their weekend.

After everyone had gone, Ava sat alone at a table as the catering staff were cleaning up trying to muster the excitement that she thought she should be feeling after a culmination of years of hard work and sacrifice had finally paid off to give her what she'd practically been begging for. She was happy her father was finally taking a well-deserved retirement and honored that he felt confident leaving the company in her hands, but there was something missing. She had been home for three months. Getting back into the swing of things wasn't easy, but she hadn't expected it to be after having been gone for a year. She'd followed how Diamond was doing in the financial news over that time. They had lost a few clients after the shakeup of her father being shot, then her leaving, and several more after the truth of Kyle's involvement, but it was expected and ultimately had minimum effect on their bottom line. Ava had just found it difficult to return to the crazy schedule she had kept before she left. Twelve-hour days were no longer possible, especially after spending her nights fighting nightmares filled with Kyle and her guilt from killing him.

After weeks of insomnia when it got to the point that she was getting no more than three hours of sleep, on a good night, she finally relented to Paige's pleas to seek professional help. They spoke via video chat daily in the weeks after Ava returned to Chicago, but it became less frequent as both of their schedules became busier. It also didn't help that they had gotten into an argument when Paige wouldn't give Ava a definite answer for when she could come to Chicago for a visit. Ava had accused Paige of being too afraid to step out of her comfort zone and that she was using the ranch as her crutch to hobble along through life with the unrealistic belief that nothing could exist beyond that world. Paige had accused her of acting like a spoiled heiress in thinking that the world revolved around her, and that Paige was just supposed to drop everything to hop on a jet at her whim. Hurt and angry, Ava told Paige that if that's what she thought of her after everything they'd been through together then there was nothing left to say. Paige agreed and they hadn't spoken for almost a month. The last she heard was that Paige was in Europe on a case tracking down a couple that had skipped town after conning a widow out of her life savings. The only reason she knew that was because her mother had become friends with Adele who she spoke with regularly.

There had been so many times Ava had been tempted to call or text Paige, but her damned Prescott pride wouldn't let her, so she quietly nursed her broken heart while trying to maintain her sanity in therapy and her obligation to the Prescott legacy at work.

"Why are you looking like someone stole your joy?" her father asked as he sat beside her. "I thought you'd be thrilled about this. Your old man is retiring and you're finally getting a seat at the grown-ups' table."

Ava tried giving him a happy smile, but she could tell by the concerned look on his face that it hadn't worked.

"Talk to me, Ava. What's going on? You haven't been yourself since you've gotten back, which is understandable considering what you've been through, but even with your therapy and being given what you've worked so hard and long for you still seem unhappy."

Ava was hesitant to talk to her father about her love life. She hadn't even spoken to her therapist about her and Paige's tentative romance. Although Ava was pretty sure her therapist had figured out something had happened between them; she couldn't bring herself to officially talk about it.

Her father took her hand. "Look, I know we've never had the kind of father and daughter relationship where you felt comfortable in sharing the more personal aspects of your life with me, but I'd like that to change. I'm here for you, no matter what. You're my child, my heartbeat. If you're in pain, then so am I. Tell me what's going on?"

Ava fought the pinprick of tears at the back of her eyes. He was right, they had never had that kind of relationship. Her mother was the one she sought advice and comfort from in anything regarding her personal life. But when it came to matters of the heart, Ava felt she was more like her father than her mother and had always wished she could talk to him and seek advice. But he had been so dismissive of her sexuality that she never felt she could. Now, as she gazed up at the love and concern in his eyes and had seen how his brush with death had changed him into a more caring and loving husband and father, Ava knew she could trust her heart in his hands.

"My appearance wasn't the only change that happened while I was away." She smoothed her hand over the waves in her still close-cropped hair. "I had a lot of time to be with myself, away from the pressure of being a Prescott and devoting my life and time to upholding our legacy. As much as I love my family and this company, I need more. Despite how you went about trying to solve the issue, you were right about me needing to find a life outside of Diamond. I had spent so much of it trying to be Marcus Prescott's daughter that I never learned to be Ava Prescott, the woman."

"I blame myself for that. I saw so much potential in you that I burdened you with a legacy that had more to do with my ego than your future. I'm so sorry not only for that but for putting you in the position to feel as if you couldn't be you, to openly love who you choose to love, and to be harmed because of mistakes from my past."

Ava gave his hand a squeeze. "I accept your apology and love you for taking the blame, but I'm just as much responsible for the direction of my life and what happened, but none of that matters now. What does is that you're alive, we're all safe and don't have to worry about Kyle Edwards ever again." Thanks to her therapy, Ava found saying that didn't cause her anxiety or bring on paralyzing visions of what she'd done.

"Then tell me what you need, and I'll get it for you."

"Dad, this isn't one of those situations where dropping the Prescott name will make a difference. As a matter of fact, it's what's causing the issue."

"Does this have anything to do with that private investigator?"

Ava looked at him in surprise. "How did you know?"

He gave her an understanding smile. "You don't think I recognize that lovelorn look so well known in the Prescott clan? It's the same look my mother had whenever I found her looking at pictures of my father, despite what he'd done to us. The same look Max had when he realized he was in love with your aunt Anita, and the same look I see in the mirror at the very thought of your mother. You had that look when you talked about Paige Richards after you first returned home and it's gotten more obvious as time has passed."

Ava shook her head with a sigh. "It doesn't matter. We, and our lives, are too different. She's lived a life full of violence and danger, has finally found her sanctuary and isn't willing to leave it, not even for what we could have. And as much as I care for her and being a part of her little piece of Heaven, I don't want to leave my life behind either. We live in two different worlds with no way to bring them together without one of us sacrificing everything we've worked for." Ava couldn't stop the tears that began falling even if she tried.

Her father pulled her into his arms. "Why does it have to be all or nothing for either of you? There must be a way to compromise where you're both able to have your lives and each other."

Ava sat up and picked up a napkin to dab at her eyes. "Dad, it's Mounds, Oklahoma. It's not like a major city where Diamond has offices that I could possibly move our head offices to. Even if it was, it wouldn't be fair to just relocate the executives and their families for my own satisfaction."

"That's not what I meant. The two of you could set up home offices both here and Oklahoma and alternate living and working from those locations on a six month or quarterly basis. Whatever works best for both of you. With technology the way it is today, you could work remotely from the ranch and fly here for any major meetings on the jet and be back home before the rooster crows," he said with an amused grin.

Ava chuckled. As her father's idea wiggled its way into her doubts, she could see it possibly working. She could even have an adjoining office added on to hers at Diamond for Paige to work out of. And maybe

Paige would be willing to convert some of the space in the library for Ava to use as a home office.

"I see the wheels turning," Ava's father said knowingly.

Ava shook her head. "Paige and I have barely determined what this is between us, let alone discussed living arrangements."

"Buttercup, do you love her?"

"It's crazy to think so after such a short time, but yes." She knew there was no sense in continuing to deny the truth.

"Then the only thing left for you to do is to find out if she feels the same way. Once you determine that, then go from there. Don't let that foolish Prescott pride cause you to lose the woman you love. I almost lost your mother because of it, and I'll be damned if I let you make the same mistake. You've got your whole weekend free. Go home, pack an overnight bag, and I'll arrange to have the jet ready for you in an hour."

Her father was already pulling out his phone and texting. Ava didn't see any reason why she couldn't go and at least talk to Paige, in person, about whatever it was that had begun between them before she'd left Oklahoma. The worst that could happen was that Paige didn't feel the same way or wasn't interested in pursuing what would start as a long-distance relationship. Ava would walk away hurt but with no regrets because she had at least tried.

Her father grinned broadly. "Everything is set. Are you ready for your grand romantic gesture?"

Ava smiled. "You're really enjoying this, aren't you? I didn't even say if I was going."

"Oh, you're going, even if I have to hog-tie and put you on that plane myself," he said, trying to appear stern despite his amusement.

Ava just shook her head, still amazed by how much her father had changed from the serious, no-nonsense numbers man he was before she'd left to the lighthearted, smiling, affectionate one he was now. It took a near-death experience for Marcus Prescott to realize what was most important in life. All Ava needed was a month isolated on a little piece of heaven with a knight in buffed cowboy boots.

It was late afternoon when Paige pulled into her driveway so relieved to be home that she just sat in her truck with the windows open, breathing in the crisp fall air. She'd spent the past few weeks traipsing across Europe trying to track down a couple that had scammed a wealthy older widow out of almost a million dollars then disappeared. Too embarrassed to get the police involved, she'd hired Paige to just locate them, and her private security would handle the rest. Paige had a good idea who her client's private security was considering she'd done her own research on the woman and found connections to some questionable familial organizations, but she didn't ask any questions. She just did what she'd been paid to do, reported back to her contact, and hopped on the first flight she could get home.

A familiar bleating drew her attention. She stuck her head out the window to find Lucy and Ethel standing nearby waiting for her to exit the truck.

"Hello, ladies."

Paige rolled up her windows then got out to greet them, but before she could they took off down the path leading back behind the house. She watched after them curiously and shrugged because unlike the nickname Ava had given her, she couldn't read their minds to wonder why they did what they did. Even if she could, she was too tired to do anything but warm up whatever leftovers Adele had stored in the freezer then sleep until morning. She knew she should probably check in with the menagerie, especially since Lucy and Ethel knew she was home, but she didn't see any reason why that task couldn't wait until she'd slept off the jet lag from the red-eye she'd taken.

Paige grabbed her luggage from the bed of the pickup, tiredly trudged to the back door, punched in the code and was just about to walk in when she heard the clip-clop of hooves. She gazed at the surprising reflection in the glass door of Zorro walking beside Amina who carried an unexpected rider coming up behind her. She turned slowly, wondering if she was more tired than she thought but found that her tired mind wasn't playing tricks on her.

"Welcome home." Ava greeted Paige with a broad smile as she sat atop Amina holding Zorro's reins.

"Uh, thanks." Paige was too dumbfounded to think of anything else to say.

She and Ava hadn't spoken in a month because Paige had been too much of a coward to admit the truth to her. That she regretted letting Ava leave without trying to find a way to explore what was between them further. At one point she had even researched land available in Chicago's neighbor, Indiana, but nothing there rivaled the peace Paige had here in Oklahoma. Although lately she had begun to wonder what the point of her little plot of peace was with no one to share it with. Ava had only been there for a month yet when she'd left, the ranch hadn't felt the same. Even the menagerie missed her. Brutus had moped around for weeks, Amina refused to let Paige ride her, as if she blamed her for Ava not being there, and Lucy and Ethel would run right past her out of the barn standing in the doorway looking expectedly toward the house then turning to look at Paige with what she could only describe as a look of disappointment.

Adele had made it a point shortly before Paige had left for Europe to tell her that she needed to just let go of her foolish pride and call Ava, but Paige didn't see the point in it. Neither was willing to budge when it came to their lives outside of their relationship so there was no way it could work. Now, seeing Ava sitting atop Amina as if she were born to the saddle dressed in cowboy boots, jeans, a T-shirt with COWGIRL spelled out in rhinestones, a denim jacket, and a cowboy hat, she wondered how she had managed to survive these past months without Ava by her side.

"I thought we should talk, figured Zorro would probably want a little attention from you after being gone so long, so here we are. But now, seeing how tired you look, I'm thinking this might not have been a good idea after all."

Zorro strolled forward and butted Page's shoulder with his nose. She smiled and reached up to give him a scratch on his forelock. "No, this is fine. Let me just put my bag in the house and I'll be right out."

Their gazes locked and Paige knew there was no way she was going to let Ava leave here again without being honest.

Ava looked relieved. "We'll be here."

Paige gave Zorro one last scratch before entering the house, tossing her bag just inside the door, and walking back out. She wasn't quite dressed for riding wearing Jordans, khaki pants, a T-shirt, and khaki jacket but at least she was comfortable. She took the reins Ava offered, placed her foot in the stirrup and pulled herself up in the saddle.

"Lead the way," Paige offered.

Ava smiled and tapped her heel against Amina's side to get her moving. If Paige didn't know any better, she'd swear the horse was smiling just as happily as her rider. Paige followed as they galloped down the main path of the ranch then Ava turned off to the path leading to the west gate. When they arrived, she leaned over in the saddle to unlock it, surprising Paige with how well she held herself up as she did so. The gate slid open, and Ava exited, leaving Paige to close it behind her. They rode the two miles to the stream they had last ridden to together. Ava halted Amina at the tree closest to the water and surprised Paige again by managing to smoothly dismount before Paige could get down and help her.

She dismounted from Zorro. "Has someone been practicing her dismount technique?"

Ava gave her a shy smile. "I found a riding school in Chicago and have been keeping up on my lessons."

Paige gazed at Ava curiously as she tied Zorro's reins to the tree. "Really?"

Ava nodded then turned away and unhooked a blanket from Amina's saddle. She walked to the exact spot where they'd had their picnic and spread the blanket over the area. Paige watched Ava for a moment, still finding it hard to believe that she was there, then took a seat on the blanket beside her.

"How long have you been here?" Paige asked.

"Since Adele and my mother are besties now and talk practically daily, I knew you would be getting back today so I arrived late yesterday."

"I'm surprised to see you here considering how we'd left things."

Ava looked guiltily down at her hands folded in her lap. "Yeah, I'm sorry about that. I let my pride get the best of me. I didn't mean what I said about the ranch being your crutch. After everything you've lived through, you deserve the peace you get here."

"I owe you an apology as well. I don't think you're spoiled or that you believe the world revolves around you. I lashed out at you out of pride and fear and that was wrong. I'm sorry."

Paige reached over and took Ava's hand. There was a sense of rightness from the innocent contact. She missed the warmth and softness of Ava's smooth manicured hands within her rough callused ones. The look Ava gave her told her that she missed her as well.

"I think we both have been alone and so focused on our careers and being the strong, independent women, we needed to be that we handicapped our own love lives. I think the only reason I maintained whatever it was between Selena and me was because it didn't require a real commitment. It was convenient and mutually beneficial when it needed to be, like every other business agreement in my life." Ava frowned.

Paige squeezed her hand in sympathy. "I know what you mean. At least you had something consistent. The longest romantic relationship I've had as an adult lasted a month. Fighting in a war and working counterintelligence doesn't leave room for a romantic relationship. If you already had one when you started, sooner or later the job affected it. Then, after I got out of the service, I was too broken to even be thinking about a love life. I didn't want to burden someone else with having to share my trauma."

"It's not a burden if the other person loves you and sees you surviving your trauma as a strength. What you've been through has made you the strong, empathetic, caring protector that you are...and the woman I love who I would gladly battle any demon for and help carry every burden with." Ava finished her sentence looking bashfully down at their clasped hands.

Paige reached over, placed a finger under her chin, and raised Ava's head so that she could see her eyes. She saw Ava's love reflected in her gaze and Paige's heart soared.

"I love you too, Ava. I've felt an overprotectiveness for you that I've never felt for any informant or client I've worked with in or out of the military. Then you arrived here without a complaint about having to trade in your high fashion style for denim and cowboy boots nor did you hesitate in getting your hands dirty by helping around the ranch. Despite your fortune, you're far from being a spoiled heiress. You've managed to stay down-to-earth and humble and shown that you genuinely care about others around you. You're smart, beautiful, funny, and passionate and I can't imagine my life without you in it or sharing each other's burdens with anyone else but you."

Ava smiled broadly then closed the distance between them, pressing her lips against Paige's. The kiss was passionate and full of promise. Paige ignored the niggling of doubt trying to push its way through the depth of love she felt for Ava. Would it be enough? That little voice asked. How could they make this work when they had such different goals and were at such different places in their lives? She abruptly broke off their kiss before it consumed what little common sense she seemed to have left when it came to her feelings for Ava.

"How are we going to make this work?" Paige asked.

Ava smiled. "My father, who was the one that convinced me to come here, had an idea that just might work if you're willing to try it."

"Really?"

"Yep. He's become an old softy since his brush with death. He doesn't care who I choose to spend my life with as long as I'm happy."

"And you want me to be that person?"

"Yes…if you want to be that person."

There was a wary look in Ava's eyes. As if she were waiting for Paige to tell her she didn't want to be, but that was the furthest thing from Paige's mind. There was nobody else for her but Ava and she would do whatever it took to make their relationship work.

Paige kissed her softly then grasped Ava's face so that their gazes met. "I've never wanted anything more. So, what's this grand plan of your father's?"

About the Author

Anne Shade indulges in her passion for writing from the idyllic suburb of West Orange, New Jersey and is the author of *Femme Tales: A Modern Fairytale Trilogy*, *Masquerade*, *Love and Lotus Blossoms*, and *Her Heart's Desire* and has collaborated with two Bold Strokes Books anthologies, *In Our Words: Queer Stories from Black, Indigenous and People of Color Writers* and *My Secret Valentine: 3 Romance Novellas*. Her other passions include supporting women's professional football and making plans for her future bed and breakfast where she plans to spend her days writing and hosting old, new, and future friends and family.

Books Available from Bold Strokes Books

Almost Perfect by Tagan Shepard. A shared love of queer TV brings Olivia and Riley together, but can they keep their real-life love as picture perfect as their on-screen counterparts? (978-1-63679-322-1)

Corpus Calvin by David Swatling. Cloverkist Inn may be haunted, but a ghost materializes from Jason Dekker's past and Calvin's canine instinct kicks in to protect a young boy from mortal danger. (978-1-62639-428-5)

Craving Cassie by Skye Rowan. Siobhan Carney and Cassie Townsend share an instant attraction, but are they brave enough to give up everything they have ever known to be together? (978-1-63679-062-6)

Drifting by Lyn Hemphill. When Tess jumps into the ocean after Jet, she thinks she's saving her life. Of course, she can't possibly know Jet is actually a mermaid desperate to fix her mistake before she causes her clan's demise. (978-1-63679-242-2)

Enigma by Suzie Clarke. Polly has taken an oath to protect and serve her country, but when the spy she's tasked with hunting becomes the love of her life, will she be the one to betray her country? (978-1-63555-999-6)

Finding Fault by Annie McDonald. Can environmental activist Dr. Evie O'Halloran and government investigator Merritt Shepherd set aside their conflicting ideas about saving the planet and risk their hearts enough to save their love? (978-1-63679-257-6)

Hot Keys by R.E. Ward. In 1920s New York City, Betty May Dewitt and her best friend, Jack Norval, are determined to make their Tin Pan Alley dreams come true and discover they will have to fight—not only for their hearts and dreams, but for their lives. (978-1-63679-259-0)

Securing Ava by Anne Shade. Private investigator Paige Richards takes a case to locate and bring back runaway heiress Ava Prescott. But ignoring her attraction may prove impossible when their hearts and lives are at stake. (978-1-63679-297-2)

The Amaranthine Law by Gun Brooke. Tristan Kelly is being hunted for who she is and her incomprehensible past, and despite her overwhelming feelings for Olivia Bryce, she has to reject her to keep her safe. (978-1-63679-235-4)

The Forever Factor by Melissa Brayden. When Bethany and Reid confront their past, they give new meaning to letting go, forgiveness, and a future worth fighting for. (978-1-63679-357-3)

The Frenemy Zone by Yolanda Wallace. Ollie Smith-Nakamura thinks relocating from San Francisco to her dad's rural hometown is the worst idea in the world, but after she meets her new classmate Ariel Hall, she might have a change of heart. (978-1-63679-249-1)

A Cutting Deceit by Cathy Dunnell. Undercover cop Athena takes a job at Valeria's hair salon to gather evidence to prove her husband's connections to organized crime. What starts as a tentative friendship quickly turns into a dangerous affair. (978-1-63679-208-8)

As Seen on TV! by CF Frizzell. Despite their objections, TV hosts Ronnie Sharp, a laid-back chef; and paranormal investigator Peyton Stanford, have to work together. The public is watching. But joining forces is risky, contemptuous, unnerving, provocative—and ridiculously perfect. (978-1-63679-272-9)

Blood Memory by Sandra Barret. Can vampire Jade Murphy protect her friend from a human stalker and keep her dates with the gorgeous Beth Jenssen without revealing her secrets? (978-1-63679-307-8)

Foolproof by Leigh Hays. For Martine Roberts and Elliot Tillman, friends with benefits isn't a foolproof way to hide from the truth at the heart of an affair. (978-1-63679-184-5)

Glass and Stone by Renee Roman. Jordan must accept that she can't control everything that happens in life, and that includes her wayward heart. (978-1-63679-162-3)

Hard Pressed by Aurora Rey. When rivals Mira Lavigne and Dylan Miller are tapped to co-chair Finger Lakes Cider Week, competition gives way to compromise. But will their sexual chemistry lead to love? (978-1-63679-210-1)

The Laws of Magic by M. Ullrich. Nothing is ever what it seems, especially not in the small town of Bender, Massachusetts, where a witch lives to save lives and avoid love. (978-1-63679-222-4)

The Lonely Hearts Rescue by Morgan Lee Miller, Nell Stark, Missouri Vaun. In this novella collection, a hurricane hits the Gulf Coast, and the animals at the Lonely Hearts Rescue Shelter need love, and so do the humans who adopt them. (978-1-63679-231-6)

The Mage and the Monster by Barbara Ann Wright. Two powerful mages, one committed to magic and one controlled by it, strive to free each other and be together while the countries they serve descend into war. (978-1-63679-190-6)

Truly Wanted by J.J. Hale. Sam must decide if she's willing to risk losing her found family to find her happily ever after. (978-1-63679-333-7)

A Good Chance by Ali Vali. Harry, Desi, and Desi's sister Rachel are so close to getting everything they've ever wanted, but Desi's ex-husband is coming back to get his revenge and rip apart their chance at happiness. (978-1-63679-023-7)

A Perfect Fifth by Jaycie Morrison. Streetwise pianist Zara Keller and Lady Jillian Stansfield couldn't be more different; yet their connection brings a new awareness of who they are and what they truly want in their lives—including each other. (978-1-63679-132-6)

Catching Feelings by Ana Hartnett Reichardt. Andrea Foster expected to catch a lot of pitches from the Alder Lion's star pitcher, Maya, but she didn't expect to catch feelings. (978-1-63679-227-9)

Defiant Hearts by Lee Lynch. In these stories, you'll find your lovers, friends, and lesbians you wish you knew—maybe even yourself. (978-1-63679-237-8)

Love and Duty by Catherine Young. All Princess Roseli wants is to marry her three lovers, but with war looming, she must instead marry Princess Lucia to establish a military alliance between their planets. (978-1-63679-256-9)

Murder at Union Station by David S. Pederson. Private Detective Mason Adler struggles to determine who killed a woman found in a trunk without getting himself killed in the process. (978-1-63679-269-9)

Serendipity by Kris Bryant. Serendipity brings jingle writer Annie Foster and celebrity pop star Bristol Baines together, and their undeniable attraction keeps them close, but will their different paths drive them apart? (978-1-63679-224-8)

The Haunted Heart by Jane Kolven. A ghost, a ring, and a quest to find a missing psychic—it's a spell for love. (978-1-63679-245-3)

The Rules of Forever by Nan Campbell. After reconnecting at their high school reunion, Cara and Lauren agree to embark on a textbook definition friends-with-benefits relationship, but trying to keep it uncomplicated is harder than it seems. (978-1-63679-248-4)

Vision of Virtue by Brey Willows. When virtue and desire come together, be prepared for sparks in this next installment of the Memory's Muses series. (978-1-63679-118-0)

Cherry on Top by Georgia Beers. A chance meeting leaves Cherry and Ellis longing for a different life, but when Ellis's search for truth crashes into Cherry's insta-filter world, do they have any hope at all of a happily ever after? (978-1-63679-158-6)

Love and Other Rare Birds by Angie Williams. Ornithologist Dr. Jamie Martin and park ranger Rowan Fleming are searching the Alaskan wilderness for a bird thought to be extinct and they're about to discover opposites really do attract. (978-1-63679-108-1)

Parallel Paradise by Mayapee Chowdhury. When their love affair is put to the test by the homophobia of their family, community, and culture, Bindi and Rimli will need to fight for a chance at love. (978-1-63679-204-0)

Perfectly Matched by Toni Logan. A beautiful Cupid named Hannah, a runaway arrow, and just seventy-two hours to fix a mishap that could be the best mistake she has ever made. (978-1-63679-120-3)

Royal Exposé by Jenny Frame. When they're grouped together for a class assignment, Poppy's enthusiasm for life and love may just save Casey's soul, but will she ever forgive Casey for using her to expose royal secrets? (978-1-63679-165-4)

Slow Burn by Missouri Vaun. A wounded wildland firefighter from California and a struggling artist find solace and love in a small southern town. (978-1-63679-098-5)

The Artist by Sheri Lewis Wohl. Detective Casey Wilson and reclusive artist Tula Crane are drawn together in a web of passion, intrigue, and art that might just hold the key to stopping a killer. (978-1-63679-150-0)

The Inconvenient Heiress by Jane Walsh. An unlikely heiress and a spinster evade the Marriage Mart only to discover true love together. (978-1-63679-173-9)

A Champion for Tinker Creek by D.C. Robeline. Lyle James has rescued his dad's auto repair business, but when city hall condemns his neighborhood, Lyle learns only trusting will save his life and help him find love. (978-1-63679-213-2)

Closed-Door Policy by Erin Zak. Going back to college is never easy, but Caroline Stevens is prepared to work hard and change her life for the better. What she's not prepared for is Dr. Atlanta Morris, her gorgeous new professor. (978-1-63679-181-4)

Homeworld by Gun Brooke. Headed by Captain Holly Crowe, the spaceship Velocity's crew journeys towards their alien ancestors' homeworld, and what they find is completely unexpected—and they're not safe. (978-1-63679-177-7)

Outland by Kristin Keppler & Allisa Bahney. Danielle Clark and Katelyn Turner can't seem to stay away from one another even as the war for the wastelands tests their loyalty to each other and to their people. (978-1-63679-154-8)

Secret Sanctuary by Nance Sparks. US Deputy Marshal Alex Trenton specializes in protecting those awaiting trial, but when danger threatens the woman she's falling for, Alex is in for the fight of her life. (978-1-63679-148-7)

Stranded Hearts by Kris Bryant, Amanda Radley, Emily Smith. In these novellas from award winning authors, fate intervenes on behalf of love when characters are unexpectedly stuck together. With too much time and an irresistible attraction, anything could happen. (978-1-63679-182-1)

The Last Lavender Sister by Melissa Brayden. Aster Lavender sells her gourmet doughnuts and keeps a low profile; she never plans on the town's temporary veterinarian swooping in and making her feel like anything but a wallflower. (978-1-63679-130-2)

The Probability of Love by Dena Blake. As Blair and Rachel keep ending up in the same place despite the odds, can a one-night stand turn into forever? Or will the bet Blair never intended to make ruin their happily ever after? (978-1-63679-188-3)

Worth a Fortune by Sam Ledel. After placing a want ad for a personal secretary, a New York heiress is surprised when the woman who got away is the one interested in the position. (978-1-63679-175-3)